my life uncovered

my life uncovered

UNRAVELED, REVEALED...BARED

LYNN ISENBERG

RED DRESS INK™

First edition December 2003

MY LIFE UNCOVERED

A Red Dress Ink novel

ISBN 0-373-25043-6

Visit Red Dress Ink at www.reddressink.com

Printed in U.S.A.

For my mother,
who teaches me to be open-minded.
For my father, who taught me to be discerning.
For my sister, who teaches me to trust myself.
For my brother, who taught me to appreciate
the good things in life.

With thanks to...

John Laurence, my best friend,

Mary Hanlon Stone, Corie Brown and Diane Wilk
for their unwavering support
and valuable feedback,

Kathryn Lye, my amazing editor,
who saw the diamond in the rough,

Laurie and Bobby LaZebnik,
my favorite cousins,

Ron Moler, my longtime colleague,

my dear friends Chelsea and Rosemary Low,

and all those who generously gave me
idyllic places in which to write this novel.

CAST OF CHARACTERS

Accent Film Co.: Porn company.

Adam Berman: Corie's husband, a business mentor and friend to Laura.

Ann Taylor (Stern): Laura's older sister, who is engaged to marry the guy Laura rejected and who's about to live the perfect life in Malibu.

Annie: A fluffer.

Austin Stern: A former California state assemblyman, father of George.

Barry Burnstein: A renowned Hollywood acting coach. Laura hires him to teach porn stars in her quest to advance the quality of porn.

Bennett Taylor: Laura's older brother, a fashion buyer who invents leather socks.

Bob Tinkerton: President of the National Swingers Club.

Brad Isaacs: An STA agent who champions Laura's script until his wife, competing superagent Natalie Moore, gets ahold of it and then he drops it like a hot potato.

Cliff Peterson: One who exudes sex. Prolific award-winning director-producer of porn for the Accent Film Co. Also, the cousin of Joseph, the very nice car mechanic mentioned later.

Cole Tanner: A cinematographer of feature films who used to work with Mitchell Mann. He remeets Laura and along the way he becomes Laura's third Hollywood-related boyfriend, but this time, thank God, he's a good guy.

Corie Berman: Laura's best friend, an assistant to STA agent Jason Brand.

Darlene Green: The epitome of rude. A manager-producer who gets Laura's script from Natalie Moore and tries to set it up without ever talking to Laura.

Elaine Dover: Former STA assistant turned creative executive and one of Laura's Hollywood friends.

Eric Leve: An ambitious, yet insecure literary agent who was once Laura's boss. Instead of helping her, he expresses his sexual fantasies about her.

Eva Taylor: Laura's mother. A natural-born storyteller with a flair for anything organic. She wants the best for her children. Happily divorced.

Gavin Marsh: A Hollywood boyfriend of Laura's, and not any better than the others. He's a manager-producer on the fast track to nowhere.

George Stern: Ann's husband-to-be. A supernice guy who'd rather please his father and be a politician, than be the entrepreneur he's always dreamed of being. Unfortunately, all his attempts to entrepreneur fail, until...keep reading.

Ian Bujinski: A porn makeup artist.

Jason Brand: Synonymous with slick and sleek. An STA agent who will stop at nothing to make his deals happen.

Jeremy Kincaid: A Hollywood producer of big-budget action-adventure films.

Jose: A South American hunk attending the Intimacy Workshop at the nudist colony.

Joseph the Mechanic: A very nice car mechanic who introduces Laura to his cousin Cliff.

Lacey Larson: A porn star.

Lance Vaughn: A gorgeous male sex surrogate.

Larry Solomon: Laura's former college English professor who is now editor of *Inside Hollywood,* a popular trade publication.

Laura Taylor: Our heroine. A really nice Jewish girl who is trying hard to make it in Hollywood but inadvertently finds success in porn. She sets out to write the great American screenplay but ends up writing great American adult movies.

The Law of Malus: Laura's opus screenplay, a romantic family epic and metaphor for overcoming personal obstacles to reach one's greatest potential. It garners Hollywood attention like a carrot on a stick.

Lily Laurence: Deceased. A former patient of Walt Taylor's, and the inspiration for Laura's prized screenplay, *The Law of Malus.*

Lola Stormrider: An old-time porn writer with a horrible cough.

Maya: Leader of a Tantric sex workshop and the inspiration for Laura's new screenplay, *The Surrogate.*

Mickey Colucci: Owner of Accent Film Company. And one of the few people who truly respects Laura.

Mitchell Mann: Another Hollywood boyfriend of Laura's. B-level movie director who is always trying to get back together with Laura, even after he got another woman pregnant.

Natalie Moore: Superagent at OTA (Organic Talent Agency), married to Brad Isaacs at competing STA.

Oliver Kleimeister: A stock market guy who somehow managed to become a studio executive. Strictly into numbers, he has no penchant for story and lacks manners.

Rabbi Weiss: A great giver of sermons, which inspire Laura.

Rand Chessick: Scott Sher's assistant, who rebuffs Laura, then later helps her as he advances up the creative executive ladder.

Richard Marksman: President of STA who befriends Laura and becomes instrumental in her career, or rather, she becomes instrumental in his retirement.

Sara Stephenson: Another studio executive. She saves Laura from a Mitchell Mann episode and takes a liking to Laura's writing and to Laura.

Scott Sher: Hollywood agent who makes false promises to Laura and disappears from the story before we ever meet him.

Sex Ed Couples: See couples 1–4 in Part Two.

STA: The Significant Talent Agency, the hottest talent agency in town. For those in Hollywood, think CAA under the reign of Ovitz during its heyday.

Stiff Wand: Hot new male porn star in one of Laura's films.

The Surrogate: Laura's screenplay for Hollywood that becomes an adult movie hit, which then gets noticed and bought for a mainstream Hollywood movie.

Tess Knight: A porn star.

Things Change: Laura's first award-winning porn film. It receives rave reviews and goes on to become a cult classic.

Tom Kaplan: Head of marketing for the Accent Film Company, who likes Laura, but only gets close enough to gift her with a dildo.

Tony Lombardo: A celebrity publicist only in one paragraph in the book.

Unnamed Teenager: A seventeen-year-old going on seventy. *Very* wise.

Walt Taylor: Laura's dad. Soon to be retired, this podiatrist put Laura through college so she could have a wonderful career and wonderful marriage opportunities.

prologue

Who is Bella Feega? That's what I wonder whenever I begin to reflect on the strange course of events that led to my standing before five porn stars in an acting class I organized in an attempt to do justice to my dialogue, to speaking to an audience of swingers at a Holiday Inn banquet room for the ostensible purpose of making sex education videos, or to sitting in a limo negotiating my own four-picture X-rated writing deal. Every time I ask myself, "Who is Bella Feega?" and "How did I get here?" I try to trace my story, try to find some semblance of meaning in what was to be an otherwise ordinary but honorable life. I just didn't know my own odyssey to tell stories would become the story I would tell, but here it is, a naked truth, a life of good intentions…uncovered.

part one

WRITING ADULT ENTERTAINMENT JUXTAPOSED WITH WRITING AND SELLING HOLLYWOOD MAINSTREAM ENTERTAINMENT

1

take one

THE HOLLYWOOD STRUGGLE

I can't believe what I have just heard. I repeat the words that I think rolled off the studio producer's tongue because I am suddenly unable to decipher the meaning of them.

"What do you mean there's no deal?" I ask, my heart pumping furiously.

"There never was any deal," he says, leaning back in his chair beside a pile of screenplays, contracts, and production budgets. "Who'd you say your agent was again?"

"Scott Sher at the Significant Talent Agency," I repeat.

"Hmmm. I thought I knew all the agents at STA. Never met him," says Lee Weston, a high-profile movie producer on the lot of a major film studio. "What exactly did he tell you...Linda?"

"It's Laura. Laura Taylor. And he told me the deal was done months ago," I affirm. My memory can't be that bad. After all, why would I quit my job at STA, the hottest talent agency in town, if there hadn't been a deal? Scott had told me to leave and stick with writing. I wonder, can Alzheimer's strike at twenty-nine? Maybe it's some sort of studio conspiracy against struggling writers. Or perhaps this guy is an imposter and the real tanned-face Weston has the contract for my screenplay with him on a sandy-white beach in Fiji. "Scott said I was supposed to hand in the second draft today and pick up a check for $25,000—less the ten-percent commission."

"Sorry, but he stretched a truth that never existed."

"You mean, he lied?"

"He's an agent, Laura, they all lie."

My eyes drop down to gaze at my screenplay *The Law of Malus.* It's my opus, but now it's lying limp on my lap, an injustice clearly having been done to it. I close my eyes, trying hard to make reason out of the insanity I've just heard, as the lump in my throat grows with panic and now utter humiliation.

"Do you have other writing work?" Lee asks.

"I'm supposed to do a rewrite at Satellite Studios. That's all," I say.

"I'd offer to look at your script, but from your description, there's no way I'd make this. It's not high-concept and the new head of the studio only wants action-adventures. Romance and family dramas are dead."

At this last line I stop breathing. Romance and family dramas are dead. Everything I write, everything I stand for on behalf of the human condition is no longer wanted.

Lee leans forward and gazing at my chest murmurs, "I've got a meeting now, but I can...discuss it with you later. Come over for drinks at my place tonight."

I know I'm dazed, but I could swear Lee Weston has just hit on me. I stare at him uncomprehending, still spinning from round one of immense disappointment and unexpected betrayal.

He continues to glance at my chest. "If the writing doesn't work, maybe you should consider becoming an actress."

"Me?" I ask, stunned, wondering if someone else just walked in. I see no one else and for a moment I'm flattered. After having months of work abruptly tossed aside, I consciously crave any compliment I can get.

"Why not? You're pretty, smart, and you've got a great smile. My secretary will give you my address. How's eight o'clock?" He leers.

I stare at him, unable to respond. I look out the window. Is it spring? My mother always loved saying that when the ice would melt the boys would flock to me. Was it my pheromones? I'm no sizzling 6'0" model; I'm 5'2", petite and lithe, sporting dark-brown hair matching dark-brown eyes, with an approachable personality and an absentee fashion style. Of course I wanted to look good, but I never labored over my wardrobe like other girls did growing up. I preferred tackling new words to shopping at the mall.

I didn't see how my outfit could have contributed to Mr. Weston's advances. I was wearing my usual white tank top with an untucked bone button-down short-sleeved silk shirt hanging over a pair of charcoal gray slacks with casual black leather boots that were going on three years old. I'm a pragmatist. I don't believe in buying new shoes until I have to replace the ones I have. Much to the annoyance of my older brother, Bennett, the fashion king. He prides himself on wearing only designer brands, and always being the first in line every time one hits the store's shelves. I dress for comfort, not trends. Maybe that's why I was out of sync with the studio's current script-seeking mandate.

"Uh, no thanks," I reply.

Shit.

Shit.

Shit.

Despite my confusion I find the studio's parking lot. My ten-year-old silver Toyota Corolla hatchback appears dull and aged among a fleet of shiny, leased luxury cars. Still in a trance, I drive down the block and around the corner to STA. I can't believe that this is what starving for six months to write a script about loss amounts to, what a master's degree in literature from the University of Michigan provides, and what, having written every day from the age of six, results in.

The Law of Malus was to be my first, or at least my first significant, movie deal. My first script was *The Magic Mitt,* a family adventure tale, which received a semi-finalist screenwriting award and has the best studio synopsis I'd ever read, epitomizing it as the perfect blend of all things Americana and giving it a strong recommend to buy. And yet it still could not get sold or made. So I decided to up the ante from a PG-rated story to an R-rated one with *The Law of Malus,* a harmonious synthesis of the struggles relayed to me by an elderly female patient of my father's, named Lily Laurence.

My college summers were spent as a podiatric assistant in my dad's, Walt's, office where I had come to adore Lily. During her ritual footbaths, I came to understand the sacrifices she made in her life, the dreams lost in self-recrimination and the vast love gained in the quiet solitude of surrender. I was deeply touched by her story, steeped in loss and self-renewal. Knowing of my desire to write for the movies, Lily asked me to tell her story. My problem wasn't in the telling of her story, but in the fact that I had made a vow to get it produced.

Of course I wasn't so naive as to believe that I'd write it and Hollywood would find me. First, I'd go there and meet people who could finance it and distribute it. So after graduation I packed my bags, drove out west, and landed a job at the Significant Talent Agency. That's where I spent three years as an assistant to literary agent Eric Leve. And that's where I met the people with the resources to make things happen. It was Eric who introduced me as an up-and-coming writer to the hyper-aggressive agent Scott Sher, who in turn would later promise me a deal on *The Law of Malus.*

It would be an understatement to describe the lobby of STA as daunting. Smug receptionists man the desk sitting front and center. Courtesy phones on either side of simple leather couches offer the potential for human contact. No privacy exists but you are invited to sit on one of the couches and feel a false sense of significance. In addition, the ceiling rises forever, like a giant beanstalk. This space, between the floor and roof, charges the atmosphere with sovereignty. Hallways weave around the walls of its perimeter where small men strut through like heads of state believing they manipulate deals as important as national security secrets. Celebrities breeze in and out escorted by top agents. The plot of land this lobby rests on sees more deals close than any other piece of real estate in Southern California. And my deal, I thought at the time, was about to become one of them, of which I had been foolishly proud. I promise myself I won't make that mistake again as I pick up the first courtesy phone I can get to.

Rand Chessick, Scott's assistant, answers, "Scott Sher."

"Hi, it's Laura Taylor. I'm in the lobby and I need to see Scott. It's important."

"Scott no longer works here," the words rapidly roll off his tongue.

"What?" I ask, astonished.

"Well, in the last sixteen hours he's left the entertainment industry and joined the Peace Corps in South Africa. Hang on. I've got another call."

In a state of shock I call my best friend, Corie Berman, an assistant at STA. "Corie," I plead. "Where's Scott? What's going on?"

Corie whispers back, "Rumor has it he's entered a drug

rehab center somewhere in North Dakota. That's all I know for now. I'm rolling calls for Jason. Later."

Jason is Jason Brand, Corie's boss, one of the slickest, sleekest agents in town. Corie's been manning his desk for thirteen months, two weeks, three days, four hours, and sixteen minutes, which puts her in the Guinness Book of World Records for the longest employed assistant Jason's ever had. She knows how to keep him in balance, unfortunately at the risk of abandoning her chances to advance her own career. I've learned the best time to talk to Corie during work hours is when Jason's out of town or at a meeting, and if they're rolling through his phone sheet, well, it's a no go. Jason prides himself on returning every call he receives even if it's to say, "Can't talk now, let's try tomorrow."

I take a deep breath and dial Rand again, "So, Rand. I don't mean to sound disinterested in Scott's sudden career shift, but, uh, what happened to my deal?"

"To tell you the truth, I'm not sure there ever really was a deal," he says.

"But Scott said…"

"Well, I guess he misled you," Rand says curtly.

In staccato style I cry, "Can another agent take over for me? How about Eric Leve?"

"Not for just hip pocket clients, you had to have officially signed with the agency, besides Eric's out of the country for four weeks. And Richard's already put the word out that he doesn't want the agency to keep any of Scott's clients, unless they're grossing over a million a year. Sorry, Laura. I gotta take these other calls. Good luck, but well, uh, adios."

Devastated, I find my way to my car and climb inside, dashed dreams cloud above me anesthetizing my body and soul. My cell beeps indicating I have three voice mail messages.

"Hey, Laura—Hank Willows from Satellite here. Bad news. The rewrite we wanted to hire you for is on permanent hold due to production problems in Prague on another picture. I'll call you when things calm down, but don't hold your breath."

I sigh and hit the skip button. Next message.

"Hi, honey. It's Mom. Let me know when I can pop the organic champagne to celebrate your deal!"

I cringe at the thought of explaining another failed Hollywood story to my family. I quickly hit the skip button. Next message.

"Laura. It's Mitchell Mann."

The sound of Mitchell's voice instantly triggers my body into a momentary state of numbness. I wonder why he always tags his greeting with his last name as if I wouldn't know him by his first name alone. Suddenly, our years of intimacy seem much less intimate.

"I want to know why we can't at least be friends," he pronounces. "I know I got another woman pregnant, but still I don't see why..."

I hit the erase button. I take a deep breath preparing for the onset of monetary desperation. I turn the keys in the ignition. Nothing happens. Along with my dead dreams, I now have a dead car. This does not bode well for my journeying through the urban sprawl of Los Angeles. I feel as if I've become the lead character in a never-ending nightmare horror flick.

Triple A tows my car to a nearby gas station. The mechanic, a stocky, avuncular guy named Joseph, according to his patch, diagnoses my problem as transmission failure and quotes me twelve hundred dollars for automotive surgery. That's when I break down and weep. "I don't have that kind of money."

"Well, what do you have?" asks Joseph, taking pity on me.

I throw my hands in the air to signify nothing. Too choked up to speak.

Joseph calmly peers inside my car. "What's that?"

I look. My script lies on the floor mat. I pick it up and wave it at him. "This? This is it. This is all I have left. A 110-page screenplay. This morning it was worth $25,000 against $250,000! Or so I thought. But I got screwed. Fuck! Excuse me for swearing."

"No problem," says Joseph, remaining unruffled. "So what's the script about?" he asks, sounding genuinely interested.

"It's a love story, with romance and drama, and *family values,* but of course Hollywood doesn't care about that! Hollywood only wants *high-concept* fear and suspense saturated with special effects!"

Joseph stands there, quietly letting my words bounce off his chest. "Tell you what I'm gonna do," says Joseph. "You give me the script. I'll fix your car. We'll talk again tomorrow. In the meantime, I'll have one of my guys drive you home." I wasn't going to look a gift ride in the mouth, so I accepted.

My apartment building is located at the corner of Westminster and Abbot Kinney in Venice—L.A.'s tiny counterpart to New York's Soho. I navigate my way past a homeless person camping out on the front steps. Inside the foyer, I retrieve my mail hoping there might be an old-fashioned postcard or letter from Gavin Marsh. Gavin is a Canadian talent manager-producer I have been dating for four months. For two weeks he's been on location in Vancouver with a client and isn't due back for another two. So he's hardly available to help me solve the problems of the day. One tiny bit of communication from him would mean so much at this moment, but there are no words from him, only more bills from more creditors.

I enter my apartment and flip the lights on, but only darkness prevails. At first I think it's a dead fuse, but the hallway lights are alive and well. Then I recognize a pink slip compliments of the S. California Gas Company lying on the hallway carpet outside my door. I feel prostalgic for the end of this day, which has yet to come, and look across the hall at the door of my best friends' place. I hope their couch is comfortable.

Corie and Adam Berman's apartment is bright and well-lit in contrast to mine. I'm pulling a plaid pillowcase over a down pillow while Corie spreads a pair of matching sheets across the couch in her living room recounting the drama of Scott Sher's sudden departure from STA.

"Rumors about his drug habit were flying around the halls of STA for months. When Richard Marksman finally confirmed them, it was adios amigo before you could say *ecstasy.* You should have seen the reactions, Laura. The place was in a tizzy—every agent with a secret to hide scrambling for the nearest phone. Not to mention the bottleneck of flushing evidence away that would land them in the same state as Scott Sher."

"Is it that rampant?" I ask.

Corie finishes tucking in a sheet corner and looks up at me, "You've been in a cave writing too long." She tosses me the remote control to the television set. "Here, watch a few music videos, get caught up on today's pop culture."

"Gee, thanks. Is that how you stay in the loop?"

"Of course not. I get my info during coffee breaks and from Adam who reads four newspapers a day."

"News-synopses-on-demand. How convenient. Speaking of which, when does Adam get home?" Adam manages the licensing and distribution of music at a large production company.

"Not 'til late, as usual, unless his meeting goes over and he misses his flight from San Francisco, which is the most likely scenario." A whistle sound hails from the next room over. Corie looks up. "I'll get us some hot tea. You relax." She retreats into the kitchen. The day catches up with me and I collapse on the couch. Corie returns with two steaming cups of chamomile tea.

"What am I going to do, Corie? Everything's upside down. How can I face my family at Ann's engagement party tomorrow?"

"Don't even think about that right now," she says, and then softly adds, "Give yourself a break. The best thing you can do for yourself is get a good night's rest."

"Okay, thanks. I think I'll call Gavin."

"Sure, but I don't know what good that will do," she murmurs, trying hard to downplay the trace of disdain she holds for him. "Tell me again what you see in him?"

"Besides being charismatic, outgoing and sexy, at least to me, he's the perfect antidote to Mitchell Mann—a logical businessman in entertainment, instead of an ego-driven artsy director."

"Right," says Corie.

I climb into my makeshift couch-bed and recall how Gavin and I met at the Telluride Film Festival four months ago. I was with Elaine Dover, another former STA assistant turned VP of Acquisitions for a small film company. She invited me along on her quest for the next box office hit—assuming she could outbid the competition. We traipsed from theatre to theatre watching movies and from coffee shop to coffee shop schmoozing with filmmakers and film distributors. I met all sorts of people and when the moment was appropriate I let them know about *The Law of Malus.* They all wanted to see it and asked me to have my agent send it over. But I didn't have an agent. It was that old catch-22, no deal until there's an agent and no agent until there's a deal. That's when Gavin overheard the conversation and stepped in to vouch for me. Frozen in that moment of time, he was my prince in shining armor, at least that's how I liked to interpret it. Corie preferred the version of a guy gambling on an easy commission. But for the rest of the festival we hung out and sealed our interest in each other inside a sleeping bag during an outdoor midnight screening.

I dial Gavin's cell phone number. "Gavin," answers a gruff voice on the other end against the din of loud rock music.

"Hi, it's Laura. How are you?" I ask. My voice betrays my frailty from the day.

"Great. What's up?" he replies.

"Well, nothing really, except that my deal for *The Law of Malus* just unraveled. And now I think I'm unraveling, too."

"Hey, listen, I can't really talk right now. I'm out with the crew. It's work. Gotta keep them happy. I'll talk to you later."

"Okay, 'bye." I hang up telling myself it's just bad timing. It's midnight and he's still working. My problems certainly can't get in the way of that. I stop myself, realizing that Gavin doesn't even have to make up excuses for himself; I'm much too willing to do it for him. And then I let the fleeting thought fleet.

Hours later I lay awake on Corie's couch thinking about the good night's rest I can't seem to manage. I flip on the television set scanning channels, but it only leaves me feeling agitated. I stop on the E! Network to watch the story of legendary producer Robert Evans, who gave us *Love Story, The Godfather,* and many others. I'm consoled by the battles he had to endure to get his movies made. His persistence and risk-taking paid off and I hope someday mine will, too. I flip some more, this time to AMC, playing *Gone With the Wind*. I watch as Scarlett O'Hara stands defiant and determined to survive. Magically I'm mesmerized, as if seeing it for the first time as opposed to the forty-sixth.

I calm down, reminding myself why I'm doing what I'm doing. My father inspired a love of movies in me. Films offer strength and courage, provide life's lessons, spark laughter, elicit tears, and create the feeling of being part of something bigger than yourself, experiencing the vicissitudes of someone else's journey, which helps you appreciate your own. I exhale and settle into a remedy of escape from my own problems in total solidarity with Scarlett.

It's 8:00 a.m. when Corie graciously drops me off at the mechanic's shop, letting her feelings about Gavin slip out again. "I still don't see why he can't help you get a writing job, or even *a* job. He manages the star of a hit TV show. Why can't he help you?"

"It's not his job to get me a job, Corie." We've been through this before.

"Yes, it is," she says. "You've just been around too many creeps and you've forgotten what it's like to be with someone who really cares about you."

"Gavin cares," I say. "He's just busy taking care of his own business."

"But you are his business so stop defending him," she exclaims, then softens, "Look, don't worry," she bids. "Things change." I force an ephemeral smile before she drives off, thinking about the power of those two words. That would be a good theme for a story, I think. But why write anymore? I'm beginning to think the universe is sending me a message and maybe I should listen. Though not writing would be the equivalent of not breathing. Words strung together to make images are my oxygen.

The first thing Joseph tells me is that he's got this cousin in the San Fernando Valley with a production company who's always looking for good scripts. "I gave him your script last night. He thinks you're a talented writer," says Joseph.

"He does? He read it in one night?" Maybe the universe does want me to write!

"Yeah. He wants to meet you. Go see him. You can pay

me back in a month." Joseph hands me my car keys, a bill reduced to a thousand dollars, and the address to the Accent Film Company. I've never heard of them. Must be an independent I think; after all, when I worked at STA, I had only dealt with production companies that were part of the studio system. I thank Joseph profusely and without delay head north to the valley.

The 405 Freeway is jammed. Maybe this is a good time to call STA again. You'd think after all my time at STA as Eric Leve's assistant, I'd know the best time to phone. Ah, the phones. When not answering them I was typing phone sheets, deal memos, cover letters, filing, organizing, opening mail, taking notes, handling personal errands and enduring the mood swings of the ambitiously insecure. And I did get to exercise some creative writing skills. Whenever Eric was running late to meet his newlywed wife, which was always, he'd ask me what to do to pacify her. I came up with a litany of romantic gestures, going so far as to prepare midnight picnic baskets for him loaded with wine, berries, caviar, massage oils, romance classics on DVD along with one-page love essays relating the theme of the movie to his love for her. He gave me carte blanche on his credit card and I subsequently became well versed in the finer things. When his wife found out that I was the one who was orchestrating the scenes and penning the love essays it all came to an abrupt end. She wanted those words and actions to come from him, but when he tried to write down his feelings or think of passionate scenarios on his own it was clear he didn't have a single romantic gene in his body. Their marital bliss soon began to disintegrate, which was evident during his morning greetings; satiated smiles replaced by frustrated scowls. This led me to taking exorbitant amounts of coffee breaks, which in turn led me to develop relationships with other agents and agent trainees who could provide information on demand. I call STA and ask for Charlie Roberts, the sole agent in charge of independent film companies. Alas, Charlie is out of the office and his assistant is a temp who's never heard of the Accent Film Company. I am left to wing this meeting without any prep and to wonder on my own who the principals are, and what kind of movies they like to make.

Joseph did say his cousin liked my screenplay. Maybe this would be my chance to finally get my screenplay made, restore my personal vows, and make my father proud. After all, movies represented for me an important connection to my father, podiatrist by day and avid moviegoer by night. He loved movies and instilled the same in me. It didn't matter whether it was Clint Eastwood in *Dirty Harry* or Sean Connery in James Bond. For me, it was about sitting next to my father with a tub of buttered popcorn and getting swept away.

Sociologists describe the phenomenon of movie watching as "group dreaming," a time and place when members of a society adhere together as they gather in the dark to share an experience. My family bonded over movies in the theaters of suburban Detroit. In the dark, with popcorn and lemonade, we shared in the compassion of Atticus Finch in *To Kill a Mockingbird*, in the adventures of Dorothy in *The Wizard of Oz*, the revelations of George Bailey in *It's a Wonderful Life*, and countless others. The ritual as we transitioned out of the group-dreaming phenomenon occurred as the film's credits rolled and my father invariably announced his rating of the movie on a scale from one to ten. "I give it an eight," he'd say, and that would be that, the full summation of his critique in five words.

If my father, child of the depression era, represented an escapist's view of film, it was my cultured mother, a classical pianist and drama major that inspired the critical thinking aspect. This was evidenced by a mandatory discussion initiated by her after my parents took my siblings and me to see *Summer of '42* before either of them had read the reviews. My older brother Bennett, 14 at the time, displayed latent homosexual tendencies and saw no reason to discuss the hetero sex scenes. Instead he predicted that saddle shoes would soon come back into vogue. My 12-year-old sister, Ann, was shocked by the adolescent boys' immature and clumsy approach to sex. Even though she was one year older than me her life experience had begun with instant familial bliss whereas I had been jilted upon birth, spending my first three weeks alone and touch deprived inside a sterile incubator, my tiny hands locked in fists fighting to survive. It's no wonder I found the film riveting, intrigued by how that one tender sensual encounter of love and loss had changed Hermie forever. To be touched and transformed was what I was after, or so I thought. I found myself determined to connect and inspire through movies. But so far, while my efforts accumulated industry accolades in the form of verbal praise, my bank account accumulated personal debt. I hoped this might be the chance to turn it all around....

Cliff Peterson, tall, handsome, thin, in jeans and a pressed T-shirt, sits behind a glass desk. An air of intense sexuality lingers around him. I see no ring on his finger, and can't help but wonder if he's single. The guy exudes sexy, yet too sexy, almost too hot to handle.

"Sorry I can't offer you a cup of coffee. We're expanding our space and moved into these offices last week. We haven't unpacked all of our boxes yet."

As the producer of the Accent Film Company peruses my resumé, I sit attentively across from him carefully studying his office. Black leather chairs tell me he likes comfort with style. State-of-the-art CD, DVD, VCR and five-foot-long hi-definition flat-screen monitor all haphazardly lie on the floor. No art on the walls. I assume it's also yet to be unpacked. I deduce that I don't have enough information to make a valid deduction about anything.

"I'm impressed," he says. "You've got experience working with the studios. Writing awards. Represented by STA. I've heard of them."

That should have been my first clue, but his sultry voice distracted me.

He tosses my resumé to the side and looks straight at me. "You're a great writer—and I want to elevate the work around here. I want better stories, better plots, better characters. I want my movies to have meaning with all kinds of romance and broad appeal."

"Something for the whole family?" I naively ask.

"That's only overseas. They're much more liberal over there." I wasn't sure what he meant, but I didn't have time to figure it out. He kept going. "Do you have any risky romances you're working on right now?"

"Sure," I say.

"Tell me one," he says. That's when the workmen enter carrying huge frames of artwork.

"Where do you want us to hang your movie posters?" one of them asks.

"You don't mind, do you?" Cliff inquired. I shake my head no, grateful for the interruption that gives me a chance to flex my writing brain for a story idea.

"Just spot them evenly across the walls," Cliff tells the workmen. "And be gentle, those represent my best movies." The two guys then turn the frames around to reveal Cliff's prized cinematic moments.

My jaw drops and my purse hits the floor. I quickly feign a cough to cover my shock as I scan titles and graphics. *Austin Prowler, The Kissing Match, Under Dressed, Something*

About MaryAnn, Biker Babes, Memoirs of a Lady, and *Strap On Molly.* Holy shit.

I reach for my open purse and its contents of overdue bills and termination notices lying scattered on the floor. I scoop them up glancing between them and the porn posters. Thinking. Thinking. Cliff looks at me, clearly waiting for my answer. I'm thinking fast but drawing blanks so I go for the broad plot description. "It's a love story inside a love story with a twist."

But he waits for more. Obviously, he's not one to explore three-act structures or the virtues of Aristotle's *Poetics.* That's when I notice the framed photograph on his desk of two pretty women, arms wrapped around each other, smiling for the lens. They look like good friends; maybe they're Cliff's sisters. Who knows? But for me right now, they have just turned into lovers and the protagonists of my embryonic story.

"Well, it's about two women," I tell Cliff. "They're deeply in love with each other but then one wants to leave the relationship, to, uh…"

I glance at the women in the photo again wondering if the person behind the camera taking the photograph is a man—perhaps it's Cliff. What if one of the women finds herself attracted to him and becomes confused about her sexuality?

"To, uh, explore her heterosexuality because she's, um, she's never been with men before," I say, sneaking another peek at the image, knowing I need to throw in some drama, wondering what her lover would do to create conflict. Manna drops from the heavens and I've got it. "Her lover's devastated," I continue. "So she hires a guy to date her now ex-lover, and then dump her so she'll come back. That's the basic premise."

Cliff sits still, thinking about it. Moments pass. "I like it," he states. "I like it a lot. What's the title?"

"The title? Um, the title is... *Things Change.* It's a working title."

"I only pay five hundred for a script. A thousand on a rare occasion."

I'm shocked. "Guess you're not a signatory to the Writers Guild." He gives me a funny look. "It's okay. I'm not in the union...yet," I quickly add.

"Since your writing is exceptional and you owe my cousin a grand for the transmission job, I'd be willing to pay a little more," he says in that sultry voice.

"Isn't this the part where you're supposed to negotiate with my lawyer?" I ask. Not that I have a lawyer. Scott Sher never got around to that referral.

Cliff dismisses the statement asking, "How fast can you write?"

"How fast do you need it?"

"Five days. Four would be better. We start production in ten."

He must be out of his mind. No one writes a screenplay in five days. "That's doable," I say, wondering what I've gotten myself into. I know I'm fast once I've got a story down but this would be world record-breaking time. I'll have to bury myself in my apartment and chug caffeine around the clock. "Is a director attached?"

"Me," he says.

I glance at my bills. Adding up all that I owe I decide to risk it. "Okay. I'll do it for twenty-five hundred including one rewrite, but if you want a second rewrite or a polish it will cost a thousand more." Okay, so at least I remember how to structure payment fees for writing assignments thanks to all those deal memos I typed for Eric Leve.

Cliff gives me another funny look, as if he's never heard these terms before. I'm thinking he must be a really bad poker player or a really good one.

"Okay," he says. "I'll give you a thousand now and fifteen hundred more if you can deliver me a script in four days. Here's a sample video to look at in case you need to study the formula. Bottom line—make sure you give me a lot of romance. Sorry, but I don't know where the box covers are." He hands me a naked videotape.

"What about your business affairs department? Aren't they going to contact my lawyer to draw up a contract?" I ask with trepidation, wondering if this might kill the deal since he hasn't brought it up.

He smiles and holds out his hand. We shake. "There's your contract." He pulls out his checkbook, writes a check out to me for one thousand dollars and hands it over. "Here you go."

"Thanks." I turn to go then stop myself. "I forgot to ask you about sequel rights."

"If it sells over 100,000 units, you can have sequel rights. But just so you know, we've never made a sequel before."

"Units?" I ask. That's a new term on me.

"Straight-to-video talk," he says.

"Oh." Then, I remember the most important question of all, as other deal memos come to mind. "What about a back-end deal?" I ask, before I realize I've made a faux pas, or a pun, depending on how it's received. "I mean, a percentage of the royalties in case the movie's a hit," I quickly say.

"Very cute," he chuckles. "No back-end deals on straight to video."

"Do I get sole screenplay credit?"

"You can have it."

I've never heard of a production company not hiring writers to rewrite the work of other writers. Where am I?

"Turnaround rights?" It's my last question. Turnaround represents purgatory for any screenplay if the studio decides not to make the movie. The script can languish on a shelf until it literally disintegrates.

Cliff looks at me with a blank expression on his face.

"If you decide not to use the screenplay," I explain, "can I buy back the right to sell it somewhere else at the same cost you spent to have me write it?"

"Sure. But I always make the screenplays I commission. When you come back I'll give you the grand tour of the offices, editing bays, stages, and warehouse. Right now I've got a box cover shoot to go to. Good luck with the writing."

What just happened out here in the deep, deep valley? I couldn't believe how straightforward getting this writing job could be, compared to studio deals. No battle. No posturing. No paperwork. No agents. No lawyers. No commissions. And no sexual passes. Yesterday morning I lost two deals and an agent. Today, I had a go movie with a director attached and a guaranteed production start date before I touched the keyboard. Life was weird, I thought, and yet, I had no idea just how weird it was about to get.

2

take two

RULES OF ENGAGEMENT

All the way to my sister Ann's engagement brunch I keep glancing at the naked videotape peeking out from inside my purse on the passenger seat. Hey, it's important for me to expand my horizons, right? Look at Anais Nin and Henry Miller. Besides, I'm an adventurer, like that time I went to the Cannes Film Festival with Mitchell and decided to go to the beach. As soon as I stepped off the hotel's porch, the paparazzi chased me all the way to the shore, convinced I represented some famous actress or famous actress-to-be. I went along with it, wanting to know what it felt like to be a person whose private boundaries had been stripped away by purveyors of the public. However, I quickly discovered that paparazzi are worse than a plague of locusts, worse than a fleet of Alfred Hitchcock's "Birds" or a mosquito-infested jungle from which there is no escape. I finally shooed them away after they, camera-ready, collectively motioned for me to take my bikini top off.

As for writing an adult movie, it's just another adventure, I remind myself in mantra-like fashion. It's only temporary, *yes,* it is only temporary. It's not like I've got an addictive personality and am going to get hooked on penning porn. I'm a writer. And writers write.

I pull into the car-packed driveway of my sister's new 3,000-square-foot home in Malibu, which overlooks the Pacific Ocean. The house was purchased by her husband-to-be, George Stern, whom she met because I turned him down. I stare at the perfectly coiffed yard surrounded by a white-picket fence and take a deep breath. This might be harder than I think. Before I can dig through my purse to find my lipstick, George appears, gallantly opening my door for me.

"Hey, you," he smiles, and then greets me with a big bear hug. He's a decent-looking guy with a kind face. What was I thinking? He's so nice in comparison to the Hollywood men I've dated since.

"Hey, you, back," I smile.

He closes my car door for me and takes my hand in his. "You know I owe you, don't you? I really liked you, Laura, still do and always will."

"Come on, George, I spared you. My ambition would have driven you crazy."

"Maybe. But you sure were fun. Even though you broke my heart."

"I mended it, didn't I? I didn't have to introduce you to my sister when you told me you were off to Michigan for a graduate degree in engineering. Of course, I didn't think you guys would fall in love, but hey, now I've got family out here. First my sister, and now my dad's thinking about retiring nearby. So maybe I should be the one thanking you."

"Don't ever give up those dreams of yours," he says, grinning. "Unlike me," he adds.

"George, you're giving up your dreams and going into politics? But you told me you hate politics," I say. The truth is I'm not surprised. Austin Stern, George's unyielding father and a former state assemblyman, carries a force too strong to be resisted by a sweet and malleable guy like George. It was one reason why I couldn't be with him. George didn't respect his own dreams and goals. He dabbled in them, but he never got in the sandbox to really play.

He shrugs. "After ten entrepreneurial failures in a row, I don't think I've got the instinct. I thought engineering would give me a leg up on new inventions, but I just keep picking the wrong designers with products that serve no purpose. I probably should have gotten my MBA."

"You still can, you know? You're only thirty-four."

"It's too late for that. Besides, sons should make their dads happy, right?" He says it seeking reassurance. It's painful to see him brush aside what he really wants to do with his life. Thankfully, he changes the subject. "You hungry? We've got a ton of food, come on!"

Inside George and Ann's immaculate craftsman home, an entourage of family members greets me, taking my coat and purse, guiding me to a huge buffet table loaded with lox, bagels, cream cheese, capers…the works.

My mother, Eva, looking sophisticated and beautiful at sixty, takes me by the hand. "Hi, honey! We were worried about you. We thought maybe your car broke down again."

"I'm fine, Mom. Car's fine. Apartment's fine. Weather's fine."

"Gavin?"

"Fine."

"Your movie deal?"

I stab a piece of lox. "A slight altercation, but fine."

She hones in on me. "What kind of altercation?"

I really wish I could lie, now would be the perfect time, but I'm not very good at it, "Just one less zero on the end, no big deal."

Eva rolls her eyes and whispers in Jewish-mother support style, "Honey, I hate to see you struggle so much. Maybe you should give up writing and be a teacher."

"Mom, if I don't write every day I'll go insane."

"What's wrong with writing lesson plans?"

It's no use. I placate her, "You know, Mom, you're right, I'll ponder it." Satisfied, she leaves me at the tuna salad when my not as yet openly gay brother Bennett, who has flown down from San Francisco, slides in. He's dressed in spiffy black shoes and a supple black leather jacket.

"Nice outfit, Bennett." This always makes him feel good. I try to get specific but blow it. "Is that Armani?" I guess.

"Try Prada," he replies, smirking as if everyone should know the difference. He looks me over. "Where have you been shopping? In an attic?" he asks, revealing his critical trademark tone.

I look down at my outfit from Banana Republic...okay, it's five years old, but there are no stains and it still fits. I wonder what's so offensive and respond, "I'm experimenting with retro-nineties, do you mind?"

"Retro is only retro when it's over twenty years old," he snaps with a mollifying grin.

"Well, this is an abridged version of retro," I proudly counter. "Not all of us have time to practice fashion combining like you have since the age of three, experimenting with Mommy's closet, coordinating her outfits every time she left the house."

"Touché," he smiles. "Where's blue-eyes?"

"Still on location," I reply. "Where's the bride-to-be?"

"In the living room, all a-twitter. I had to redo her makeup three times. She was overdoing it on the blush."

I cross over to the living room navigating my way through George's multitudinous cousins ranging in age from two to ninety. Three five-year-olds whiz by me but not before leaving chocolate stains all over my ivory-colored shirt. I sigh, as Ann intercepts me before I can do anything about it.

"There you are," she beams. "I thought maybe you wouldn't make it."

"Why? You're my sister, Ann."

"Well, you gave me George when you could have had him and all…this," she says whipping her gaze around the room. "I thought maybe it would be too much for you, especially when I tell you I'm quitting my job because I can. Speech pathology was never my thing anyway, actually full-time work was never my thing, I'd much rather be a housewife."

"How much have you had to drink?"

"A lot. I'm sorry. Go mingle." Ann teeters off, when George's father approaches me. His myopic views on the world always made me nervous. And besides, who ever heard of a Jewish Republican?

"Well, hello, Laura. I suppose I owe you a thank-you for having introduced my son to your charming sister."

"Oh, it was nothing really," I say. "Congratulations. So how's the politicking business?"

"Wonderful, now that I have my son joining me. With the right grooming I think he could even make it to the Senate one day. That is after he becomes state assemblyman. How's the writing going?"

"Fine, fine. Who knows, maybe one day I'll be able to write the A&E biography of George's political rise to the top."

"Now wouldn't that be something?" He smiles. "In the meantime, you could do mine," he chuckles, much more serious than not. "Let me know when you're ready." And then he turns toward the other guests.

My dad, Walter Taylor, 62, handsome in a Humphrey

Bogart/Jason Robards kind of way, comes up to me and grips my cheek with a strong pinch. I've come to interpret it as a subtext of endearment. My father was always pinching us kids. My siblings hated it. They complained that it hurt. But not me, I loved it. I knew it was my father's way of saying he loved me. "Hi, hon. Where's Gabin?" he asks.

"Gavin," I correct him. "He's on location. Hi, Dad," I say rubbing my cheek.

"Why do you look so worried? Are you nervous about what to do with your big check? You should invest in stocks. I know a good broker you can talk to."

"Aren't stocks a bad idea?"

"Always go against the trend." He winks.

"Oh, you have no idea how much I'm bucking trends," I reply.

"Why are you biting your nails?" he asks.

My nervous habit is a dead giveaway that something's up. I alter reality once again. It's not lying, just rearranging. "It's nothing. The check's just not as big as it was supposed to be." I omit that it's for writing porn.

"Great!" he shouts, trying to be supportive. "Things could be worse. It could have been even less. Just do the best you can," he declares, and then holds my hand in his. "You know I love you, no matter what. But maybe you should consider going to synagogue. Get a little faith going in your life."

"I don't have time for faith, Dad...."

My impromptu speech is suddenly interrupted by a loud screech on the giant home theatre screen. I turn around to see the three five-year-olds with chocolate-stained fingers playing with the VCR and volume controls. Then I notice my purse lying wide open and the naked videotape gone from within, as the kids proudly phoneticize the main title credits, "Fris-kee Bus-i-ness!" they scream. I make a mad dash for the eject button, tackling a few relatives along the way.

"Hey, you guys! That's not—" I freeze, suddenly aware that all eyes in the living room are upon me. The videotape pops out of the machine and the screen goes black. I grab it. They're all waiting for an explanation for my odd behavior. "That's, uh, not finished yet," I fumble. "It's just a rough cut...of my new film...the one I sold...that I've been writing for six months and two weeks and four days...but who's counting?"

"Mazel tov," says my dad. "Why are you holding back on us?"

"Well, I uh, I didn't want to upstage Ann's moment," I offer.

"You're so considerate," my dad says as he pinches my cheek again. "Let us know when it's all done and we can come to the premiere!" There's a round of applause from all the anonymous new relatives in the room.

I smile sheepishly and roll my eyes. I have a new career all right, the backtracking liar, and apparently, I'm not so bad at it.

On my way back to Venice, I cash the check from Cliff Peterson and pay my electric bill. At least it didn't bounce. That was a good sign. At home, my power surges back on. I retrieve an old stopwatch, pen and paper. I am ready to view the tape and study the formula when Adam and Corie enter unannounced with a six-pack of Asahi beer and a box of tantalizing pizza.

"We're treating you to dinner tonight," announces Corie.

"Along with ten bad jokes from the office to lift your spirits," adds Adam.

"Thanks. That's so nice of you guys, but um, look, I've got this movie I have to watch for a writing job, so now's not a good time..." I say, eyeing my ticking clock on the writing deadline. I glance at the pizza, smelling the wonderful aroma. I sheepishly grin, "But feel free to leave a slice before you go."

Adam beams a smile and raises his beer bottle. "To Laura's

quick comeback. It's amazing. You always land on your feet. We'll help you watch it."

"No, really, guys. I can't thank you enough for letting me crash on your couch last night and taking me to the mechanic and being so encouraging. But I really need to do this. I'm going to have to pause it a zillion times plus I have to time the sequences so it won't be any fun for you to watch. Really. Trust me."

"Never trust anyone who says, 'trust me,'" chides Adam as he plops down on my couch making himself comfortable. He flips open the box of pizza. The smells of barbecue chicken and mozzarella cheese waft through the air.

"Well, what's the movie called?" asks Corie. "Maybe we can help you."

"It's just some obscure home video title," I say, closing the box of edible temptation. But before I can deflect another question, Adam reaches for the remote and queries, "How'd you get the writing job anyway or from whom should I ask?"

I leap in front of the television set to block his view. "It was a referral. And um, I don't think the remote works anymore. Here, let me take that from you and put in some new batteries."

But Adam hits the play button and the VCR whirs to life. "It's fine," he says. Credits roll with funny names like Dickey Fire and Woody Tall. The title reads FRISKY BUSINESS.

"Is this a rip-off of *Risky Business?*" asks Corie.

"It's a parody, I think. Look, you guys, I really need to watch this alone. Plus, the producer asked me not to show it to anyone because it's not finished yet."

"So far the soundtrack is horrible and the actors can't act," Adam remarks, oblivious to my request.

"It looks like it was shot on video," Corie adds.

"What's the budget of this movie?" asks Adam.

"Whatever direct-to-video budgets are," I reply as I sit for a moment to jot down notes about the structure I'm supposed to follow and inadvertently grab a piece of the pizza.

"That's usually between one and three million, assuming it's shot on film, but the production value here looks like fifty grand," he comments.

"Look, you guys, you really have to go," I implore, reaching for the off button on the remote that Adam has finally set down on the coffee table. At this point, the room goes silent. All of our jaws simultaneously drop because the actors are now completely naked and ferociously giving each other blow jobs.

Adam giggles first. "You got a job writing a porn film, Laura."

"Well, at least it pays the rent," Corie adds. "When it's finished could we borrow it?"

"Very funny," I say in full confession now. "I've never seen a porn film in my life. And now I'm writing one. I can't do this. What's everyone going to think?"

"Who cares what everyone thinks," Adam says emphatically.

"You don't think it's gross and disgusting and immoral?"

"You need to pay your rent. There's nothing wrong with it. If you need any music licensed, let me know. I'll give you a good deal."

I glance at my purse of bills on the kitchen table, thinking Adam is right. Why should I berate myself? But I still have my dreams to pursue so I beg them, "You guys have to swear to secrecy about this. Promise me! I don't want this to affect my nonexistent Hollywood writing career."

"Okay, okay. Mum's the word. But did you sign a contract with this company?" inquires Corie.

"Just an oral commitment. And no back-end deals either—pardon the puns."

"What's the director's name?" she asks.

"Cliff Peterson."

Adam looks wide-eyed at me, astonished and impressed at the same time. "He's the most prolific porn director around. He used to star in them before he started making them."

"How do you know that?" asks Corie.

"During college I interned at a small production outfit that supplied music to porn companies," he replies.

"Great. So now I'm working with the porn industry's version of Steven Spielberg," I comment.

"In a way, yes. So, what kind of film are you going to write?" Adam asks.

"What do you mean? As in porn comedies, porn westerns or porn adventures?" I retort.

"No," he replies, "as in bondage, bust, gay, gonzo, spanking, gang bang..."

I roll my eyes, "I can't do this."

"Yes, you can," says Adam. "It's that or file for personal bankruptcy and destroy what remaining credit you have. Just make sure the company doesn't have any connections to the mob and you'll be fine."

"The mob?" Corie and I shout simultaneously.

"The mob is notorious for being connected to pornography. But they don't control all of it."

I look out the window for a moment, then turn resolutely to Adam and Corie. "Well, if I'm going to write an adult film," I announce, "I might as well write a damn good one."

I take the first sip from my sixth cup of coffee and glance at the porn codes I've jotted down, when my phone rings. I debate whether or not to answer it as I'm fiendishly trying to work out the story line for *Things Change*. I've got three days left to start and finish this screenplay for Cliff Peterson. Every minute is precious writing time now and I can't afford to do another airport run for George's relatives whom I don't even know. I ignore the ring and keep going. The answering machine clicks on. "Hey, you, it's me. Pick up if you're there."

My heart brightens at the sound of Gavin's voice and I grab the phone. "Hi! How are you?" I ask.

"Great," he replies.

There's a long pause as he neglects to ask how I'm doing with the fallout of my opus script or how the engagement party was for my sister. No matter, I'm not one to stand on ceremony, so I offer it up on my own. "Me, too. I'm much better now. Things are looking up and Ann's party was a success. Everyone asked about you."

"Right. Listen, I'm coming in tomorrow night," he says.

"Want me to pick you up at the airport?"

"No, I've got a meeting to get to right away and then my lawyer's dinner party. Why don't you meet me there? I'll have Henry e-mail you directions."

"Okay," I reply, "but I'm not sure how late I can stay. I've got a writing deadline."

"Can't you work around it?"

"I can try," I say, wishing Gavin would at least ask what it's for. But then I recall the visit to his home in Palm Springs. He reluctantly helped me piece together a writing desk out of plywood and bricks. And whenever I rose early to write he claimed I was abandoning him.

"Oh, and wear something…hot," he adds. "It drives me crazy for you."

"Something *hot,*" I repeat. Gavin likes it when I dress up, which is not all that often, and not that we need it. We had a never-ending supply of passion between us. Jokingly, I add, "No footsie pajamas?"

"No footsies," he says.

On our second date Gavin took me to the Playboy Mansion's Midsummer's Night Party and forewarned me that everyone shows up in pajamas. He purchased a brand-new silk robe for the occasion and I showed up in floral patterned cotton footsies amid glamour girls sporting see-through teddies with high-heeled pumps. I was grateful to meet junior studio executive Hank Willows there, also in footsies, only with a cowboy theme. We bonded over our wardrobe and I'm convinced that's one reason why he tries to hire me for those ever-elusive rewrite deals.

Before I can say goodbye, Gavin hangs up. I put the question of what to wear to the dinner party on hold, unplug the phone, and get back to the writing deadline looming in front of me.

Based on my study of the video Cliff Peterson gave me, I decipher a formula for writing porn. Working on the same Hollywood premise that each written page equals one minute of screen time, I discover that I need a sex scene every seven pages. Unlike the film Cliff gave me, I intend to create a plot with well-developed characters, no pun intended, that provide the reasons for the romance (aka sex). I also determine that writing porn is like designing a puzzle. You have to mix up the variety of sex scenes. Coding B for Boy, G for Girl, and M for Masturbation, I get the following combinations going. B/G, G/G, B/G/G, and GM.

You can also work the story to encompass a limited number of characters and a limited number of locations that you can use several times. You must take into consideration the acting ability of the talent, so plan your dialogue accordingly. From there, you map the characters' relationships to one another and how they are going to lay out, again no pun intended, over the course of the story with logical reasoning injected into each sex scene. Finally, all this needs to be done in ninety minutes. But ninety minutes in porn time equals approximately 40-50 pages in script length. That means a good forty-fifty minutes are devoted to the playing out of those sex scenes. So they had better be well motivated.

And that is how I come up with *Things Change.* I plot

the twists and turns of the story to build a lengthy cohesive outline for my blueprint. The hours pass away. I lose track of time as my characters come to life. Dawn flows to dusk and dusk to dawn. I take catnaps all the while dreaming up more scenes to follow.

Three quarters of the way done on the actual script with one more day to go, I'm interrupted by an incessant knock at my door. I put my characters on hold and answer it. Corie stands there with worry lines on her forehead and a first aid kit in hand.

"Are you okay?" I ask.

"I'm fine," says Corie. "Apparently, you are, too. But your hair's a disgrace."

"Who's that for?" I ask, glancing at what she's holding.

"You," she says. "You don't answer your phone, you don't check your machine, you don't come to the door. I thought you might have OD'd on writing. I was about to call the paramedics. Do me a favor and check in with me from time to time."

"Okay," I sulk obediently, truly touched by her concern.

"When did you last eat?" she asks.

I shrug, "I don't remember, but I'm definitely saving on grocery bills."

"You need nourishment. Come over for dinner in an hour."

"Dinner? What's the date today?"

"The fourteenth. Why?"

"Shit. I'm meeting Gavin at a dinner party. I gotta go, Corie. Thanks for knocking! I'll call you later! 'Bye."

I jump into the shower allowing hot water to cleanse my skin and clear my mind. Inside my head I sift through my wardrobe trying to compose a hot outfit I can put together in a hurry—I know, the black Tara Jarmon pantsuit with a sheer top, a charcoal leather duster and black leather calf-high boots that Bennett gave me last year. It was my one really great thing from a store called Really Great Things. He said it was the kind of quality outfit that would never go out of style. I put it on, adding a touch of makeup, grab the e-mail printout with the directions and scoot out the door. I start the car feeling proud of my progress on the script, anxious to finish it on time, and excited to see Gavin all at once.

The Hollywood dinner party is tucked away in the hills of Lookout Mountain. The house bears a modern design comprised of wood, glass and steel boasting nonstop spectacular city and mountain views from a variety of balconies that cover the entire circumference of the house. The structure is beautiful, but I wonder why the architect built a glass house on stilts on top a mountain near a fault zone. I fear for its inhabitants.

A variety of industryites mill about taking a moment to size each other up before deciding on conversation-participation. That's the part I hate about Hollywood and it's always most evident at the parties Gavin takes me to.

I scan the small crowd looking for Gavin and spot his ex-girlfriend, Ria, who models for Versace. I see the real estate developer who invests in Gavin's overseas-financed film projects, but I can't remember his name. I recognize John Zane, president of the latest studio in town called Avant-Garde, an oxymoronic name since its leading investors come from a cheese conglomerate in France. I see Charlie Roberts, the STA agent in charge of indie film companies, well, no point in asking him about the Accent Film Company now. I spot Bert West, Gavin's entertainment attorney and host of the party. It would be easy to feel intimidated by all these successful and powerful people, but after days holed up writing, it's good to interface with humanity again, and besides, breaking stories makes me invincible, even if it's temporary, and even if it's porn.

I can't find Gavin anywhere and then I see him hand his keys to the valet and walk up the driveway. "You look hot," he says, and greets me with a kiss.

"Thanks, so do you. How was Vancouver?"

"Incredible," he says. "I found a surgeon there for my chin implant, too."

"A chin implant? Why do you want to do that?"

"To even out my facial proportions," he answers matter-of-factly. He neglects to ask me about me which is actually a relief. Maybe it's better he not know about my new clandestine assignment. He quickly moves toward his investor who he pulls aside to boast about the next film he wants to produce, and have the investor finance the screenplay to be written by a friend of his. Gavin's told me how talented I am but I have too much pride to ask if it's me he has in mind. Charlie Roberts joins in, "Hey, Laura. Hey, Gavin. When's the house in Palm Springs going to be ready to party in?"

"The contractor's finishing the kitchen remodel right now," says Gavin. "Be right back."

As he heads for the bar I quietly approach him. "I thought you were having trouble paying your employees this month."

"So?"

"Then how can you afford the kitchen remodel?"

"It's all in the way you move money, Laura." Gavin returns to the group. I wonder why his employees stay with him. His ex-girlfriend slides up next to him and whispers in his ear. I'm not one to practice jealousy or possessiveness, though I think it's rude to whisper. I give Gavin all the space he needs, but I think what I heard was "Scored some hot shit."

During the five-course sit-down dinner, Gavin talks about his new client, Elle Hunter. "She's awesome. Wait until you see her in this next movie. Her quote's going to double."

"What about *The Law of Malus* for her?" I ask.

"I want her to do a comedy next," he replies.

The president of Avant-Garde Studios, John Zane, replies, "Invite me to a rough cut so I can get a lead on her," and then he politely turns to me and asks what I do.

"I'm a writer," I reply.

"She's 'trying' to be a writer," says Gavin, emphasizing the word *trying.* It doesn't feel good. When people only try, they don't do, and I was doing. I decide I need to correct this faux pas.

"But I've written lots of scripts," I say in my own defense.

"Anything that's been produced?" asks Ria.

An unproduced screenwriter is synonymous with being persona non grata in Hollywood. You might as well erase your birth certificate and hope for a better life through reincarnation. The thing is, everyone has to start somewhere. So I decide to mention my start. "I wrote a children's educational film called *Coping with Stress.*"

"That's not fiction," says Gavin. "It doesn't really count."

"Well, actually, Gavin. I am writing," I say. I decide now's the time to tell him, well, sort of. "I got hired to write an original screenplay while you were gone," I explain. "Based on a pitch."

"Congratulations," say the others at the table. But Gavin seems to be fuming.

"I thought you told me the whole thing came apart."

"I got another deal with an independent production company."

"Which one?" pries Charlie Roberts.

"Oh, just a little company called AFC," I reply. Who said an acronym can't suffice for the truth?

"Who are they? How did you get the job? And when did this happen?" prods Gavin.

To recount the tale in front of this crowd feels detrimentally wrong so I deflect with, "It's a really long story. I'll tell you later."

"What's it about?" someone asks.

I take a sip of wine, stalling to figure out the best reply. "It's um, really hard for me to talk about it until after I'm done writing."

"I can understand that," says Charlie. "I tell all my clients the same thing. Don't talk, or you kill the instinct to write."

"I have so much respect for writers," states John Zane. "If you think about it, they are the underpinning for all media companies. They are the bellies of the beast. Without them we don't exist."

"Here, here," toasts Charlie, "and by the way, Gav, you were supposed to get me a writing sample of Laura's two months ago."

I look at Gavin. "He still hasn't gotten it?"

"I did send it," says Gavin, "I'll have to check." But I'm not so sure I believe him this time.

I excuse myself and head for a bathroom only to get lost on the way back via one of the many balconies. A good-looking teenage boy stands alone staring out at the city's twinkling lights. "Hi, there. Taking a break from the dinner party?" I ask.

"Me? Nah. My only association with that crowd is my dad who's hosting it."

"Not following in his footsteps?" I grin.

"Oh, I was until a year ago. Now I want nothing to do with it." He leans back against the wall. "Things change."

"Yeah, they sure do."

He exhales and cocks his head toward me, "My girlfriend since third grade died in a car accident. Now all I do is think about the meaning of things."

"There is no meaning in life until you give your life meaning." I pause. "My dad says that."

He looks at me and grins, then repeats my words with a bemused expression.

Surprisingly, Gavin appears, "What are you guys doing? There's no talking about serious crap now."

I am shocked by Gavin's response.

"Come on, let's get back to the table. I'm trying to grow a business here."

The kid and I share a goodbye glance steeped in mutual understanding. What a good man he is, I think, and wonder how much more grand he'll be when his true age catches up with his spirit.

As dessert and coffee roll around at eleven, I politely turn to Gavin and the others. "Excuse me. I have a deadline on my script so unfortunately I have to leave now to get up at 4:30 to finish it." I look at Gavin and quietly add, "If you want, you're welcome to sleep over."

Everyone wishes me luck, except Gavin.

Once I'm in my car, my body starts to relax. The people at dinner were pleasant enough, but these parties where women are treated more like adornments always cause my Midwestern sensibilities to freak out.

I glide past billboards for new movies while checking my cell phone for messages. The recorded voice tells me I have three messages.

First message: "It's Corie calling and I hope you ate a lot and are storing it up in your fuel cells because you're going to need it. I scored two tickets from STA to the hottest premiere in town tomorrow night. Adam can't make it so excuse the by-default invitation, but you're going to want to go with me. Why? So I can introduce you to a new executive looking for family dramas. I've already hinted to him about *The Law of Malus.* See you then." I smile at Corie's message and hit skip.

Second message: "Hi, honey, it's Mom. I thought you'd want to know that I made it back to Michigan just fine. I'll be back out next month to help with Ann's shower so I'll see you then. By the way, have you finished pondering yet?" At least she has a sense of humor, my mother. I hit skip again.

Third message: "Hi, Laura." I nearly get in an accident. The voice is so sexy it steers me off course. "It's Cliff. Just want you to know I'm looking forward to getting the script tomorrow." Tomorrow? Did he say tomorrow? I thought I had one more full day and night. Exhausted, I step on the gas.

Waking from a deep sleep, I realize that Gavin is knocking on my door and yelling for me to open up. His face looks tight with stress.

"What's wrong?" I ask as he starts pacing the room.

"I can't see you anymore. How could you leave? I can't date someone who would leave a dinner party early."

Shaking, I reply, "I honestly don't get you, are you insane, Gavin? You're a control freak on a power trip!" I shout.

"You are so wrong!"

"And you are so impervious to criticism or self-growth, you just don't get it. Let's just call it quits."

"You can't break up with me," hollers Gavin.

"Okay, then you break up with me, because I have a writing deadline and I can't let you screw it up unless you want to move money into Laura Taylor's debt reduction program. Otherwise, there's the door."

I open it up for him and motion for him to make his exit. He leaves huffing and puffing like a big bad wolf whose hot air was simply not strong enough to blow my house down.

take three

THE IRONY OF IT ALL

"Sorry," I say, nervously handing my screenplay to Cliff Peterson. "I meant to get here earlier but then I inadvertently took a nap and hit rush hour traffic. Um, do you think you'll be able to give me the rewrite notes in a couple of days?"

"I'll give them to you in an hour," he says. Wow, I think, in Hollywood it takes a minimum of two weeks to get script notes back from an executive. Cliff plops himself down in his chair and devours the first pages of the script. He glances up at me.

"Hey, I can have someone show you around the place while I read the script."

The next thing I know, a very cute guy in charge of marketing named Tommy Kaplan is escorting me around the Accent Film Company. Tommy is a sprightly guy with a lot of energy for the end of a workday. Exhausted from writing, I politely ask for a cup of coffee. I figure the least I can do is keep my eyes open during the tour. Tommy happily leads me to the makeshift kitchen and pours me a cup of instant coffee. Already I see stark differences between Hollywood production companies and adult entertainment ones. When we continue with the tour I notice the hallways are adorned with posters of stacked naked women as opposed to the studios' expensively-framed one-sheets stacked with credits.

As Tom guides me through 25,000 square feet of space used to churn out, market and distribute porn, he explains to me that the posters are used to promote the films at trade conventions. The biggest convention is in Vegas every January. Tom continues to broaden my knowledge by telling me that the "girls," which I deduce means actresses, stand behind the company's booth and sign the posters for fans who line up in droves. I notice that Tom seems really normal, except for all the words coming out of his mouth.

I follow him into the post-production bays where a couple of longhaired disheveled guys named Wolfe and Brandon work on computers editing scenes of naked people. The action in every scene seems the same, the only difference being their surroundings.

Tom leads me past rows of video duplicating machines into a vast cavern of space filled from floor to ceiling with shelves of adult videotapes. He hands me one as an example. The picture on the cover flaunts two naked women with white hats fawning over a half-naked guy. I can't believe that even in porn men don't reveal as much, at least not on box covers. The title reads *Nurses in Love.* Inside the feeble box, a piece of flimsy molded plastic contains the videotape.

"Why is the box so big and flimsy?" I ask.

"It's standard for the industry. I'm not sure why. It's always been like that. But take a look at these new box covers from Europe. They're much nicer." He hands me a much sturdier box than the other one. It easily flips open from the side like a book instead of folding open from the top. I notice that Tom's quite proud of these new boxes.

Off to one side on a shelf, I glimpse a giant stack of video-tapes labeled *Jesus Loves You*. "You do religious porn, too?"

"Oh, that," says Tom, "those are videotapes from a local church group. We handle some of their video duplication for them."

The more I learn, the more fascinated I find myself becoming with this strange new world until I spot some funny looking boxes in another corner of the warehouse. "What's that?" I ask.

"Those are dildos, sometimes we bundle them with merchandise as a sales tool."

"Oh," I say.

"Here, have one."

"Why would I want a dildo?" I ask shyly.

"You should have one," he states.

"Gee, thanks, but you really don't have to."

"It's okay, I want to." I can tell he likes me, but this is a strange way to show it. He quickly retrieves some boxes, insisting I look at them. "See, there are all kinds of shapes and sizes and colors. Which one do you like?"

Tom displays for me pink dildos, brown dildos, flesh-colored dildos, ribbed textured dildos, smooth dildos, large and small dildos, and one giant double-sided dildo. I can't even imagine what you do with that one.

"I'm not sure I like any of them," I say horrified, but then I notice how authentic they appear. "How do they get them to look so real?" I ask as my curiosity takes over.

"They take a mold of a guy's penis," replies Tom, as if it's common knowledge.

"Oh," I say, nodding my head. "Of course."

★ ★ ★

Tom drops me off at Cliff's office and leaves. I suddenly feel like I'm without a safety net. Cliff asks me to take a seat and then sits across from me. His deep voice drips with sexual energy and it's making me nervous.

"I really like your script, Laura," he says. I breathe, relieved. "But it's a little long. Usually these scripts are thirty pages. Yours is fifty-four."

"I can edit it down if you want."

"No. I'll tell you what I'm going to do instead. I'm going to make two movies out of it. Part one and Part two. And because the script is exceptionally good, I'm going to shoot it on 16 millimeter film and increase the budget. It'll be $150,000. I'll use two of the hottest girls, Tess Knight and Lacey Larson. They're all natural. No fake anything, you know? I think you'll be very pleased with it when it's done."

"Wow, that's great," I reply, not knowing what else to say. Suddenly aware that now I'll have two produced movie credits to my name with apparently two of the biggest female stars in the business.

"The only thing you need to change is the ending. Since this is a co-production with Erotica, the girl has to end up with a guy."

"Erotica?" I ask, surprised by this new information.

"They get the soft-core cable version and we distribute two hard-core versions."

"Oh," I say, suddenly aware that my two movies have now turned into three. "Are there any other changes you want me to make?"

"Just your name. You'll need a pseudonym."

A pseudonym, I think, stumped. I wonder if there's a Pseudonym Store you can go to, to pick one up. Maybe I could enlist Corie's help. I'll have to remember to ask her later tonight.

* * *

"Decadent," I say. "Definitely decadent."

"I'd add debauchery, self-indulgent and hedonistic to the list," says Corie, as we flex adjectives to best describe a typical Hollywood studio's premiere party. In this case, Avant-Garde Studios has transformed its back lot into a giant igloo to match a key location in the movie it's about to release.

Corie and I have dressed up for the occasion. I'm repeating my outfit from the night before and Corie's coordinated a Donna Karan pantsuit with a pair of shoes from a discount chain, of which she's quite proud. "Ever since STA signed a shoe diva to rep the discount brand, everyone at STA receives a thirty percent discount to shop there," she explains, "it's not how much you spend, it's how you put it all together."

"But what if the shoe falls apart?" I ask.

"What will it matter? At the rate things move these days, the new trend will be in and I'll be able to afford the next new shoe. Thinking you're only as good as the amount of money you spend on a product is just part of the marketing conspiracy to get people to pay more!"

"You're so convincing, Corie, and such a good company loyalist. I shudder to think what you'll be able to sell when you become an agent."

"I heard the ultimate is getting people to buy their own car," she quips.

Our focus returns to the decadent premiere party as we meander into the star-studded crowd.

"Do they have premiere parties for X-rated movies?" Corie asks.

"No, and they make more money than Hollywood and television combined. In fact, adult entertainment is a leading export of this country."

Corie stops and looks at me. "You've been doing some homework, haven't you?"

"Yes, I have. And that's not all I learned. The number of video rentals has been rising steadily. It's a growth market."

"That's amazing. Think of all the people that industry must feed," replies Corie.

"You're not kidding," I say. "Speaking of food, let's shift direction and go feast on the hors d'oeuvres." I lead the way.

"So in all your research did you find out how industry-standard pseudonyms are invented?" asks Corie.

"Actually, I did. I found out that porn stars often get their names by combining the name of their childhood pet with the name of the street they grew up on, in which case, I would be Freckles Stansbury."

"And I would be Bambi Feathers," laughs Corie.

"But then I'm not a porn star," I say. "Somehow, I've become a porn writer—in need of pseudonym—by tomorrow at ten. So you gotta help me, Corie."

"What about Luscious Lips Laura?"

I look at her like she's out of her mind. "You know what? I love you, but it's okay. I'll find inspiration elsewhere."

We maneuver past the movie mascots dressed in mint-green Eskimo outfits parading around the perimeter of the igloo.

"I hope there aren't any designers here or we'll have *Nanook of the North* fashions again this fall," Corie comments.

"That's one thing about adult movies," I mention. "They never have their clothes on long enough to create a fashion statement. Unless of course, you consider nudity its own unique fashion statement." I ponder this last thought as we continue along. Maybe I could write an adult film making nudity a fashion statement, sort of a twist on *The Emperor's New Clothes.*

As we head for the moveable feast, Corie's mini-cell phone rings. She digs through her purse to find it as I guide us through the throng of celebrities and celebrants.

Corie listens and relays, "It's Adam. ASE Sports Network wants to license his music for all their shows." She returns to the mouthpiece, "That's great, Ad. Hey, Laura needs a pseudonym ASAP. Any ideas?" She turns to me and repeats, "Adam said to use the name *Bella Feega,* that it's perfect for you."

"What, did I suddenly become Italian?" I inquire.

"I like it," comments Corie.

"What's it mean?" I ask, finding myself oddly excited at the idea of adopting an alter ego.

Corie repeats my question to Adam, pauses a moment with a stunned expression, then looks at me, "He said it's Italian slang for *pretty pussy.*"

"That is disgusting!" I howl.

"But it is a nice alliteration," chimes Corie, then addresses her cell phone looking more than perturbed. "Since when did you become bilingual?"

"How 'bout something a little more mellow—what's Italian for *beautiful breasts?*" Corie hands me the phone so I can speak to him. "Are you crazy?" I ask.

"There is no slang for the upper chest," says Adam. "I'm telling you, Laura, go with *Bella Feega.* But I'd spell it with two *e*s. I promise it'll come in handy one day."

"Adam, how do you always know this stuff?" I ask.

"I had an Italian girlfriend in Florence when I did my junior year abroad. She taught me everything."

I hang up and hand the phone back to Corie. She offers me a sly smile and asks, "Shall we move on—Bella?"

"Not funny," I say. "I now have dual personalities growing inside my one body and you're making a joke out of it."

Corie laughs.

We pass by Hollywood's elite; top agents, producers, and celebrities, all there to attend the premiere of Jeremy Kincaid's latest film extravaganza, *Morning to be Reckoned.*

Jeremy Kincaid passes by and politely smiles at me. There's a tinge of recognition, but only for a moment. He keeps walking.

"He doesn't even remember our meeting. And he was so close to optioning my first draft of *Malus.* Remember? It's just as well. What would I say if he asked me what I was writing these days?"

"Good point. Have you considered learning how to fib?" asks Corie.

"Not one of my better skills," I reply. "Though necessity seems to be helping."

"It's so *not* Kincaid, anyway," says Corie as she lifts bruschetta sprinkled with caviar to her mouth. "Can you really see him making an intimate family drama?"

"Why do people need to pigeonhole each other? You don't see directors working in only one genre," I retort. The pigeonholing trait really frustrates me. And it feels like a double standard. Directors can direct a wide range of genres while writers, according to one agent I know, have to stick to one. But what if your talent expands into other types of stories?

I look around at the industryites and movie stars in attendance and sigh. "Face it, Corie, the only movies that get made are the ones that can guarantee a big return, and that doesn't include an emotional romantic epic like *The Law of Malus.*"

"*The Law of Malus* deserves to be told. So don't give up, Laura. I believe in it."

"Do you think this new studio will, too?" I ask hopefully.

Corie cringes. "I doubt it. I did some digging and found out their mandate for now is action-adventure. But it's just one studio so don't despair. Oh, there's Jason. Wait here while I say a quick hello."

I watch Corie get wrapped up in a long conversation with her boss, the slick Significant Talent Agency's talent agent, Jason Brand. I see Hank Willows from Satellite in the distance, but I don't have it in me to say hello. Ever since the rewrite he promised fell through, I don't trust myself not to sound desperate for work. I glance at the meandering crowd and decide it's time to explore the illustrious Avant-Garde lot.

I realize I've wandered too far from the giant igloo when I feel a tap on my shoulder. I spin around to come face-to-face with Mitchell Mann, my old boyfriend. Four years ago I delivered a script to him from Eric Leve at STA. At the time, Eric had just signed Mitchell, a young, charismatic British music video director with a burning desire to direct horror films. Eric got him his first gig directing *Zombies Cometh* for a mini-studio. As I handed Mitchell the script on set, Cupid struck before I could detect that Mitchell's confidence was merely a disguise for arrogance.

For all of his cultural bravado and European appeal, being romantic, sensual or interesting in bed eluded him. Mitchell was a one-note lover. I desperately sought to counterbalance this, to expand his sexual horizons and fulfill my longing for a gentle, loving nature supported by a deep emotional connection. So I tried enticing Mitchell with romantic stories. I didn't know then that they would be the underpinning for my future writing career. I created stories full of plot that always turned him on but never achieved the effect I wanted.

After I attempt to cover my gasp, my mind races. What's he doing here? He turned into a B movie director of really bad horror films that go straight to video. The fake blood looked real enough but the actors were poorly cast and the stories always fell apart somewhere between the opening credits and the beginning of Act One. *Morning to be Reckoned* is an A-list party. The two just don't go together. Then again, maybe I shouldn't talk. I *used* to work in the world that packages A-list movies, but look at me now, far below B, I was now at X, triple X to be precise.

"How are you? You're looking good." He's got that lusty

look in his eye. After three years of an on-again off-again relationship filled with emotional turmoil, I can't believe the magnetism between us is still there. It's not pure chemistry, but a heady mix of lust and fear.

"I can't really talk to you right now, Mitchell," I say, remembering my therapist's admonition to stay away from any dialogue with him. I had to keep reminding myself why, oh yes, because any semblance of rational thinking refused to be a part of it.

"I'm not doing coke anymore," he announces like a little boy seeking approval for his redeemed behavior.

"Good for you." Memories of his Jekyll and Hyde behavior patterns flood my thinking. Only I never knew he had a coke problem. It wouldn't have made sense. He was Mr. Health. Tofu hot dogs and beans for breakfast, he was a profound anti-dairy activist and proponent of anything soy. A strict vegan, he wouldn't even wear leather other than a belt his grandfather gave him during his pre-vegan years. In addition, he exercised every day with weights or practiced some form of cardio. So the fact that Mitchell had become addicted to cocaine was incongruous with who he was, except that who he was, was a hypocrite.

Moving closer, he whispers, "I miss you. Tell me. What are you writing now? I'd like to know."

"You would?"

"I'm always looking for good material."

"Right. Well, I…I got a three-picture deal."

"No shit. Need a director?"

"They come attached with one," I say.

"What kind of stories are they?" he asks.

I couch my answer, "Erotic psychological dramas."

Mitchell grins, seductively boxing me into a corner. "Not your usual milieu. A young girl leaves home in search of her dog."

"Funny, very funny, Mitchell. I'd like to go now."

He holds up his arm to stop me. "Look, Laura, Shelly tricked me. She told me she was on the pill. The truth is I didn't want to wait any longer for a kid. You did. But it was on my agenda before I hit thirty. She's due in two months. It's just that I don't really trust her, I'd rather be with you."

"And I don't really trust you. You're the one who slept with her while you were talking to me about wedding rings."

"Come on, Laura. You know I'm crazy about you. Let's get out of here. I'll go rent us a room at the Bel Air Hotel and we can really talk about all this."

"A hotel room?"

"It's just that your place is far and Shelly and her mother are living with me now. Come on. I really miss you." He starts to pull me into his arms. His British brogue adds to the allure. "I promise I'll open up. And then you can tell me one of those great romantic fantasies you're always coming up with. You never did finish the one where I'm fucking you in a barn."

I feel myself diminishing into his vortex again. The seduction of his accent and smooth mannerisms speak to me. I have to get away, but he draws me closer. I wish for someone to save me from the destructive magnetism that's moving into play here.

Suddenly, Mitchell lets out a short screech and pulls away. His skin sizzles, exposing a tiny burn on his arm. Behind him stands a beautiful blond woman in erudite glasses, who tosses her cigarette on the ground with a pretentious apology.

"Oh, sorry, I'm afraid my cigarette grazed your skin," she says. And then ignoring Mitchell, she turns to me. "Are you Laura Taylor?"

I twist around, accidentally bumping into her chest as I distance myself from Mitchell.

"I've been looking all over for you," she says, giving Mitchell a get-lost look. Underneath sophisticated clothes, an extremely confident woman exhales the last of the smoke with hints of smoldering sexuality. She smiles at me as I collect myself from the embarrassment of Mitchell's surprise come-on.

"I couldn't help but overhear your conversation. I'm Sara Stephenson."

Mitchell immediately interrupts, "From Eagle Films." He extends his hand for a shake but she ignores it. "I'm Mitchell Mann. The director. I'm being considered to direct one of your…"

Sara ignores Mitchell and turns to me. "I'm very interested in the genre you're writing."

"Really?"

"Yes." She glances away. "I have to use the rest room. Let's talk there."

Sara and I walk off leaving Mitchell in our wake. He blurts out, "I'll talk to you later." And then as quickly as he appeared, he disappears.

Inside a tiny back lot bathroom, Sara looks at me with genuine concern. "Are you all right?"

"Yes," I say, mortified.

"You sure? We can rest here or leave altogether so he doesn't bother you again."

"No, I'll be okay. Thanks. How did you know to look for me?"

"Hank Willows from Satellite pointed you out. He said you're a great writer and I should know you." She dampens a paper towel and hands it to me. I cool myself down. Once she sees that I'm okay, she pulls out her eyeliner and begins applying it to her left eye. "So tell me, what's the premise of your movie?"

"It's a trilogy. They're all journeys of self-discovery, women empowering themselves after humiliating encounters with men," I reply.

She offers a knowing grin, then pulls out her lipstick, "Sounds intriguing. Can your agent send them over to me for a read?"

I watch, fascinated with her transformation as she sensuously applies red lipstick, top lip first, bottom lip second, then neatly fitting them together like two perfect halves of a whole for a perfect blend. "I don't have an agent anymore and they're uh, not available. The uh, studio, doesn't want anyone duplicating their production plans."

At the words *not available,* her interest level drastically rises. She stops her routine and looks at me, impressed. "They're going into production? On all three?"

I nod.

"Good for you." She stops and looks at my face. "Let me put some makeup on you." I obediently tilt my head back as she applies blush. "So who're the director and talent?"

In the interest of self-preservation, I decide to continue practicing the art of the fib, a slight variation on the white lie. "I'm under contract not to say…until they do a press release. I think they're still ironing out everyone's contract."

Sara's interest skyrockets. Then she focuses on my eyes. "You've got beautiful long lashes," she says. "Look down for me." I do, feeling the mascara thicken and lengthen them. "You must be quite a writer," she adds. I humbly shrug as she takes the lipstick and gently holds my chin up. "Promise me you'll let me be the first to see your next spec script."

I look back into her eyes, "Uh-huh."

"Good. Now part your lips for me."

I do as I'm told, staring into Sara's face as she applies red lipstick on me. I pucker, connecting the halves to make a whole, and then split them apart again. Red looms out at me, reminding me of the Red Sea, which in turn reminds me of a sermon at synagogue that Rabbi Weiss once gave. "The Red Sea taught us that only when we stepped into the water, did the waters part. This is a defining value of

Jewish life," he stated. "For there is a natural human desire to understand what we undertake before committing to it. But only by doing the act, committing to the act, do we truly understand it." I wonder about Cliff Peterson, Tommy, what had I committed to? And would I ever understand it?

We exit the bathroom and Sara turns to me once again, "You didn't mention the title," she carefully digs.

"*Things Change.* It's a working title," I mumble as Corie finally reappears. "Uh, Sara, this is my friend, Corie Berman. She works at STA with Jason Brand."

They exchange perfunctory hellos. Sara pulls a business card out of her wallet and hands it to me. "Why don't you call my office this week and we'll get together for dinner. I'd like to hear what else you're working on."

She leaves and Corie gives me a look. "I'd say that's major, dinner—not lunch, not breakfast, not even drinks—dinner. What did you tell her?"

"That I had just written an erotic psychological drama that's going into production next week. I didn't know it would pique so much interest—apparently, I've been writing in the wrong genre all this time."

Seeping through a rare cloud, afternoon sunlight hits our lunch table. Elaine Dover, no longer doing acquisitions, is now an MOW (Movies of the Week) executive, producing stories primarily about DOMs (Diseases of the Month). She treats me to a meal at a popular Italian eatery.

It's been three weeks since Scott Sher became persona non grata at STA and it's still big news in Hollywood. Elaine whispers to me, "I heard that the Peace Corps in South Africa was really a cover for a rehab center in North Dakota."

"Really. I hadn't heard that," I say, disinclined to get involved in the gossip.

"Did you hear about Richard Marksman, president of

STA? He's trying to buy that weird nightclub on Melrose as a venue to launch STA's emerging music acts."

"Really. I hadn't heard that either," I say. Thinking to myself, no wonder he needs a floor of one million on every client.

"There's a rumor that he's going to retire soon," she adds.

"That I don't believe. He's a deal guy, Elaine. Deal guys never retire. He may exit the STA building but guys like him never leave the deal behind, even if it's to negotiate a golf package inside a retirement plan."

"You're right. Oh, I almost forgot to tell you. I heard back from the Ladies' Network," she says. My eyes widen with hope. Elaine is a big fan of *The Law of Malus* and given her new position she asked me if she could present it as a movie of the week. "They loved it! And they thought the writing was exceptional," she says.

"Really?" I ask, my emotions leaping forward with joy.

"Yeah. But they have to pass because they just bought a story similar to it a month ago," Elaine explains. I let go a sigh.

"I think you should keep trying to set it up as a feature," she adds. "It's totally Oscar material."

"I'm trying," I say.

"You just need a new agent to get you out there. That and a lucky break."

"Yeah, I hope you're right. But waiting for my lucky break is getting costly. I may have to find a way to help move it along. Excuse me—I have to go to the rest room, Elaine. I'll be right back. And then I want to hear about you and Dennis."

I stroll past tables laced with agents, studio executives and talent. Former newbie agents at STA turned junior studio executives gesture hello to me. I wave back, wondering if I might not be better off changing tack and finding a cushy executive job rather than depend on the odds of getting a screenplay produced.

When I return from the bathroom Elaine asks me, "So who's Bella Feega?"

"How do you know about Bella Feega?" I whisper incredulously. I hadn't heard from the Accent Film Company since I handed in the first draft of *Things Change* two weeks ago.

"While you were in the bathroom your cell phone kept ringing," she says. "It was making a lot of noise so I answered it. Someone called asking for Bella Feega. He said it was really important. I thought it was a wrong number. But I have to admit, the guy sounded really sexy. If I wasn't engaged to Dennis I might have asked for his number."

My cell phone rings again and I quickly answer it. Before I can say a word, a voice on the other end shouts above some background noise, "Is Bella Feega there?!"

"Yes, this is Bella Feega!" I say, equally loud, by accident.

A short waiter with dark hair stops dead in his tracks and looks at me with a strange smile, which is astutely caught in Elaine's encompassing vision. I immediately lower my voice. "The copy machine ate them? Yeah, sure, I can drive it out to you. Pages 12 to 17. Where are you shooting? Okay. See you soon." I hang up and turn to Elaine. "Elaine, I'm really sorry, but I have to go. It's an emergency of sorts."

"You have a movie in production, don't you? Why wouldn't you tell me?"

"It's sort of complicated," I say.

"Well, who's Bella Feega?"

"I'll have to tell you another time. I, uh, I really have to go."

"Why can't you tell me now?" she asks.

"You know production budgets, Elaine. Every minute costs money, right? So I better run," I reply, hoping that will satisfy her.

As I'm leaving the table, Elaine shouts out again, "But

who's Bella Feega!?" And all the Italian waiters and waitresses turn to stare at me. Yet I press on.

I drive through Coldwater Canyon toward an exquisite home near the top of Mulholland Drive. Later, I find out that the homeowners are on vacation and have rented their home to the Accent Film Company. I park on the street. Only a few cars reside nearby. It hardly looks like a film crew is here. I see no honey wagons or five-ton grip and lighting trucks. I check the address again. This is it.

I knock on the door but no one answers. I walk along the side of the house toward the backyard, which is completely hidden from the nearest neighbor. A small crew of half a dozen people surround a pool that looks like a grotto. I see Cliff Peterson standing behind a cameraman. The cameraman weaves around a particularly secluded area.

As I approach, I hear a lot of moaning and groaning. Some crewmembers shift positions and I suddenly see two women—fully naked and on top of each other. Cliff says, "Okay, Buck, get ready to enter the scene when I say."

Off camera, I see a handsome hunk standing naked; his huge engorged penis hangs next to a young woman kneeling beside him, rubbing it, to keep it that way.

"Action," says Cliff.

Buck enters the scene and joins the two women. I realize this is the scene where Denise's character, aching out of loneliness over her lover Lisa's departure, has a threesome with her client and her client's husband. A G/G/B.

All three seem to be enjoying the sexual interlude and are begging for more. This includes Denise's character, which works against the story line.

Buck starts to enter Denise. My mouth drops, I've never witnessed a penis that big before. I throw my hands over my eyes and then slowly peek through my separated fingers.

"Okay, Jake, get a tight shot of Buck and Denise," barks

Cliff. Jake swings the camera around and zooms in on the action. "Now get her reaction, let's see her in ecstasy," adds Cliff.

I can't help it. I take my hands off my face and blurt, "Cut!"

Everything freezes, even the humping. Cliff turns around. "Who said that?"

"Me?" I humbly offer, meagerly holding up my hand.

Cliff marches over to me. "You know I'm the director, right?"

"Right," I say, and quietly whisper to him, "but um, Cliff, Denise's character is enjoying this way too much."

He looks at me funny. "We're making a porn film, she's having sex. She's supposed to like it."

"No, she's not," I say.

He rolls his eyes, exasperated. "Laura. Who's the virgin here?"

"Okay, wait and hear me out. She's supposed to be missing Lisa. So, even though she's there, she's not supposed to really be there, in her mind I mean, she's just supposed to be going through the motions."

The funny look on his face does not shift, so I continue, "Look, if she's enjoying it so much, then we're not going to believe that she really misses Lisa and goes to all the trouble to hire some guy to get her back. Besides, she's not supposed to be the one who's into men—that's Lisa's character arc," I say.

The actors and the crew overhear me. Everybody looks up. I realize I have overstepped my boundaries. Writers are never supposed to make a suggestion that could upstage the director. At least not in Hollywood. In Hollywood, the director is *auteur.* I had no idea if this credo applied to adult films, but I was about to find out.

"It's in the exposition on the missing pages," I say, pulling extra copies of the missing pages out of my bag. This might even save face for the director and keep the scene intact.

Denise looks up from the frozen ménage à trois. "Cliff...that does kind of make sense. If I'm still in love with Lisa, maybe my eyes should wander off or something, like I'm thinking about her."

"It might be a good idea to have a tight shot on her face that's full of sadness and regret," I suggestively add.

Cliff looks over the pages I hand him. A contemplative expression takes over. He leans his head back and closes his eyes. Everybody remains silent.

Quickly, Cliff juts his head back to its normal position and announces, "Okay. Let's try it. In fact, Ian, put some tears on Denise's face for the close-up when she starts missing Lisa. Okay, everyone, let's pick it up where we left off."

Buck looks down at his crotch then back up again, "There's nothing to pick up anymore."

Cliff peers around. "Who's the fluff girl today?"

The young woman on the sideline steps forward, "I am."

"Okay, Annie, please take care of Buck," says Cliff.

Annie rushes over to Buck and starts sucking his penis. In a matter of moments Cliff declares, "Action."

I stand there in shock over the graphic scene being played out before me. The actors reach a climax together and Cliff Peterson yells, "Cut."

Cliff turns and, as if nothing unusual has happened, saunters up to me. "You've got balls, Laura, but I like that. You're welcome to stay and watch if you want." He faces the crew. "Okay, everyone, let's set up for the goodbye scene between Denise and Lisa. Ian, freshen up their makeup. Jake, I want to go with soft, diffused lighting. Laura, can you give the actresses their missing pages? Thanks," he says and walks off toward the house.

Denise and a brunette girl I haven't seen before are now in their bathrobes. I assume the other girl must be the lead character, Lisa. A male makeup artist applies lip liner and powder on their faces. He calls out to me, "Excuse me, could you please bring me that other box of makeup by your feet?"

"Sure," I say and lug it over.

"Thanks, I'm Ian Bujinski," he says as he opens the box.

"I'm Laura Taylor," I reply. "I uh, wrote the script, here are the missing pages." I hand them over to the brunette and the blonde beside her.

The Lisa character looks at me, and smiles, "Hi, I'm Tess. I really like your script," she says. Her petite frame and tender air of vulnerability enhance her already established beauty. The blonde, equally as gorgeous with an air of self-assuredness says, "Me, too, I'm Lacey, by the way."

"Thanks," I say. "Nice to meet you."

The two actresses look over the missing pages of the script. "Wow, this is a lot of dialogue," remarks Lacey. Her face scrunches up in concentration. "I'm not sure I can remember all of this."

"I can help you," I offer, "we could do a quick rehearsal right now. Start with Lisa's line—'Something happened…'"

Tess flatly delivers the line, "Something happened at work today."

"Um, Tess, try to say that as if you know you're about to break up with Denise. You're a little scared to tell her, but you know you have to. You can't lie to yourself anymore, even though you know it's really going to hurt Denise."

"'Something happened at work today,'" says Tess, mixing painful hesitation with full disclosure.

"That's perfect," I say. Tess smiles. "Keep going."

"'Jonathan kissed me and…and I felt…something,'" Tess looks directly at Lacey now and adds a touch of sexual excitement, "'He really turned me on.'"

Lacey looks at me, confused.

"Okay, Lacey," I say, "your character knows deep down what this means—you know that Lisa is second-guessing her sexuality and that this might mean she'll leave you, so your response has to have tones of denial underneath it."

"'So what,'" says Lacey as Denise. "'Now you're ready for us tonight. Come on, give me a kiss and you'll forget the whole thing.'"

"That's great," I say. "All you have to do is remember that those are the emotions driving your characters. Lisa knows she needs to leave this relationship and Denise is going to do everything she can to stop it, but not without first feeling hurt, angry, and resistant. Lisa is going to be as kind and honest as possible, yet she doesn't give in. She knows this is something she must do."

"Then why does the scene end with them making love?" asks Tess.

"It's a bittersweet goodbye. It's the most tender love-making they've ever had and Denise is determined to make Lisa feel so good that she'll want to come back to her. That, and I needed another sex scene," I explain.

One of the crew walks up to us. "We're ready for the goodbye scene in the bedroom," he says.

I follow Tess, Lacey, and Ian into the house. Cliff directs the actresses as to where he wants them to stand. A woman, who I assume manages the wardrobe department, gives the women outfits to put on. The actresses casually drop their bathrobes and climb into their wardrobes. Tess slips into a pretty summer cocktail dress and Lacey wears masseuse attire. I realize in that moment that dressing rooms on an adult set are not a requirement and automatically make that line item disappear in a production budget.

Cliff calls out, "Action." I'm about to leave. I can't bear to see my dialogue ripped apart. But then I hear the women flawlessly execute the scene. I circle around to watch the rest of it.

Lisa

Ever since my father left I wrote men off. Never even gave them a chance. Then you came along...and you took me in...and I realized I've never been on my own, you know.

Denise

You don't have to punish yourself for the way you live.

Lisa

I'm not. I just need to move out and explore my sexuality. I need to find out if I'm really gay or not.

Denise paces the room, hurt, scared and angry.

Denise

I don't believe this. You're leaving me.

Lisa

(with great sensitivity)

Don't say that. I have to find the answers to some questions. Please...try to understand.

Denise acts numb, unable to speak. Lisa comes up behind her, gently brushing the hair from the nape of her neck, then softly whispers in her ear with deep affection and love.

Lisa

Hey, if I get through this then we'll be together and I'll never have doubts again.

Denise perks up at the possibility of hope in the future.

Denise

Promise?

Lisa softly kisses the nape of Denise's neck.

Lisa

I promise.

Denise takes Lisa into her arms and kisses her on the lips, deeply and passionately. The women portray the fear of losing each other and are unable to break away at the lips. The kiss builds. Denise sweeps Lisa onto the bed and begins to undress her as their passion grows. Lisa is completely naked now. Denise sensuously strokes Lisa's hair off her face, then hungrily kisses her again.

Denise

I'm not going to let you forget how good it is, Lisa.

Lisa relishes Denise's touch.

Lisa

(murmurs)

I don't want to forget, Denise.

I've never seen two women together before. I had only imagined it for the script. Now, suddenly, the reality is in my face. Both women kiss and fondle each other, even suck each other's breasts, embracing each other as if they never want the moment to end. I am extremely uncomfortable. It seems the scene has mesmerized everyone. And the guys all have bulges in their pants.

As Cliff directs the cameraman in and around the women in bed, I realize that the actresses no longer speak coherent words. The dialogue has dried up for now. At this point, my job has come to an end and witnessing the extracurricular activity is embarrassing, so I politely excuse myself and escape to my car.

On the street, I notice a big black Lincoln idling beneath a maple tree nearby. As I start my car, the Lincoln's backseat window descends several inches and a lone billow of smoke pours out. I didn't know it then, but I would come to know that Lincoln and its mysterious inhabitant soon enough.

take four

THINGS CHANGE

I'm studying the want ads of Hollywood's premiere trade paper, *Inside Hollywood*. Next to me is my notepad appropriately labeled JOB HUNTING LOG SHEET. Eric Leve's name is on top with an "LW" next to it. Underneath his name is "Larry Solomon." I pick up the phone and dial.

"Hi, you've reached the cell phone of Larry Solomon, editor of *Inside Hollywood*. I'll be in corporate meetings all week. Leave a message and I'll get back to you as soon as possible," says the ephemeral voice of my former English professor turned editor. He had come through for me with two freelance articles before a corporate merger involving the trade paper, reached its finale. He even supplied me with a temporary press pass. Larry's job had been spared in the staff cutbacks and I thought maybe he could provide me with more work. It was worth a chance.

The beep sounds and I take my cue, "Hi, Larry. It's Laura Taylor. I was just wondering if you happened to have any writing assignments available or any staff positions that need to be filled… Okay, well, keep me posted. 'Bye."

"Left word," I say, and mark "LW" next to his name when my intercom buzzes. I flip it on.

"Mom and I are waiting curbside," booms the voice of my sister Ann.

"Coming," I answer. My mother's back in town for the continuation of Ann's wedding preparations. I swiftly turn my laptop off and scurry around my apartment searching for my purse, slipping into a pair of clogs, and snatching a Zone bar when Corie enters.

"What's the rush?" she asks.

"Lingerie sale," I say, still looking for my purse.

Corie studies me, dubious of my motives, "You? Did you get back with Gavin and you're on your way to the Playboy Mansion?"

I roll my eyes at her, "Can I have a little more credit than that, please?"

"You got another porn-writing gig and it's research?" she tries.

"Hardly," I say. "My porn prose career was short-lived. I haven't heard from Cliff Peterson or Tom Kaplan in weeks. Not since they started filming *Things Change.*" I lift my jacket on the couch and find my purse hiding beneath it.

"At least you got caught up on your bills," she comments.

"Only to be swimming in red again," I say, heading for the door. "I've got sister-duty now. New chapter. The Shower Registry."

Corie steps aside as I pass by, then calls out to me, "Hey, when are you going to be ready to start dating again?"

"When I see black," I shout from down the hallway.

★ ★ ★

Victoria's Secret couldn't be more crowded. Nevertheless, the onomatopoeias, Eva and Ann, manage to pick out some choice items and obtain a large dressing room. Eva and I sit side by side on one of those cushy dressing-room benches while Ann starts trying on the goods. She lifts a hanger clamping a skimpy red leather g-string and stares at us.

"Okay, who picked this out?" she asks accusatorily, and then stares at me.

I turn to Eva, trying hard to camouflage my smile, "Mom! How could you?"

"Don't look at me," exclaims Eva. "I wouldn't know what to do with that thing."

I smile back at Ann. "I thought you should expand your horizons."

"Very funny, Laura," says Ann.

"Try this on, Ann," says Eva, holding up a beautiful long ivory silk bathrobe.

"Oh, now that is gorgeous," declares Ann, taking it off the hanger. "I think George will love this." She puts it on and poses for the mirror. The onomatopoeias fawn all over it. I add an "ooh" and an "aah" as part of the chorus. Then Ann turns to me. "Don't worry, Laura, your turn will come. But just so you know, we're all thrilled it won't be with Gavin. The truth is none of us really liked him."

"Oh, well, thanks, that's good to know…now, Ann."

"One day you'll find a nice guy like George," toots Eva.

"I did," I remind them. Before either one can respond to what I consider a great comeback line, after all they were talking about finding, not keeping, the wall of the dressing room adjoining ours suddenly begins to cave in. This is followed by some heavy panting. Then two pair of skimpy leopard-colored g-strings drop to the floor in plain view. The following hushed dialogue is heard between two women on the other side.

"You are so hot in that bra." Smooching sounds follow. "Your breasts are to die for," shadowed by an echo of kisses. "Come on, let me rip it off of you, right now." A few moans trail, then, "Oh, please do...take me," chased by succulent noises.

My mother and Ann both turn beet-red with embarrassment, then look to me, as if I'm the only one who can do something.

I sigh and bang on the wall. "Hey, uh, excuse me, but could you keep it down in there...not down, I mean...quiet." The uncensored lovemaking ceases. I turn back to Ann and Eva hoping they're satisfied, "Okay, where were we?"

"Hey. You sound familiar," says the voice behind the wall.

"I don't think so," I say.

There's a knock on our dressing-room door. Eva timidly opens it, thinking it's a Victoria's Secret salesgirl and says, "We're not done."

"Neither were we," says another voice with a giggle. Then the porn star, Tess Knight, from *Things Change,* dressed in the most revealing teddy there is, pokes her head inside our dressing room and stares at me wide-eyed, "It's you!"

"Me?" I exclaim, as Ann and Eva's faces expand with shock.

Tess pulls her girlfriend over, also in revealing garments, and points at me. "This is the writer I was telling you about. She's going to make me a legend."

I blush, not from grateful yet humble recognition, but from the absolute horror that the onomatopoeias will find out about Bella Feega.

"You know each other?" asks Eva.

"Well, not quite," I say, pointing to the two half-naked girls. "Mom, Ann, this is uh, Lisa. I mean, Tess."

Tess smiles, "Nice to meet you. This is my girlfriend, Megan." Megan nods hello. There's a long pause. Tess continues, "I knew I knew your voice. Well, see you." She takes hold of Megan's hand and they leave.

"You have a *movie* that got *made?*" asks Ann, her eyes squinting in discernment.

"No, it was just a rewrite for a commercial, no, that was something else, it was uh, a low-budget student film...some USC or UCLA or USB student thing, one of those U's, you know. I didn't even know they actually found more money to uh, finish it."

There's another knock on the door. Eva opens it. Tess, now dressed in street clothes yet still managing to bare her cleavage, pops her head in. "I forgot to tell you the movie's done and rumor is it's going to win some awards."

Ann looks at me. "What kind of awards?"

I gently guide Tess out the door. "Thanks for letting me know." I turn back to the onomatopoeias. Ann's waiting for an answer. I shrug and say, "How should I know, some student award."

"That's wonderful news," says Eva. "What's it about?"

"Just your typical formulaic love story," I say. "Can we finish up in here?"

"Well, maybe we can show your movie at Ann's bachelorette party," offers Eva.

"Oh yeah," I say with mock deference under my breath, "that would be great."

Two months have passed since the writing of *Things Change.* And my bank account continues its decline. I call Eric Leve again, my former boss at STA, to see if I can get my job back. After two cancellations he finally squeezes me in for a late-night drinks meeting following a dinner he has with one of his clients. It went something like this: Me, trying to hold onto my pride without sounding like I have entered begging-mode, him, demonstrating an altogether different agenda.

"Ever since the writing deal Scott Sher claimed he negotiated fell through because it never existed in the first place, things have been tough and I was wondering if I could get my old job back."

"What about that rewrite deal you had at Satellite? The one Hank Willows promised you?" asks Eric.

"That fell apart the same day Scott Sher did. Not to put any guilt on you, Eric, but you were the one who set me up to become a hip-pocket client of his."

"Hey, who knew?" shrugs Eric. "He was a hot, aggressive, high-strung agent STA (Significant Talent Agency) poached from CTA (Combined Talent Agency) who stole him from OTA (Original Talent Associates). He was supposed to develop emerging writers, not emerging drug habits."

"Yeah, well, he told me to quit working and keep writing, that the money was coming. So I did, writing for endless hours in the tiny office in my kitchen, while watching my savings dwindle to minus digits."

"Wasn't there any option money?"

"The only thing that made it into my bank account was the lesson that you can't trust a young, ambitious agent's lexicon, let alone his moral fiber," I spout.

"Why didn't you call me?"

"I tried. I left word four times."

"You did? Well, I was in Ireland signing a new writer. Look, I can't just fire the girl on my desk now, Laura."

"Do any other agents need an assistant?"

"I'll check with Human Resources and let you know."

"What about the Creative Group meetings? I could come in and run those on a full-time basis."

The weekly Creative Group meetings had become my one and only source of joy while working for Eric. Having volunteered to take the minutes in the meetings, I had secured sole assistantship to this private enclave of a select few talent and literary agents. Eric led the discussions that I discovered were the primary way in which movies are born in Hollywood.

Each week the Creative Group convened and agents took turns going around the room with "ideas" for movies. Fitting right in with an agent's penchant for acronyms, I titled my minutes IGP (for "Idea Generation Process"). IGP origins came from magazine articles, newspaper clippings, books in galley, lyrics to songs, or sometimes an agent's own imagination. Typical dialogue in a Creative Group meeting went something like this:

Agent 1: I read an article in *The New York Times* about campus entrepreneurs. I think this could be a clever ensemble comedy like *The Breakfast Club* about a group of college kids who create businesses competing against each other while getting their degrees.

Agent 2: My client Eddie Quinn used to be president of his entrepreneur club in college, he might be very interested in writing and directing this.

Agent 3: My client Rachel Moore is launching several side businesses. She's incredibly entrepreneurial. She might be great to attach as a lead.

Agent 4: I cover Dreamworks and it so happens that Jodie Pritchard who is poised to take over as head of the studio is on the board of a program like this at Princeton. She's actually a judge in the university's entrepreneurial contest.

Eric: Great, Agent 1 take the lead on packaging this with Eddie Quinn attached to write and direct, Rachel Moore attached to star and we'll set it up at Dreamworks. Next idea?

Back in the present moment, Eric responds, "I don't think so, Laura. The agents themselves barely have enough time to prepare, let alone turn that into a packaging program for someone to work on full time."

"Well, how about if I stroll the halls of STA as a walking Rolodex? I could shout out any needed phone number or address on the spot." I'm only half joking. Three years at

STA and I had become excellent at memorizing numbers and addresses. I didn't think I was too far-gone for him to consider creating the position.

"Nice try," he says, smiling.

"I already spent six months in the mailroom, designed to weed out the frail and meek, plus three years on your desk. There's got to be something for me at STA."

Eric smiles again, "I remember you in the mailroom. Buried under heavy stacks of scripts unceremoniously dumped in your lap. You barely made it."

"But I survived. Once I discovered the shopping cart as an applicable means of transporting the glut of scripts to my car."

"You were definitely resourceful."

"I got the job done, didn't I? Wherever those scripts had to be in the vastness of L.A. I got them there even if I was too tired to write at night."

"Meanwhile, how is the writing going?"

"I finished another draft of *Malus*. Will you look at it?"

"Sure," he says. I hand it over to him neatly bound and protected by plastic cover sheets. He sticks the script in his bag then boldly looks me in the eye, "So do you still see Mitchell Mann?"

"Not for over a year now, though I did bump into him at the *Morning to be Reckoned* screening. Is he still a client of yours?"

Eric shakes his head no. "I could never find material weird enough to interest him. He's not that good of a director either and he's kind of a creep. He was no good for you anyway."

Yes, I think to myself. He's a dangerously charismatic addictive psychopathic liar with visions of grandiosity. Like most of the men I have met in Hollywood.

"Thanks for your support, Eric."

"So are you dating anyone now?"

I shake my head no. "Not anymore." I decide not to

bother mentioning the short-lived Gavin-Laura union. I couldn't help but think of all the sour relationships I'd had since arriving in Los Angeles. I had given up a perfectly great college boyfriend back east to pursue my dreams in the west, having no idea how fraught Hollywood would be with pretentious ego-driven men.

"To tell you the truth, Eric, I'm beginning to give up on L.A. guys," I reply.

Eric nervously fiddles with his spoon. "You'll find someone," he says, leaning closer toward me. "But in the meantime, I have to tell you something." He furtively glances around us then focuses on me. "I have feelings for you that have been building up inside of me for a long time. Ever since you wrote those love essays for me, I mean for my wife. I read them all the time. That's why it's not a good idea for you to work for me again or for me to see you every day at the office. Laura, I'm crazy about you. You're my fantasy. And I want to know if we can act on my feelings."

I'm stunned. I look at him in disbelief. "Are you nuts? You're married."

"This has nothing to do with my wife."

"How can you say that?"

"Look, Laura, I've already discussed this with my therapist and he agrees that it's okay for me to broach this with you and act on my feelings if it's mutual."

"Eric, I'm sorry, but it's not mutual. And you've got a really screwed-up therapist. If you want to help me the script's in your bag."

"And what do I get in return?"

"A commission and a thanks."

"Come on, Laura, I know you can do better than that."

"Okay, help me get a deal on this script. I don't care if it's a studio film or an independent. If I make fifty grand on it, I'll send you and your wife to Hawaii for a week of never-ending room service, with a stack of porn films."

Eric winks at me. "There you go again, getting me all hot and bothered."

I throw my hands in the air. "Oh for heaven's sake, Eric, get a fantasy of your own!" I grab my purse and start to go.

"Why? When you're so good at it?" he innocently asks.

"Well, I don't want to be good at it, at least not for someone who's already married." And I'm out the door.

A week later, I take a break from my troubles when my dad returns, searching for a townhouse to buy in Marina del Rey. He's with his latest girlfriend, Helen, a blond dental hygienist from San Francisco. We're at Anaheim Stadium sitting behind home plate watching the Detroit Tigers play the Angels. I'm the only one of my siblings who bothers to go to these games with my dad and his beau of the month. To Ann and Bennett it's just a boring spectator sport. But to me it's a father-daughter ritual and a chance to recapture sentiments of approval from my youth. Inevitably, an Angel will hit the ball to the Tigers' left fielder who will make the throw all the way to home plate for the out. That's when my dad will turn to his date, beaming with pride at me, "You should have seen Laura play baseball in high school," he'll exclaim, "What an arm! I've never seen anything like it. Boy, can she throw!" Then he'll pinch me on the cheek, making the whole trip worth it.

I'm happily rubbing my sore cheek when Helen asks me, "Are you excited for your sister's wedding?"

"I've got six months to get excited," I answer.

"I guess you've got six months to put together the toast, too, huh?" she adds.

I turn to my father. "I'm writing the toast?"

"You're the writer," he says.

"But I don't write toasts."

"Sure, you do," he retorts, his eyes trained on the game.

"Great," I comment on deaf ears, then waving my hand

in front of him add, "just don't expect me to do the delivery. Smelling salts or no smelling salts."

My dad nods, but I'm not sure if it's at me, or the fact that the Tigers' first baseman just snagged the batter's line drive bringing the sixth inning to an end. Helen excuses herself for the rest room as fans rise for the seventh-inning stretch.

"So, how are you doing, hun?" Walt asks me, as he stretches his arms. "Bennett said you were no longer seeing that fellow named Gabe."

Apparently the onomatopoeias have passed it on to the consonant brother who has passed it on to the patriarch. "It's Gavin, or it was Gavin, and yes, we're no longer dating," I confirm.

My father remains silent for a long moment, then comments, "I'm sure it's for the best. Besides, I never cared for him. You just have to move on and you will." I'm starting to recognize a pattern. None of my friends or family liked Gavin. And if I look a little closer, neither did I.

I spot Helen who's on her way back to us and so I pose the rhetorical, "So, do you like her, Dad?"

"Yeah, she's nice. But I met another one yesterday at the airport lounge." He winks at me.

"Another *one?*" I ask, wondering why women are relegated to numbers. I think about what I could do to change that perception through writing. Though what's the point, no one ever sees what I write anyway. Maybe it's not too late to follow my father's footsteps, n.p.i., and become a podiatrist. I could still tell stories, only instead of doing it on celluloid or digital video to thousands at a time, it would be orally over the surgical removal of an ingrown toenail to one person on occasion. And if you can say or do something that helps even one life, isn't that what counts in the end? Isn't inspiring one person just as powerful as inspiring the masses? After all, the masses are made up of many persons put together. But then I remember my promise to Lily along with my science grades and realize that's just not going to work.

Two days later, Corie and I are at the library on a self-improvement kick. I'm looking for books on "The Ten-Minute Toast sans Procrastination," while Corie leafs through a paperback she found on "How to Manage your Boss."

I'm reading about how it's best to begin a toast with a joke when Corie taps me on my arm and whispers, "Hey, cute guy at eleven o'clock."

I look up. "Yeah, he is cute," I say, until his girlfriend appears and he wraps his arms around her. "Not anymore," I add, and return to my book.

"What about Charlie Roberts?" Corie whispers. "He's single now."

"I'm done with guys in the entertainment industry," I quietly announce.

"Really? Then you might want to consider moving," says Corie.

"Believe me, I have," I say.

Corie suddenly looks sad, "Don't do that. Life won't be as much fun without you here."

I look at her appreciatively and smile. "Thanks, okay, I'm staying."

"Good," she replies, and turns back to her book.

Not since I faxed over my pseudonym and witnessed "a day in the making of..." have I heard from the Accent Film Company. I figure the whole writing experience was a lark that provided some badly needed income.

Meanwhile, I still haven't given up on *The Law of Malus.* I believe in it with all my heart and soul. Sara Stephenson's office has set up a dinner for us in two weeks. All four previous attempts to get together were pre-empted by emergency production meetings at the studio. This time she has her assistant promise me there will be no cancellation since the head of the studio left town for a vacation in the Alps. I intend to give her the latest draft of *Malus.*

The phone rings, and Tom Kaplan from the Accent Film Company greets me. "Congratulations," he says.

I don't know what he means. "For what?" I ask.

"*Things Change* has been nominated for Best Screenplay. In fact, it received twelve nominations all together."

Now I really didn't know what he was talking about—how could they edit, score, market and distribute so quickly—so I got right to it and asked, "What are you talking about?"

I soon discover that the adult film business has its own version of the Academy Awards called the AVN Awards. *Adult Video News Magazine* sponsors it every year during CES, the Consumer Electronics Show. Apparently, it's an intense annual ceremony, with its own celebrities making speeches and presenting the awards. Some people even use it as a forum to express their political views, which mostly center on free speech issues rather than foreign affairs. The press comes out in herds and everyone dresses in their finest alluring outfits. Even a red carpet adorns the entrance to the festivities.

Okay, so it was in Vegas, not Hollywood, and maybe there weren't three billion people watching, but 3,000 plus the tabloid journalists. And maybe they weren't the celebrities you see in *People* magazine and *Entertainment Weekly,* but there were stars. The ones you see in *Adult Video News Magazine, Playboy,* and *Hustler.*

Things Change had received nominations for Best Screenplay, Best Picture, Best Director, Best Actress (for each lead), Best Love Scene (for three different scenes), Best Cinematography, Best Editing, Best Music, and Best Overall Marketing Campaign. Furthermore, in its first month of being released, *Things Change* had broken sales records in both video rentals and sell-through.

With all these nominations and record sales, had I had any impact on changing people's lives? While writing the story I had tried to remain cognizant of exploring themes of honesty and self-acceptance. I had hoped that in doing so I might impart the importance of these everyday values to the viewer's self-growth and inspire the willingness and ability to begin again. Okay, maybe this hadn't happened in some prophetic way, but hey, I must have had some kind of effect because reviewers raved about it.

One critic, yes, apparently there are movie critics in the adult industry. One critic went so far as to call my work "a thinking person's porn classic." Another critic referred to the "strong emphasis on story," adding, "It's possible to watch these two films without holding your cock in your hand." A third critic wrote, "*Things Change* gives dignity to its characters heretofore unequalled in adult entertainment." And, if you don't think that made me proud, well, it did. At least I was making a difference—somewhere. And whether I received an award or not, here was an industry that had the balls to recognize me for it, pun intended.

Tom faxes me the glowing reviews along with the record-breaking numbers for video sales and rentals. I slowly begin to reconsider the power of validation. After soaking in all the accolades from the stats and the film reviews, Tom promises to get me copies of my movies, which I have yet to see. Then he asks me if I'm going to attend the award ceremony next month.

"We never do this, but my boss has offered to take care of your airfare and hotel room. And if you want, I'll escort you down the red carpet," he offers.

It hadn't occurred to me to go until he mentioned it. "Let me think about it," I reply, but the more the idea seeps in, the more I think how can I not go? After all, it may be the only time I ever get nominated for Best Screenplay.

Tom continues with the second reason for his call. Mickey Colucci intends to fly out from Connecticut to Los Angeles and wants to meet with me. I have no idea who Mickey Colucci is, but somehow I have a feeling this porn plot is about to thicken.

"Who's Mickey Colucci?" I ask.

"He's my boss, the original investor in the company, and the one footing your bill to Vegas. He put together an IPO and took the company public. In fact, it's the only adult film company on the New York Stock Exchange."

I have to admit, I am impressed by this information. "How's the stock doing?" I inquire.

"Not bad. It's up half a point today. He's coming out here for business and he wants to meet you."

"Why does he want to meet me?" I ask somewhat fearfully.

"He saw the film. He thinks it's really good. And he's got a story he's been working on that he wants to talk to you about."

"He's got a story? Is he a writer?"

"No. But I guess he's got this idea and he wants you to write it. I've never known him to do this and I've been working for the guy for seven years."

"Do you know what the story is?"

"I think he's calling it *My Red Vibe Notebook*. He'll probably want Cliff Peterson to direct it."

"*My Red Vibe Notebook?* Is that supposed to be a takeoff of *The Red Shoes* or *The Red Shoe Diaries?*"

"What's *The Red Shoes?*"

"Never mind. Well, what's he like?"

"He won't bite. But just know one thing, Laura. Mickey Colucci doesn't have a funny bone in his whole body."

We set a time and date for me to meet Mr. Colucci, and before I can figure out just where my life is going, the phone rings again.

"Is Laura Taylor there? I have Brad Isaacs from STA calling from an airplane."

"Yes, this is she."

Brad Isaacs—major literary agent at STA. He's been there for fifteen years and while he has an amazing reputation for good taste, he also has an equally unremarkable reputation for follow-through. Regardless, I feel my heart jumping with excitement.

"Go ahead, Brad," says the ethereal voice.

"Laura? This is Brad Isaacs. Eric Leve gave me your script *The Law of Malus,* and I haven't been able to put it down."

"Thanks," I say, overjoyed with appreciation for his appreciation.

"I can't believe how powerful it is. This is a great story. It made me cry. You are a really talented writer," he shouts above the din of the airplane. "When I get back from the Venice Film Festival I want to sit down with you. In the meantime, is it okay if I submit the script to Maggie Reese?"

"Yes, of course," I reply. My ego soars. Finally, someone is recognizing the value of this story. But things sure are getting weird and wonderful at the same time.

take five

THE INSIDE OF PORN

I must confess, while getting dressed to meet Mr. Colucci, I am more than anxious.

What do you wear to a meeting with the owner of a publicly-traded porn company?

For reasons only my subconscious can rationalize, I decide on a black skirt, white silk blouse and black heels, no hose. I have to keep up an L.A. casual chic.

I drive into the industrial parking lot of the Accent Film Company and take a deep breath.

Tom arrives to greet me in the lobby. "Hey you, don't be nervous, but so you know, Cliff can't make it. He got tied up on set directing another movie. This meeting will be just you and Mr. Colucci."

I trip but quickly regain my footing. I'm not used to the heels. And I'm certainly not used to meetings of this sort, despite my Hollywood track record.

"You're not sitting in on the meeting?" I ask, surprised.

"He didn't invite me. Just make sure you see me after the meeting though."

I follow Tom to a large office where he introduces me to Mr. Mickey Colucci. Mickey remains seated behind a massive black desk and his mouth never moves. I soon learn that when it comes to speaking, Mickey prefers the minimalist approach. He barely nods his head as he reaches for a fresh cigar. He snips the end off like a professional moyle performing a routine circumcision. The lost end piece somersaults in the air, landing on the floor. Rather than leave it there, I observe Mickey lift his rotund figure from the desk, revealing a black polo shirt neatly tucked inside black pants. He lumbers over, picks up the lost end piece, and places it in his pants pocket. Then he sits down at a round table in the corner of the office and motions for me to sit beside him.

Tom is right; Mickey doesn't once crack a smile during the introductions, nor for a very long time after that. He tells me he likes my movie a lot. Then he cuts through all the unnecessary pleasantries that Hollywood spends so much time on and gets right down to business.

"I want you to write the sequels to *Things Change*—Part III and IV. Only you can't use Tess Knight in the story 'cause she's leavin' the business," he says in a gruff voice.

"Why is she leaving?" I ask, somewhat disappointed. After all, she was a star in this world and she did attempt to make my dialogue ring true, at least in the one scene I witnessed.

"Too many donuts," says Mickey Colucci, and before I can try to figure out what that means he says, "I want you to write a story based on these notes of mine."

He pulls out an old stenograph notebook and flips through several pages of handwritten notes all in uppercase letters. I watch closely as he clears his throat preparing to read. He stops to glance at me. "You can take notes," he says.

I get the hint and swiftly haul out my notebook and poise my pen.

"It's called *My Red Vibe Notebook,* see?" he says, showing me the notes he's jotted down. "It's about a married woman who writes down all her fantasies in a diary. While her husband's away working, she starts to act on them. I want it in two parts."

I can't say all this did not flatter me; Mickey Colucci was basically offering me a four-picture deal. On the other hand, this was really pushing my morals. If it's one thing I know, it's that I do not want to write about adultery. It's against my principles. It's also tacky. But how on earth do you say no to a man in his position?

"What do you want for it?" he asks, not wasting any time.

Now I know why agents receive commissions. You really need a tough stomach for this kind of stuff. I swallow hard, hoping he can't possibly hear the saliva pass over the lump in my throat. I throw out the number that will clear me of all my debt and give me two months' respite. "How about eighty-five hundred, plus five hundred shares of stock in the company?"

He stares at me for a long time.

I even start to perspire. "Well, we are talking about four scripts here," I say.

Then he asks me, "You got a pen name?"

"Yes."

"What is it?"

"Bella Feega."

And that was when Mickey Colucci not only cracked a smile, but released a hearty chuckle. "I like that," he says. "I'll give you ten thousand. No stock."

"Thanks," I utter and then in my head say a hundred thank-yous to Adam Berman. Based on earlier conversations with Tom Kaplan, I've just become the highest paid writer of adult movies.

We shake hands and I tell Mr. Colucci that I'll send over a deal memo with a work agenda and a payment schedule. This causes a peculiar look to appear on his face. I'm beginning to get the picture here. There are no deal memos—for anything. Just a good ol' fashioned handshake. I wonder how long that would last in Hollywood. When working on Eric Leve's desk at STA I discovered the existence of not one set of entertainment lawyers, but two. One set to do the original deals, and a whole other set to protect the original deal once the buyer inevitably decided not to honor it. I can't tell you how many times I would bear witness to the utter frustration of writers and directors who had closed lucrative deals with the studios only to have them reneged at different stages of the game, whether it was over gross box office receipts or network syndication sales. In the end, after thousands more dollars had been spent on lawyers' fees, the talent would be lucky to settle for half of what he or she had originally and contractually been promised. I was so disgusted by this practice that one day I marched down the hall to the head of business affairs at STA and asked how the studios can get away with this? "Because they can," said the lawyer, who immediately went back to work. Where the hell had all the ethics gone? I asked myself and wondered in abhorrence why school curriculums didn't teach the real business of life. Back in Mickey's office, I surmise that the ethics, as far as honoring a deal was concerned, had gone to the adult film industry.

Tom Kaplan asks me how the meeting went and I fill him in. Then he gives me several presents, gift-wrapped, and asks me to open them. Inside are three videotapes of *Things Change,* Part I and Part II (the hard-core versions), the soft-core version for the Erotica Channel, and...a dildo, just as he promised.

"Would you like to go out sometime?" he asks me.

"Oh. Um. I'm not sure," I answer. The truth is I'm kind

of freaked out by this whole thing. I think Tom's a great guy, funny, smart and really cute. But even though I'm not one to talk, I'm not sure I can get past the fact that he works day in and day out in the adult industry. I decide to be frank with him.

"Can I ask you a question?" I ask.

"Sure," he says.

With a degree of trepidation I inquire, "Do you date the women that, uh, act, in these movies?"

"No," he says flat-out. "Listen, it bothers a lot of girls that I work in this industry. I can understand if it bothers you, but for the record, I do not date the women you think I date."

"Okay, well, can I think about it?"

"Sure. Just let me know if and when you want to get together. I make a great Caesar salad. In the meantime," he grins, "enjoy the presents."

Corie, Adam and I are at their place watching the hardcore version of *Things Change.* Adam and Corie seem to be engrossed in it. I'm looking at it from a writer's angle and I can't believe that I am actually impressed. Everything I wrote exists as I wrote it. I have no ill feelings toward the production for battering and butchering my dialogue that I have often heard many Hollywood writers complain about. Furthermore, the music sounds not bad, not great, but not bad. The actresses are beautiful and actually do justice to most of my dialogue, especially their goodbye love scene.

"I saw a porn film once before and it was disgusting," says Corie, "but this is really good."

"You're really talented at this," Adam says.

"Thanks, I think," I say, not sure how else to respond. The film continues.

"I thought you never slept with a woman?" asks Corie.

"I haven't. I just transferred the feelings I have for men into a different relationship to give the story a twist."

"You're a good writer," says Adam, "because you sure fooled me."

"It's called imagination and watching the world around you," I say.

I watch them let my words sink in while the sex scene onscreen continues to a crescendo of exhilarating moans.

"I think you're right," says Corie.

"I think I have to go take a shower now," Adam says abruptly. He leaves the room. Corie and I trade looks.

"I kissed a woman once," admits Corie.

"You did?" I ask, astonished.

"Sure. Who hasn't?"

"What was it like?"

"It was…nice," she says, remembering. "Of course, it was only a brief intoxicated moment in college, but yeah…it was really nice." She drifts off in her reverie, then quickly returns to the present. "But in the end I decided it's about the person and I ended up with Adam." She waits for a moment, turning back to the movie. "You know, I think I'll go help Adam with that shower," she says, casually, then asks, "Would you mind leaving the film here overnight?"

It's a good thing Tom Kaplan called me the following week to see how I liked the film. I told him I was pleasantly surprised and asked if I could get a few more tapes, because I never did get that copy back from Adam and Corie, though they did thank me profusely the day after they watched it.

Tom said he'd get me five more copies and offered to give them to me over dinner at his place. I thought it was time I take a chance on men again and so I accepted his offer.

Tom's place is deep in the western part of the valley, an hour's drive from Venice. It's a small quaint brown brick house with a freshly mowed green lawn. Tom greets me at the door from behind his apron, "Hi!" he beams.

I enter with a bottle of Sangiovese red wine. It's one of

my favorites. I discovered it during my prolific wine-buying days on behalf of Eric Leve. "I brought this for us."

He looks it over. "Thanks! I know nothing about wines, but the label's pretty. Come in the kitchen, you're just in time for the show." He opens the bottle, pours me a glass, and then sits me down at the counter. He's got all the ingredients for the Caesar salad laid out. I nervously sip my wine, watching him perform cheflike wonders, theatrically breaking a raw egg in one hand to create a waterfall of egg yolk into the mix.

"So how did you get into this business?" I ask.

"I distributed sex magazines to bookstores during college, and then I just fell into it," he answers.

"What were you studying in college?"

"Poly-sci," he says.

"Oh. Is any of it applicable to what you do now?"

"Nope. So, I have to ask, did you try your dildo yet?"

"I can't figure out how to operate it," I fib, beginning to feel the effects of the wine on my empty stomach. The truth is that I hadn't yet opened it. He notices my transitory sway and offers me some cheese and crackers until we sit down to eat.

The salad is amazing but it's the only item he's prepared and not heavy enough to soak up the rising level of alcohol in my system. I feel myself getting tipsier. "So what's the inside of a porn marketing guy's house look like?" I ask, more than curious.

Tom proceeds to answer by giving me a full press court tour. We reach his guest bedroom and that's where I see wall-to-wall stacks of cellophane-covered girlie magazines, posters, sex toys and adult videos. If he weren't in the porn business I'd think he was a pervert. I cock my head at the contents of the room. "You're expecting an orgy? Or starting a museum?" I ask.

He laughs. "I'm a collector. I have faith that one day these items will be worth a lot of money." He picks a super duper dildo off the shelf, a duplicate of the one that he had given me and removes it from its box. I notice it has the airbrushed photo of a woman's face on it. "This is called the Whale Dildo. I'll show you how it works," and so he unscrews its base. "This is where the batteries go." He plops in three double A batteries and then flips a switch hidden behind a rubber flap of skin.

"Wow," I say, impressed by its engineering and design. The penis portion suddenly whirs to life in large circular motions. Below that is what looks like an additional mini-penis that vibrates incessantly. "What's that thing?" I ask.

"That's to stimulate the clitoris," he offers, again in that matter-of-fact manner as if this should be common knowledge to the entire planet. I am staring wide-eyed at the size of its moving members when the doorbell rings. "Here," says Tom, handing over the hypnotic whirring instrument. "You can play with it while I see who's here." I wonder if this is how all his dates begin.

Standing in the sea of adult accoutrements I also wonder where I would be right now if I had gone to a different mechanic. A loud ruckus interrupts my thoughts. I exit the guest room and peer around the corner into the foyer. A large buxom brunette towers over Tom flailing her arms in anguish. She looks familiar but I can't place her.

"I don't care if you're on a date. How could you do this, Tom? You were supposed to check with me first!" she screams.

"I did," says Tom in self-defense. "Your manager told me it was okay. I swear to God."

"He did? That bastard. That's it. I'm firing him." She's still steaming mad when she spots me by the wall.

"Hi. I'm the date," I offer.

Tom turns around, sees me, and attempts to smooth things over with a polite introduction. "Laura, this is Ashley Wade. Ashley, this is Laura." A long pause ensues.

"So, uh, what's the problem?" I ask, breaking the silence.

"Ashley's the spokeswoman for the Whale Dildo," explains Tom.

"They have spokespeople for dildos?" I ask.

"Product is product," he says. "She just got back from Europe and saw her photo on the box cover."

"And I'm not happy about it," she barks.

Now I know why she looked familiar. "Why? I think you look really pretty on it," I say.

"Really?" she asks.

"Oh, yeah," I repeat, feeling light-headed again and ready for this unexpectedness to end.

Ashley looks at Tom. "Next time, skip my manager and come straight to me."

"You got it," says Tom.

Ashley leaves and I soon follow, explaining to Tom that between the wine and the whir of the dildo, I'm not feeling well and it's time to call it a night. I'm not sure how I made it home, but I did remember dreaming about giant dildos at sea.

The time has come. I am beginning to take some pride in my work, even if it isn't mainstream filmmaking. After all, the return on investment for my movies surpasses that of most box-office hits, comparatively speaking. Of course, I have no back-end deal, so I wasn't getting any royalties or residual fees when they played on cable or when they were rented throughout hotel chains as pay-per-view. I daydream, wondering if there could ever be a union for porn writers, when my father, in L.A. to close escrow on the townhouse, finishes ordering his bagels, lox and poached eggs. We are at his favorite breakfast place in Marina del Rey and I haven't yet told him about my recent success.

"Where's Bennett?" I ask. "I thought he was joining us."

"He's been invited to some Prodo warehouse sale," says Walt.

"You mean, Prava?" I ask.

A waitress passing our table chimes in, "It's Prada."

My father and I look at her and reply in unison, "Thanks."

"I saw *Morning to be Reckoned,*" says Walt.

"What'd you give it?" I ask, waiting for the critique.

"I gave it a six," he says. My dad had a penchant for action. They had to be horrendous to score lower than a six. "How's your work coming along?" he asks.

I decide that with the credibility of all the movie's nominations, perhaps it is time I come out of the closet and tell my father that I have become a porn writer, at least temporarily. But how do you tell your father, the man who helped raise you, who taught you to tie your shoes and throw a baseball a hundred yards to land on a dime, the man who taught you to ride a bicycle, balance a checkbook, and monitor the oil in your car, the man who helped put you through college so you'd have a good education and a good life...how do you tell him, your father, that your talent and your best intentions have landed you a career as a writer of adult entertainment? After all, I was supposed to be raising his grandchildren by now, not anonymous penises in the dark, though inside that thought I wondered how many other people's grandchildren my movie might have inspired.

As he bites into his bagel, I drop it on him. "Dad, the movie I wrote that got made, well, it's received twelve nominations, including Best Screenplay, but um, what you don't know, is that it's a, uh, well, it's an adult film." I see the hope he had for me become disappointment and it kills me inside. I always felt like his favorite child—the one who could throw the ball farthest, run the fastest, wrestle the longest, the kid who always laughed at his corny jokes when the other family members would groan. Ann and Bennett seemed more comfortable living their own lives, whereas I always remember worrying about my dad. I laughed at his corny jokes not because they were funny but because *he* thought they were and somehow I sensed he needed to share the laughter, that underneath was a sadness he had become proficient at hiding. Now I consciously risked my version of a happy childhood for brutal honesty.

Even worse, without thinking, I say, "I've got copies of the film, if you think you might be interested in watching it."

To my surprise, my father replies, "Sure," and accepts my indiscreet offer.

But then I am not sure which of the movies to give him. Even though the soft-core version went easier on all of the sex scenes, the editor butchered the story line in the process. As a writer and a purist when it comes to storytelling, I prefer the hard-core version even though the sex scenes are interminably long and beyond graphic description. At least justice is given to the screenplay. So I decide to leave it up to him.

"Do you want the soft-core version or the hard-core version, Dad?"

"The hard-core version," he says gruffly. With a combination of apprehension and pride, I promise to send the videotapes to him. I drive home somewhat panicked over my actions.

A week later my father calls from Michigan. "I watched your films," he says. "I have a couple of questions for you."

"Okay…shoot," I say, trembling, unable to imagine one possible question my father might ask me.

"Did you write the sex scenes?" he asks.

I breathe a sigh of relief. That's not so bad and it lets me off the hook. I can handle that one easily enough and reply, "I wrote the dialogue that's the foreplay to the sex scenes, but when they stop talking, I stop writing and the cameras take over."

"Oh," my father says. He pauses, and then continues with his second question. "Do you think I abandoned you?"

I immediately remember the scene where the lead character tells her female lover that ever since her father left, she's given up on men and now needs to leave her lover to explore men for the first time. It's true my father divorced my mother, and in the most unexpected way because no one saw it coming, including my mom. One day, my sister and I came home from high school and he was gone. It's true that I felt terribly abandoned by him. And it's true that I gave up on men for some time.

My brother and sister made terrible allies. Each one of them abandoned the fight to preserve our family before a plan could be devised. Bennett was in his second year of college and refused to get involved. Ann chose to spend her senior winter of high school abroad as a foreign exchange student in Geneva, Switzerland where everything was white and neutral. My mother went into a deep depression from which she eventually emerged a stronger, happier person. But at the time, her bedroom hideout left me constantly worried for her well-being.

In my pain, on my own, I turned to literature for courage and found it in the novels of Lillian Hellman, Ayn Rand, Herman Hesse, and Henry James. I determined to never allow myself to be left behind; instead I would become a woman of independent means, unavailable to potential abandonment. I would secure my own goals first, unlike my mother, Eva, and my father's patient Lily, women who sacrificed their dreams to support their husbands only to see their worlds come undone.

And so I wrote about what I didn't know, but sought to understand. At my Hebrew school of Conservative Judaism, I wrote a paper about the themes in the book of Genesis.

I read all the stories and contemplated their symbols and metaphors. Adam and Eve, Noah's redemption, the Tower of Babel. I sought connection in their meanings and discovered that the point wasn't to begin, but to begin again.

This underlying theme became the basis for my life. Yes, my parents divorced, the first in the neighborhood. Though it tore me apart, I found solace in the discovery, that the disruption of life as I had known it would not in the end keep me (or my parents and siblings) from finding a means in which to begin again.

I stare into the receiver of the phone where my father waits on the other end for my reply. I decide it's now or never and go for the truth.

"Yes, Dad," I say, "I feel like you abandoned me."

"I'm sorry," he says. Tenderness coats his voice; it feels both foreign and beautiful at the same time. "Don't ever think that. I hope you can understand, if not now, then one day, that I left the relationship I had with your mother. It had nothing to do with you. And I think your mother's a better person for it. We married young. Neither one of us were growing anymore. I never meant to make you feel like I abandoned you. I love you, hun. And I give your movies a ten."

And there you go—a porn film brought my father and me closer together. If it hadn't changed anyone else's life, it had just changed mine.

Hollywood can do a number on anybody's self-esteem. It pumps you up with accolades, creates momentum for surging success, promises you writing deals and production bonuses that inevitably fail to come to fruition, then when you hit bottom, the whole mess starts all over again. It's an evil cycle. In the end, as my scholarly cousin who spent three years helping her talented daughter launch a failed acting career remarked, "Hollywood is a multi-million dollar business that is based on random chance. There is nothing that you can do that will insure success. No matter how hard you work or what road you follow or who you know."

But now, thanks to porn, my self-esteem has skyrocketed. Thus, I think it will be safe to start seeing guys again. Though I'm not ready to go on another date with a bona fide employee of the adult film industry, so I choose not to call Tom Kaplan. Instead, I start asking friends to fix me up.

My first blind date commences with a guy named Ronnie Green, a mild-mannered real estate lawyer from Indiana, fairly new to the L.A. landscape. He still has a Midwest naiveté about him, and not a scent of Hollywood, which I find refreshing and unfamiliar at the same time.

Ronnie treats me to a simple Chinese dinner. He appears to be a nice, uncomplicated guy. I am not immediately attracted to him, but I am hoping that by the end of the night his personality might win me over.

After dinner, Ronnie suggests renting a movie at the local mom-and-pop video store near his new townhouse in Brentwood. We start picking through videos and finally find an innocent comedy. He offers to go next door to get a bottle of wine while I continue to explore back-up options.

While Ronnie fetches the wine, I start getting curious and decide to casually sneak into the adult section to see if they carry my movies and if so, see how they are doing. In the back corner of the store I rummage through the sea of titles and there they are—in the heterosexual column, *Things Change,* Part I and II. I reach up and pull them down off the shelf to take a closer look. I'm checking the wear and tear on the boxes when I feel a presence behind me, a quickening of breath. I turn and see Ronnie, bottle of wine in one hand, leftovers from dinner in the other, and a huge beatific grin on his face.

"Hi," he says. A lusty quality now invades his tone.

I look at the videotapes in my hand and then murmur, "This is not what you think, Ronnie. Really."

"Then what is it? I'm dying to know."

"I can't tell you."

"Yes, you can. I won't tell a soul. Promise."

"Well, okay," I whisper, mistakenly flattered by his interest. "I um…I wrote these."

Ronnie's eyes suddenly expand and begin to take on more and more of a lecherous tint.

"Wow," he says, impressed, glancing at the tapes. "Do you have a fetish for porn? Do you like watching women? It's okay, you know. We could call an escort service and ask some chicks to come over."

"Look, Ronnie, you're getting the wrong impression about me." I must have raised my voice for emphasis because the owner of the store appears in the adult section next to us, ready to squelch a potential scene of domestic violence.

"Can I help you out with something?" he asks.

"We're fine," I pronounce, putting the videotapes back on the shelf.

"She wrote those," Ronnie declares with pride.

"No shit?" says the owner. "Those are my biggest-selling tapes. In fact, people keep stealing them. I've had to reorder them three times now. Would you mind autographing them for me?"

"Of course she will," offers Ronnie, behaving somewhere between a proud father and a pompous pimp.

As I'm signing the videotapes at the front desk, I see Hank Willows and his boyfriend walk in. I try hiding my face. But it's too late. Hank strolls over for one of those polite but meaningless Hollywood hugs.

"Laura! So good to see you! This is J.J. J.J., this is Laura, she's a fabulous writer! Her stories are always so authentic!"

I quickly step on Ronnie's foot, hoping he's not too green to get the drift and keep quiet. "Hi, um, this is Ronnie, Ronnie this is J.J. and Hank. Hank works at Satellite."

By now J.J. and Hank's eyes begin to drift. They've immediately picked up on Ronnie's lack of Hollywood-ness, obviously they think he's no one they need to know, and instead focus on the videotapes in my hand.

"Oooh, Laura, what's that?" inquires Hank.

"That. That is for my research," I fumble. "You know how I'm such a stickler for facts, Hank." Those acting classes I took are now starting to come in handy and I pick up some speed. "Listen, Hank. You can't tell anyone. I'm writing an erotic psychological thriller set in the adult film industry. It's for a major studio, obviously not Satellite. Ronnie here is one of the major co-investors." I step on Ronnie's foot again and he nods on cue.

Hank's eyes quickly shift from the videotapes to Ronnie. "Really?" he says. "Here's my card if you ever want to talk about investing in some of Satellite's media projects."

"I hope you mean that only if I'm attached to write, Hank." I add, "Since I did make the introduction."

"Of course! Only if Laura writes them!" he blurts out.

We leave the store and Ronnie starts grappling with me as soon as we get inside his car. He says the whole adventure turned him on and he can't help himself. And he didn't. That was the last I saw of Ronnie Green.

"Leather socks? Who's going to wear leather socks?" asks Ann. "You should know as the son of a podiatrist that's bad for your feet and great for a fungus infestation. How are your toes supposed to breathe?"

Bennett rolls his eyes in disgust, "The sock is a wool-cotton blend. It's the ankle to the calf part that's leather!"

I'm staying out of this one. Not that Bennett would value my opinion on anything worn by humans anyway.

We're at the Getty Museum looking at the outdoor garden as a possible reception area for Ann's wedding. The weather is turning windy and cold and I'm starting to shiver.

"Can we go now? I'm freezing," I say.

"You wouldn't be so cold if you had on a pair of leather socks," chimes Bennett.

Ann downs the rest of her double latte and glances at him. "Is Dad actually going to invest in this?"

"He said he'd endorse it," replies Bennett. "The authoritative voice of a foot doctor. It can't hurt."

"So you want George to invest in this?" she asks.

Bennett nods. "Why not?"

"Is there a prototype?" she asks.

Bennett produces a sample "leather sock" out of his leather bag. Ann and I have a look. Not sure what to make of it.

"How do you market something like this?" poses Ann.

"Product placement in movies," he replies. "That's where Laura comes in."

"Me?" I ask, surprised.

"You know enough people in Hollywood. Can't you get it into the hands of some costume designer?"

"I'll get right on it, Bennett. What am I supposed to call them? Is there a name for these leather socks of yours?" I ask.

"I'm still working on it. You're one with words. Got any ideas?"

"Hmmm. Let's see." I think, brainstorming brand names for leather socks. "Leather plus warmth plus feet…or skin. How 'bout Skin Tight, Leather Touch, Leather Sole or…I know—Leather Footish?"

Bennett nods, thinking. "That's not bad…."

"Good. Now can we go, my teeth are clattering and I have a meeting at STA."

"I hope it's not another jerk-off meeting," Ann says.

"Nice support there, Ann. I didn't want to jinx it, but for your information, STA wants to give my script to Maggie Reese," I announce.

"All they do is talk a lot. Maybe what those people really need is a good speech pathologist," she says, smiling at her own wit.

Bennett hands me the leather sock, "Here, see what you can do with it. Maybe you can get Maggie Reese to wear it."

I stare at it and then stick my hand inside to keep it warm.

Exciting. Emotional. Stimulating. Words that describe what I witness as I sit on Brad Isaacs's couch on the third floor of the Significant Talent Agency. Brad paces across from me. His arms flail when he speaks, which is incessantly. His extremities are constantly in motion. Novels and screenplays clutter his desk. Framed pictures of his wife and toddlers adorn what little space remains unoccupied. He leaves his office door ajar providing me with a clear shot into the hallway. I glance at the diminutive agents strutting by as Brad showers me with superlatives about my screenplay. "I love this screenplay. It's brilliantly written. It's powerful. It's deep. It's provocative. It has Academy Award written all over it."

In the corridor, Rand Chessick, Scott Sher's former assistant, marches by and sees me. I watch as he does a double take, stunned to see me sipping a cup of something on Brad Isaacs's couch. I smile sweetly at him, a hint of gentle retribution in the corners of my mouth, and turn away to face Brad again.

"I'm setting you up to meet with Joe Schwartz," insists Brad, bringing me back to the present. "He's running Nick Blake's company now. I want you to meet him."

"Nick Blake!" I scream, trying to hide my excitement since he's the hottest star in Hollywood.

Brad shouts out to his assistant through the crack in the door, "Anita, make sure you set up a meeting for Laura and Joe Schwartz."

"What ever happened to the submission to Maggie Reese?" I ask.

"I haven't done that yet," he says. "My cat scratched my hand and I was in the hospital for a week. It was a nightmare." Then he turns toward the door and hollers again, "Anita, make sure you prepare a package to send this to Maggie Reese and put her development exec on the call sheet." He spins back around to me, "So what else are you working on?"

"Oh, nothing. I'm writing some low-budget features for a very tiny independent film company."

"Are they paying you?"

I nod yes, trying not to draw attention.

"How much?" he asks.

Well, since I'm finding out how Hollywood prides itself on presentation, I decide it can't hurt to add a few zeros. I could tell him they paid me $100,000 for two back-to-back movies. That would come to a fictitious $10,000 commission for him and for what? Agents are supposed to get the work for you; instead they enjoy collecting the commissions on the work that you get yourself. And besides, I couldn't see Brad Isaacs or Eric Leve negotiating with Mickey Colucci. I decide that having an agent collect my porn commission is simply not worth it. Besides, in reality, it would only be a thousand bucks, hardly worth his time.

"$10,000," I say.

Brad nods his head as if to say, "not bad." "Who did the deal for you?"

"Me," I say. "It wasn't complicated and at the time I had no agent."

"Well, now you do," he states. "You let me know if you need me to negotiate for you next time. You shouldn't be negotiating for yourself. You should be writing."

Right, I think.

Anita enters the room. "Joe Schwartz can meet Laura next Thursday afternoon at three o'clock."

Brad glances at me. "Can you make it?"

I check my Pocket PC, my one indulgence since closing the four-picture deal with Colucci. It sends out the right signals: that I am part of progress, part of the changing technological landscape, that I am capable of adapting, that I am keenly interested in the value of the economics of time-saving devices, and lastly, that I, too, can create the perception that I make enough money to have expendable income.

"Isn't the Pocket PC great?" asks Brad.

"Oh, yeah, sure, it's great…uh, that time and date work for me," I say, marking it down. "What exactly should I do to prepare?"

"Nothing," says Brad. "I'll make sure he reads your script before the meeting and we'll see if we can package a couple of big names on this."

As I leave the room, Richard Marksman, the president of STA, stands in the corridor quietly gazing down to the center of his domain, yes, the formidable lobby. He's much taller than most agents, probably five seven and a half, and he's young for his position, probably thirty-eight. This is the guy who indirectly gave me the heave-ho by not keeping me as a client after the Scott Sher fiasco. Even though I'm at the Significant Talent Agency, brushing past him as a less than million-dollar-a-year writer makes me feel totally insignificant, and for all their current interest in my work, it still feels like I am being pampered with platitudes.

I am trying to find something to wear to Sara Stephenson's dinner party. Not an easy task since my Bennett outfit is at the cleaners. And when I'm immersed in creating ideas out of words, the last thing I can think of is how to create something fashionable out of my wardrobe.

The clock moves again and I don't want to be late. My one and only all-purpose sleek black cocktail dress jumps out at me. I slip on black loafers and leap in the car to head north for the beaches of Malibu.

Sara has cooked a delicious dinner for four. But the other two guests, Hank Willows and his boyfriend J.J., have cancelled at the last minute, so it is just Sara and I standing on her spacious deck overlooking her backyard, the Pacific Ocean.

Sara wears a simple white sundress speckled with pastel stitching. Her blond hair hangs loosely over her shoulders and she has discarded her glasses. The erudite woman I had innocently met and been rescued by has transformed herself into a serene feminine goddess in repose.

"I'm really sorry about all the cancellations," she says.

"It's okay," I say. I had never been to a studio executive's house before and frankly I felt nervous without knowing why.

"Dinner was amazing," I say. "Thanks."

"You're very welcome. Can I get you anything else?"

I decide the time has come to make my request. I reach into my fashionable combination backpack and purse and pull out the latest screenplay of *The Law of Malus.* It rests safely inside a plastic zip-top bag.

Sara looks at the bag and gently laughs. "I see you have it safely wrapped inside a condom," she says.

"Yeah, I guess so," I say, laughing with her. Then I clear my throat, throwing in as much confidence as I can muster. "This is my opus," I declare. "You asked me what else I was working on and this is it. It's a dramatic love story—a cross between *Ordinary People, The Big Chill, Prince of Tides* and *The Way We Were,* or so I like to think. I know Hollywood thinks the public is only interested in fear-based movies, but I disagree. I think it's time Hollywood promoted movies that define a different kind of emotional courage and inner strength. Okay, I'm done with my sermon now."

"Quite an opening," she says. "How'd you come up with it?"

"It's based on the marriage of a woman named Lily Laurence, a gifted and passionate singer during World War II up to the eighties."

"What's the title mean? *The Law of Malus.* It's got a poetic ring to it," Sara comments, as she leans her back against the porch railing, thereby giving me her full undivided attention.

"It's a metaphor borrowed from the world of optics, having to do with rotating the polarization of light to create maximum intensity. Impressionist painters used it when they pushed aside the traditional notion of central perspective and replaced it with new ways of perceiving light. Pulling Malus' Law referred to achieving intense light depending on your angle of rotation. I believe the spiritual metaphor has to do with the search for your greatest beam of inner light. This story is about the events in a character's life that alter her perception of herself until she's able to relate to these events and thus discover a new sense of self."

"Sounds intriguing," Sara says, nodding her head in thought. "Tell me about the theme," she requests as she sips some wine.

"The theme deals with loss and the simple gifts of life that are universal. It's a story of adversity that tears you apart, then provides you with insight into how two people deal with heartache in two very different ways."

I try to read Sara's thoughts, but she reveals nothing. So I continue. "For me, the moral of the story is acceptance, accepting ourselves, accepting our differences, and accepting that as human beings we cannot only begin, but that we can begin again." I finish and nervously down my wine in one gulp.

She takes it in, nodding again, then in a genuine voice says, "I'd love to read it," as she fills my glass again. "But I was hoping you'd tell me more about the erotic psychological dramas you're working on."

"Oh. Well, what do you want to know?"

"Tell me about them," she says.

"They're just a series of dramatic love stories. Your typical lover gets lover, loses lover, and then gets lover again."

"Are you sure you don't mean girl gets girl?"

"Why do you ask that?" I reply, hoping this is not going where it is obviously going.

"Hank told me about your research. I did a little digging on my own and then I rented the films. You write well-developed characters, no pun intended." She smiles. "They really turned me on."

"Oh. You think I wrote those! That's very funny. I didn't write those. Someone named Bella Feega wrote those. They were strictly for research purposes," I blurt out.

"Research. Hmmm," she says, and then changes the subject. "I felt bad for you at that party," she says. "Who was that guy?"

"An old boyfriend. I never did thank you for uh, getting me out of a fix there."

"It was no problem," she insists, gliding up to me. Then she whispers in my ear, "But you can thank me now if you want. Consider it research." She wraps her arms around me and I feel a rush go through my body.

Before I can say a word she kisses me gently on my mouth. Her lips are soft and sweet. She pulls me closer and I feel myself succumb to her embrace. She kisses me again on the lips and on my neck. I hear myself murmur, oblivious to anything but her touch. Between her tender kisses her hands gently caress the contour of my body, slowly finding their way to my breasts.

And then my mind races with competing thoughts, emotions, and questions that go something like this: "Oh my God, a woman is kissing me." "Hmmm, I can't believe how nice it feels." "What am I doing? I'm not gay!" "This is wrong for me." "God, I miss the arms of a man, a man who loves me." "What is the meaning of this?" "Maybe I'm here for a reason." "But I don't belong here." "How do I know she's not using me?"

At that moment I must make a decision. Do I leave right now or investigate the reality of what *The Law of Malus* has taught me? But I am not ready. And these sensations are simply too frightening.

"Sara," I say, "I can't do this." She stops and looks at me. She gently sweeps the hair away from my eyes and dazzles me with her beauty.

"You have a beautiful smile…are you sure?" she asks.

"I've never done this before," I say.

Her hands suddenly pause along the surface of my skin. She looks perplexed. "Then how did you write those movies?"

"Bella Feega wrote those movies. And how does any writer write? They have active imaginations and get inspired by what's around them."

"Well, I'm around you. Why not let me inspire you, Laura, you might really like it. I promise I'll be gentle." Her hands move back into play. And for a moment, I recall my college boyfriend, our bodies locked together, his hands tenderly caressing my face, his lips gently kissing my breasts. God, I miss him. He was so perfect. But then Sara's lips graze my ear and I begin to feel myself melt. I try to superimpose my memory of men over the sensations she elicits in me. Her sensual voice interrupts my reverie.

"Let yourself go. That's it. Relax," she hums. I feel her fingers sensually scan my skin. "I believe in unlocking all those beams of light. Don't you?" she murmurs between more kisses.

I gently pull her hands down. "Sara, I'm too afraid, and I like men, sometimes, when they're not dickheads. I, uh, I really have to go now."

"Come on, Laura, stay with me the night. I can still please you like a guy. Just let me get the strap-on."

"Okay, now I'm freaking out." I grab my purse. "Uh, thanks for dinner, Sara."

"Wait one minute, Laura. Let me at least kiss you good-bye."

She takes me in her arms and I turn into mush.

I leave Sara's house confused and relieved, and really missing a male lover, someone who's simply not around. The whole drive home I am consumed with "what ifs." Between the moonlight's reflection on the ocean water, the beam of my headlights, and my longing for reliable love, I move through my imaginings of Sara Stephenson seducing me on her patio, an evening filled with nurturing caresses, heartfelt emotions and…a strap-on.

Back at my sturdy desk in the corner of my kitchen, I try to recoup by focusing on the sequel to *Things Change.* I try not to think about Sara Stephenson, but she has left a mark on me. And somehow, she manages to invade my adult screenplays.

Since Tess Knight chose to leave the business and her character, Lisa, possessed center stage as the main protagonist, I decide to keep her in the sequel by using clips of the original movie as flashbacks from Denise's point of view. This helps me transition Denise into becoming the main protagonist and slowly bleed Lisa out of the plot.

To recap the original story, Lisa leaves her relationship with Denise to explore her heterosexuality. Denise decides that if Lisa can be with a man, so can she and denounces all ties to her former homosexual life.

I create a scene at a heterosexual bar where Denise meets an honorable guy named Tray, the kind of guy I would love to meet, but then she ends up rescuing a pretty young woman named Julia from her obnoxious abusive boyfriend by burning his arm with her cigarette. An obvious reference to the first time I met Sara Stephenson. Circumstances justify Julia temporarily staying with Denise until she can get on her feet again. Of course, all sorts of exterior and interior obstacles get in the way of their eventual union; Denise's attempts to be with Tray; Julia's attempts to get over her ex-boyfriend and the realization that she's falling in love with Denise.

Julia's ex-boyfriend becomes an amalgamation of all the insufferable men I have known, but mostly he represents the cathartic release of my own pain from Mitchell Mann and Gavin Marsh. I know I need to forgive and forget, well, forget, and I sincerely hope that writing these scenes will help me get there.

In the meantime, between Sara and the script, I decide I'm in need of male company.

Tom smiles at me from across the hand rolls of spicy tuna and sautéed asparagus in a downtown Japanese restaurant. "So what are you looking for in a guy?" he asks.

"Tenderness and compassion, intelligence…and…" I start.

"Sounds like you need a good woman," he interjects, before I can finish.

"Please don't say that," I quip. "And why *would* you say that?"

"Most guys I know don't have those qualities," he explains. "And besides, the most intelligent women I know have all been with other women."

I wonder if his comment bears any truth and then return to defending my list of desires, "Well, my college boyfriend had those qualities. Therefore, I know they exist. Anyway, I was going to add loyalty and a sense of humor," I say.

"Aha! Then maybe what you need is a dog," he says with a straight face.

"You're not serious, are you?" I ask.

"I know a lot of women who are into dogs…and horses," he says with that common-knowledge face again.

"I think my open-mindedness has its limits," I say.

"Well, if you ever feel like exploring beyond your limits, let me know and I'll be your guide. I know just where to take you."

"Gee, thanks," I say. And with that I know that Tom and I might become good friends, but never full-time lovers heading to the chupah. I might not be totally clear on what I want or in what form I want it, but I still have enough instinct to know what I don't want.

Sitting next to Ann in her living room collecting discarded paper wrapping from her shower gifts amongst her giddy girlfriends and newfound relatives was also something I knew I didn't want. If I ever got married and had a shower I'd make it a bowling party and include the guys. This was one ritual I just did not get. But I was determined to play the role of dutiful sister, gracefully adding to the chorus of *oohs* and *aahs* and making notes as to who gave Ann what for her thank-you cards. Another waste of time and resources, I thought. Why not just stop with Ann thanking everyone there? Why waste the trees, the cost of money on stamps, and the mailman's footwear?

I watch as Ann opens her gifts of predetermined lingerie and pretend I am seeing it all for the first time.

"Isn't that lovely," shouts Eva, as Ann delightedly holds up a long ivory silk bathrobe.

I offer an *oooh* followed by an exclamatory "That is just sooooooo beautiful!" I may have overdone it because a moment later Eva casts a glance my way indicating for me to tone down the theatrics.

Later at the coffee table, Ann introduces me to her friend Sandra. "I told Sandra all about you. She works for the *Malibu Post,*" says Ann.

Sandra corners me. "Ann says you're a writer. I could see about getting you an internship writing obituaries. There's no pay for the first six months, and then after that it's minimum wage, but at least it's a foot in the door."

"Gee, thanks," I politely respond. "But uh, those aren't the kind of deadlines I write for." I turn to Ann. "So how are the meetings going with the florist and the caterer and seamstress and the rabbi?" I ask.

"Takes forever. When you get married, let me give you some advice. Elope."

"Okay, thanks," I say.

My mother crosses over to me. "You're coming to brunch tomorrow, aren't you? The rabbi will be there. He wants to talk to us about our relationship with Ann, for the wedding sermon."

"Oh, I won't be here," I reply, to which I'm met with questioning glares. "I have to go to Vegas. Research," I add.

"I hope you're getting paid for it this time," says Ann.

"Actually, I am," I respond, to which I am met with more questioning glares. "Why doesn't anyone believe me?" I ask.

"Because you have more flarshegennuh meetings in Hollywood and they always fall apart," replies Ann.

"It's not my fault they crumble. It's the way the business works," I say in my own defense. "That doesn't mean I give up my dreams because the universe isn't responding to my perceived timetable of success."

"We just worry about you," says Eva.

"Well, you don't have to. I'm getting paid to write these little psychological dramas for cable until I get *Malus* off the ground." As is par for the course these days, I omit the details. Instead, I point outside to the driveway. "See the yellow Beetle. It's a new lease."

Their glares become sighs of relief. "It's adorable," comments Ann.

"Why didn't you tell us?" asks Eva.

"Because it's Ann's time to shower and shine, not mine."

"You don't have to be that considerate," says Eva.

"But Mom, you raised me to be that way," I counter, to which she cannot object.

take six

THE ADULT ACADEMY AWARDS

The Las Vegas hotel banquet room is tasteless, kitsch and, well, tacky. Walker Smith, a very famous R&B musician, escorts me down the main hallway leading to the ballroom where the ceremony will take place.

How Walker Smith came to be my escort is another story. It turned out that Jason Brand is the best friend of Michael Hartzman, who is this guy's entertainment lawyer. Apparently, staying in hotels over the course of a twenty-three-year musical career had made Walker Smith a porn film aficionado.

Jason overheard Corie on the phone with me, asking "What do you mean you're not going? You have to go. You've been nominated. Just think of the stories you can tell your grandchildren. No, forget them, think of all the stories you can tell Adam and me." She personified the persistent advocate. The conversation continued. "I have no idea what one wears to this kind of function," declared Corie. "I would think since you're a writer you should wear something on the demure side, but it's got to be sensual and sexy, because you are after all going to the porn awards."

"Who is going to the porn awards?" shouted Jason from inside his office.

"No one you know!" quipped Corie from her cubicle in the hallway.

The next thing I know, the musician, who happens to be in Las Vegas this week, has gotten a gentle grip on my elbow.

As I witness the decked-out stage where the ceremony will take place, I begin to conjecture, what kind of awards do they pass out anyway? Are they Golden Dick Awards? I really have no idea. I can't help wondering how I've gone from being a writer of children's adventure and romantic epics like *The Magic Mitt* and *The Law of Malus* to *Things Change* and *My Red Vibe Notebook.* Suddenly it dawns on me; my genre has expanded, I'm a G-X screenwriter.

Walker and I sit at the Accent Film Company table near Tom Kaplan and Cliff Peterson. Mickey Colucci has not flown in for the event. Apparently, he's a devoted family guy and never comes to these affairs.

Tom whispers to me, "Nice escort, Bella. Does he meet all your requirements?"

I grin at Tom, "This is a favor, not a date."

"Oh," he smiles. "Well, in that case you should know that I've started reading the dictionary."

"Learn anything interesting?" I ask.

He thinks it over. "Not really. I fell asleep at *doze.*"

"Cute," I laugh. "Intelligence plus a sense of humor, I better watch out."

Next to Walker sits an older woman named Mona V. Walker recognizes Mona immediately and tells her what a fan he is of all her movies, the ones she starred in and the ones she subsequently directed. Walker reveals a litany of titles followed by a lengthy and descriptive synopsis of each film's story line and the names of all the stars. It occurs to me that here exists an industry where women can actually have steady careers as directors. Mona smiles graciously, flattered by the recognition. And then I watch Walker Smith whip out his evening's program and a pen and ask for her autograph.

The awards program lists all the films and videos nominated and their categories. Studded with glossy photos, the program also provides short bios of stars, directors and producers who've made a significant impact on the history and development of the adult film industry. An inserted pamphlet tells the story of Reuben Sturman, the renowned Cleveland businessman credited as the founding father of the porn business, who for years beat obscenity charges brought against him, but in the end died at 73 in a federal prison while serving a four-year term for tax fraud and extortion.

I am fascinated with Sturman's story and wonder if anybody has optioned the right to adapt his life into a feature film. This would have been something to bring up at an STA Creative Group Meeting. I skim through more pages and find the bios of Tess Knight and Lacey Larson, each with over a hundred films to their credit in less than three years.

Walker and Mona are deep in conversation still going over her biography, so I politely excuse myself and wander around the gigantic room filled with buxom women and ogling men dressed to the nines. I pass the bar and recognize a Hollywood literary agent I know, who co-represents a client of Eric Leve's.

"Lyle, what are *you* doing here?" I ask incredulously.

"I'm nominated for Best Video Writer," he grins and places his finger to his lips and murmurs, "Shhh." I smile to myself. Apparently, I'm not alone.

I decide I need a drink and get in line behind a handsome dirty-blond-haired surfer dude in a tuxedo. We smile at each other.

"Are you here for a nomination?" he asks.

"I'm up for Best Screenplay for *Things Change.*"

"That's great," he says. "By the way, I'm Louie."

"I'm Bel—I mean Laura. So are you here for a nomination?" I ask.

"Not me. My girlfriend's nominated for Best Actress in *The Harder They Come.* You want to meet her? We're always looking for good scripts I can direct her in."

"Sure."

We pick up our drinks and head over to another table. I never drink hard liquor, but I order a double vodka and tonic to get me through this evening. Louie tells me about himself as we cross the room. He's really a film/video editor, who's temporarily directing low-budget porn videos to save enough money to buy an editing system. Then he plans to leave the adult industry and edit commercials and television programming. It occurs to me that while most people use the adult industry to launch their mainstream careers, I've managed to do it all backwards.

Louie introduces me to a dark-haired woman named Summer Wind who tells me she's really not an actress. She's a dancer.

"Really?" I say. "I used to study African American dance in college. I love dancing. I almost became a choreographer. What kind of dance do you do?"

"Exotic dance," she says.

"Oh, that's great," I respond enthusiastically, covering up my embarrassment over not realizing the obvious, while acknowledging how truly naive I can be.

"Why don't you come see a performance of mine sometime? I'll give you the address and afterwards we can talk about some of your script ideas," she says.

"Sure," I say, realizing that it feels good to be wanted for your work.

Louie taps me on the shoulder and points. "There are the stars of your movie." Sure enough, Tess Knight and Lacey Larson enter the room, each with a male escort.

"Do you know why Tess is leaving the business?" I ask him.

"I think she's going back to Washington University to get her degree in Physical Therapy. That's her boyfriend. He's in medical school."

"What about Lacey, who's she with?"

"That's her husband. He's not a great actor, but he gets all the male roles with her because she refuses to do male intercourse scenes with anyone else."

Now I understand why my dialogue in a few scenes of *Things Change* was not delivered in the most, well, let's just say it could have sounded better.

"Has anyone ever considered starting an acting school for the talent?"

"I suppose you could try," Louie says, "but that's not exactly where their gifts lie. It's not easy to make love on camera, ya know."

I'm hiding out in the bathroom, taking a moment to collect myself. Taking a moment to step back and consider the events that have led me to this evening when I notice two slot machines on either side of the vanity. One machine reveals vivid yellow lemons and bright oranges, the other luminous green apples and shiny blueberries. I look from one machine to the other and realize that I'm in the middle of a déjà vu and really, at the core of it all, there's the reason that has brought me to this moment.

It was in Ms. Reinhard's third grade class that my daydreaming began to take shape as stories. And it all started with the Crayon Wars raging inside my desk. Orange and yellow crayons battling constantly with blue and green ones for my attention, leaving the red crayon caught in the middle. I couldn't help it. I was biased. I didn't like yellow or orange and while I didn't mind red, I had a penchant for blue and green. Blue offered me the sky and clean water. Green gave me lush forests and soft grass that cushioned me while I lay on the lawn gazing up at the big blue sky.

It was while the crayons were having it out that Ms. Reinhard interrupted, asking the class to pull out their pencils and begin writing a story, any story we wanted. "You have one hour," she said. "Go." I wrote *The Tall Tale of King C* and thus began my odyssey to write, inspired by an assignment in third grade. My story, about a giant dog named C, who saves a town of innocent cats from a nasty dragon and falls in love along the way, was chosen to represent the entire school at Oakland University's Young Authors' Conference.

My little story, conceived and executed in one hour at the age of eight, managed to possess a beginning, middle, and end, a protagonist and antagonist, a hero with a journey, and a point of view. Those eight pages inhabited conflict and drama, symbols and irony, humor, and a romantic subplot.

And that is why, I surmise, I now sit inside a Vegas bathroom at an AVN award ceremony waiting to see if my jackpot might be "Best Screenplay."

All of a sudden the bathroom door opens and Tess Knight and Lacey Larson enter. I don't know why, but I suddenly feel like I'm in the presence of adult entertainment royalty. Celebrity energy definitely surrounds them. They are stars in their world. And I am all too aware that that energy has permeated my reality. I decide I can't let this moment pass without re-introducing myself. The two of them politely nod to me as they reapply their lipstick.

"Hi," I say, "um, I don't know if you remember me…"

They look at me with a combination of defensiveness and boredom. I realize they must think I'm either a psycho fan or a lesbian trying to make a pass at them.

"I'm the writer of *Things Change,*" then looking at Tess add, "and your former lingerie dressing room neighbor."

They immediately break into warm, genuine smiles. "Oh, hi! I didn't recognize you all dressed up. You look great," says Tess.

"You really helped us out that day," adds Lacey.

"Yeah, I was able to get into the character in a whole different way than I've ever done before," says Tess. "It's the best script I've ever worked on."

"We've gotten so many compliments from it. And you know, it's really done a lot for so many women," adds Lacey. "You should know that."

"Thanks. Well, you guys were really good in it, you made it what it is," I say, aware of and embarrassed by my starstruck attitude.

"I really hope you win," says Tess.

"Me, too," says Lacey. "The industry needs good scripts like yours."

"Thanks. Well, I hope we all win."

And then, like beauty queens in a pageant, we hug and wish each other good luck on all of our nominations.

I'm about to follow Tess and Lacey out the door when I take a last glance at the slot machines. Feeling a little light-headed from their compliments or from the alcohol, or maybe from both, I decide what the hell and pull out a quarter. I've never played a slot machine before. I drop in the coin, close my eyes, and anxiously pull down on the lever. I open my eyes to watch a whir of colors and numbers rapidly rolling by like a Ferris wheel on an acid trip. It comes to a halt on a row of three blueberries, a cacophony sounds as quarters endlessly spill forth. I smile broadly as I collect my winnings, I can't help myself. Before I exit the bathroom, I take one last look at the slot machine and for a moment, it looks like the colors of the fruit have shape-shifted into colored crayons. I shake my head and push my way outside and into the present.

Back in the ballroom, the ceremony begins. The emcee is introduced and the show comes alive. A variety of adult industryites present the awards, mostly stars and a few directors and producers. The awards themselves turn out to be made of gold, but I'm disappointed to find out they're ordinary looking trophies. There's absolutely nothing about them that would indicate a connection to the adult industry, which destroys my chances at more self-deprecating humor. Speeches are made. The audience claps and cheers.

So far, *Things Change* takes every award. Tess Knight and Lacey Larson win for Best Actresses. They accept their awards and make small speeches thanking the director and producer. To my surprise they add, "And we'd like to thank the writer, Bella Feega, for her wonderful story and really inspiring dialogue." Tom Kaplan winks at me. Walker smiles and whispers, "All right, Bella—I mean Laura!"

When they finally get to Best Screenplay, I'm not only nervous, but I have a strange feeling inside me, a feeling of desire, and it's intensifying. I realize two things. One, that while I don't want to want the award, I do in fact want the award, and two, I want it in a big way but am petrified that anyone might find out.

Walker turns to me. "Did you prepare a speech?"

I shake my head no.

"By the way," I ask Walker, "this isn't going to be televised is it?"

"No way," he says, "or I couldn't be here. My wife would kill me."

The presenter leans into the microphone to announce the winner for Best Screenplay. I hear the name Bella Feega, followed by an applause sprinkled with chuckles from all the Italian-speaking individuals in the room.

I find myself at the podium. The only thing I fear more than being a porn writer, is public speaking. I gather courage from my acting class and intermittently attended Toastmaster sessions, which I took to conquer my fear of pitching stories in creative meetings.

One of our assignments was to conduct interviews and write a speech about it. I had decided to interview the top interviewers about interviewing. When I spoke with a popular morning show host, her parting words offered me a source of strength and courage. "And don't be afraid of public speaking, Laura," she said.

It wasn't what she said so much as how she'd said it. Her words were filled with endearment and understanding, and became my symbolic amulets in a hero's journey crossing the threshold.

I take a deep breath and begin. "Gee thanks, everyone. I, um, I don't know what to say. I've never written this kind of film before. And well, I find myself standing here feeling really, really honored. First, I'd like to thank Cliff Peterson for bringing my words and sentiments to life and for transforming my descriptions into amazing images and, to all the actors, especially Tess Knight and Lacey Larson for making my characters so believable."

I can't stop myself. This may be the only recognition I ever get for my writing. I continue, my confidence building. "To Mickey Colucci and the Accent Film Company. I would also like to thank Tom Kaplan for his beautiful box covers and great marketing campaign. I'd like to thank the academy for putting on this awards ceremony."

Oh, hell, I think, I might as well go for broke. It would be wrong to forget to thank anyone else at this point. And so I continue, "I'd like to thank my mother for teaching me to be open-minded and my father for teaching me to be discerning. And especially to all the fans out there who rented or bought these videos—that were shot on film—and um, I'd like to add that to be recognized for what you do and how you do it, well, it's pretty remarkable. It makes all those sleepless nights worth it. Because in the end, what we really want is to be noticed and accepted. And I think everyone in every profession should get to come up to a podium at some point in his or her life and have the honor of graciously accepting recognition from their peers."

My peripheral vision captures a figure nearby hyperactively crossing his neck with his finger, but I continue. "As writers, we're the storytellers of our time and we bear an important responsibility for that task. We speak for humankind about humankind and attempt to push new innovations of thought and perception. With that in mind, I really hope this film inspires not just women, but every human being, to be strong, to be independent, and to have the courage to follow your truth and alter your circumstances or your self, or whatever it is that needs to transform, because what's really, really important here is to know that God's gift, and I mean God in whatever way you want to interpret it, but to know that God's gift to humankind is not to begin, but to begin *again,* to know that *things can change!* Thank you, the Academy of Adult Entertainment!"

Okay, so I got a little carried away and went on record for having one of the longest speeches in the history of this ceremony. But the crowd cheered when I walked off that stage.

Tom Kaplan comes up to me, gives me a big warm hug and whispers through laughter in my ear, "Laura, so you know, there is no Academy of Adult Entertainment."

"Oh," I say. "Well, maybe I'll just have to start one."

After all that, *Things Change* took home every award except for Best Picture. It didn't make sense. And it bothered me. Not only that the film didn't win, but it bothered me that it bothered me that it didn't win. I was beginning to really care about this otherworldly career of mine. And that made me nervous.

Just like in Hollywood, the after-parties take place in a variety of hotel suites and last till dawn. I meet the critics of my movie who fawn all over me.

"You're Bella Feega!" they exclaim. "It's an honor to meet you." I think I must really try to get a grip and not let this go to my head. This is just a porn film.

A docile, sweet woman in her mid-sixties approaches me. She takes my hands in hers and ferociously shakes them. "Congratulations, Bella Feega," she says.

"Thanks," I say. "What's your name?"

"Lola Stormrider," she answers between onslaughts of coughing.

"Hey, are you all right? Can I get you some water?"

"I'll be all right, honey."

"Wait a minute, weren't you also nominated for Best Screenplay tonight?"

"Good memory," she says, continuing to hack away.

"That doesn't sound good, Lola. You should get that cough checked," I tell her.

"Well, maybe if I cracked the glass ceiling on writing salaries like you I could. I hope it creates some changes around here. In the meantime, who can afford decent health insurance today? I've tried a dozen health insurance companies and health insurance agents. I even wrote a spec adult political detective parody about the current state of our health insurance industry."

"What's it called?" I ask.

"I call it *The Green Dick Who Licked Blue Cross.*"

"That's hysterical," I say. "Do you have more like those?"

"Oh, yeah, I have a lot of adult political parodies in my drawers," she says. "You know, I used to run Reuben Sturman's first adult production company and in those days, political satire and drama with an adult entertainment twist did well. To tell you the truth, I think we helped a lot with the war effort."

"How?" I ask intrigued.

"Ever hear of the *Adam & Eve Under Cover* series?" I shake my head no. She continues, "*Adam & Eve under the Iron Curtain, Adam & Eve get down in Cuba*. There were more. But no one will ever know."

"How long have you been writing adult movies?" I ask.

"Forty years now. I tried to write features in Hollywood fifteen years ago—if nothing else, it would have been nice to be in the Writers Guild, for the insurance alone, but it's impossible to break in, not to mention getting past all those snotty assistants when you're looking for a literary agent. I liked myself too much to be treated like that. The pay in adult films may not be Hollywood mainstream numbers, but at least it's steady work and more than once in awhile you get recognized for it. You can't beat that. Maybe your breakthrough will raise the bar for the rest of us. Congratulations, Bella Feega."

She coughs again and then politely excuses herself. I try to keep my eye on her as she drifts into the crowd, her body convulsing under a stream of incessant coughs. And then I lose her. Lola Stormrider disappears in the throng of partygoers.

It turns out that Walker Smith not only makes for a famous escort, but he also displays graciousness and thoughtfulness. He astutely points out who everyone is in the after-party suites, like the guy in the cowboy hat, notorious for his "gonzo" porn flicks; and the woman in the sarong, known for her feminist femme fatale videos. He looks after me when producers approach me and ask me to call them; at least I think they are producers until I realize they are actually the owners of the other major adult film companies, namely, Accent Film Company's biggest competitors.

An executive from the Erotica Channel introduces himself to me.

"I'm the one who approved your script for Erotica. Congratulations on your award," he says. "Here's my card. I would love it if you'd give me a call sometime. We're gearing up to do a low-budget soft-core feature film in Maui for three hundred thousand. Do you think you might be interested in writing it? It's called *Hot Hawaii*. It's a behind-the-scenes look at photographing a magazine's swimsuit edition. We would be willing to fly you to Maui for a week of research, too."

"That would be great," I say, "I'll call you next—"

We never finish our conversation because a commotion happens near the elevators. Crews with lights and video cameras barge into the suite. Erotica's discreet video crew covering the after-parties sensitively captured only the adult film stars on tape. But this infiltrating camera crew and others like them are mercenaries on a mission. JKL Cable Network, known for their sensationalized rip-off of HBO's "Real Sex," has sent their aggressive "Authentic Sex" video news team to get a story here.

Walker ducks away and disappears. He tries to pull me with him but I get trapped between two porn stars and a critic. I stand, squeezed in the crowd, watching as the JKL crew rudely flash their lights and microphones in the face of one of the stars. Someone points in my direction and a crew member shines his spotlight on me. A second pimply-faced reporter almost shoves his microphone up my nose, "So tell us, Bella Feega, what does your name really mean?"

Thank God I never leave home without it, that is, since I received "it" from Larry Solomon. I promptly flash my temporary press pass from *Inside Hollywood* and snap, "Excuse me, but do I look like a person who pens porn? I'm on duty, too. Do you mind? Thanks for blowing my cover."

"Oh, sorry, I thought you were someone else," he says rather skeptically, eyeing the award I'm attempting to shove into my clutchbag.

"Next time, try some manners," I holler at him before making a break for the closest elevator.

Walker and I find each other in the lobby and stop for a nightcap.

"What a mess," says Walker. "Glad you got out okay." He turns to me. "Hey listen, you gonna write any more of these films?"

"Maybe. I guess it depends on Hollywood. I get a lot of praise but it rarely comes with cash."

"Well if you ever need me to score a movie for you, you let me know."

"Okay, thanks Walker, I will, and I hope it's a studio movie."

"Either way is cool with me," he says. "So how's it feel to be a winner?"

I swish the port in my glass and stare at it for a long moment thinking about my answer. "Weird. Bella Feega got the recognition, not Laura Taylor. Only Laura Taylor is Bella Feega. And Laura can exist without Bella, but Bella can't live without Laura. On top of that, Laura can't tell anyone about Bella, but everyone who knows Bella, knows Laura. I'm really confused."

"I hear you," says Walker, supportively. "Walker Smith ain't Walker Smith."

"Really? Who is he?" I ask, wide-eyed.

"Just a kid from the streets who got lost in his music…and stayed there. But you gotta remember something. This is your voyage, your trip, and no one else's. And there's a reason for this that you can't see right now, but one day, it's gonna show up and you're gonna know what the experience was for. You just have to trust that and keep your eyes open to see it." Then he tilts his glass of scotch at me, smiles, and finishes it quickly.

"Thanks for those words," I say. "They mean a lot." And then in a moment of camaraderie, I repeat his actions and down the rest of my port in a gulp with a grimace.

"You want to come up and stay with me?" he asks. I get the sense that he asks more out of loneliness than anything.

I smile at him. "No, thanks, I'm not very good at sleeping with married men, but thanks for thinking of me." I kiss him on the cheek with my golden statue in hand. "Good night, Walker. Thanks for being such a nice escort."

And that was my first adult film awards ceremony, comprised of elation, gratitude, and bittersweet eudaemonia. In the cab on the way back to my hotel I reflect on Walker and decide he was right. I need a little more faith and a lot more patience to enjoy this journey.

take seven

NEW DEVELOPMENTS

I am at a love boutique in Santa Monica on a mission for Elaine Dover's bachelorette party, which I am hosting. When she begged me to throw her one I couldn't refuse. Then Ann found out about it and the next thing I knew, I was throwing a small intimate double bachelorette party for both of them.

While researching one of my erotic stories I stumbled on this store, which specializes in love paraphernalia. I figured it would be a good place to start. Though I am amazed at the stuff that lines every available inch of space. I have my shades on as I shyly peruse the gift options.

A pretty salesgirl approaches. "May I help you?"

"Uh, just looking for stuff for a bachelorette party. What can you recommend?"

"Follow me," she says, as she sashays down the aisle. With

a grin she points to a poster of a gorgeous naked man missing a penis.

"That's called Pin-the-Penis-on-the-Hunk," she says. "It's very popular. You blindfold the girls and see who comes closest to pinning the enclosed 'cocks' on the bull's-eye."

"Oh—that's nice," I say, trying to act nonchalant.

The salesgirl swiftly turns around and lifts up a box. "This is a dirty word game," she explains. "You throw the dice and make erotic sentences out of the dirty words while drinking margaritas. Speaking of margaritas, you might want to try serving them in a slightly more unique fashion," she adds, smiling as she picks up an ice mold in the shape of a penis. "It has other uses, too," she says, winking mischievously.

I am guided through rows of lingerie, dildos in a variety of sizes, vibrators in an assortment of colors, strap-ons, incense, and an endless row of books like the *Kama Sutra*. I decide on the poster, the dirty word game and the penis mold, since they are the least expensive and I think the most appropriate for Elaine's and Ann's friends. For the hell of it, I throw in a red vibrator as a gag gift and for my writing inspiration until the party.

I open the door to my car when I spot Sara Stephenson looking as beautiful as ever. She smiles, happy to see me. I quickly shove the bags in the driver's seat as she walks up.

"Hi, Laura," she says. "How come you haven't returned my calls?"

"I'm sorry, Sara, I've just been so busy writing, going to 'nowhere meetings,' and then I was in Las Vegas."

"Oh, what was in Vegas?"

"Um. Business." She scans me like a metal detector and I can tell she knows that I'm omitting certain facts.

"Please don't be afraid of me," she says with the kind of sincerity I haven't heard in years. "You know it's okay if you're not into women. It's not about gender or labels for me. We can just be friends."

"Okay," I say.

"How about a croissant and café au lait next door?"

"Sure," I reply.

In moments we are sipping our coffee drinks and chatting about screenplays and movies. "You know I really love *The Law of Malus.* It's a difficult sell for Eagle Pictures, but I'm trying to find a way to help you with it. It deserves to be made. All the characters are so wonderfully drawn."

"Thanks. Which character do you see yourself as?" I ask. When I had finished interviewing Lily and mapping out the story, I told it in detail to my sister to make sure it had a logical conclusion. She told me she saw me as Gale, a friend of Holly's, the protagonist. Gale is a former gymnast, married with children, and curator of an important photographic museum. She told me she saw herself as Ari, Holly's witty ten-year-old son who dies in a boating accident in Germany. I saw my sister as Audrey, Holly's estranged older sister who leaves her family at a young age to marry a diplomat and live in Switzerland. Holly felt abandoned by Audrey. I, too, felt abandoned by Ann when she left home to study abroad. I related to Holly, a mother and singer, who's married to a composer—her best friend, the kind of man you can whisper secrets to in bed.

Without missing a beat, Sara answers, "I see myself as Joy because she has the courage to leave an identity behind that no longer works for her and explore new experiences. And you, I bet you see yourself as Holly, always striving to be better than she thinks she is."

"That's pretty intense," I say. I politely excuse myself and head to the bathroom.

I throw some water on my face and take a good long look at myself in the mirror. Am I really always striving to be better than I think I am? Do I really believe I am not enough?

Sara enters the bathroom. Startled, I kick over my bag and its contents spill to the floor.

"Let me help you," she offers.

Of course Sara sees it all. The erotic word game, the penis mold, and the red vibrator. She helps pick everything up, everything but the red vibrator, which she holds in front of me. She never says a word, coyly waiting for the right moment.

"This is not what you think, Sara. It's for a bachelorette party."

She looks at me, grinning, knowingly, and then gently leans forward. My back brushes against the bathroom wall. She locks the door and lightly kisses me on the lips, sending a bolt of electricity through my body as she glides the red vibrator between my thighs and over my cleavage.

She whispers in my ear, "You are good enough just as you are, Laura. You don't have to try so hard."

But I've been trying ever since incubation, I know no other way, I think. Somehow, the pure act of survival has gotten mixed up with a need for approval, but from whom and for what? It couldn't be as simple as receiving an accolade for throwing a baseball, creating the perfect wardrobe, or marrying a nice guy. Was it a misplaced misconception derived from my own psyche? My thoughts dissipate under the traveling vibrator with Sara at its helm.

She uses its tip to draw an imaginary heart over my heart. "Your wound is your gift," she calmly states. "It's what makes you unique."

Just exactly what was my wound? Abandonment? Rejection? Conveniently repeating them in the realm of Hollywood? And what was with the sudden sexual awareness of women? Did it have its origins in the emotional absence of my mother, depressed and unavailable after my birth with a reprise at divorce-time? And if these truly are my wounds, then what's my gift?

"Let yourself be nurtured," Sara gently hums.

"I'm so tired," I say, letting myself fall into her arms. "I'm so tired of trying."

"Don't try," she says, holding me. "Just be."

Oh hell, if I could do that I'd win a Taoist medal for curing type A personalities.

She interrupts my thoughts once again, quietly urging me, "You can start by looking at yourself in the mirror and declaring, 'I love you.' Do it," she seductively whispers, "Do it for me, right now."

I stare into the mirror. "I..." Why is this so hard? I watch my eyes dilate. "I...love..." I take a deep breath, and then exhale. "I love you," I utter, watching my eyes search for the soul behind their own reflection. I focus on the mirror again. I am alone. Sara is not there. She never was.

Sara pays for the coffees and walks me to my car. I am carrying my purse and a cappuccino to go. I barely manage to pull out my car keys and tap the unlock button without spilling my drink. The car doors click open.

"You don't think women can be chivalrous like men, do you, Laura?"

"I never said that."

"Good, then you'll let me open your car door for you. In public."

"No, you don't have to do that, Sara, really, it's not necessary," I plead.

But it's too late. She opens the driver's door and the bags from the love boutique store come tumbling out, as if the bathroom scene had been a premonition.

I immediately grab the erotic word game and the penis mold. Sara, however, snatches the red vibrator. I am mortified. Her lips curve into a salacious smile.

"I can take that now, really. I'll just put it all in the back," I sputter.

"Good, then I'll open the trunk for you, too," she says. "I can't wait to see what else you've got in here."

I have forgotten about the poster of *Things Change* lying in the trunk of my Beetle. The color photograph shows Tess Knight and Lacey Larson in unbuttoned blue jeans and lacy black bras about to embrace. An exceptionally large image, it spans four feet by three feet and takes up the entire trunk space.

As she opens the back, I am stunned and embarrassed by the poster. Sara sees the image as I dump the erotic word game and penis mold next to it.

She smiles again. "And you want me to think you're not into women." She gently leans into me and whispers, "I'm not giving up on you, Laura." She glides the tip of the red vibrator over my breasts. I feel as though it is casting a spell over me. Sara leans close, pulling me into her arms and murmuring, "One day, you'll let me show you what it's like to float among the stars." She tosses the vibrator next to the game and the mold. Then she squeezes my hand and confidently walks off.

Confused by my own curiosity, I'm not sure how to respond. The ringing cell phone temporarily eradicates my unease.

"Hello?"

"Laura? It's Tom Kaplan. Mickey Colucci is coming to town in two weeks and was wondering if you might be able to have the scripts ready a few days early."

"Sure, yeah, no problem."

"You don't sound so good."

"What makes you say that?"

"The intuitive tender side of me, which you haven't had a chance to explore yet," he quips.

"Nice," I say, catching my breath more than responding to his clever repartee.

"You sure you're okay?" he asks, no more joking around now.

"Yeah, I'm just…driving and I can't really talk now."

"Okay. Call me later because there's a new director on *Red Notebook* and he wants to go over the script with you."

"What happened to Cliff Peterson?" I ask.

"He double booked himself," explains Tom. "I'll leave the new guy's number on your home machine. 'Bye."

I sit in my stationary car, paralyzed by the impending deadline of four adult screenplays. Then I realize that what just happened has inspired the opening scene for *My Red Vibe Notebook.* I start to see my main character, Samantha, come alive. She's sexually frustrated, making her vulnerable to new experiences, because her husband is largely gone. She wants to remain loyal to him and decides the only way is to learn to take care of her own needs, so she goes to a sex shop and buys a red vibrator. I can also use the location and actors twice by having Samantha return to the shop when her vibrator breaks, at which point, Samantha will be seduced by the more experienced saleswoman. And she will have a best friend, JoAnna, who represents singlehood and shares all of her sexual adventures with her, including the one with the gorgeous college-aged pool boy. At their favorite restaurant, Samantha excuses herself to go to the bathroom. JoAnna follows and discovers Samantha with her red vibrator, then locks the bathroom door and pleasures Samantha with it. She makes Samantha float among the stars. Okay, I think, I've got my story line and at least half the scenes taken care of.

I agree to meet Jimmy Hesse, the replacement director for *My Red Vibe Notebook,* at a local hamburger joint for lunch. He's addicted to their mushroom burgers and requests that we go over the script there, which is conveniently close to where I live. What I find is a raggedy-blond-haired hippy Harley-driving rough-and-tumble guy.

What I discover is a total sweetheart jock filling in for Cliff Peterson with aspirations of using porn to transition into Hollywood. I show him my outline and he asks me to think about adding bizarre costume ideas for the fantasy sequences. I can't help but think of my brother Bennett's adamant request.

"How about if one of the characters has a fetish for leather socks?" I ask.

Jimmy's eyes light up, "That is so cool! We can do all sorts of sexy stuff with it. Especially if they're knee-high." Then he switches gears. "Hey, I've got ADD. Do you mind if we finish talking about this at my rock climbing club? It's only ten minutes from here."

Exactly twenty minutes later, Jimmy and I are hanging from ropes on belay, climbing up pseudo rock formations while continuing our discussion of *Red Notebook*.

"I want to keep the color red going on as a theme throughout the piece," he says, as he finds a small crevice to dig his fingers into and lifts himself up another notch.

"Okay," I reply, "I'll find out if I can get the leather socks in red." I locate a fissure in the counterfeit rock and hoist myself up to his altitude. "Hey. I like the way you work," I say.

"Next time we can do it surfing some waves if you want," he adds. "So Tom Kaplan said you write for Hollywood. How are those projects going?"

I watch a rock climber dangling in midair between the pursuit of the rock and the trappings of the floor. "They're on belay."

For all his unbound enthusiasm, no new news has come from Brad Isaacs's office regarding Maggie Reese. He did leave word once asking me if it was okay for him to pitch it to Hollywood luminary, Lester Crawford, to direct. Of course, I called back immediately and told his assistant,

Anita, that that would be fine. My two-week-later follow-up call resulted in Brad's sudden attack of amnesia. He had absolutely no recall about Lester Crawford. He was thinking of the director Peter Fastow and told me he'd get back to me on it. I ask him if there is anything I can do, like take a meeting with any of these directors. He tells me that's a great idea and to just sit tight and he'll take care of it.

Days later I am still sitting tight when Elaine's three friends and Ann's two newfound Malibu friends, whom I barely know, appear at my apartment for their double bachelorette party. They are all impressed by the penis ice cubes in their margaritas. The pin-the-cock-on-the-hunk game provides a lot of laughs for about three minutes and the erotic word game proves to be pretty dull.

Ann corners me in the kitchen while I remove more penis ice cubes from the freezer. "Laura, where on earth did you find this stuff?"

"Oh, um, a friend told me where to go," I reply.

"Which friend?" she asks, munching on a celery stick.

"My friend...Bella...Feega," I say meekly.

"Hmmm. What does she do?"

"Um. She works in sex...education," and then I quickly change the subject by handing Ann a tray of fresh margaritas. "Here, can you pass these out?"

"How do you know her?" Ann asks, taking the tray from me.

"Oh, uh, I think it was from research I did on that student film...which um, had to do with sex education." I notice Ann make a mental note.

"Speaking of which, when can we see it?" she asks, staring at the ice molds.

"I don't know. I'll let you know when I hear something," I say, nodding at the tray, "Ann, the penises are melting." She finally turns to go.

Hungry for erotic excitement, the women decide to play a storytelling game where everyone has to write down her fantasies on paper, then shuffle them in a hat and read each out loud and guess who wrote it. Exhausted from prepping for the party, I decide to repurpose the stories I have already written. This creates quite a stir, particularly for Elaine, who has had five too many margaritas and by this time cannot drive home.

Ann's *Malibu Post* friend Sandra, also well inebriated, decides it's time to share her surprise offering. She grabs her purse and pulls out a paper bag.

"What's in there?" asks Elaine.

"Since things are about to change for our bachelorettes, I thought this was an appropriate party favor."

To my astonishment, she pulls out *Things Change* Parts I and II. Everyone laughs and giggles while I gasp for air.

"We're watching pornos?!" asks Ann. "I think that's against my religion."

"Award-winning ones. That's what you're supposed to do at a bachelorette party," Sandra replies.

"Who says?" I screech. "I mean, where is it written that you have to watch…those things…at these things?"

"Let's watch them," says Elaine. "I've never seen one before."

"Me neither," says everyone else, including Ann now.

At the crowd's insistence, I pop Part I into the videocassette player.

Ann reads the name Bella Feega under the screenwriter credit and looks at me. "Isn't that your friend's name?"

I shrug. "That is really some coincidence, huh? But I think she spells it differently." I thank God no one in the room is Italian.

"It sounds familiar," comments Elaine, still swaying from the alcohol. I shrug again. In a moment it no longer matters because they are all wide-eyed and engrossed in the action.

"It's not as disgusting as I thought it would be," says Sandra. "In fact, it's pretty damn good."

"The men and women are gorgeous and there's a…story," declares one woman.

"Gee, I bet they go all the way now," mumbles another.

"Actually, they only go halfway," I unconsciously utter.

In the next minute, the action stops and takes a different direction.

Sandra looks at me, impressed and curious. "How did you know that?" she asks.

"Well, um. If it's award-winning it probably has a less predictable story line," I say, checking to make sure Ann is buying it. But she's got her head down and she's crying. "Ann, what's wrong?" I ask.

She shakes her head and wipes her hands like window washers, then drunkenly sputters, "George and I don't have sex like that. It's not even close."

Everyone is silent. I put my arm around her. "Ann, I'm sure it will get better. Sometimes it takes time," I offer consolingly.

"You're both under a lot of pressure right now," chimes Sandra. "Pre-wedding jitters always dampens the sex. I know. I've been through it twice."

"Besides, it's a porn film," I add. "It's supposed to up the ante on one's sexual prowess."

"But the way they talk to each other in bed while they make love is so… beautiful," she blurts. "Is it okay if I keep the films?"

"Ann, how many margaritas have you had?" I ask.

"Six," she burps. "Do you think maybe I could talk to that friend of yours…about upping my ante?"

"What friend?" I ask.

"That sex education friend, Bella…Riga," she says.

"I'll, uh, look into it," I say.

Sandra drives Ann home and after everyone else leaves, Elaine, still too smashed to drive, decides to crash on my couch, but not before insisting on watching the rest of the film. Ann took Part I and Elaine got to keep Part II. She pops Part II into the VCR while I brush my teeth in the other room.

She yells out, "I forgot to tell you. I gave *Malus* to this director I met."

"What did you say?" I shout back. "Hold on. I can't hear you." I finish brushing my teeth and cross over to her on my couch. "Did you say something?"

But Elaine sees the name Bella Feega on screen again. She forgets whatever it was she wanted to tell me and persistently manages in her intoxicated state to question me further. "Aren't you going to tell me about Bella Feega? I know you know something from that lunch at Orso's."

In her condition, I figure tomorrow she won't remember a thing, so I finally disclose my secret identity. "Okay, I'm Bella Feega," I say. "Happy now?"

"Yeah, right," she says, "I'm not gullible, ya know?" She takes a closer look at the screen. That's when I begin to realize the power of the tape, how it seems to change the chemical behavior of the viewer, first in a small dose with Adam and Corie, and now in a much larger format, metamorphosing Elaine from a passive being into a sexually stimulated life form. When Elaine glances over at me in her inebriated state I know I am in trouble. She assumes that I have been with a woman and confesses to me that she would like to sleep with me as her one last fling and will I please accommodate her wishes. I look at her exasperated. What is it about women coming on to me? I don't have to say much after that, because about thirty seconds later, she conveniently passes out on my couch. The next morning her hangover insures complete amnesia of the night before. All she remembers are the penis ice cubes.

★ ★ ★

Two weeks later I am proudly hanging the newly framed one-sheet poster of *Things Change* in my bathroom. I decided to have it professionally framed, which was not easy. First, it was costly because of its size. Second, I had to get over the embarrassment of bringing it to the custom framers. But I was bent on hanging it up because it represented my first produced movie. And in the lower right-hand corner of the poster, it even read Shot on Film, apparently a rather impressive point in the adult industry. Every executive or writer I know has one-sheets from their movies framed and hanging in their offices. Even the Feng Shui books I'd read at the library declared the importance of hanging your professional accomplishments on the walls of your office. But because of the nature of this particular photograph and because my office is in my kitchen, the only other place for it is in the bathroom.

Adam and Corie drop by the next night for a visit. Adam excuses himself to the rest room and to see the latest addition to my home.

"So how was the double bachelorette party?" Corie asks while digging into the buffalo mozzarella dish I quickly prepare.

"Great. The penis ice cubes made a big splash."

Corie laughs. "Maybe you can use the experience for your next adult script."

"I am—the part where I go to a love boutique to buy all the, uh, goodies. So what's new with you guys?"

"We got a brand-new sixty-inch TV set from Adam's boss and we need another copy of *Things Change*."

"Why are those two things in the same sentence?" I ask suspiciously.

"Because Adam received the uh, gift, after he gave his boss our copy of *Things Change.* Apparently, it saved his boss's marriage and he wanted to thank Adam, so he sent us a sixty-inch set."

"Oh. Nice to know they're having a positive impact on the world."

"Yes. And we'd like to give you our thirty-inch set because after all, none of this would have happened if you hadn't written the story to begin with."

"Wow. Thanks," I say. "Hey, you think Adam got lost in the bathroom?" I ask, aware that he's been gone for a long time now.

"I'll find out." Corie knocks on the bathroom door. "Adam, are you okay?"

"Fine," he says. When he rejoins us he looks at us and says, "That's quite a poster you have there, Laura. I'm afraid when your guests go to the bathroom, you might lose some of them—forever."

"What are you going to do with it when your family comes to visit?" asks Corie.

"Leave it for my dad and take it down for the others," I reply. "I'm an out-of-the-closet porn writer with respect to my dad and he's fine with it, though we did make a pact to keep it confidential since it's only temporary. It's professionally that concerns me."

"Speaking of your Hollywood career, what's the update on *The Law of Malus?*" asks Corie while she goes for another piece of mozzarella.

"Let's see," I say, "the meeting with Joe Schwartz has been postponed twice. Brad Isaacs hasn't followed up with Maggie Reese yet, nor set up any other meetings for me with the directors he says he's sending it to, and he owes me a call from a week ago. I'm afraid by the time he actually follows through the actors will be too old for the part. On a happier note, Sara Stephenson read it and loved it. Alas, she took it to her boss who said until there's a name director and star attached he won't touch it because it's not an Eagle Pictures kind of movie in the first place. In the meantime, she's looking into other writing assignments for me over there."

"She's really taken a liking to you, hasn't she?" says Corie.

"Yeah, I uh, guess so," I say, trying to pass it off.

"What about the porn career?" asks Adam. "I find that far more interesting."

"*My Red Vibe Notebook* is in production and Vibrant Video wants me to write a story about two of their female stars, 'Mia and Callie.'"

"I've heard of them," says Adam. "They're under contract there. It's like the old studio system. The female actresses aren't allowed to work for other adult film companies."

Corie looks at Adam astonished. "How do you know all this?"

"They were on Lyle Sherkan," he replies.

"Well, thanks for the info," I say, "because they want me to interview them at a strip club in Pompano Beach, Florida."

"Why there?" asks Corie.

"I guess they're on some sort of strip club tour and I happen to be going to Florida for a family bar mitzvah. I'll be ten miles from them."

Adam and Corie start giggling.

"It's not funny. I've never been to a strip club before."

"The whole thing is funny," says Adam. "Did you ever find out why *Things Change* didn't get Best Picture?"

"Tomorrow. Mickey Colucci is flying in to visit the set of *My Red Vibe Notebook* and to meet with me to explain why—especially after the *Financial Journal* article."

"What *Financial Journal* article?" asks Adam.

"You were in Austria, or London, I don't remember," replies Corie, "but they wrote about Colucci having the only publicly traded adult film company on the stock market."

"And they pointed to the success of *Things Change* as a

turning point in the quality of storytelling from the adult entertainment industry," I add rather proudly.

"I'm impressed," says Adam. "I'd like to see a copy of the article. Whatever happened to those animated kids' films that dealt with stress and grief and forgiveness?"

"Oh, those. I finished them while writing *My Red Vibe Notebook*. The company makes you do a ton of rewrites and they barely pay you for it. They're hardly worth the trouble."

Adam and Corie start giggling again. "Are you laughing because I was writing for them and porn at the same time?" They nod yes between more infectious giggles.

"There's a way you can celebrate the irony of it all," says Adam, "I've heard of black market cartoons that have their characters doing it together."

They burst into fits of laughter. This time I cannot suppress it either. The irony my life has become is finally catching up with me. Through tears of joy Adam screeches, "Maybe we should develop a Bella Feega theme park!"

Some remaining pride finds its way to the surface and I declare, "Out! Both of you, now!"

The following day, I arrive at a fancy restaurant in the valley. It's Monday and the place remains closed to the public. Inside, I watch as Jimmy directs a scene from *My Red Vibe Notebook*. He's cast the movie with adult stars Pamela Valentine and Daisy Steam, whose names mean nothing to me but a lot to those in the know. Apparently, word is spreading through the adult film industry that this will receive an "erotic rating" of "volcanic." And even though the women are beautiful, their acting skills are far below Tess Knight and Lacey Larson's, or maybe Jimmy isn't as skilled as Cliff Peterson when it comes to working with the talent.

Mickey Colucci saunters onto the set of the high-class bathroom scene. He motions me over with a slight nod of his head.

"Good morning, Mr. Colucci."

"You know why your film didn't win Best Picture?" he asks.

I shake my head no.

"Because we cut it in half and made two movies out of it. The industry doesn't like that. They slapped me in the face. Sorry you got slapped, too." He waits a moment and then continues. "The truth is *Things Change* sold more units than the film that won Best Picture. It's still selling. It's becoming a cult classic. I thought you should know."

"Thanks for telling me," I respond.

"Action!" shouts Jimmy.

The actors lean against the inside door of the bathroom and immediately drop their robes. They are acting out the scene where Samantha, aroused after hearing the details of her friend's sexual adventures with the poolboy, hides herself in the bathroom with her new red vibrator only to be discovered and seduced by her friend, JoAnna.

Jimmy directs the actors by their character names. "Okay, JoAnna, I want you to tease Samantha now. Make her really want to know what it's like to kiss a woman."

JoAnna brushes her lips against Samantha's face and stiffly repeats the dialogue, "'Do you want to know'—what's the line again? Oh yeah, 'don't you want to know what it's like to float among the stars?'"

"Cut," says Jimmy. "Okay, that's a wrap. Keep the lighting the same and let's get the busboy ready for his sex scene with JoAnna. And let's be sure to use the leather sock this time with a red filter on the lens."

Colucci noticed me grimace at the delivery of the lines.

He turns to me. "Bella Feega. You're my star writer. I want you to be happy." He pauses to look at me again, closely now. "You don't look happy. Something's going on behind your face. Tell me what's gonna make you happy."

I turn to him, a little shocked. How do you tell Mickey

Colucci that, well, the actors suck, no pun intended. But I figure that honesty is the best ace I've got and so I respond appropriately, "Well, okay, I don't like what they're doing to my words and I think, well, I mean, I'd like to start an acting workshop for the talent. You know, get a real professional Hollywood acting coach in here to help some of them."

Mr. Colucci considers this for approximately one minute, then pulls out his wallet and hands me a thousand dollars in cash. "Show me the results onscreen."

"Thanks," I say. "I better put this someplace safe." I head over to my knapsack in the corner of the room, when I see none other than Mitchell Mann and another guy enter the restaurant. Before I can duck, Mitchell spots me.

"Laura?" he asks. "What are you doing here?"

Before I can answer, Jimmy calls out to me from the set, "Hey, Bella, can you come over here? The busboy thinks he's a star and wants to know what his motivation is for seducing JoAnna."

"Bella?" asks Mitchell, somewhat suspiciously.

"Yeah. It's my, uh, my new nickname," I say. "It means beautiful."

"I think it fits," says the handsome guy next to Mitchell. "I'm Cole Tanner, Mitchell's DP. We met once before on the set of *Zombies Cometh*."

"Oh. Right. Hi. So, what are you guys doing here?"

"Scouting locations," says Mitchell. "So what's your movie called?"

"It's, um, called... *The* uh, *The Red Notebook*."

"Sort of like *The Red Shoes?*" asks Cole.

"Sort of. Yeah, a woman is obsessed with her diary and eventually it starts to possess her," I reply.

"Let's watch some of it," Mitchell proposes.

"No, you can't do that," I swiftly say, pointing toward the door, motioning them to leave. "It's a private set. There's some nudity in this next scene and the actress is really shy about showing her body."

Just as I get Mitchell and Cole to the door a loud argument resounds from the set.

"How's *this* for motivation?" yells a female voice.

Mitchell, Cole and I look over to see smug-faced JoAnna completely naked, flaunting her breasts in the face of the actor playing the busboy.

Mitchell and Cole give me a look. "That's part of the dialogue," I promptly add. "So you better go now. Bye-bye."

I close the door on them and sigh. Laura. Bella. Laura. Bella. Who am I? I feel like I've willingly gone into exile in a strange and foreign land to pay a price, so that I can immigrate back to the land I came from. But I wonder if the price I pay means losing sight of who I am without having any idea who I will become.

After the third postponement, I am now seated in the office of Joe Schwartz, sipping coffee and staring at the framed one-sheets of all the movies that Nick Blake has starred in. I wait for Joe to finish what seems to be a pressing phone call.

"I heard you. But he's not doing it!" hollers Joe. "What do you mean why?! I told you why. Nick doesn't like German shepherds. He's not doing a buddy picture with a German shepherd. Change the dog to a Saint Bernard and maybe he'll reconsider. Hey, it's not my fault they don't use Saint Bernards for police work. I know for a fact they use them in the Red Cross because one of 'em pulled my uncle out of an avalanche in Switzerland. You could change the setting from Brooklyn to Geneva. Look, I've got a meeting. Later."

Joe hangs up the phone, shakes his head and sits down next to me, intermittently shaking his leg. You'd think he'd had five cups of coffee by now, but he tells me he only drinks herbal tea. I peg him for about thirty-two years old. He acts cocky about his five-month-old position as head of Nick Blake's production company and his deal with a well-known studio, which will remain unnamed because of what is about to transpire.

Joe wears faded blue jeans, a black button-down Armani shirt with black loafers and white socks. He represents a weird mix of New England prep meets fresh L.A. actor's executive.

After overhearing that last bit of conversation I decide I'm better off being demure and hiding behind continuous sips of coffee.

"So..." says Joe, "it's a pleasure to meet you."

"It's a pleasure to meet you, too."

His assistant opens the door again, "Uh, Joe, Nick's publicist, Tony Lombardo, is on the phone. Says it's urgent."

Joe excuses himself and picks up the phone. "Yeah," he says. A beat. "Well, if that's what he said then that's what he said." (Another beat.) "Right. He's not going on *The Today Show* until you get him on the cover of *GQ*. He's still pissed off that it went to Matt Duncan whose movie comes out the same week as his." (Another beat.) "No. He doesn't want *Vanity Fair,* he wants *GQ*. Get it? Good. Gotta go, I'm in a meeting. Oh, but hey..." his voice suddenly drops to sotto voce level.

"I forgot to ask you," he whispers. "How was that babe you picked up at the screening last night? Was she a *bella figa* or what?"

Shocked, I spit my coffee halfway across the room. What did he just say? My eyes are slit like daggers poised to fly. He sees my expression, and with embarrassment quickly covers the headset mouthpiece with his hand and asks me, "You Italian?"

"Jewish. Very, very Jewish."

Guilt washes over him, he tilts his mouth into the phone and murmurs, "In a meeting. Later, dude." He hangs up and sits back down.

"Sorry about all those cancellations," he says as a platitude, with one leg shaking. "Nick needed to go over a lot of business on the set for his latest movie. I had to meet him in Toronto one week and Paris the next and then we were in Berlin for the Film Festival there and after that we got hit with this press junket...well, you don't want to know all about that," he says. "The good news is we're finally meeting. The bad news is I haven't read your screenplay because Brad Isaacs never sent it to me."

My lungs deflate, again, and I wonder what I'm doing here. "So, why would you want to meet with me if you haven't read the script yet?"

"I didn't want to waste any more of your time or mine, so I've got Oliver Kleimeister coming down to join us. He's our executive at the studio. I figured you could pitch us the story and that would save us all a lot of time."

This is the worst news that could possibly happen. While *The Law of Malus* certainly represents a good story and well-written screenplay, it is not the kind you pitch. For one thing, it's not a high-concept movie, and secondly, it deals with death, a very hard notion to convey to studio executives who believe unequivocally that they're immortal. I feared they wouldn't be able to see its universal representation of loss. Everyone knows loss in one way or another, whether it's the death of your favorite frog when you're growing up, the death of a job, the death of a loved one, or the death of a marriage resulting in the loss of family life, as one teenage girl had known it.

Joe's assistant knocks on the door and pokes his head in. "Oliver's here."

"Send him in," says Joe.

Oliver Kleimeister's a little guy, with blond hair, thick glasses, and an adolescent face. He wears an oversized gray suit and looks like a miniature youth from the Aryan nation. Joe makes the obligatory introductions, adding that Oliver recently graduated from Harvard with an MBA and joined the executive ranks of the studio approximately six months ago.

This is more bad news. Ever since the junk market on Wall Street went bust, all those MBA guys opted against investment banking and threw themselves into what they figured is the next best moneymaking machine—Hollywood. They have no literary background, no sensitivity toward story and are concerned only with projected numbers, which, in the world of art meets commerce, consists of nothing more than a crapshoot. The trouble is that these guys think their Harvard MBAs give them some sort of crystal ball that cracks the code and results in a gold mine of ticket sales. All sorts of horror stories were spreading through town about these guys.

One writer told me he was adapting a short story by Nathaniel Hawthorne, and during a story meeting when they were grappling with a plot issue the MBA turned studio exec asked him to bring in the author to help resolve the issue.

Oliver Kleimeister looks harmless enough, but my instincts tell me to get up and hike it out of there. Though being trained not as a ruthless MBA, but as a human being with manners and good behavior, I foolishly stay to grin and bear it. However, nothing could have prepared me for the disastrous scenario that followed.

Joe and Oliver politely give me their undivided attention as I begin to pitch my most prized piece of work.

"This is the story of a woman who—"

"Hold it right there," interrupts the diminutive Aryan-looking greenhorn executive. "There's no way we're going to make this movie."

"I haven't even begun to tell you the story. May I ask why?" I inquire incredulously.

"It's a female protagonist. We'll never make it," he proclaims.

Joe doesn't say a word. He impishly sits there nodding his head.

"But her husband, Peter, is an equal protagonist. It's just that the story is told from Holly's point of view."

"I'm sorry, Miss Taylor, but the demographics just aren't big enough," he explains, standing up to leave. "The majority of moviegoers are male and they have no interest in female protagonist driven films."

"What about movies like *My Big Fat Greek Wedding?* That had a female protagonist and plenty of men went to see it. The grosses speak for themselves," I counter.

"No comment," he flatly says.

I really wanted to kick the little Harvard shit. He didn't have an artistic bone in his entire body. Numbers, numbers, numbers. Whatever happened to legendary MGM president Irving Thalberg's famous cry of, "Story, story, story"?

Like a slap in the face it was suddenly clear to me that while Hollywood had abandoned solid storytelling, the adult film industry had placed a premium on writers with good stories and the dividends were paying off with hard-core numbers.

I am soaking in a hot bubble bath trying to wash away the day's grime. It is the first time in a week when I start to feel my body relax.

I am imagining what it must have been like to live in Roman times discussing the politics of the day in steamy bathhouses when midnight strikes and my phone rings. I answer to find an infuriated Brad Isaacs on the other end. I realize this day is far from over. Brad furiously shouts at me and I have no idea why.

"What is going on with *The Law of Malus?*" he says in an angry whisper.

"What do you mean?" I reply, completely baffled.

"All I know is, I'm in bed with my wife and she's reading a copy of your screenplay. Do you know how bad this is?" he exclaims.

"No. And I have no idea what you're talking about or who your wife is or how she got the script."

"My wife is Natalie Moore."

"Natalie Moore, the super agent over at OTA (Organic Talent Agency)?"

"Yes. And she represents Brooke Anders. She's crazy about your script and already submitted it to Brooke!"

"That's great, isn't it?" I ask, realizing my script has gone to Hollywood's biggest female star, at least for this month.

"No. It's bad. It's very, very bad!"

"Why is it bad and why are you whispering?"

"Because I'm on the street in front of my house in my pajamas on my cell phone so Natalie can't hear me. Because we have a serious conflict of interest here. Because for one thing Natalie and I are at competing agencies, and for another, I made the submission to Maggie Reese last week with a hard sell. If they both like it we're in trouble."

"Isn't that what you call an embarrassment of riches?"

"It's what you call various agents fired by volatile ego-driven celebrities. You can't have two female leads competing for the same script at the same time! So tell me, did you make a deal for someone to produce the movie?"

"What?"

"Well, according to Natalie, Darlene Green is attached to produce your screenplay."

"How can someone attach themselves without making a deal with me, let alone contacting me first?"

"It's Hollywood."

"That's unethical."

"What? Like I said, it's Hollywood. Look, I'm going to have to pray that Maggie didn't read the script last night and I'll have to make up an excuse for her development executive to take it off her reading list. It's too risky. I can't be pissing off clients like this."

"But nothing's happened."

"But it *could* happen. And that's what I have to protect. I'm sure Natalie will be calling you in the morning."

"Let me do some digging into how Darlene Green got the script. I'll call you back in the morning."

I hang up and get out of the tub to make some calls.

"Elaine, I'm really sorry to call so late, but did you by any chance give *The Law of Malus* to anyone lately, like Darlene Green?"

"No. I don't know Darlene Green. But oh, yeah, I gave it to a director, Frank Hall, to get his read on it. He liked it a lot and asked me if he could give it to his new manager so she could get an idea for the kind of films he would like to direct. I didn't think it would do any harm for him to show it as a writing sample. Why?"

I describe the mess it's created and Elaine says, "Just go with the flow."

"Excuse me? How can I go with the flow when Darlene Green blatantly claims to be the producer and doesn't even call me and tell me of her intentions? This is worse than bad manners. This is worse than rude. This is wrong."

I sink into the couch while Darlene Green sits elevated from behind her desk. Underneath her skin, I am convinced a pit bull is waiting to bare its teeth. From the get-go, I find nothing nice about her.

I have just come from Natalie Moore's office at OTA where she has told me that whatever I decide to do is fine by her; that with or without Darlene Green attached, she will still happily send the script to Brooke Anders.

I watch Darlene very carefully and not once does she bother to apologize for her behavior. She simply declares, "This is a fabulous piece of writing and I'm attaching myself as sole producer of the film with my client to star and Frank Hall to direct with one of Natalie Moore's clients to also star, most likely Brooke Anders. Then Natalie and I will take it to a studio to set it up. Frank will do a polish on it, which means you'll have to share the writer credit. Other than that, I can only offer you a shared co-associate producer credit in the end titles. So do you want this package or not?"

Darlene Green has never produced a film in her life. She doesn't even know what celluloid looks like. She simply attaches herself as a producer in return for the use of her high-end clients. On top of that, Frank Hall has only one feature film credit to his name and it's for some really bad teenage romp flick.

"What about putting up some option money before taking it to the studios?" I ask.

"Why would I do that?" says Darlene, as if I have greatly offended her, which I probably have.

"Because it shows you're committed to the project and this isn't a happenstance deal. What if the studios say no, are you going to go the distance and raise independent monies, keeping the talent attached and committed?"

"Why would I do that?" repeats Darlene.

"Well, has your client read the script?"

"He'll do what I tell him to do," she pronounces, "and so will you."

I feel a wave of disgust wash over my face.

"Think it over and let me know what you want to do," announces Darlene. "I have to get back to work now. Oh, and you can clean your coffee mug in the kitchen on your way out."

My hand accidentally knocks the mug over spilling what remains. "Oops," I say, not sorry that a little passive-aggressive behavior has come to the surface.

Darlene becomes flabbergasted and starts foaming at the mouth. "Never mind, I'll have my assistant get it. Just go."

When I step outside into the light, I face Corie waiting for me at the curb. "How'd it go?" she asks excitedly. "Are the rumors about her true or false?"

"They aren't rumors for nothing!" I shout.

"What happened? You look a little pale. Are you okay?" she asks.

"That woman, no that beast, is lethal! You know, she never once apologized for running off with the project. I waited the entire meeting for one simple apology and it never came. I'll bet anything she was an absolute terror in junior high. I don't want to work with her, Corie. I can't work with her. It's just an indication of how miserable the experience will be. I would rather write porn than put up with her crap."

"I don't blame you," says Corie. "I don't get it. How do people like her wield so much power?"

"Apparently, in Hollywood rudeness is the prevailing force. The ruder you are, the more respect you get. It's sick."

Corie does not argue with me. She's heard enough.

Of course, in true Hollywood form, Natalie Moore did not keep her word. As soon as she heard that I chose not to accept Darlene Green's imperious attachment, she swiftly killed any chance of involving Brooke Anders or any of her other clients, or any of OTA's clients for that matter.

What was worse was that Brad Isaacs got cool on the project. He said he would reinstate the submission to Maggie Reese, but nothing ever came of it. Meanwhile, as Hollywood played politics at my expense, I had porn films to write and an acting session to coordinate.

8

take eight

HOLLYWOOD MEETS PORN

The five stars of *My Red Vibe Notebook* help themselves to my famous buffalo mozzarella dish. I have hired my former acting teacher, Barry Burnstein, to coach the girls for three hours in return for five hundred dollars cash. Adam and Corie attend for support, but I think they're really there to be voyeurs. Nevertheless, Barry needs Adam, as the only other male, to participate in some of the exercises, which Adam is of course only too obliged to do.

Barry has the reputation of being a no-nonsense acting coach. He mixes a number of different techniques, Meisner, Stella Adler, Uta Hagen, Method Acting, etc. He has worked with every major actor in town and feels a direct connection to the success of his students and consequently takes great pride in their achievements. I had to do some serious negotiating to get him to do this and swear on my life that I would never tell a soul. As for the girls, I had to pay them each one hundred dollars to commit to showing up.

Barry gathers everyone in my living room and begins the first exercise. "Now, this is all about learning to release emotions in order to bring feelings to the surface," he begins. "Once feelings are on the table, we can create a variety of responses and interactions—that's why I call this exercise Cause and Effect Improv. It's essentially about loosening the emotional muscles so we can be flexible in our acting. Think of it as the asana of acting."

This comment appears to go right over the girls' heads.

"Let's start with Daisy and Adam," says Barry. "I've brought along some tools." He points to a bat, a punching glove and a large pillow. "Now, Adam, I want you to stand on that side of the room and feel free to use those items. I want you to connect with a particular feeling you've experienced and release it. And then I want Daisy to enter the scene and react to whatever Adam does with his feelings. Improvise with each other to create a scene using real emotions. Let's go."

Adam stands off to the side and takes a deep breath and another, and then a third. He freezes.

"Adam, try to work off of your current feelings. Think about what's been going on with you in the last week. Has work created unusual amounts of stress lately or maybe you've got a lot of happiness inside you or you're remembering a relative who passed on," coaches Barry.

Adam picks up the bat and gingerly hits the pillow, then progressively launches into a full attack with an intense display of aggression. The anger increases and Adam completely loses himself in whatever his deepest hidden emotions are, which have now surfaced.

I turn to Corie and whisper, "I've never seen him like this."

"Neither have I. It's weird."

"What do you think is going on?"

"Well, we did have a fight last night. We always do this

time of year. He gets real testy and he's never told me why. I don't think he knows himself."

Adam grunts and sobs and hyperventilates at the same time. Corie starts to move toward him. Barry quietly holds her back. "Let him work through this, there's obviously something very cathartic going on." Corie sits back down.

Barry gently coaches Adam through his unrestrained emotions, "Start talking, Adam. Let whatever it is come out."

Through tears of anguish Adam screams, "Why did you have to go? Why? Why?"

He smacks the pillow again. This time feathers erupt into the air. Then he breaks the bat and falls on the pillow, spent, still in an emotional trance of some sort.

I whisper to Corie, "My God, he's good. He could be an actor."

"No shit," replies Corie.

Barry motions to Daisy. "Enter the scene and work off his subtext."

"His what?" asks Daisy, perplexed.

"His actions. Work off of his actions."

Daisy nods and awkwardly enters the side of the room where Adam lies. "Hey, um, are you okay? I mean, like, why are you crying?"

"I don't know," murmurs Adam. "I can't help it." Feathers from the pillow now drift in the air between them.

Daisy stands next to Adam not knowing how to respond. Barry chimes in to coach her, "You can comment on what you think he might be feeling."

"You seem really, um, angry. And um, really sad."

Adam barely nods his head, still in a daze from his emotional release.

Daisy looks to Barry for more help. "If he doesn't talk, then respond to his body language," coaches Barry.

Daisy nods self-assuredly and starts stroking Adam's legs. Then she holds him in her arms and he starts to relax.

And then with an extraordinary display of natural talent, Adam reveals the motivation for his pain: "I'm mad at my father for dying. I was twelve. I didn't understand it. I'm mad because he left me. And I never got to say goodbye. Today's the anniversary of his death."

Daisy looks blankly at Adam who begins to cry. Corie and I share a look. Now she finally understands the annual outbursts. She leans toward him but Barry signals for her to wait.

"Try to connect, to pull emotions out of him," whispers Barry.

Daisy's face lightens, as if she finally understands what Barry means. She proudly turns to Adam. "I can make you feel better. I can give you a blow job." She places her hand on his crotch and gives him a seductive smile.

I watch Adam's eyes perk up, Corie's narrow, and Barry's roll inside his head.

After two more unsuccessful exercises, the evening finally ends. Barry refuses to accept any money, claiming he has failed miserably, which leaves him questioning the entire foundation of his training and coaching prowess.

In the end, I decide I will be better off giving Colucci his money back. But Colucci surprises me. "It's a good idea. I don't want you to give it up. Keep working on it and tell the acting coach I'll double his fee."

A few days later, I leave word with Tom Kaplan at the Accent Film Company that the acting classes are suspended until I return from my trip to Florida. But I omit the part about my doing research for an adult film...for one of their biggest competitors. Vibrant Video.

Corie's behind the wheel rounding the bend into the airport departure lane. "So how come Ann's not going to your cousin's bar mitzvah?"

"One, she hates to fly. Two, I think she's having panic attacks about the wedding."

"She's having second thoughts about George?" asks Corie.

"No, more like paralysis over green versus blue invitation background colors, what kind of flowers to order, and how big the centerpieces should be."

"I remember going through that. It's a nightmare," comments Corie.

"I know. She's advised me to elope."

"I concur," Corie adds, as we reach my terminal. She pulls up to the curb and hugs me goodbye. "I'll call you if I hear of any new developments on *The Law of Malus.* And Laura, try to take some time to lie out on the beach and soak up a few rays."

"Will do. Thanks for the ride. I'll see you in four days," I say hugging her back, grateful for her friendship.

The next thing I know, I'm sitting in a synagogue as a second cousin once removed completes his bar mitzvah. My father sits beside me along with Bennett, whose suit outfashions the wardrobe of the entire congregation. It's good to be with family again. Aside from Ann's recent move to Malibu, and possibly my dad, I have no family in Hollywood and it often feels like I have no anchor, no place to rest my soul.

My father asks me how it's going. I try to explain but it's futile. He only wants to see me happy. I secretly pray to God to help me find meaning in my life.

Toward the end of dinner, I ask my uncle for directions to Pompano Beach. "Why do you want to go there?" he asks. "It's a bunch of strip clubs."

"Well, actually, I have an interview with two strippers for a movie about, uh, about strippers."

"Oh," he says. He has no idea how to respond. The "oh" sounds like a mixture of shock and excitement. "Sort of like a documentary?" he asks, trying to put it into some form of palatable context.

"Sort of," I reply.

Lascivious would describe the dark cavernous room as my eyes adjust to the lack of light. This strip club offers a high-end Vegas-like casino ambiance with neon lights decorating the stages. The clientele are extremely well dressed. Men range in age from eighteen to sixty, but I'm not the only female in the crowd. A few other women presumably with their boyfriends dot the premises. People drink and the strippers have their bottoms on.

This strip club isn't what I anticipated. There are no crude remarks, no raucous behavior from the sidelines. Maybe it's because there are lots of tall, beefy guys roaming around in black T-shirts wearing headsets with microphones attached. I learn that they are security, in constant communication with each other to make sure nothing and no one gets out of hand. I inform one of them that I am here to interview Mia and Callie.

He nods at me and speaks into the microphone, "Got a lady out here supposed to interview Mia and Callie... Ten four." He turns to me. "They're backstage prepping for their act. I'll find you when they're ready." Out of the corner of his eye he spots potential trouble. "Put Marcus on the southeast corner, guy in blue shirt getting too frisky with one of the girls." He takes off.

I nervously stand among the crowd studying my surroundings. I watch as a stripper finishes her performance to a round of applause and then heads over to a corner of the room where a long line of men has begun to form. Several men guide one young blind man who has two canes to support himself into the line along with another man in a wheelchair. Curious, I head toward the corner of the room to see what's caused the commotion. The men have queued up to have their pictures taken with the stripper. She wraps her arms around each man, banters with him and smiles for the camera. For a few minutes of direct female attention, these men have gladly handed over their twenty-dollar bills.

A gorgeous guy with a warm, friendly smile stands next to me. "Can I buy you a beer? You look a little nervous."

I accept his invitation and we start talking. His name is Tev Davis, and he's a nice Jewish dermatologist from Pittsburgh, Pennsylvania—my mother's hometown. Of all the places to meet a nice Jewish guy. Unfortunately, he's not single. He's accompanied by his girlfriend, Nadine, who used to be a cocktail waitress here. They came tonight to see some of Nadine's friends who still work here but have aspirations to make more money on the stage or meet a nice Jewish doctor like Nadine managed to do. Tev and I discover how much we have in common from our similar upbringings to familiarity of summer camps while growing up, and after playing Jewish geography we discover that my Hebrew school classmate's college boyfriend was in the same dermatology program as Tev. A few minutes later, the young Nadine appears. Her unpretentious sweet attitude enhances her beauty. We take an immediate liking to each other. Within an hour, I am surprised at how comfortable I feel with them, as if Tev is family.

The beefy guy in the black T-shirt finds me. Patrons pack the club, now making it difficult to maneuver around the place. Tev offers to save me my seat until I finish my interview with Mia and Callie.

In the dressing room, I am introduced to two half-naked busty blondes. Mia and Callie graciously offer me a seat while they put on their makeup and costumes. A fruit platter big enough to feed ten people arrives at their dressing room and they politely offer me anything I want. They are thrilled to be interviewed for a film being written solely about them. I pull out my mini-tape recorder and turn it on as a backup to my note taking.

"So tell me about your act and how you guys met," I begin.

And I'm launched into another world. It turns out that Callie is married to a man and has a young child. Mia is gay but not seeing anyone right now. The two of them met in a high school gymnastics class and reconnected a few years later in a theatre performance class. They decided to combine their gymnastics with theatrical dance, spice it up by simulating lesbian love and take their show on the strip-club road.

I try digging, searching for hints of dramatic conflict. "Who choreographs your acts? Do you ever get jealous of each other? Have you fallen in love with one another?" They confess that at one time they had been intimate and that they love each other.

Callie expounds, "When I act in movies, I have a standard rule and the production companies know that. I simply don't make love to any men, only my husband and that's off-screen. On film, I only make love to Mia."

She plants the seed I am looking for. In the days that follow, I write their story, bend truth into fiction, inject it with conflict, and call it *Three Days of Blondage: Nothing can come between us.*

Following the interview, I rejoin Tev and Nadine to watch the show, again taking notes to incorporate into the script. The crowd attentively watches Mia and Callie. Their costume changes and variety of props keep everyone's attention fixed on them, especially when they melt hot wax on each other while gyrating to the blasting music in a 69 pose.

When the show reaches its conclusion, Tev and Nadine ask, "Would you like to come over for dinner tomorrow night? We want to invite our friend Darryl over, too. He's a nice single Jewish optometrist."

"Thanks," I say, "let me check so it doesn't interfere with any family get-togethers and I'll call you tomorrow." I leave feeling connected, feeling like I have made new friends. In a town like L.A., made out of glitter and gold, you don't realize how vital a genuine connection to another person can be until you have it again.

The next morning, my father suggests that he, my brother, and I all go to brunch together. The mere suggestion brings a scowl to Bennett's face.

"What's wrong, Bennett?" I ask him.

"Nothing," he says in his typically critical voice. It is nearly impossible to please Bennett. He has a high standard of excellence and expects others to share the same view. Most of us have come to accept this about him. In fact, we find it amusing. Only Bennett could feel completely justified at sparing no expense on himself when it comes to clothing, design and air travel. He once told me, "It's very important to surround yourself with beautiful things so that you feel beautiful." I strive to live by that, but unlike Bennett, I do so within my means.

All during brunch, Bennett barely pays attention to me. Somewhere between the French toast and the coffee refill I ask, "So what did you guys do after dinner last night?"

"We saw *As Good as it Gets,*" says my father. "I gave it an eight."

"I loved that movie," I say. "What did you give it, Bennett?"

"What do you care?" he scowls.

My father gives him a startled look.

"Dad, will you please tell me why Bennett is so pissed off at me?"

"Bennett, talk to her," says my father.

"What she's doing is gross," says Bennett. "Going to strip clubs and writing a documentary about them. It's not what you sent her to college for. Besides there's no money in documentaries."

"At least I went to college," I dig back, now on the defensive.

"That's not the point!" he declares.

"Since when are you judge and jury?" I ask as I feel my buttons getting pushed, provoked and prodded, that big 'ole button that yearns to be accepted and loved for who I am.

"I don't totally disagree with him," says my father. "I would prefer it if you did something else, Laura." He and I both know what he's talking about.

"Why don't you just become a teacher or something?" implores Bennett.

"Why don't you, instead of bopping around as a buyer from one department store to another?"

"Because teaching salaries don't pay enough for my lifestyle," he counters.

"Oh, and they do for me?"

"I am doing something else. I'm starting to manufacture my leather socks."

"Do you have buyers lined up?" I ask.

"Not yet," he says, defensively, and then looks for the waitress, "I need more coffee."

I look between my father and Bennett. It suddenly becomes clear. "Dad invested in your leather socks?"

"No...George did," replies Bennett.

"George? Does his father know?"

"Not yet. When he does, he'll have a shit fit."

Now it's even more crystal clear. "Oh, I get it now. You can't pick on Ann anymore because George is an investor, so that leaves me. Well, at least I know why."

I sometimes think Bennett's favorite sport growing up, aside from doodling fashion designs on paper napkins, was to pick on his sisters. He wasn't into baseball, which disappointed my father, and he hated that I had an arm, which never failed to elicit a smile on Walt's face. My sister and I could never dress well enough for Bennett's taste. Ann would always give in and acquiesce to his demands, but I would stand my ground and march to my own creative style, which only infuriated him more. Through the years I thought that we had come to accept each other, but obviously I was mistaken. Ann once hinted that Bennett disliked me since I came home from the hospital as a baby runt and required a lot of care and attention, which meant less for him. But she always surmised that it was because deep down Bennett didn't know how to like himself for being different.

"Maybe if you did something else with your life I wouldn't pick on you. Even living in L.A. is gross," says Bennett.

"I suppose you have a road map for me, too," I reply.

"Hey, let's stop this, both of you," says my father. "There's no reason to get so heated up over this. All Bennett and I are suggesting is that maybe it's time for you to give up the writing."

"Yeah. You need to settle down and have a baby already," adds Bennett.

"Speak for yourself. I can't believe this. I'll never be good enough for you, will I? Even when I dated Erik in high school, I let you intimidate me into dating Bobby instead."

"Erik wasn't Jewish," replies Bennett.

"I don't see either one of you dating Jews."

"She has a point there," adds my father.

"You know, you guys should think twice about the fact that at least I'm trying to reach my goals. I'm not into drugs. I'm not in jail. I'm not a menace to society. And I'm not homeless."

"What's the difference? You can barely support yourself," quips Bennett.

"Didn't you learn anything from that movie? I don't believe this is as good as it gets, that's why I keep trying. I don't intend to struggle forever. I'm going to be a Hollywood screenwriter. But what does it matter? My efforts will never be good enough for you."

"That's not true, hun, I love you no matter what you do," says my father as he gives me a hug and a pinch on the cheek. I feel the pinch but I'm not so sure about the strength of his love.

"I hope you mean that, Dad."

"I just want you to be happy," he says with sincerity and concern, and adds another pinch. This time I feel the pinch and the love.

"So do I, Dad, so do I." I turn to Bennett, "So, Bennett, what's it going to take?" I ask.

"I don't want to talk to you until you straighten yourself out," he adds. "We're tired of worrying about you."

I'm stunned. Walt looks at Bennett; even this is going too far. "That's uncalled for," he says. But my brother has planted his feet in the ground. If writing a documentary about strippers is enough for him to put me into exile, I wonder how he'd react if he knew what I was really writing.

Bennett's disregard for me becomes increasingly uncomfortable. Even when I offer him my sunblock, he ignores me. When Eva calls on my cell phone I explain the recent turn of events. She consoles me, saying "I think things didn't work out with his new friend and he must be taking his disappointment out on you. Just ignore him."

"Mom, that's what you said when we were little. And it didn't do anything but make me feel as though my feelings didn't count."

"You're right. I'm sorry, Laura, but I would try not to take his words to heart. He'll get over it. Focus on being the person that you are. Remember it takes guts to go after your dreams, and well, no guts, no story."

My mother has come a long way from the depression that once haunted her. I had so much respect for her. If she could conquer that, I could surely conquer this. If only I knew what "this" was and why I had to conquer it.

I tell my father that I am off to visit new friends who want to fix me up with an optometrist. He urges me to go and have a good time. In my rental car I call Tev and Nadine who welcome me over and give me directions.

By the time I reach their house I manage to camouflage the emotional wreckage surrounding my heart, but only for so long.

Tev shows me around the place. It's impossible not to notice the many framed photographs and posters of white leopards covering the walls. Tev sees me staring at them. "Nadine's into saving the snow leopard from extinction," he explains.

"Oh. I don't know much about them," I say.

"Don't get her started. She's obsessed with them. I think she was one in a past life."

"Why do you think there's such a deep connection there?"

"Probably has to do with her father. He was a famous naturalist. He died somewhere near Tibet trying to save them when she was a teenager."

"That's harsh," I say.

"Yeah. No shit," he says. "Now she's an expert on snow leopards and the mystical beliefs that surround them."

Tev serves me a glass of wine, and I am wondering what mystical beliefs surround the snow leopards, when Darryl, the single Jewish optometrist, calls to say he's stuck with post-surgical complications and won't be making it. I am relieved because my mind is still trying to sort out my father and Bennett's view of me. To feel even slightly unloved is devastating to me. I wonder if it has to do with those first three weeks in an incubator. I must have become familiar with struggle from the get-go. Maybe Ann was right, maybe I equate thrashing about in Hollywood with survival and I like it because it's what I know. But I refuse to believe that.

I will not allow myself to fall into a struggle addiction trap. First, I'm too smart for that, really, I didn't graduate from the University of Michigan for nothing. And second, how do I know it's not just plain ambition?

I'm still covering up my agitation, trying to shake it off with new friends and conversation. Another two glasses of wine is now making it more and more difficult to concentrate on Tev's description of his family's scrap metal business.

Nadine enters smiling, "We have a surprise for you," she says and holds up videotapes of *Things Change.* "We thought it might be fun to watch your films with you, if you're up for it."

"Sure," I say, a little tipsy from the wine.

The three of us sit on their couch watching *Things Change.* By now I'm becoming accustomed to these impromptu screenings of my films in mixed company—with people I've known for less than twenty-four hours. They are a good audience, listening carefully to my dialogue and making favorable comments here and there when the characters are not talking. Of course, we fast-forward through the interminably long sex scenes. But when we get to the scene where Lisa confesses that she felt abandoned by her father, the words and the wine merge together and my emotional camouflage quickly disintegrates. Tears leap forward. Tev and Nadine look at me, not quite sure how to respond.

"Are you okay?" they ask.

"I guess that scene was the real trigger for what happened today."

"What happened today?" they ask.

Through tears I let it out. Nadine holds me in her arms, gently stroking my back and whispers for me to take deep breaths.

"Older brothers can be the worst," says Nadine. "They want the best for you. But they don't always know how to express it."

"It's not you, Laura. The problem is that any member of your family will do whatever they can to keep you pigeonholed so they don't have to reevaluate themselves," says Tev.

"That's really deep," I say. "But it doesn't make the pain any less."

"I know," he says, "how about another glass of wine?"

"Okay," I say, but he notices the bottle's emptiness.

"I'll run to the store and get some more," he says.

"You have to try hard not to take it personally," adds Nadine, "and that's not easy to do. It helps to be aware that you're in a state of *bardo*."

"Bardo?"

"It's Tibetan. Bardos happen all the time, in life and in death. They represent that moment just before the possibility of liberation or enlightenment. I'd say you're in that moment now."

"What happens after enlightenment?"

"You transform," she says, casually finishing off her wine. "You feel a little more empowered and you revel in it. The final objective is to live and die without regrets."

"You're welcome to stay here if it's more comfortable for you," says Tev, "that is if you can handle Nadine's mystical dispersions." He takes a moment to smile at Nadine, and then turns back to me. "Maybe it's better if you don't put yourself near your family's judgment right now. I'll be back in a little while."

At this I begin to relax. I call the hotel and leave a message for my father that I'll be staying with friends tonight and leave him the number in case he needs me. I'm still shaking and Nadine gently holds me. I begin to notice how good it feels to have her touch me.

"Maybe I'll write about this," I say, finishing the last of the wine in my glass and feeling very tipsy.

"How will you do that?"

"I can put it in a story. Create a character on a journey,

searching the past for acceptance in the present. Even, what do you call them? Bardos. And it's there that she partakes in rituals that erase and abolish all judgment. It will be a cathartic release for her and for the spirits that judge her, something like that. It's just a germ of a story now," I say, inspired by the idea.

"I think you might be on to something," says Nadine. She gently reaches down and strokes the remaining tears from my cheeks, and then she gently kisses me. And this time, I accept it. I accept feeling good and feeling loved.

"Maybe your character has a female companion who helps her on her journey," she whispers. "Your character shouldn't be alone, you know. Her companion teaches her not to fear interdependence. We all need each other, Laura. To be needed is a gift."

"I like that idea," I say. And then she kisses me again and I begin to feel less weird about it.

She smiles at me, suddenly nervous herself now. "I've never kissed a woman before, but I've always wanted to. I sensed maybe you needed it. Is it okay?"

"That was really nice," I say.

"Believe me when I tell you, you are beautiful. Do you trust my touch?"

I nod my head yes.

"Do you want to kiss each other?" she asks, somewhat shy.

I nod my head yes again. And this time we both put equal energy into it and kiss each other.

"What about Tev?" I ask.

"He won't mind."

"Why do you want to make love to me?" I ask, still reeling from the wine.

"To help you know yourself." And then her lips melt into mine like soft butter, and we gently caress each other as I let myself go, thinking of *Things Change.* Was my life imitating my art or was my art imitating my life? Nadine nurtured me that night in a way I had never been nurtured before. She and Tev held me, caressed me and kissed me until my emotional pain merged into physical pleasure, and for a little while I was able to let go and feel safe and loved for who I am.

The sun warms my skin as I lie on a large beach towel and nap under a balmy breeze on the soft sand, making up for the loss of sleep from the night before.

My father finds me and wakes me up to inform me that Bennett does not feel well. Apparently he woke up to discover a strange rash around his groin causing him excruciating pain. My father's been on the phone for the last three hours unable to find a dermatologist that can see Bennett right away.

"Hold on, Dad, I think I know someone. Let me make a phone call," I say. I dial Tev at his office; he immediately takes my call. Within thirty minutes, Bennett receives treatment for his rash and his pain disappears.

When my father and Bennett return to the hotel, they both rave about what a fantastic doctor Tev is and that whenever they visit Florida they will continue to see him. Then my father turns all of our Florida relatives on to Tev as well. Suddenly, Tev has a steady stream of new patients, not that he needed any, but there they are.

No longer required, I split for a sunset walk on the beach by myself. Walt finds me a short while later on the shoreline.

"Don't let this get to you, Laura," he offers, consolingly. "One day Bennett will appreciate you and if he doesn't, then it will be his loss." My dad puts his arm around me and hugs me. Then he points to the colors spread across the horizon, "Isn't that a beautiful sunset?"

I nod; walking silently alongside him adjusting my focus away from the turmoil within and back to the outer beauty the world has to offer.

★★★

Back once again, deep, deep in the San Fernando Valley, I'm sitting in a booth at Denny's having lunch with Gayle Reed, a porn producer whose uncle, Harold Reed, owns Vibrant Video; Kat, a porn director; and Mia and Callie—five women making porn. Somehow I don't think Gloria Steinem would be too happy about this.

We are going over my script and Kat presents a litany of ideas for the shoot. She asks me if I can tailor some of the scenes to meet her location needs when Gayle remembers to tell Mia and Callie about next week's photo shoot and pre-established interviews with an industry magazine to get the promotion machine in gear.

Callie asks, "We are going to be on the cover, aren't we?"

"Not this issue. They already committed to Dakota Halston," Gayle replies.

Mia and Callie are not happy about this.

"What do you mean, Dakota Halston? We should be on the cover," says Mia.

"I want to be on the cover of that magazine, or I'm not doing the interview. And that's all I have to say about it," adds Callie.

As I listen to them whine, I start to think that maybe "things change" is inaccurate, only names and places do. Egos are egos.

We leave the restaurant and head over to a location that Kat wants to check out.

I follow the women into a desolate building and enter yet another strip club, which by day seems like any other ordinary club with a bar, pool tables, and dance floor. But then my eyes adjust to the dim lights and I discover a stage one-quarter mile long that snakes around the entire room.

Kat excitedly turns to Gayle. "Do you think we can afford a steadicam? It would be great to weave in a long shot on this runway."

"I'll see what I can pull from another part of the budget," replies Gayle.

Kat turns to me. "Bella, can you write a scene where we follow the girls weaving around the runway?"

"I'm sure I can figure that out," I say, taking copious notes so as not to forget.

Mia and Callie discover a pole on the stage with a showerhead over it. "They just keep filling these stages up with more and more surprises," comments Callie.

"Maybe balloons fall from a skylight, too," I add facetiously.

All four women stare at the ceiling searching for a skylight. Of course, no skylight exists. They turn to me, not sure whether or not I'm joking.

"Look," I say, "why don't I, uh, incorporate the showerhead as a finale in their act? We can also use stills of Mia and Callie under the shower to send to the magazine as promo photos."

The women look at me, considering the possibilities.

"That would be hot!" declares Mia.

"Yeah, I bet they'll use it on the *cover!* Move over, Dakota Halston!" shouts Callie.

Kat and Gayle look at me and nod their heads in agreement. "Not bad, Bella, not bad," they say.

But as we exit the darkness and enter daylight again, I feel conflict stirring inside me. A gnawing sensation tugs at my core.

part two

9

take nine

HOLLYWOOD MERRY-GO-ROUND

Corie hovers over my kitchen table sipping a hot cup of tea. She's crying and I'm listening. "I hate them," Corie says. "They're evil. I don't think I can do this anymore."

"What happened? Tell me the whole story."

"It's that everyone's backstabbing each other. You wouldn't believe it, poor Toby Smith. She closed two deals this week and I watched Jason Brand screw her."

"How did he screw her?"

"He took credit for both of them. I was in the weekly staff meeting taking notes and I watched him do it. I'm on his desk every day. I know for a fact they were Toby's deals. She asked him for guidance on one aspect of the negotiation and Jason twisted it around in the meeting in such a way that he got all the credit."

Corie grabs a tissue from my counter and wipes her eyes. "Right after that, Richard Marksman promoted Jason to head of the talent department. There's no way Toby's going to get her bonus now. But that's not what upset Toby so much. It's that Jason went behind her back. I watched Toby hold back her tears until she got to the bathroom."

"Why didn't she stick up for herself in the meeting?"

"She did. Jason's a master at manipulation and made her look worse. Then later on, he goes into one of his screaming sessions at me for not having his phone sheet freshly typed for the day when I had the notes from the meeting to transcribe." Corie cries some more. "I think I'm too sensitive for this."

"You're not too sensitive. You're too human. And next time you make him a cup of coffee, slip some Prozac in it. That should at least take care of the yelling."

Corie smiles. "I like the way you think, Laura. But maybe I should start looking into a career as a real estate agent or maybe a fashion designer, if it's not too late."

"I'll back you all the way, Corie," I say, giving her a big hug. "I don't care what you do as long as you're happy. But just so you know, I was hoping that one day you'd be my agent."

"Really? You think I'd be a good agent?"

"Of course. All you need is an opportunity to prove yourself."

Corie stops sniffling, considering the possibilities, when my phone rings. I ignore it until she urges me to go ahead and answer it. It's Sara Stephenson.

"Hi, Laura," she says. "I've got some good news for you. I was at a party and told Francesca West all about *The Law of Malus.* I sent her the script. She read it the next day and now she wants to meet with you right away. I think she may want to star in it."

When I hang up, Corie looks at me with a what's-up expression.

"The Hollywood merry-go-round has started again."

★ ★ ★

In the office of Francesca West's production company, the receptionist asks, "Can I get you coffee or tea?"

"Oh no, I'm fine," I say, holding *Malus* tightly in my hands while trying hard to contain my excitement. Finally, a light in the tunnel.

"You do know you're an hour early," states the receptionist.

"I know," I say. "I didn't want to risk a traffic jam or an accident on the freeway or any number of unforeseeable events."

"Right," she says, dubiously raising her brows.

Exactly at my scheduled meeting time, I am escorted down the hall into a large conference room. I sit there alone, clutching my script. Finally, a young woman in glasses walks in carrying several screenplays, a yellow legal pad and a pen. She grins at me, "Hi, I'm Ronda Reese. I run Francesca's production company for her. She couldn't make it so she's asked me to conduct the meeting."

"Okay," I say, disappointed, but still thrilled to be here.

"First, let me say that we all love your screenplay. It went all the way up the ranks from our readers to our junior executives to Francesca and me. It's exquisitely written and you should be very proud of yourself."

"Thanks," I say, blushing from the compliments.

"Right now Francesca is trying to decide if she would direct this or just star in it. But it won't be both."

"Really? Wow, that would be great. Either one, really," I say.

"There's just one problem," she adds. "Well, two actually. One, Francesca is tied up with several other projects, so she won't be available right away, and two, I want her to consider one other romantic family epic that she hasn't seen yet."

"Oh, there's another romantic family epic circulating around town?" I ask.

"Yes. Actually, I wrote it," she admits.

"Oh. You wrote a script, too, in addition to your full-time job, that's great," I offer. It's obvious that with the inside track she holds my chance for a production deal has just evaporated.

"Thank you," she says, peering at me from behind her glasses. "It's my first script. I'm using a pseudonym so Francesca won't be biased when she reads it. Unfortunately, she won't be able to do two scripts in the same genre."

"Oh, right, of course…so, when does she become available? Assuming she decides to act or direct *The Law of Malus?*" I ask.

"Oh, not for at least four years," says Ronda.

"Four years? Wow, that's a, uh, busy schedule."

"We'll let you know as soon as she makes up her mind," concludes Ronda. "I'll see about rescheduling your appointment with her. In the meantime, it was a pleasure meeting you."

Ronda walks out of the room. I look at my watch. A whole five minutes has passed. I look back at my script and sigh.

Between the constant Hollywood rigmarole, the jet-propelled porn writing career, the death of the Gavin-Laura relationship, the birth of my first time sleeping with a woman, and the emotional hang-up with Bennett, I am in need of a resurgence of faith. And so I head for the synagogue to pray for guidance and hear what I hope will be an inspiring sermon from Rabbi Weiss.

It feels good to be in the sanctuary. The ground feels firm under my feet. I pull out an old gold compass and squeeze it tightly in my hands while I whisper in my head, "Dear God, please give me guidance. Please help me find my true direction because I am confused between two worlds that make everything I've known before seem upside down, and yet it seems to make sense."

Rabbi Weiss announces, "Let me tell you a story about the importance of seeking to know." He begins by describing a man who wanted his daughter to be married, but to a special person. So he went to a Yeshiva and posed a complex problem from the Talmud for 500 students to answer, and not one of them could answer the problem for his daughter's hand in marriage. The next day, 250 students came and could not answer the problem. The following day, 50 students tried with the same result. The man got in his carriage, and as he rode away one student ran after him yelling, "Wait, wait!" The man stopped and the student ran up to him. The man asked, "Do you know the answer to the problem?" "No," said the student. "I don't. But I need *to know* the answer. Please tell it to me." The man looked at him and replied, "You will marry my daughter, for I am not interested in the man who knows the answer but the man who *wants* to know the answer."

It is a good story and I feel assuaged because I am one who wants to know. I want to know what motivates human behavior. I want to know how actions create thoughts or thoughts create actions. I want to understand the parables of life. Perhaps in the answers I will know myself better, be a better person, a happy and content person.

As I stand at the table for the blessing over the bread and wine, pondering these possible epiphanies, I see Richard Marksman nearby. He sees me and smiles. We repeat the blessings and drink our wine.

The retired STA president approaches me. "You look familiar. How do I know you?"

"In which way?"

"Which way?" he asks.

"Well, yes, there are a few."

"Why don't you tell me in chronological order then?"

"All right," I say. "First, I used to work at STA as Eric

Leve's assistant. Then I was a hip-pocket writer client of Scott Sher's. Following his, uh, departure, I became a hip-pocket client of Brad Isaacs."

A congregant accidentally bumps into me, and my compass falls to the ground. Richard leans over and picks it up, gently returning it to me.

"That's nice, antique?" he asks.

"My father gave it to me when I drove out west."

"So you don't lose your way?"

"That would be the obvious metaphor," I answer.

"So what are you doing now?" he asks.

I decide to implement the new marketing strategies I've been reading about lately.

"I'm an award-winning G to X screenwriter," I proudly declare.

Richard Marksman lifts a brow and replies, "That sounds very interesting, do you have time to take a walk and tell me more?"

Two weeks later, the rescheduled meeting with Francesca West requires postponing for the second time due to her travel schedule.

My Hollywood calendar overflows with dozens of meetings involving high-powered executives and talent, which have led nowhere, while in the land of adult entertainment, I now have five produced movies, all shot on film, and more on the way.

I wonder if I can publish that calendar. "See, look here, Dad," I imagine saying, "this is the day I pitched *The Magic Mitt* for a second time to the studio, but they changed their minds on genres during the three weeks it took to make the changes they begged me for before never paying me. Over here represents the day Satellite cancelled my rewrite after they had hired me, but before I signed a contract. Here's where I met Nick Blake's executive, who never bothered to read the script. And on this day, my agent screwed me on the facts surrounding my writing deal on a project I spent six months and all my savings slaving over..."

Hey, no one could say I wasn't trying. It was work all right, but no one's paying me to go on all these meetings. I think I might be onto something with this calendar. I could call it, "Working in Hollywood," and each meeting would reveal notes about what had happened then subsequently about how nothing happened. I'm mulling over this idea when I am hit with an onslaught of writing jobs that commands a juggling act on the part of my brain, but manages to get me out of debt and back to a bank balance of zero.

The Erotica Channel tracks me down and offers me the job of writing *Hot Hawaii,* with an all-expense paid trip to Maui for research. Since I am a curious creature and a writer of authenticity, I plunge myself into the fashion world, which, after several trips to the library, I conclude represents an industry far more morally unstable than Hollywood. However, that's not the focal point of the story, only possible fodder for character background, and for my own edification in writing a story about relationships in this milieu.

In the meantime, Sextime Network buys an old script of mine that I've doctored for their late-night soft-core lineup. A period piece called *Cat House*, I wrote it after my final breakup with Mitchell. It's a story about two people who hate each other, yet due to circumstances, are forced to make love to one another. Eventually, their mutual hate turns to mutual respect when the female lead delivers the bad guy, and the male lead delivers her freedom and a new life.

Sinful Pleasure Productions offers me a three-picture deal. They also want me to write a period piece, but this time, I am given certain guidelines. They need the story to revolve around a mansion. I set it in the past with a leading lady who owns and operates it as a single woman. She has given up on love after losing her husband, the love of her life. Unable to move on emotionally, she tends to obsess with frequent flashbacks of herself and her late husband making love. But then, enter our leading man, an undercover cop set up to take down the operation. He needs to find evidence of gambling and prostitution and of course, true to adult entertainment, he becomes part of the evidence. The twist comes when our leading lady and undercover cop fall in love, which allows her to finally release her past memories and begin again.

This flick becomes another big hit in the world of adult entertainment and so Sinful Pleasures calls upon me to write a two-part movie set in the Caribbean. Again, there are guidelines.

I am specifically asked to come up with a story where there will be minimal dialogue for a specific number of female characters that will be debuting in both scripts. By minimal, they mean virtually none. The reason is that Sinful Pleasures looks for fresh, interesting faces to brand their new films. To do so, they fly "actresses" from Eastern Europe to the Caribbean for this production—and these women speak very little English. The women willingly come to work because the money is exceptionally good and they want to make enough to emigrate with their families. This leads me to a discussion of pay scales. This lesson over, see new one below.

For once, an industry exists where the pay scale tips in favor of women. In adult entertainment, females make a lot more money than males. Their day rate starts at $1,000 and they get bonuses of an additional $500 for every blow job and another $1,000 for every intercourse scene they engage in. Whereas the men in the industry make about one-third that. Apparently, they just don't seem to command the attention and adoration the women do. Men are the service providers to the women here and well, not to be crass, but they are expendable in a certain sense, in terms of demographics, because with the exception of the gay film category, the adult viewing population has a far more developed penchant for watching a woman, a woman and a man, or a woman and a woman. Note the common denominator. Women open movies in adult entertainment. In Hollywood, it's the other way around, where male stars are considered the driving force and therefore they command bigger salaries. Tom Cruise, Tom Hanks, Mel Gibson, Bruce Willis, Brad Pitt, Arnold Schwarzenegger are all good examples. Their fees are upwards of twenty million per movie. Hollywood female stars on the other hand command far less with few exceptions. The irony is that every once in a while, a Hollywood film with a huge star opens and the movie still fails, and that's because the true star is the story.

I decide to make the two Caribbean films parodies of James Bond movies. I interlace the stories with a mix of James Bond meets *Get Smart* humor, and a political theme based on the actresses' real-life desires to emigrate. The production company loves my work and in two weeks they are already filming in the Caribbean.

Then the mother of all adult production companies calls upon me to write the biggest budgeted adult film ever. I immediately think of Tev and Nadine, and her passion for the snow leopard. Garden of Eden productions has allotted a budget of $400,000, including money for special effects that will morph technology with real snow leopards and for which I do serious amounts of research at the Beverly Hills Library. For instance, did you know the snow leopard is the only leopard that doesn't roar? And of course, I call Nadine in Florida to bring in a mystical point of view. I recall our special evening together and somehow, I can't help but see portions of that night making their way into the story.

I create a female companion who assists the female lead

on her physical and spiritual journey. The movie is shot on 16 millimeter film. The score is original and stupendous. The film becomes an immediate success.

In the midst of all this, I finally meet with Francesca West, who has decided that she wants to star in *The Law of Malus,* but the way her schedule seems to unfold, it won't be for at least three years. It doesn't matter anyway, because two weeks later Natalie Moore at OTA poaches Francesca West from STA and finds a subtle and deliberate way to talk her out of the project.

Meanwhile, Mickey Colucci has learned that the competition has been hiring me away, especially since every film I write ends up receiving rave reviews. This news perturbs Mickey. This, I discover early one morning while dreaming about snow leopards. In my dream, the snow leopards break all conventional biological findings and roar. They are about to tell me why they are roaring, why they are in need of being heard and what it is they so desperately want to say. But in my hypnagogic state, the roaring transforms into a ringing telephone.

"You can tell me," I murmur to the snow leopard in my head, but hold the receiver close to my mouth.

"This is Mickey Colucci." The words don't register, only their deep, guttural sound, like that of a snow leopard roaring. "I'm looking for Bella Feega," he hollers.

My eyes pop open. "Oh. Uh, this is Bella Fee—I mean, Laura," I say, the dream coming to an abrupt halt.

"Good. I'm offering Bella Feega a full-time job. It's sixty thousand dollars a year, plus benefits and bonuses. Starting now."

"Am I allowed to ask what the job is?" I reply.

"Talk to Tommy Kaplan."

Mr. Colucci is about to hang up when I counter, "No."

"No? No, you don't want the job, or you want stock options, again?"

"No. I want you to tell me what the job is. Please." There's a brief pause.

"You head up the new sex ed division—you write, produce, and direct if you want."

"Did you say sex ed? As in sex education videos?" I ask.

"Don't make me waste my syllables."

"Is this exclusive or non-exclusive?"

"As long as you do the job, you can do whatever else you want."

This sounds interesting to me. It's educational and could really serve a purpose in helping people. I get to be autonomous. I can still pursue my Hollywood writing deals. The money sounds decent, one job versus piecing together several to pay the rent. And, I could use a break from writing all these sex stories because quite frankly, I feared that I had turned a corner with a libido on overdrive.

As I've been churning out these uh, romance stories, I've had to create stories that I think will turn an audience on, and to do that, well, I have to turn myself on. All this writing of multiple story lines with multiple sex scenes has my hormones racing. Unfortunately, there hasn't been an opportunity for relief in sight. Well, it's been in sight, but that's all. When my bank balance hit positive digits, I was more than ready to go out with men again, so Corie set me up on several dates.

The first was with a distant cousin of Adam's who was in town from Luxembourg. He took me to see *Cirque du Soleil*. During the entire performance I whispered to him how I couldn't wait to duplicate all those contortions for him in bed. This seemed to be truly frightening to him and he dropped me off immediately following the finale.

The second date was with Corie's ophthalmologist. He took me to the Getty Museum's antiquity exhibit of Roman sculptures where I couldn't help but see, and express, something sexual in every object we looked at. He took me for a pervert and left me staring at Marcus Aurelius's naked porcelain body, while he faked the excuse of an emergency page.

The third date took me to a perfectly beautiful, elegant, and serene restaurant wherein the exhaustion from all the writing set in and I promptly passed out during the main course.

Therefore, I figure this opportunity with Mickey provides exactly what I'm looking for—a chance to get off this self-induced sexually-motivated merry-go-round. So, piqued by his offer, I decide to ask a few more questions.

"Sex education videos? You mean like those *Better Sex* Video series?" I ask.

"These are based on books written by a sex therapist. The first is *Usual Couples, Unusual Sex,* the second is *Sex Beyond Middle-Age.*"

"Have you optioned the books already?"

"I'll give you a budget for that and the production. I want it to look like *20/20.*"

"You want a news magazine style format? With polished interviews and fancy graphics?"

"Yeah, that's it, and real couples simulating the exercises in the book. Tommy will set you up with an office and an expense account."

"I haven't said yes," I remind him.

"You will," he says.

"Why me?" I bemoan.

"You've got good taste."

"How about some stock options for that taste?" Another brief pause follows, and I wonder if I have gone too far.

"It's seventy thousand a year. No stock. See Tommy." He hangs up.

10

take ten

CAREER SHIFTING

Within a few days, I have my own office and parking space on the lot of the Accent Film Company.

The only problem appears to be that when Mickey Colucci said simulated sex, he meant real sex. Part of my job consists of having to find couples willing to make love on camera. This is not an easy task. There are certain requirements, such as no tattoos, no pierced body parts, and never having worked or been on camera in the adult industry. The good news is I can offer each couple a thousand dollars a day. The ads I place in fringe magazines to attract "real couples" only result in a dribble of responses from very wacky people. In order to get the couples, I'll have to take a more active role. But where do I find real couples willing to make love on camera? And for the *Sex Beyond Middle-Age* video, where will I find real attractive couples in their fifties and sixties to make love on camera?

The most resourceful person I know, me, is finally stumped. I decide to take a Taoist approach. For the first time in my life, I stop the struggle to achieve, to prove, to perform. Following this approach, I decide to lean back and simply discuss the problem with everyone I happen to run into.

Taoism is about harmony, about non-interference with the natural course of events.

So that is what I did. I did nothing. I taoed and suddenly the information I needed came forth.

In this case, my openness to discuss my problem began to create a buzz around possible solutions.

I am sitting in my office looking out over the deep, deep valley, when Adam Berman returns my call. "Hey, Adam, I need to talk to you about licensing some of your music as background for these sex education videos I'm producing."

"That's no problem," says Adam. "I can have one of our music editors work with you on it. How's it going otherwise?"

"Well, I'm not really sure what to do. I have to find ordinary couples willing to have outrageous sex on camera and quite frankly I'm stumped."

"I see," says Adam. "Why don't you try the Swingers Club?"

"What's the Swingers Club?"

"It's a very liberal national organization that puts on private dinner parties for thousands of couples who want to swap partners for the evening. I can get you the number of the president if you'd like."

"Well, that would be great, thanks, but how do you even know about this?"

"Before I married Corie, I had a girlfriend who liked to swing and she introduced me to that world. It was quite interesting."

Adam gives me the name and number. I call and speak to the president, a Mr. Bob Tinkerton. I explain my situation and he invites me to be a guest at his table at an upcoming dinner at the Holiday Inn in Long Beach.

"Here's what we'll do," says Bob. "I'll tell the DJ to stop at one point and let you make an announcement and then people can approach you if they're interested."

I am shocked to find out how easy this has suddenly become. Taoism plus Buzz rocks.

I receive my next call from Corie. "I hear you need to find couples. Why don't you check out the nudist colony in Topanga?"

"There's a nudist colony in Topanga?"

After Corie's call, I am talking to my mother when she offers information about an organization called The Human Responsiveness Institute that conducts intimacy workshops. When I speak to the director, I am invited to attend an Intimacy Workshop taking place at the nudist colony in Topanga. To this, I convince Corie to go with me.

Two elderly men are playing tennis when Corie and I drive onto the premises of Topanga's nudist colony. The only clothes they wear are tennis shoes, and as they chase the ball their penises flop in the wind. I turn to Corie. "Well, there's an image you don't get to see everyday."

"Just think, if you didn't have this job, we would've missed out on this." She laughs.

The leader of the workshop, a man in his mid-forties named Aaron, welcomes us into a large rectangular room. We join twenty-five other people sitting on the floor, sipping hot chocolate. I pour myself a cup of hot tea when I see Mitchell Mann in the corner of the room. I nearly drop my mug and quickly swivel toward Corie.

"Oh my God, don't look now, but Mitchell Mann's at high noon!"

Corie freezes, shifts her eyes away from me, and then back

again, "Isn't he out of his league here? What do you call someone like him who comes to a place like this?"

"I'd call it an illogical plot twist. It makes no sense. Why would he be here?"

"Maybe he's doing research for a horror film that takes place at a nudist colony."

I nod, considering Corie's answer to be a real possibility.

"Welcome, everyone, to a Human Responsiveness Institute workshop," says Aaron. "How many of you have participated in one of these workshops before?"

A dozen people raise their hands. Mitchell's remains in his lap.

"Great. To get started, we're going to pair off into groups of two, with someone you don't know, and we're going to begin with our first intimacy exercise. So everyone, pair off with each other."

I turn to the man next to me. He's youthful looking for a guy in his early fifties. He introduces himself as Ray and he's got a genuine smile. Corie turns to the hunk next to her, a sultry South American from Brazil named Jose.

Aaron continues, "I want you to hold your partner's hands in yours, look each other straight in the eye, and then be completely honest and tell each other why you're here."

Ray holds my hands, looks me in the eye and says, "I'm here to learn how to love myself so that I can love others. I want to deepen the relationship with my new girlfriend and share our love with the world."

"Wow, that's beautiful," I say.

"Why are you here?"

"Oh. Um. Let's see, well, the truth is that I'm here to find real couples who will be willing to make love on camera for a series of sex educational videos I'm producing."

"I thank you for your honesty, Laura, and I believe my girlfriend and I would be very interested in helping educate others about intimacy and sexuality. I'll give you my card."

Okay, this Taoism thing works so well it's starting to freak me out. "Don't you want to know how much it pays?" I ask.

"I'm an investment banker. Money isn't my motivation."

Aaron continues, "In order to create intimacy we have to become what we want. And we have to accept what we become. Remember, freedom exists when you surrender to your choices."

I stop, arrested by that inspiring line of dialogue. I make a mental note and repeat it lest I forget it. Freedom exists when you surrender to your choices. Freedom exists when you surrender to your choices. At some point, I know that I must create a character that embodies this maxim.

"So ask yourself," says Aaron, "what choice do you want to make right now in the present moment that will bring you closer to the qualities of intimacy? Is it honesty? Is it awareness of what you're feeling? Is it letting go of trying to prove something to someone else including yourself? Now pick a new partner and ask each other what quality you are bringing to this moment?"

I rotate around to see that Corie and Jose are engaged in deep conversation and a profound locking of the eyes. Their intensity creates a thick wall of energy around them. Apparently, they have no intention of picking other partners. Before I can turn around again, I hear a familiar British accent.

"Hey, Laura, fancy meeting you here."

"Hey, Mitchell." I manage to keep my knees from buckling as the sound of his voice activates the chemistry between us. I grope for words to keep me standing. "So, um, what quality relating to intimacy are you bringing to this moment?"

"The awareness that I've still got the hots for you, and you?" he asks.

"Oh. Well, um, the awareness that unfortunately, our lust never equated to love, and it's time to stop thinking otherwise."

"Maybe you should speak for yourself. Being a father has changed me, see, here's a picture of my son." He splashes a photo of his son in my face. The image stings—that was supposed to have been our baby.

"Look, intimacy was never your strong suit, if it were, we'd be together. So why are you really here, Mitchell?"

"Who says I haven't changed? That I'm not capable of intimacy?"

"The fifty in my pocket...and be honest," I say. "It's the least you owe me."

Mitchell's eyes narrow, glancing at my pocket, and then he raises them back up to look at me with a confessional expression on his face. "Okay. I'm scouting locations for my next horror film that takes place at a nudist colony."

I glance at Corie, still with her eyes set on the Brazilian, wondering how she pegged that one. I look back at Mitchell. "You want your fifty?"

"Keep it and take a walk with me instead," he pleads.

"Through a nudist colony? Fat chance. Besides, I'm not a quid pro quo kind of girl." I reach for the fifty.

"Don't be ridiculous, Laura," he says, taking the opportunity to place his hands gently on mine, portraying sensitivity and compassion. For a moment, I think that maybe Mitchell has changed and that I have underestimated him.

"Let me take you to dinner," he says softly, but a hint of seduction laces his tone and his next sentence shatters all that I had thought a second before. "I can tell you about my new six-picture deal I'm about to close," he boasts. "I can show you the building I'm planning to buy. I'm going to name it The Mann Building. You could christen it with me, you know what I mean? And I can pay you back next week."

"Pay me back for what?"

"Dinner and a hotel room. Shelly hasn't moved out yet and I'm low on cash these days."

Aaron interjects, "Tick tock. Everyone choose a new partner now."

"'Bye, Mitchell," I say and circle around to find Corie and the Brazilian. I slice my hand through the air between their eyes. "Excuse me, Jose, but we have to go now."

Corie seems like she's in a trance.

Jose gazes at her. "Please take these gifts of intimacy with you and share them with your husband."

Corie gazes back at him. "I will. Thank you, Jose."

"Remember what Aaron says, freedom exists when you surrender to your choices," he adds.

As we head out, I interrogate Corie, "What did Jose teach you?"

"The power of being in the present moment, and you, did you get what you came for?"

"Yeah. One couple and the realization that there are some things that never change."

A heap of congested automobiles surrounds me as I watch time tick by on my watch. A pile of scripts sits in the passenger seat next to me. I have spent the afternoon driving around town dropping off copies of *The Law of Malus* to one agent after another. A costly procedure, were it not for Corie who helped me make ten copies at STA late last night. I pull out my cell phone and call Northwest Airlines, who in turn tell me that my mother's plane has arrived not on schedule, but one hour and seven minutes early. I wish there was a way I could just put motion in reverse, so I'm there to pick her up as arranged. I comfort myself with the thought that she's probably got a lot of baggage to wait for and that she'll pass the time telling stories to her fellow passengers as their luggage goes round in circles. My cell rings and I quickly grab it. It's my mother calling from LAX. I explain the current traffic situation.

"Honey, don't worry about me," she says, "I'm fine. When

I get my bags I'll take a cab to your place and meet you there. Just drive safe."

Fifty-five minutes later I make it back to Venice thinking that my mother will be comfortably sitting on the porch swapping stories with the neighbors. But she is nowhere to be found. I'm starting to get nervous. Just then, Roy, the building manager walks by with hedge cutters in hand.

"Hi, Roy, have you seen..." I start to ask but he interjects.

"Oh hey, Laura. I just met your mother. What a lovely lady. She told me the funniest story about you as a little toddler traipsing around in your favorite white rain boots and how you loved those rain boots so much you never took them off and then this plumber comes to the house." Roy has to stop himself because he can't stop laughing. I, on the other hand, still need to know where Eva went. And then I realize I forgot to take down the poster of *Things Change* hanging in the bathroom and fear for the worst.

"Roy! I know the rain boot story," I plead urgently. "I've heard it a hundred times, but can you just tell me, where is my mother?!"

But Roy is lost in his amusement, "And then, Eva, she did tell me it was okay to call her Eva. Eva tells me that the plumber turns around and says to her, 'Excuse me, ma'am, but are you expecting a flood?'" He erupts with howls of laughter.

"Roy, it's not that funny. Come on, where is she? Tell me you didn't..."

"I let her inside your apartment," he says through tears of laughter. "Are you expecting a flood?" he repeats, keeping his hilarity on a roll.

"How could you do that? You don't just let people into other people's apartments these days! How do you know she's my mother and not some terrorist? I'm sure they're training the most inconspicuous people..."

"I did check. She showed me a picture of you in your high school baseball jersey," he replies.

I roll my eyes and head upstairs hoping that maybe she didn't have to go to the bathroom and she's hanging out in the kitchen making herself a cup of tea.

I nervously enter my apartment. "Mom...are you all right?" I call out.

She comes out from the kitchen holding a cup and saucer. "I'm fine, honey," she says.

"So...how was the plane ride?" I ask.

"Fine," she replies.

"And you got your bags up here okay?"

"Yes, Roy helped me."

"And you found your way around the...apartment okay, like the kitchen?"

"And the bathroom," she says. "I brought you organic bath products," and then she gives me a sympathetic look. "Honey, why didn't you tell me?"

"Tell you what?"

"That you're gay. It's okay. Gay-shmay, as long as you're happy."

"But, I'm not gay."

"At least now I know why your relationships with men never last."

"Mom, I'm not gay. That's just a poster...my friend... Bella...gave me to hang onto for a little while...because she's moving and...she can't afford to pay for storage. Did you see how big that thing is?"

"Is that friend your partner? Why don't you bring her to the wedding?"

"Oh, my God. She is not my partner. She just happened to write that...movie."

"Is Bella gay?" she asks.

"No, Bella is not gay."

"Has she ever slept with women? How could she write that if she hasn't?"

"Well, she told me she had one experience but technically it came after she wrote that. She dates men, she just hasn't found the guy she wants to settle down with yet."

"Whatever you say, dear. I won't say a word until you're ready to come out of the closet, or should I say bathroom. In the meantime, you'd better get me to Ann's seamstress appointment. By the way, are you going to wear a dress or a fancy tuxedo to the wedding?"

"Gee, Mom, I don't know. I still have another month before I have to worry about it," I say, exasperated.

Hours later, Corie sits on my bed watching half-dressed me shuffle through drawers and hanging garments.

"Great. Now my mother thinks I'm having an affair with Bella Feega," I say, pulling out an old Gap outfit and holding it up for a yea or a nay.

Corie shakes her head nay and comments, "Well, technically, you are in a relationship with Bella Feega."

"I am not having a relationship with my alter ego or my pseudonym or whatever you want to call her," I say, frustrated, trying to match a skirt with a top.

Corie shakes her head no, again, at the combination and adds, "It's like a split personality inhabiting the same space."

"What are you saying? I've turned schizophrenic?"

"Not exactly."

I stare at my closet and throw my hands in the air. "What the hell do you wear to a swinger's party?" I ask.

"Well, since you're going as a professional outsider, I'd say a business suit."

"Thanks," I reply and grab one off the hook. "Why didn't you say so in the first place?"

"Because it's more fun watching you try to figure it out," says Corie.

"I am not your entertainment center, Corie."

"You're turning melodramatic. Can we please switch channels back to the comedy?"

I roll my eyes. "Cute, you're very cute."

I find myself seated at the head table in a Holiday Inn banquet room. Bob Tinkerton, president of the National Swingers Club is sitting next to me. Approximately one thousand couples are participating this evening. The crowd appears to be middle class. Everyone dresses up in his or her best outfit. Most of the women have hairdos reminiscent of a fifties beehive. Most of the men wear simple suits and ties. I see no one in Armani or Ralph Lauren except for one couple sitting to my left. I am immediately suspicious—they clearly do not fit the profile of the other attendees.

As bland salads are served, Bob Tinkerton eagerly explains the Swinger philosophy to me, "Swinging is a lifestyle. It's basically recreational social sex—and we help promote that way of life, we make it accessible, we create a safe place where couples can explore each other. There's no pressure and there's no touching without permission."

He takes a bite out of his limp lettuce and continues, "Now there are two kinds of swing events, on-premises and off-premises. Tonight is an off-premises event—that means no sexual interaction here. But that's why we do these evenings at big hotels like this one. Couples meet, pick and choose who they want to swap partners with, and then rent a room for the night."

"So an on-premises event is where they have sex on the premises?" I ask.

"Exactly. Those are usually formed by smaller groups of consenting adults."

A middle-aged couple approaches Bob, bringing our

conversation to a halt. They discuss swapping partners. I turn to the out-of-place-looking couple, a man in his early fifties with a woman in her early forties, both fashionably dressed. I smell Hollywood producer all the way and, anxious to see if my hunch is accurate, I turn to the gentleman and ask, "So what do you do?"

He glances around to make sure no one but me can hear him and quietly murmurs that he works in the entertainment industry.

"You look like a film producer," I say.

"How did you know that?" he asks.

"It takes one to know one," I reply. "I used to work at STA before I became a writer."

"No kidding," he says. "My name is Roger Carson. I'm here incognito, doing research for a movie."

"Roger Carson. You're kidding? I'm a friend of your development executive, Elaine Dover."

"Really? Well, I would appreciate it if you keep the circumstances of how we met between us," he adds. This leaves me to ponder the validity of what he'd said since his date is scanning the crowd.

"So what are you doing here?" he asks.

"I'm a writer, but right now I'm producing a sex education video. This is part of my research. What's your movie about?"

"I want to make a *Bob and Carol and Ted and Alice* version of the swinger lifestyle. We should talk about you writing the screenplay. Do you have a card?"

"Great," I say as I hand him one. My conversation with Roger comes to a sudden break when a young, fairly attractive man approaches me.

"Excuse me," he says, "I was wondering if you'd like to get a hotel room together for the night."

First my jaw drops. When I manage to pull myself together, I stutter, "Oh, um, I, uh, I don't think so. I'm, uh, here on business."

Before he can respond the DJ announces my name. "And now a word from a guest of Bob Tinkerton's tonight, Laura Taylor."

I nervously make my way to the stage amid stares of hungry swingers. "Hello, everyone. Um. I'm here because the Accent Film Company is producing a series of sex education videos. We're looking for couples who would like to participate by sharing their personal issues and making love on camera. I'll be in the back of the room for the next hour if anyone is interested." I pause. The audience remains silent.

The DJ whispers in my ear.

"Oh, yeah, um, we're offering one thousand dollars a day per couple." A resounding applause of hoots and hollers follows and I soon find myself accosted by a variety of swingers eager to take part in the filming.

To cleanse my soul of couples, sex, and relationships, I make another synagogue visit where Rabbi Weiss enlightens us with another provocative story.

"When God decided to create man in his image, the angels became very upset. They did not want God to give himself away, or have man mess up his image. So the angels beg God to hide his image from man and then they deliberate over where to hide it, on the top of the mountains or in the valley... In the end, they decide that God should hide his image in the hearts of Humankind, because this is the last place Man would ever think to look. The point of this story is that God resides inside of all of us and we simply have to remember where to look to find him. We look inside ourselves. We look inside our neighbors."

Richard Marksman and I hike around the block. "Great sermon," he remarks.

"Yeah. I have to remember to apply it to all the couples

I meet, and remind myself that God lives in all of us and to be kind and nonjudgmental with them."

"As well as with yourself," Richard adds with sincerity in his eyes.

In that very moment, I gain a new respect for Richard Marksman. The gem contained within his comment strikes my soul—those are the kindest words I have heard in a long time.

"I won't be here next Saturday," he informs me. "I'll be at a company retreat in Santa Barbara."

"Really? I'll be in Santa Barbara, too," I reply, "at the Red Rose Foundation. I'll be incognito searching for couples at a Tantric sex workshop."

"Would you like to pick me up when your workshop is over, say around three o'clock, and drive me to the airport? I have to fly to New York. We could keep each other company and I'll buy you dinner at the airport."

"Sure, I can do that."

"Great," he says. "We can talk about your script then, too."

A few days later, Corie is hanging out on my bed watching me do my usual wardrobe runaround while I try to pack a small suitcase. "I cannot believe that you got Richard Marksman to read *Malus,*" she exclaims.

"Yeah, well, we'll see. Saying it and doing it are two different things," I reply.

"You know he still comes to the office every single day. Even though he says he's retired, he keeps his position on the board, along with his corner office."

"What did I tell you?" I ask. "Deal guys never retire." Aggravated by the packing process, I pause and look up at her. "What the hell do you bring to a Tantric sex workshop?"

"Do I have to tell you now? I'm not done watching you." She smiles.

"Yes! You have to tell me now."

"Yoga clothes," she says.

"Thank you," I say. "Next time, a little sooner, please."

Tantric sex has many definitions and many traditions, but its one common theme emphasizes sexuality as a pathway to a direct spiritual experience.

As I enter the Santa Barbara workshop, a sign hanging at the entrance reads: "Sexuality is the vehicle, not the destination. Our true spiritual nature is the goal."

First, the leaders divide the men and women into two groups. A beautiful Middle Eastern woman named Maya leads the women to a private room where we are asked to spread out on the wooden floor and stretch. We participate in a series of breathing exercises, followed by confessions of past sexual abuses. I am amazed to hear such varied and heart-wrenching experiences. In the next exercise, we are asked to name our yonis.

"What's a yoni?" I ask the angelic instructor, Maya.

"It's the Sanskrit name for vagina," she replies.

"Oh."

"After you name your yoni," she says, addressing the group, "I want you to talk from its voice about your past. How does it feel to be your yoni? Let's start with Martha."

I check my watch and breathe a private sigh of relief. In another hour I will have to excuse myself and conveniently escape to pick up Richard Marksman. I'm glad that I don't have to lie. The truth is that I have a commitment to keep and by the time they move around the circle I'll have to leave and I won't have to think of a name for my yoni or pretend to be an alter yoni ego.

Martha, a twenty-something-year-old begins, "My name is Wanda. And I'm afraid. I'm afraid of being a yoni. Sometimes Martha likes to touch me. It makes me nervous. I don't like it when Martha touches me. I don't like it when Martha wants others to touch me."

"What does Martha tell you?" asks Maya.

"She tells me to relax. But I don't know how. I'm not supposed to relax."

"Why do you think it's not okay to relax?" asks Maya, ever so gently.

"Because my mother, I mean, Martha's mother said it was bad to play with me."

Maya takes a deep breath. She holds Martha's hands in hers and says, "Wanda, I want you to take three deep breaths and then I want you to touch your clitoris."

Silence fills the room as Martha nervously sucks in some oxygen and then slowly feels herself.

"I want you to imagine that it's okay to touch yourself," Maya says. "Now I want you to smile, Wanda." Martha smiles. She starts to relax. Maya continues, "I want you to think of a new name for your yoni, a name that will make you unafraid to smile and enjoy the pleasures of your yoni." Maya waits a moment, then, "Do you have a name?"

"Majestic," says Martha.

"That's beautiful," says Maya. "How does Majestic feel?"

"Good. Happy," says Martha.

"Wonderful. You can open your eyes now, Majestic, and say hello to Martha."

Martha opens her eyes and looks at her yoni.

"Now I want you to say, 'My name is Majestic and I am proud to be a yoni.' Say it three times, say it with pride, and take a deep breath each time before you say it."

Martha takes a deep breath and then with a bellowing force from her lungs she shouts, "My name is Majestic and I am proud to be a yoni." Tears of relief and pride stream down her cheeks as she repeats the exercise two more times. When she finishes, Maya remains silent, looking straight into her eyes.

"How does Majestic feel now?" asks Maya.

Martha smiles. And the group smiles in return as if we,

too, have all experienced a part of her transformation. All her previous hangups seem to have disappeared or at the very least dissipated. The women in the room holler and clap.

Maya turns to the next woman named Rebecca in her mid-forties. Rebecca takes a deep breath, closes her eyes and begins.

"My name is Scarlet," says Rebecca. "I hate being a yoni."

"Why do you hate your own beauty, Scarlet?" guides Maya.

"Because I'm ashamed of myself. Ever since Billy Jay touched me, I've hated myself."

"Tell us about Billy Jay," says Maya.

"He's my neighbor. He's twelve. And I'm eight. He's always touching me."

"How do you feel when he touches you, Scarlet?"

"I feel bad because I like it. I know it's wrong. He's not supposed to touch me and I'm not supposed to like it."

"What you feel is very normal, Scarlet. But your name is full of shame, like *The Scarlet Letter.* So, I want you to change your name. What would be the opposite of shame?"

"Pride."

"That's great. I want you to rename your yoni. I want you to call yourself Pride. Take three deep breaths and tell me your new name three times."

Rebecca renews herself with fresh inhales of oxygen and then states, "My name is Pride. My name is Pride. My name is Pride."

"Now turn to each person in the circle, hold their hands in yours, look into their eyes and say it to each one of us. By doing this, you begin to create new grooves in your psyche that eventually will erase the old scars that have become unwanted grooves, grooves that no longer serve you."

Rebecca takes a moment, fills her lungs with the surrounding air and tediously repeats the exercise with each woman in the circle. When she completes the circle, her whole aura manifests a dramatic change. She holds her eyes closed for a minute collecting herself and then opens them and smiles. Tranquility fills her entire frame.

"How do you feel now?" asks Maya.

"Unbelievable," declares Rebecca.

I am amazed to hear everyone's yoni stories. I realize how intense some people's sexual pasts have been. I eye the clock, preparing to excuse myself when the receptionist gently knocks on the door and enters.

"Is there a Laura Taylor here?"

"Yes, I'm Laura Taylor," I say.

"Richard Marksman called. Because of a high-speed freeway chase, he said he had to leave earlier than expected to catch his flight and that you don't have to pick him up."

"Oh. Okay. Thanks."

Maya looks at me. "Oh, good, you'll be able to finish the exercise with us."

I swallow under a camouflaged smile.

"Laura, what's your yoni's name?" she asks.

"Rosebud," I say. It's the first thing that pops into my head.

"And how does it feel to be Laura's yoni, Rosebud? Can you tell us about your sexual experiences?"

Me as Rosebud: "I feel happy and free. I feel like Laura respects me. She takes care of me. She introduces me to safe sensual pleasures. Sometimes I feel afraid of—excuse me, what's the Sanskrit word for penis?"

"Lingham. It means wand of light. Its purpose is to channel creative energy and pleasure," replies Maya.

Me as Rosebud (continued): "Sometimes I fear the linghams when I feel their motivation is not honest and forthright."

Maya takes my hands in hers. "Look into my eyes as if they are a mirror and repeat after me, 'I trust myself.'"

I look at Maya's face. Her beautiful green eyes look directly into mine. Her focus remains steadfastly trained on me. She does not pierce me with her look, but rather her gaze reflects an open invitation to use her eyes in order to see my soul. I breathe deeply and repeat her words, "I trust myself."

"Now say—I trust my instincts to know the difference between genuine love and feeling used."

"I trust my instincts..." I say, but then I can't go on. The words get tangled inside the back of my throat and I am unable to speak.

"Let it out," she coaches. "Let go of the wounds."

Tears trickle down my face. I feel the eyes of the circle upon me, supporting me, the collective women's energy sustaining me through the thick emotions that have now surfaced.

"Take a deep breath," steers Maya.

I breathe deeply and repeat, "I trust my instincts..." This time the tears gush forth. I'm not sure where the tears are coming from or why. The silence in the room provides a gentle space for my cry to be released and I continue, "I trust my instincts to know the difference between genuine love and feeling used." I look at Maya's eyes.

"What are you feeling now?" she asks.

"Safe with myself," I answer softly.

Somehow, repeating those words in the circle opens me up, and I begin to feel a transformation of fear into love.

In this search for couples, I realize that the Tantric sex adherents possess a truly sacred approach toward an advancement of sexuality through healing. Something very honest and pure supports their underlying philosophy and subsequent behavior.

I stay after the workshop to talk to Maya. She tells me she would be interested in participating in the sex education video and will find out if her current lover would be open to joining as well. Somehow, I have a feeling there is more to Maya than meets the eye. It was something I did not have to wonder about for too long.

★ ★ ★

I'm soaking in organic bubbles courtesy of my mother, and trying to relax before the start of production. I've got all my couples lined up and personally approved by Mickey Colucci. My answering machine beeps to alert me of its accumulated messages while I've been gone couple hunting. I don't have the time or energy to keep up with my Hollywood cohorts anymore. Pre-production is time-consuming hard work, even if it is in porn. I lean over the tub and hit the play button. The outgoing message repeats itself, "Hi, you've found me but I'm not here. Leave a message. Beep."

"Laura, it's Elaine. Where have you been? Call me." That can wait. I close my eyes in quiet anticipation of the next message.

"Hey, it's Corie. Just thought you'd like to know I saw Toby Smith with a copy of *The Law of Malus*...call when you come up for air." That, too, can wait, but not for long.

"Laura, it's your brother Bennett. I'm still not talking to you, but you better call Mom." Too cryptic. Not worth opening my eyes for...yet.

"Laura, it's Mom. You better call Ann. I think you know best how to talk to women these days." I sigh, eyes still closed, wondering what that's all about.

"Laura, it's Dad. Bennett's in San Francisco. Your mother's in Michigan. And I'm in Florida...with Charlene. I'm counting on you to..." But the message gets cut off, leaving one more message to go. I wonder how much longer I can keep my eyes closed.

"Laura, it's Ann. I watched that...movie again. I'm canceling the wedding." My eyes pop open.

An hour later I'm in Malibu pacing the floors with Ann. George is out of town on business, as usual for the past four months.

"You can't cancel, you just have cold feet, besides that,

do you have any idea how much Dad spent on deposits?" I plead with her.

"Okay, I won't cancel. I'll postpone."

I take a deep breath. That's a start. "So please don't tell me this is all about lack of sexual excitement."

Ann looks at me, "This is all about lack of sexual fulfillment. I don't want to die never having had an orgasm!"

I stop berating her. "It's that bad?" I ask.

Ann nods.

"Maybe you should go to a Tantric sex workshop," I offer. She looks at me like I'm crazy.

"First of all, I don't know what that is, but I cannot deal with my private issues in a public setting. I think I need to talk to that friend of yours, Bella Riga."

"She's not around right now."

"Where is she? I'll fly to her."

"Ann, she's absolutely crazed getting ready to go on location."

"Location? What's she doing?"

"Well, actually, I think she's producing a series of sex education tapes for adults called *Usual Couples, Unusual Sex,*" I answer.

"Maybe it would help if I saw them."

"I'll uh, look into it, Ann. In the meantime, I've got an early day tomorrow so I'd better get going." I put my coat on.

Ann, much calmer now, walks me to the door. "Did you hear about Bennett?"

"No. What?" I ask.

"His entire leather sock venture was about to go under. I can't even tell you how much George would have lost. Then out of the blue, his manufacturer gets an order for ten thousand red leather socks from some adult film company in the valley that wants to bundle them as promotional products with some film of theirs called *My Red Vibe Notebook!* Can you believe that?!"

I shake my head, feigning utter surprise, "Wow, that is quite a coincidence, isn't it?"

11

take eleven

BELLA FEEGA, THE PRODUCER

I'm in my office putting together the production for the series of sex education videos when Mickey Colucci calls me, "I need you to trim another twenty g's from the budget."

"I already trimmed eight thousand. Any more and we'll have talking heads."

"Then trim ten."

"Okay. What would you like me to use as leverage? Shall I offer the post-production graphic company stock instead of cash?" The stock issue always works. Colucci can't stand the idea of parting with any shares of stock.

"Just do what you can," he says. "One more thing."

"Yes?" I ask.

"I bought a line of sex toys. I want the couples to use them in the videos."

"What?!"

"Make sure you show the name of the toy, too." Great,

I think. I'm doing product placement now. "I'll send you samples," he adds. "If you run out, The Pleasure Chest carries them."

"Just what kind of sex toys are we talking about, Mr. Colucci?"

"Dildos, strap-ons, blindfolds, Kama Sutra stuff, lubricants and flavored condoms. While you're at it, include those leather socks you wrote into *My Red Vibe Notebook,*" he adds.

"Great. Why don't you just add them to the sex toy catalogue," I facetiously comment.

"Good idea," he says.

I get back to work. Mickey had firmly requested that I make sure the couples are real couples and attractive couples. So the first and most important person I hire has to be the best camera person I can find.

Of course, as a former assistant to a literary agent and as a writer, I don't know too many camera people, except the one that Mitchell Mann hired while we were dating and who I ran into again when he and Mitchell unwittingly crashed the set of *Red Vibe Notebook.* So I call Cole Tanner, whose career skyrocketed from the early horror-film days with Mitchell Mann to big-budgeted dramatic feature films. To my surprise, Cole remembers me. It turns out he's in between projects and offers to shoot the sex ed videos for me within my budget, as long as we remain discreet about it and use a pseudonym for him on the credits. Once Cole signs on, he brings with him one of the best crews in the business.

Next, I hire the makeup artist who made the actresses in *Things Change* look exceptional, Ian Bujinski. I pay him well and he pays me back with a phenomenal job and loyalty.

Only one couple sneaks past the screening process. It turns out that they covered up their tattoos the day of the interviews along with the fact that they're really second-rate porn actors. This, I discover through Ian Bujinski, while on set at the top of a Topanga mountain. This "couple" shows up two hours late looking strung out on something with their tattoos showing. Ian whispers in my ear, "She's a porn actress." She looks like she could use the money from this gig, but Mickey Colucci's word stood on the line: no adult actresses in these videos. I cancel the day's shoot and rearrange the schedule.

Couple #1: Beth & Gregory

We are in Petaluma, California, at the mountain home of Beth and Gregory. Cole sets up the interviews against a beautiful serene landscape of golden rolling hills.

The sex therapist, Adriana Simon, uses the exercises in her book as a guideline to prompt Beth and Gregory into sharing their most intimate fears and desires.

"We both wanted children very much, but we didn't know if we could conceive since we were both in our forties," says Beth. "So we created a special ritual. We wrote a poem together to welcome a newborn spirit into our world and on our first attempt, we conceived Julie."

"What was the biggest intimacy hurdle you faced after giving birth?" asks Adriana.

"I don't think either one of us was prepared for the intense shift of attention a new baby demands. It taxed the very core of our relationship," replies Beth.

Gregory interjects, "I knew the baby's needs came first, but that still didn't take away from the fact that I felt neglected, especially sexually."

"How were you able to get past it?" coaxes Adriana.

"First we decided that our relationship was equally as important as our relationship to our baby. So we scraped together the money to hire a baby-sitter one night a week and devoted that time to each other," explains Gregory.

"One night it would be Gregory's, and I would give him

whatever he wanted or needed to feel sexually satisfied. And the next week, he would do it for me," adds Beth.

An idea comes to me. I pull Adriana and Cole together in a huddle, "Let's construct this as a story. Let's recreate the ritual where Beth and Gregory conceive their child, then the conflict of neglect enters and we see how they each take care of each other's needs." Adriana and Cole agree.

We set the scene up to recapture an extraordinarily intimate moment from the past. Lit candles cover the premises. Incense wafts through the air. The luscious music of Ravel plays in the background. As the crew watches, Beth and Gregory recreate the sacred moment of their child's conception. Tears well up all over the set.

The grip, a stocky guy with a tool belt wrapped around his waist, turns to me and with tears in his eyes whispers, "I can't believe how beautiful this is. Next time my wife and I try to conceive, I'm going to do what they did."

I can't help but be affected as well and I gently squeeze hands with the grip in acknowledgement of a simulation of the miracle of creation. While Beth and Gregory take care of each other's sexual needs, everyone blushes with joy.

Couple #2: Gary & Suzette

We are on set in Santa Barbara at a local bed-and-breakfast. Perky, pretty and young best describes Suzette. By day, she cleans houses in lingerie, a true exhibitionist at heart. By night, she satisfies Gary, her rich businessman husband. Their relationship issues stem from their quest to keep their romance alive and how they use fantasies to excite one another.

The props are in place. Pillows, blankets on a futon, candles, music, incense, and sex toys adorn a corner of the living room. The lights are all in position. Cole turns to me, "We're ready to roll."

"Okay, let me get the release form signed," I reply.

Suzette is the only one so far who has not signed the release form, which allows the Accent Film Company to market and distribute the videotapes. After Ian finishes putting on Suzette's makeup, I quietly knock on the bedroom door.

"Suzette, it's Laura. May I come in?"

"Are you alone?" she asks.

"Yes," I reply.

She lets me in, and then locks the door behind me. It's just the two of us.

"How do I look?" she asks, suddenly appearing bashful for a woman who likes to clean houses in lingerie. She sports a delicate white silk robe and Ian has highlighted her features to make her look stunning.

"You look great, really beautiful," I say. "I just need you to sign this release form—"

"I'm really nervous," she says, interrupting me with a hand on my shoulder. "It's just that a lot of people are going to see me naked out there."

I face her, ready to switch roles from producer to therapist, anything to get the release form signed and this show on the road. "Yes, that's true, but we'll all be very respectful of you, Suzette. Is there something I can do to help you not be nervous?"

"Well," she says, shifting to timid and demure. "I want you to be the first to see me naked." She gently grabs the edges of her silk robe around her shoulders. She pulls the robe wide open, revealing all of her naked body. And then she lets go, allowing the robe to drop around her feet. She stares at me with lusty eyes.

"Wow. Um, well, Suzette, you, uh, you have a, uh, really beautiful body. I am, uh, really honored that you wanted to share that with me, um, first," I utter, as I stall for time to think of the best way to get the release form signed and keep my integrity intact.

"Would you like to touch me?" she asks, attempting to lace her words with a seductive glow.

"You know, I'm really flattered by your, uh, offer, but see, the crew is waiting out there and if I get started touching you then I, uh, I, uh, I won't be able to stop and it could turn into a really embarrassing scene. So if you could just sign this release form and film this bit then we can talk about it later, okay? Here's a pen."

Suzette smiles and bats her eyelashes at me as she takes the pen and paper in hand.

But I'm not off the hook so easily. During filming, while Suzette lies naked in Gary's arms, she decides to modify the script and describes a new and different fantasy.

"What would you do if I brought home a present for us?"

"What kind of present?" asks Gary, as he strokes her back.

"A woman."

"A woman? What kind of woman?" he asks, his penis starting to expand.

"A really pretty woman. She's petite, beautifully proportioned with perfect breasts, dark hair and sensual lips."

Cole looks at me, and smiles as I turn beet red. Suzette glances at me as her body gyrates into Gary's.

"I slowly take off my robe for her and kiss her," murmurs Suzette.

The rest of the crew stares at me. I am mortified.

After the shoot, Suzette approaches, "Gary and I want to know if you'd like to spend the night with us."

"That's uh, really kind of you, Suzette, but, um, well..." I'm a horrible liar.

Cole picks up on my predicament and interrupts, "I thought you were taking the crew to dinner tonight?"

"Right. That's exactly right. I did promise to take the entire crew out tonight," I tell Suzette.

"To the best steakhouse in town," adds Cole with a wink.

★★★

Two hundred and fifty dollars later along with a lot of teasing, the crew thanks me for an amazing meal. Cole and I stroll back to the bed-and-breakfast where we parked our cars.

"It would be a shame to waste this B-and-B room for the night," he says. "Why don't you stay here and enjoy it?"

To my surprise I respond, "Why don't you stay with me? We could figure out which sex toys to use for the next shoot." I look at him suddenly shy and embarrassed, "Did I just say what I think I said?"

He nods at me with a friendly smile.

Cole stays and we lounge in a hot bubble bath together, laughing about the absurdities of life. We playfully attempt to test some of the sex toys, but our laughter gets in the way. We decide to abandon them and rely on our own mutual biological attraction. Being with Cole doesn't necessarily erase my memories of Gavin Marsh or Mitchell Mann, but lying in his embrace helps shift them to the background. Cole holds me close to him as we make tender love. He confides in me that he's always found me attractive from the first day we met on the set of *Zombies Cometh*. I smile at him, his words and the sentiments supporting them fill my heart. Exhausted, we drift off to sleep in each other's arms.

Couple #3: Ray & Carla

We are in a private home in a lush part of Sherman Oaks, filming real-estate developer Ray and his new girlfriend Carla. I am in the garage with the grip, the gaffer, and the editor who mans the monitors. I wear a headset so I can talk directly to Cole who adjusts the lighting in the living room with Adriana, Ray and Carla, and the camera operator. The confined space in the living room prohibits the entire crew and all of the equipment from fitting inside, so the rest of us work from a preset station in the garage.

Ray and Carla are heavily into the practice of Tantric sex. They enjoy spending a majority of their time together pleasuring each other.

Adriana asks them, "Tell me how Tantric sex deepens your intimacy with each other and with yourselves?"

"Well," begins Ray, "we use Tantric sex to explore the yin and yang energy. When you merge these energies together, you can experience joyous transcendence and mystical ecstasy."

"Ray is exceptionally gifted at arousing my kundalini," says Carla. "In fact, I'm able to ejaculate because of our Tantric asanas and pranayamas."

"That's beautiful," comments Adriana. "That you're able to be transported into the divine realms of consciousness."

Ray and Carla exchange beatific grins. "Yes, we like to make love for ten hours at a time five days a week," says Ray.

How do they get any work done? I wonder. Let alone eat and shower. Do they ever see their friends and families? Celebrate holidays? Maybe they don't have any. Tantric sex must be for orphaned agnostic trust fund babies.

We cut to Adriana in front of a closed bedroom door talking directly to the camera. Her grave voice lends a serious approach to her work.

"What you are about to see, outlined in Chapter Six of my book, is the ancient and sacred spiritual practice of Tantric sex. This practice represents sexual principles underlying all human existence." Adriana takes a breath and switches from her weighty tone to an inviting smile for the camera. "Ray and Carla unite the evolutionary force of kundalini energy to deepen their levels of erotic pleasure throughout their nervous systems, which in turn creates electromagnetic fields around their bodies allowing them to enter the divine realms of consciousness."

We cut to Ray and Carla preparing in their bedroom. I direct the scene from the garage. Cole is inside the house. He yawns. I playfully pant into the headset and he immediately perks up.

"Sorry, boss," he whispers into his headset.

Ray and Carla begin by practicing strange breathing patterns and a mixture of what appear to be awkward and uncomfortable poses.

"Okay, Cole, can you pull back," I direct. "Give us a wide shot of this pose. Mike, can you push in, give me a close-up of Carla's mouth as she breathes in and out. Now pan over her body and pull back to a wide shot. Cole, move in on Ray's hands."

We stare in amazement as Ray pleasures Carla into a state of transcendence. Suddenly, it appears as if her genitals are inverted, protruding toward us.

"What is that?" asks my editor.

"It looks like an alien," adds the grip.

"Cole, can you get a tighter shot?" I ask.

"I'm zoomed in all the way," he murmurs.

And then, out of nowhere, Carla lets out a loud moan and a huge spray of liquid smatters the lens.

"What the hell is that?" cries the editor.

"I think she just ejaculated," I say. "You okay, Cole?"

"Just a little wet. I need to stop so I can clean the lens," he whispers.

"Okay, Mike, zoom out for a master shot while Cole swabs his lens," I say.

"Well, that's something new," says the editor.

"Where can I get a book on how you do this stuff?" asks the grip.

"Here. It's in Chapter Six," I say and hand him an extra copy of Adriana's book. "Have a ball."

We finally wrap for the day. Cole sighs, exhausted.

"Do you need me to stay, boss?" he asks, barely able to keep his eyes open.

"No, you go. Get some rest. I can finish up here. But thanks for asking."

"You sure?"

"Yes. I need you wide-eyed and bushy-tailed tomorrow," I smile back.

"That's all?" he grins.

I look up from my paperwork again. "Well, actually, as soon as this shoot is over, I will need a shot of kundalini energy so I can enter a divine realm of consciousness with you. Think you can handle that?"

"No problem," he smiles, and kisses me good-night. "See you tomorrow, Taylor."

"Oh, you can sleep in, Cole. I moved the call time to 10:00 a.m."

I stay to prep for the next day only to discover that we're out of sex toys and flavored condoms. Since I control the budget on this set and I nixed any allocation of monies for production assistants, I am the only one I can designate to get more supplies before tomorrow.

At ten o'clock at night, tired and worn-out, I head over to the famous Pleasure Chest in Hollywood to purchase all the necessary accoutrements for the next day's shoot. As I park my car in the lot, I do a double take. I'm almost certain I see the manager-producer Darlene Green exit the store in shades and load her car with several hefty packages. I shake my head in disbelief.

I push a shopping cart through the tiny aisles loading it up with flavored condoms, even glow-in-the-dark ones that say "Rise & Shine," plus assorted-sized dildos, vibrators and a strap-on.

I round another aisle and am astonished to see a large billboard for *My Red Vibe Notebook, Part I* and *Part II.* Multiple RVN videotapes line the wall for sale. Sure enough, it boasts the added inclusion of a pair of red leather socks. I pull a set down and am surprised to see that it even says penned by award-winning writer Bella Feega on the back of the box. That must have been the work of Tom Kaplan—I complained that adult writers deserve box cover credit. I add it to the cart when I suddenly feel a tap on my shoulder.

"More research?" a voice asks.

Sara Stephenson confidently peers at me over a pair of lowered shades. Next to her stands a pretty woman with hair slicked back, and a touch of pink lipstick, also in shades.

"Hi, Laura. This is Janine Tate. Janine, Laura Taylor. She's an amazing writer." As she glances at the items in my shopping cart, Sara adds with a grin, "I'd call Laura a method writer."

Janine checks out the items and smiles. "I'm dying to know what you write."

"Laura writes erotic psychological dramas, right, Laura?"

"You could say that," I reply, "I also write dramatic family epics with deep underlying universal themes."

Janine hands me her card. "I run the art house division of Maestro Studios. I'm looking for a classy steamy story that pushes the envelope, like *Last Tango in Paris* or *Basic Instinct*. Why don't you call me sometime?"

"Sure," I say, taking the card and slipping it in my back pocket. Then they notice *Red Vibe Notebook* in my cart. Before Sara can comment I hold the tape up. "Is this not amazing?" I ask. "I had to get this for the red leather socks, but more for its ingenious marketing idea, don't you think? I mean, who would have thought of putting together fashion with porn? It's such a witty oxymoron."

Sara and Janine look at the videotape box, intrigued. "You get a free pair of red leather socks?" they ask, more than interested.

I nod. Sara looks at Janine. "Why don't we bundle product placement like that with some of our movies?"

"I believe this is product integration," I add. "I'm making sure to write all my new screenplays with that in mind."

If that's not enough, hiding behind more shades, Hank Willows and J.J. saunter in. "What's taking you girls so long?" asks Hank. Then he drops his shades and sees me. "Oh, hi, Laura! More research?"

"Yeah, Hank, as a matter of fact, this story has to do with Tantric sex, the kind of sex that transports you into mystical ecstasy that only a few people ever achieve in their lifetime. Being a method writer, I can tell you it's beyond your imagination."

Hank, J.J., Sara, and Janine all quiet down. A moment of extended silence surrounds us. "Well, have a nice evening, you guys," I say as I guide my shopping cart toward the checkout counter.

That's when I see Rand, Scott Sher's former assistant, trying to hide behind yet another pair of shades. He looks at me, embarrassed beyond belief. By now, nothing fazes me anymore.

"What the hell are you doing here?" I ask, noticing an interesting array of cock rings he's planning on purchasing.

"Running a personal errand for Jason Brand. He doesn't have the guts to come in here himself. What about you?"

"I'm producing a series of sex ed videos. These are my props."

"That's cool," says Rand. "At least you've got nothing to hide."

"Yeah. You're right about that, Rand. I've got nothing to hide. Here, have a couple of flavored condoms on me." I toss them on the counter and he sort of grins at me.

And then it hits me. Hollywood's best intentions take forever to materialize because its pretentiousness often gets in its way, while the adult entertainment industry has no pretensions, and therefore always accomplishes its intentions—good or bad.

I'm trying to sleep in, just a little, when my phone rings.

"Good morning! It's a beeeeeeeeutiful day!" beams the voice on the other end.

"Hi, Dad." I murmur, rubbing the sleep from my eyes.

"Come meet Ann and me for coffee," he says.

"Dad, I have to work. We're shooting that…thing of little mini-dramas at ten."

"It's only seven-thirty. You've got time for a cup of coffee. We're at The Pickle & the Pea in Santa Monica. We'll see you there."

I hang up and sigh.

The sun shines, as usual, in California. And while Walt's face beams with perennial optimism from inside the coffee shop, Ann's looks like there's a dark cloud over her head.

"Are you okay, Ann?" I ask.

"I really need to talk to your friend," she whispers, as Walt arrives with our drinks.

"Thanks, Dad. Okay, so what's up? Why the sunrise meeting?" I ask, sipping my vanilla latte.

"You're so hard to reach these days," says Walt.

"Dad needs you to look over his spokesperson copy that Bennett's friend wrote," explains Ann. "Bennett wants to use it for an infomercial for the Leather Footish socks."

"Bennett went with Leather Footish? Nice. Okay, hand it over." In that moment, I realize my family of origin is starting to recognize me as a writer, of sorts. Even though Bennett never acknowledged the brand name that came from me or personally asked me to help with any writing, it feels good to have something to offer. Walt hands it over and I quickly peruse the copy.

> Buy Leather Footish Socks, fashionable socks for the feet. I'm Dr. Walt Taylor, D.P.M., and I recommend Leather Footish Socks, safe to walk in or run in, safe from athlete's foot, fungus or toejam. You can't go wrong with leather. It's not pleather. It's leather…

"This is horrible and infomercials are expensive. Who's paying for it?"

"George. That is if the wedding stays on," adds Ann. "In which case George wants you to produce it."

"Me, and infomercials?" I shake my head taking a red pen from my bag and quickly start rewriting. "This is just a rough idea of where I'd go with this," I say, and then I read it aloud for them.

> In today's fast-paced hi-tech world of art and commerce we all need to move in a lot of circles, and it's your feet that take you where you want to go. I'm Dr. Walt Taylor, Doctor of Podiatric Medicine, and the one thing you can do for your feet is to protect them, comfort them, and even enhance their appearance with Leather Footish, the best in sock design today. Between the foot and the shoe, lie the socks. So combine footwear with fashion and do your sole a favor, get Leather Footish. Its blend of supple leather and 100% cotton provides organic and natural liberation for your sole, so you can perform better in everything you do. I'm Dr. Walt Taylor, D.P.M., for Leather Footish.

"That's fantastic!" claims Walt.

Even Ann smiles at me. "I'm impressed," she nods. "Bennett will be, too."

"It's just a rough copy, but I really have to go now. We're shooting in Malibu and I can't be late."

"Oh, good," says Walt. "Then you can drop Ann off and I'll go to the Marina."

"But…" I gulp, remembering that my car is loaded with bags from the Pleasure Chest. I quickly try to cover them up while making room for Ann to get in. I succeed until we're on the road. My cell phone rings inside my knapsack in the back and Ann, ever so helpful, tries to get it for me, only to discover the bags' contents.

"What are you doing with all these sex toys, Laura?" she asks, startled.

"Well, actually, Ann. I, uh, I finally got a hold of Bella Feega. And she told me to get these for you and George. Not all of them, of course. She just wants you to start with an assortment of samples. Whatever you don't pick I'll just take back to the store."

"Really? You did this for me?" asks Ann. "I'm really touched, Laura." She scrounges through the products. "But why do I need a strap-on?"

"Because…because Bella said you should get…creative."

"How am I supposed to do that when George is always out of town?" And before I can answer she finds the *Red Vibe Notebook,* with the leather socks included. "Oh my God, you found the porn film with the leather socks. That is so gross!" she says. "How could you buy this?"

"I thought I'd get it for George and Bennett as a memento for their first big sock sale," I say.

Ann reads the synopsis on the box, intrigued by the story line. "A sexually frustrated woman whose husband is always gone… Hey, it's written by that friend of yours."

"Really? Maybe that's just another venue for her to educate…about sex," I fumble.

Ann stares at the box, and then looks up at me. "Can I borrow this?"

"Yeah, sure," I say, surprised. "Borrow away."

★ ★ ★

Couple #4: Maya & Jeremy

I am on set in Malibu at a beautiful home overlooking the Pacific Ocean and filming the Tantric sex teacher, Maya, and her current boyfriend, Jeremy, as they share their truly spiritual approach to intimacy.

Cole and I flirt between camera setups. For once, I realize how nice it is to really like the person you're attracted to. I notice that below-the-line talent in Hollywood, the people who make up the crew, are much more genuine and real than the above-the-line talent, the people whose names shine in neon lights.

I mention this to Cole as he works with his gaffer to adjust the lighting. "Hey, Cole, how come crew people are so much nicer and more down-to-earth than the talent?"

"Because we don't have anything to fight over, like who gets a bigger credit on the screen. We're just hard workers looking for an honest day's work."

While Cole sets up the next shot, I lean quietly against the trunk of a tree next to Maya, still curious about what secrets she must hold.

"Maya, can I ask you a question?"

"Sure," she says. "My secrets are open to you."

I wonder how she reads me so well. "How did you know that?" I ask.

"You've got curiosity written all over your face. Don't worry. It's a good thing. Persistent curiosity keeps you young. So tell me what you're curious to know."

"How did you become a Tantric sex teacher?"

"Well, it was a natural offspring from my work as a sex surrogate," she replies.

I've never heard that phrase before. Sex surrogate. I am immediately stung with more curiosity. So I ask.

She takes a moment, collects herself, and then answers, "A sex surrogate is a trained specialist who works in conjunction with a sex therapist to help people overcome certain sexual dysfunctions through sexual practice."

Her answer only intrigues me and for the next hour I bombard her with questions about the details of her life as a sex surrogate. I didn't realize then that the contents of this conversation would lead me to my next screenplay.

That night, Cole stays over at my place. We talk about the shoot and cuddle in each other's arms. For a reason that neither of us understands, a sexual interlude at this time feels unappealing to both of us. I ask Cole if he's ever heard of sex surrogates before.

"Well, yes," he says, "when I lived in Paris. I knew a woman who was a sex therapist and she would hire surrogates to work with her patients."

"Did it help them?"

"Absolutely."

"What kind of sexual issues did they have?"

"Oh, I remember one young woman had been raised as a strict Catholic and her mother brainwashed her into believing that having sexual relations was evil," he answers.

"What happened to her?"

"She went to see my friend who had a sex surrogate work with her. Now the woman's happily married with two kids."

"That's amazing," I remark. "I wonder what the surrogate did."

"I see a story brewing in your head, Taylor."

"Can I tell you a secret?" I whisper. He nods at me to go ahead. "Promise you won't laugh?"

"I promise."

I turn on my side to face him. "When I left Michigan and drove out west, I could feel the heat of adventure in front of me. I knew then that writing movies would be my way of creating social change."

"And personal ones as well, no?"

"You're so wise." He smiles at me. "The truth is, Cole, I believed that my aspirations for success and happiness lay in my determination to write the great American screenplay."

"But instead you wrote the great American porn film," he giggles.

I teasingly punch him in the arm. "You promised not to laugh."

"Sorry, but you set me up," Cole replies. He quickly gives me his full attention.

"It's that back then," I continue, "I had the naiveté of invincible youth. I thought that nothing could stop me." I pause, remembering those feelings. "It's just that now, I think this story about surrogates could really mean something."

"Your motivation is beautiful, Taylor. But don't think that your porn films haven't changed people's lives. There's yours and your father's." He strokes my face. I feel emotionally connected to him as he leans in to kiss me.

"Hmmm. That feels nice. Please don't stop," I say, glad to finally feel a small stir of sexuality rise inside me. But then the phone rings. Only because we are still in the midst of production do I pick it up. I glance at the clock. It's eleven-thirty at night.

"Hello?" I ask.

"Laura? It's Mitchell Mann."

My heart skips two beats. The mere mention of his name spins me emotionally off balance.

"What's up?" I fumble. Cole looks at me, only too aware of my shift in energy.

"I closed some financing deals and I want to talk to you about writing a script for me to direct."

"Now?" I ask, suspicious of anything he has to say.

"Yes. I also wanted you to know that Shelly moved out.

So can I come over now and see you, to talk about the script idea?"

"I can't see you, Mitchell, it hurts too much. I have to go now." I hang up. Cole looks at me. My body tenses with aching memories.

"Let's table the sex for now, Taylor. We're both exhausted from this shoot. Besides, what you need right now is another hug," says Cole.

"Thanks for understanding," I say.

Too tired to make love, or at least that's what I thought at the time, I drift off to sleep obsessed with the compelling world of sex surrogates.

Couple #5: Diane & Zack

We are in San Diego at the home of the last couple on the shoot. Diane and Zack are swingers. In the interview with Adriana, Diane reveals how Zack talked her into trying out a swing party. Once she got over her initial fright, she became addicted to the excitement of new sexual encounters. Zack couldn't be happier because now he had carte blanche to be with other women.

During the on-camera love scenes, Zack freaks out. It turns out that maintaining an erection proves to be more difficult than he had expected. On top of that, the sun begins to set, casting a coveted glow on all its subjects. Everyone's dragging their last foothold of energy through the day, hoping to wrap soon and go home.

Zack asks to have a private conversation with Cole. They consult for a while and then Cole walks toward me. He motions for me to meet him off the set.

"What's up?" I ask.

"It's more like what's not up. With all that swinging, I guess Zack's become immune to his wife as a turn-on."

"Oh no, his poor wife."

"Well, then again, it's not easy to get a hard-on in front of a camera crew," Cole points out.

"Well, at least now we can truly appreciate the talents of a porn star," I say. "So what should we do, find some *Erotica* magazines to put on the floor of the set?"

"That's not going to work. He wants to know if you would stand behind the camera and take off your shirt."

"What?"

"I'm just the messenger right now," says Cole. "It's your call. You can lose them as a couple for the series, which will seriously compromise the program, or try to salvage the day."

From a distance, the crew shuffles around the set, eager to wrap. Adriana left after the last interview. I am the only woman on set.

"There has to be something else we can do. What about blasting some erotic music?"

"Okay, let's try that."

Moments later, Cole arranges for one of the crew to blast a CD that Adriana left us from his car and we are shooting again, alas with no more luck than before. The crew is getting more impatient and the light is beginning to diminish.

Cole approaches me once again. "What do you want to do?"

I glance at Zack in the distance, appalled. He stares at me, his eyes pleading, hoping I'll redeem his manhood. "Fine," I say, "but Colucci's going to pay for this. With stock! Give me a minute," I say.

I borrow some of the crews' extra T-shirts and sweatshirts and hurriedly layer myself with tons of garments. I have no intention of ever getting to the bottom one.

For the next five minutes, I stand next to Cole, who's behind the camera, and gradually remove my layers as Zack pierces me with a locked stare. I suddenly feel like I'm part of an absurd strip show. I uncomfortably remove a shirt and then yell, "Cut!" Everyone looks at me. I turn to Cole, "Um, I'm having a little trouble getting into this role. Can someone please turn up the music?" Cole signals a crewmember. The music plays louder and we're immediately up and running.

One by one, I awkwardly peel my tops off to the rhythm of the music as Zack works himself up. I witness pure lust in his eyes that seems to be fueled by anger. I didn't realize it then, but his behavior would become a character trait of a prime murder suspect in a new screenplay brewing inside me.

Cole, eyes trained on the camera, whispers to me, "How you doing, Taylor?"

"Okay," I mumble, keeping my eyes locked with Zack's. "How are we on light?"

"We got about a minute left of it," says Cole.

I stare back at Zack, taking off another layer, faster this time, and challenging him with my eyes. I'm down to my last shirt. I'm tired and so is everyone else. I whip it off. Zack is in a frenzy, still trying, and time's running out. Fuck it. I pull my breasts out of my bra and shake them at him. Zack finally "performs" the golden shot and we call it a wrap as the remaining light disappears. I swiftly pull myself back together. Cole offers me a big hug. The crew high-fives me and immediately starts dismantling the set.

I murmur to Cole, "Well, no one can ever say I don't know how to get the job done."

Cole chuckles, and then smiles, "You're a real trouper, Taylor."

I laugh. "I need to go home and take a long, hot bath. Can I call you later?"

"Of course," he says. "But do me a favor and promise me you won't overthink this."

"Promise," I say. But before I can take off, Zack comes running up to my car.

"Hey, Laura. I just want to thank you for saving my manhood back there," he says. A lascivious smirk begins to form around his lips, as he adds, "Your breasts are really gorg—"

But I cut him off. "No problem, Zack. It's all in a day's work." I offer a temporary grin, step on the gas, and split.

It's late as I'm walking down the hallway toward my apartment. Corie's also coming home. She looks as exhausted as I imagine I must look.

"Hey, Corie, how was work today?" I ask, as we trail down the hallway together, carrying book bags and knapsacks.

"Degrading," she says.

"Hmmm. What did you have to put up with?" I ask.

And then, as if by rote, she replies without emotion because at this point what's the point, "Jason screaming at the top of his lungs because first class was booked, then humiliating me in front of Eric Leve because I mistyped the spelling of a new client's name on the phone sheet. The phone sheet, I *repeat.*" Her voice wearily trails off. "How was your day?"

"Same," I reply.

"Really, what did you have to put up with?" she asks, as we both reach our apartment doors and unlock them.

"Flashing my boobs for a cum shot," I say, as if it's an ordinary event.

"Hmmm," replies Corie.

"Hmmm," I ditto, as we acknowledge in code that it's all just part of the job. We both enter our separate apartments to collapse and then rejuvenate to do it all again tomorrow.

I am at synagogue, hoping the sermon will help me find ways to deal with my duality. But my attention, occupied with the events of yesterday and the story brewing inside me, weaves in and out of portions of Rabbi Weiss's sermon.

I try to concentrate while the rabbi orates about why Jacob wrestled with the angels. "He was wrestling with his consciousness, with his divided soul. Or perhaps he was wrestling with who he had become and that was no longer good enough. The lesson Jacob learns is that even though his integrity may be briefly shattered, he can repair it. The significance is that he wrestles to know himself and to change into a man of renewed integrity."

I realize that I, too, am wrestling with my consciousness. Wondering how I allowed myself to get sucked into two diametrically opposed worlds. How did a nice middle-class upbringing and a master's degree in literature bring me to this moment? Oh, yes, *Things Change.* But before I had found myself a success in porn films and as a producer of adult sex education videos, I was a really nice Jewish girl trying really hard to make it in Hollywood and I wondered—how had *things changed?* But change is inevitable. It's natural, part of evolution. After all, if things didn't change how boring would that be? People would stop growing. Jacob would not have found self-renewal for himself. And just think, no changing colors of leaves. No births. No deaths. And the thing in between called life.

Now choice about change is a whole other matter I think. The bigger question is why had I *chosen* to allow things to change in the direction they had. Was I not willing to see the consequences of my actions? But how do you know what the consequences are until you commit to the action? That was the theme of Rabbi Weiss's sermon last Yom Kippur. "Only by doing can we truly know ourselves," he had lectured. I had willingly jumped down the rabbit's hole. But I wasn't yet willing to see all that was down there. And maybe that was okay…for now.

On the way out of the sanctuary, Richard Marksman tracks me down. "Hey, you. How've you been?"

"Oh, hi, Richard," I say, collecting my thoughts for now.

"I never did get to tell you how much I liked your script," he says. "I gave it to Toby Smith to work on. You should be hearing from her next week."

"That's nice," I say, too tired to care anymore and unconvinced that anything will come of it.

"How about a walk? You can tell me what you've been up to."

"Sure," I reply. I think he seems to mistake my calmness for a lack of enthusiasm over seeing him.

During our post-synagogue walk, I educate Richard about sex surrogates. "I'm fascinated by them. And after doing quite a bit of research, I believe they play an extremely valuable role in society. I want to write a screenplay about a sex surrogate that puts them in a good light. I have an idea in mind."

"What is it?" asks Richard, more than intrigued.

"It's a story about a woman, a former investigative journalist, who's been betrayed by love. She goes undercover as a sex surrogate to solve her sister's murder mystery—and in the process she learns to trust in love again until she realizes she's fallen in love with the prime suspect."

"I like that. I like that a lot," he says, contemplatively. "I think you should write it."

"Thanks. So do I," I reply.

Later that evening, Cole and I meet for dinner at a local sushi spot. We share a large bottle of sake while picking at a bowl of Edamame.

"So how are you feeling?" asks Cole.

"Better. I went to synagogue to forgive myself for baring my breasts."

"You can't turn it around on yourself, Laura."

"I know. But, I did. For a little while at least," I reply.

"Well, did you at least get your stock from Colucci?" he asks with a smile.

"Maybe tomorrow," I say. Then I look at him. I feel sad. "Cole, I think I need a break from us."

"Why is that?" he asks.

"I have absolutely no sex drive anymore. Not even an ounce."

With regard to a lack of interest in sex, allow me to expand. The opposite of writing fictional romance to being on set and producing non-fictional education videos has taken a toll on my sex drive. Suddenly, instead of overactivating it, it's become underactivated, as in vanished, like nowhere to be found. I suspect it's a hazardous side effect in this part of the business. I tried looking at my award-winning porn films and got no reaction. Maybe that's too hard-core for me. So I tried flipping through channels on network television, but even a nice romantic interlude between Bacall and Bogart left me blank. I couldn't handle any of it, not Gere and Winger in *An Officer and a Gentleman*, not even James Bond. I clicked the set off, wondering if I should see a sex therapist.

Cole replies, "Me, too. And the crew. I think it's an occupational hazard."

"Do you think we can see where we're at in a month?"

"Sure," he says. He raises his sake cup and clinks mine. "To next month."

I'm not sure if the sex issue was the only reason I chose to take a break from an embryonic love affair. I think some of it truly did involve the lack of a sex drive, some of it was the fear of having a happy successful relationship, and some of it reflected an intuitive knowing that I had to learn to love myself in order to love another. And in that department, I needed a little more time.

That night I call Mickey Colucci at his home back east and wake him up. "Mr. Colucci. I thought you'd want to know, we finished production on time and on budget. But this work is destroying my—well, it's no good for me anymore. I quit. I—"

"Too many donuts, huh?" Colucci says, interrupting me.

"What? Who said anything about donuts?" I ask, slightly irritated.

"The donut syndrome caught up with you," he explains as a platitude.

"Mr. Colucci, I'm not talking about donuts."

"Donuts. Sex. What's the difference? You eat too many donuts you don't want donuts no more. You see too much sex you don't want sex no more. But you can't quit now or the horse syndrome will get ya."

"What do you mean? I'll never be able to get on a horse again?"

"Something like that. Tell you what. Finish overseeing post-production on the sex ed videos, then go back to writing your Hollywood movies. Trust me. Stay away from porn sets for three months. You'll be good as new."

"Yeah? Well, this time it's going to cost you some stock," I say, still feeling the after-effects of the last shoot.

"Okay. How much you want?"

My mouth drops open. I can't believe Mickey Colucci has offered to give me stock. But in that moment, I realize it's not the stock that I really want.

"I, uh, I don't want any of your stock, Mr. Colucci," I say. "I just wanted to know that you thought I was worth it. Good night."

Colucci kept his word and I continued full-time as the writer-producer during post-production of the videos. And I still made more money than my Hollywood writer friends, who were getting ripped off by production companies that refused to become signatories to the Writers Guild.

During post-production, I give Ann an advance copy of the sex ed tapes. George comes back from his work travels and very soon after that Ann calls to beg me to thank Bella Riga, because the wedding is now happily back on. It will be a sunset ceremony at the Getty Museum's outdoor garden in four months.

In the meantime, the distribution machine kicked in for the sex education videos, and the tapes went on to make over a million dollars in sales. To my surprise, and without my ever saying a word, Colucci expressed his gratitude by sending me an envelope with five hundred shares of stock.

take twelve

KNOCKING ON DOORS

It was time to return to my roots and see if I could get my nonexistent Hollywood writing career on track. So when Corie called to invite me to the Peak Films lot for the premiere party of *Evening to be Reckoned,* I accepted. Yes, you guessed it, producer Jeremy Kincaid's latest, the sequel to *Morning to be Reckoned*.

By now the party-going faces are very familiar as Corie and I sweep through the hors d'oeuvre line.

Scanning the crowd I recognize Darlene Green, Oliver Kleimeister, Joe Schwartz, Jason Brand, Eric Leve, Brad Isaacs, Natalie Moore, Hank Willows, Sara Stephenson, and Janine Tate. Eric Leve and Brad Isaacs glance my way with perfunctory nods. Darlene Green and Natalie Moore whisper in co-conspiracy as they scrutinize the crowd of which I am a part. Oliver Kleimeister trips on his oversized suit. Joe Schwartz rudely reaches over me for a shrimp cocktail and knocks me over. He glances at me and then says nothing as he swallows the shrimp whole.

I turn to Corie as I down the glass of Pellegrino in my hand, "Why are we struggling to be a part of this?"

"Maybe we're addicted to struggle," she says.

"I don't think I can take it anymore, Corie. It's all so frustrating. And it feels so unjust, the way they toss you and your work around like a piece of meat. How come I get so much more respect from the porn, I mean, adult industry? They would never treat me or my work the way people in Hollywood do," I say, feeling a surge of anger rise within me. "I'm going to tell them they can't treat me this way anymore."

"Are you crazy?" Corie asks. "You'll ruin your Hollywood writing career!"

"What Hollywood writing career?!" I reply as Nick Blake pours himself a cappuccino next to me. I feel my mouth start to open. Corie tries to stop me. But it's too late.

"Excuse me, Mr. Blake," I say, "but I think you should know that the people who work for you are idiots. Furthermore, they have no manners. And on top of that, they wouldn't know a good story if it hit them on the head. They should all be ashamed of themselves."

Suddenly, everyone turns around, asking to be scolded some more. I realize that this town thrives on sadomasochism. The more you yell at them, the more they respect you. It's like one big bad porn film.

I come out of my reverie—it was just a fantasy. Everyone around me mingles and schmoozes and Nick Blake sips his cappuccino. I tell Corie I've got to get out of here.

As I reach the perimeter of the parking lot, I bump into Richard Marksman.

"Where are you off to?" he asks.

"I don't belong here, Richard. I have to go."

He looks straight at me, reading between lines I don't even know exist. "Remember that compass your father gave you?"

"Of course," I reply.

"Pull it out sometime. Put your faith in it. It will tell you where you need to go. I'll see you at temple," he says. Then he leisurely walks into the throng of industryites at his own quiet pace, like Robert Redford in *Out of Africa,* moving to his own drum. I watch him vanish into the mob like an enigma.

That night, I light a candle, pull out my father's old compass, set it on the table next to my phone log and stare at it. Nothing happens. I stare at it some more, as if my forced gaze will compel long awaited answers to be revealed. I stare until exhaustion takes over. My head drops and I fall asleep on my desk. I wake up an hour later and notice that the needle on the compass now points to Maya on my phone log. Okay, maybe my arm knocked it around a bit when I crashed on my desk, but I decide to take it as a sign anyway and get to work on the new screenplay idea.

To research my story, because I am after all a stickler for authenticity, I decide to go to a sex surrogate myself to see exactly what it is they do. Maya puts me in touch with a male surrogate named Lance Vaughn.

Lance turns out to be a gorgeous, soft-spoken, kind-hearted man of Native American descent. I ask him to put me through the process while I tape-record the session.

First, he begins by explaining to me the certification process required to become a member of the PSSO, the Professional Sex Surrogate Organization. Approximately 150 sex surrogates exist in the world; most of them reside in California, France, Australia, and Canada.

"What we do here, I do with my clients in the same order," explains Lance. "The sequence is designed to create trust. Without trust, no one heals." He pauses and I let that sink in, repeating in my head that "without trust, no one heals."

"The first thing I do," continues Lance, "is teach my clients how to touch by starting with a Hand Caress. Close your eyes and give me your hand."

I tentatively hold out my hand and close my eyes. He places it in his palm and gently strokes me; it's not a massage, but a light touch.

"The point is not to think or wonder what the person you're touching is feeling but to get in touch with what you're feeling," says Lance. "Focus on giving yourself pleasure."

"Seems simple enough. What's the purpose of this exercise?" I ask.

"People get so caught up in performance anxiety they forget to feel," he answers.

He gently releases my hand and takes a deep breath.

"What's next?" I ask.

"The Face Caress. It's the same principle as the Hand Caress. Close your eyes. Don't say anything. Just allow yourself to feel."

I shut my eyes. I feel him touch me with kindness. I imagine my protagonist, a strong woman deprived of compassion, betrayed by her husband, and now learning the tools of surrogacy work to avenge the murder of her sister. It is through this part of her journey that she unwittingly begins to heal herself.

Lance touches my brows, cheeks, and lips. "The tools to heal others are inside our own wounds," he says.

"That's profound," I reply, feeling a déjà vu from my own inner resources coming forth. "But what exactly does it mean?" I ask, opening my eyes for the answer.

"Let's say your wound is that you gave up trusting what was best for you by seeking the approval of others. Your gift is learning to trust yourself."

I soak it in, thinking about my character. Betrayal represents her wound. Her gift becomes the ability to trust in love again. Can I trust in love again? I wonder.

Lance adds, "The purpose for the wound is to heal others by being in relationships with others. Let's move on to the 'May I Will You' exercise, where we take turns asking each other questions that begin with 'May I' or 'Will You.' For example, 'May I touch your hair?' And you can answer, 'Yes, you may,' or 'No, you may not.' The point is to teach a common courtesy and respect for each other's boundaries and bodies."

Being the method writer that I am, Lance and I practice the exercise. We go from "will you hold me," to "may I kiss you," to "will you caress my breasts." That's when I stop. I think I've got enough of the picture.

"I see how that really helps build trust between two people," I say, putting my coat on.

"Yes, it's very powerful and very healing."

"So I imagine your clients must fall in love with you."

"Yes," he says. "It's one of the side effects of the job. I have to be very firm with them and keep reinforcing the difference between therapy and a real relationship."

As I pack my notebooks to leave, Lance gently looks at me, adding, "I'm glad you're writing a story about this. It's important for people to know the difference between surrogacy work and prostitution."

"Thanks," I say. "I'm glad I am, too." I head out the door wondering if my work will make a difference. If I can write a story about broken hearts and trust in love regained, and make a difference in just one person's life, then won't that be living a life that matters?

Now if only Hollywood would value *that*. Surely, there must be one Lot among the Sodom and Gomorrah of Hollywood that can help bring these stories to life. And if Hollywood doesn't get it, well, I know Mickey Colucci will.

★ ★ ★

Dusk settles in the sky, shedding pastel hues. Cole and I sit poolside at the chic W Hotel in Westwood. We share a bowl of guacamole and chips under a pair of heat lamps that causes the air around us to shimmer. It's been a month since we've seen each other. Cole has just completed cinematography work on a feature film in New Mexico. His skin is tan. His hair longer, a little more unruly and wild than before. The shimmering air seems to frame his face in a halo. He looks good.

"According to Colucci, one more month and my libido should be back in business," I say with a smile.

Cole laughs, "Should I mark my calendar?"

I share my research on surrogates with him. He listens attentively until I finish and then he showers me with unexpected wisdom.

"Sounds like you need to heal something inside yourself," he says with kindness.

"What do you mean by that?"

"Well, it's just that I don't think anyone creates a screenplay or a book or a poem, or any form of art really, without the need to heal something inside themselves. Even a porn script."

I remain silent, taking it in, remembering the memories I had unconsciously blocked out for so long.

"We all have wounds," says Cole. "That's part of life. It's the reason for the wounds that inspire our gifts in life."

I cock my head at the professional cinematography gear in his bag. "So what inspires yours?"

"Judgment," he replies. "I don't own any. When you don't own or have judgment you get to hold the souls of the world in your palm." He holds up his palms for me, and smiles. "When you don't judge, what's left is trust. Without trust, you can't take someone's portrait. You know what I mean? When you're photographing someone, you have to look into their eyes and they have to let you see into their soul."

"Okay, I have two questions. One. This is really deep stuff and I want to know if you wouldn't mind my using it for my male lead character in *The Surrogate?*"

"No problem," smiles Cole.

"Okay, and two. How does this relate to you and me?" I ask.

He leans in close to me. "I'm not judging you, Laura. You're judging yourself. I think this is all great what you're doing. Writing this story is going to be cathartic for you."

"Where will you be when I come out on the other side?"

"Ah," he says, holding my hand in his. "Have faith, Taylor, have faith."

Friday morning. Six o'clock. I am fast at work on the writing of *The Surrogate* when the phone rings. Tom Kaplan greets me with a sense of urgency in his voice.

"Laura? Sorry to call so early, but we've got a bit of an emergency here. Mickey Colucci needs you back on staff right away."

"Why me?"

"Because you're really talented and he trusts you," says Tom. "You don't judge him. He likes that."

"Gee, thanks."

"You also bring him critical success and a lot of money."

"Thanks for the offer, but I can't do this anymore, Tom. I'm too divided inside. And it's killing my sex life. What's so important that he needs me right away anyway?"

"Cliff Peterson defected to the competition. He's going to Sinful Pleasure Productions. Mickey wants you to take over his position," says Tom.

"He wants me to direct?"

"And write. And produce. I'm just the marketing guy."

"What about Cliff? Is his life in danger?" I ask.

"Why, for quitting his job? Only if he stole from the kitty, which I think he did, so he'll probably be dead in an hour," says Tom.

"Really?!" I ask, petrified, revealing my gullibility.

"I'm kidding, Laura!" shouts Tom. "So when can you come back in? I'll have a vase of flowers waiting on your desk."

"I'm sorry, Tom. I've got to finish this screenplay and repair my libido."

"What do you want me to tell Mickey when his plane lands at LAX?"

"Tell him I promise not to sell his stock for at least two years."

I return to my writing, but ever so slowly, I start to feel the urge to direct. I think of all those college classes I took, writing, directing, and acting, even a comedy improv class. Maybe it was all part of a plan to prepare me for this. Maybe I could have a real hand in transforming the quality of adult entertainment, and well, entertainment in general. What if I could create divisions within the company that each specialized in a variety of genres—adult films that explored family values, social issues, coming of age, and conspiracy theories? Of course, I would have to remove myself from the hard-core sex scenes. But I could leave that to a second unit director. A wave of excitement expands inside me as I begin to consider the possibilities. I look at myself in the mirror. Then I shake my head no. What am I thinking? I'm finally back to being my old self, Laura Taylor. Laura Taylor, I repeat inside my head. My name is Laura Taylor. And I get back to my writing.

An hour later the phone rings. "Laura Taylor," I answer.

"Mr. Colucci would like to speak to Bella Feega," says a strange voice.

"Bella Feega died about an hour ago," I say.

"Then he would like to speak to Laura Taylor about bringing Bella Feega back from the dead. You can perform a séance downstairs in his Lincoln right now."

I look outside my window. The big black car sits on the street outside my building. An oversized chauffeur stands next to it speaking into a cell phone staring straight up at me. I look at my compass. The needle points at my door.

"I'll be down in a minute," I say. I throw on a pair of jeans and a sweatshirt and head over to Adam and Corie's apartment. Corie answers in her pajamas with a toothbrush in hand.

"I have a meeting with Mickey Colucci downstairs, now."

"Do you want me to call the cops if you don't come back in an hour?" she asks, sounding genuinely concerned.

"No. I think I'm going to need an agent. Would you like to represent me?"

"Me? Are you sure you don't mean you need a witness?" she asks through toothpaste mouth.

"Maybe both," I say.

"What are we negotiating?" she asks.

"Some sort of senior creative executive position. I'll fill you in, in the car. Just get dressed and meet me down there."

"Maybe I should bring a hot cup of coffee with me."

"What for?"

"Self-defense. In case we have to throw it on him for a quick escape."

"I'm sure he'll have a nice hot pot of coffee in the car for us."

I saunter over to the Lincoln. The chauffeur graciously opens the door for me and I slide in next to Mickey Colucci as he clips off the end of a fresh cigar. I watch him take the clipped end and slip it in his shirt pocket as a matter of routine.

"Hi, Mr. Colucci. How was your flight?" I ask.

He lifts his lighter to the end of his cigar, snaps a flame to life and sucks on the cigar, causing the end tobacco to crinkle into hot ash.

"Bumpy," he says, shifting for comfort in his seat and puffing the smoke out. "Coffee?"

"Sure, thanks," I say.

The chauffeur pours a hot cup for me. Mickey looks at his watch. "Is an hour long enough for you to reconsider? Or should I come back in another two?"

"Why did Cliff Peterson leave?" I ask. I have learned from Mickey it's best to get right to the point on these matters.

"Why does anyone leave?" he asks.

"Greed. Power. Creative differences. Change of scenery," I say.

"Let's just say it was a little of everything. I wish him well," says Colucci. He pauses. "So what's it gonna take for Bella Feega to come back?" he asks. "And don't tell me you want more than five thousand shares," he adds.

"You're right. I've been thinking," I answer. "And I have some ideas on how this might work."

"Wait," says Colucci. "I got a feelin' I'm gonna need a pen." He turns to the chauffeur, "Sammy, take notes."

A knock on the car window interrupts us. Mickey looks up suspiciously, wondering who it is.

"It's a female with a cup of hot liquid in her hand," says Sammy, the chauffeur.

"That's my agent," I say. "Can you let her in, please?"

Mickey gives me a look, then turns to his chauffeur, "Let her in."

The automatic locks lift and Corie, now dressed in her finest business suit, climbs inside, squeezing next to me.

"Mickey, this is Corie Berman. Corie, Mickey Colucci."

"It's a pleasure to meet you, Mr. Colucci. I've heard wonderful things about you," says Corie, nervously clutching her cup of coffee as the automatic locks click back into place.

"Nice ta meecha, too," he says.

"You can put your weapon down," I tell Corie.

I think I see the slightest curve of a smile on Mickey's mouth, but I can't be sure. Corie puts the cup down and pulls out her pen and paper.

"Here's what I would like." I take a deep breath and plunge in. "I start at $200,000. I get a back-end deal on everything I write and or direct. Production bonuses if they exceed pre-determined sales and rental expectations. I own the copyright on everything I write. By the way, that's standard in Europe. I create an R-rated division to expand the Bella Feega line, so some of the movies can air on cable networks with possible theatrical distribution—domestic and or overseas. And I would like to create a tiny division devoted to adult political satire or conspiracy theories that Lola Stormrider will write."

Between time spent at STA acquiring negotiation techniques and all the acting and speech classes, I hit my stride and it feels good. I continue my roll, "Also, mandatory acting classes for talent with a professional Hollywood acting coach. And lastly, I would like to start a union for adult entertainment writers with real solid health benefits that the Accent Film Company will be the first to join as a signatory—a union that I can fold into the Writers Guild of America six months from now. And I want Lola Stormrider to be its first active member. Come to think of it, when that's done, let's do the same for the talent and create an Adult Screen Actors Guild with pensions, especially for the women. Oh, yeah. And five thousand shares of stock is fine. You got all that?"

"You done?" he asks.

"One more thing. I would greatly appreciate it if you wouldn't smoke cigars in my office—please. If that's agreeable for you, Bella Feega will start right now with a hot new release ready for you next month."

Mickey stares at me, keeping his poker face intact. "You're out of your mind."

"Yes, you're probably right about that, but it's not cheap to raise the dead."

Mickey maintains his poker face and Corie gives us both a strange and apprehensive look, then interjects, referring to her notes, "Excuse me, I think we should bring the salary down to $150K, with an expense account, but with non-exclusive status on anything non-adult. After six months, when company profits jump by ten percent, then you bump Bella up to $200K. You all right with that, Laura?"

"Sure," I say.

Corie continues, "Good. As for the R-rated division, I think it's a great idea and we can make those co-productions contingent upon co-financing deals. Of course, Laura should have a minimum of a 2.5% royalty on all merchandise related to the Bella Feega line, including right of first refusal on any sequels and novelizations. As for the Adult Writers Union, I think you should consider the positive press that will create for you, Mr. Colucci, as a man who cares about the rights of others. It will make you a hero and increase your profit margins."

Corie ends with a rather severe bout of coughing. And for the first time, I watch Mickey stamp his cigar out. He stares at the two of us for a long time.

"Okay...deal," he says. He holds out his hand. We shake.

Upstairs Corie lights a cigarette and blows the smoke out the window looking at the vacant space where the Lincoln sat a moment ago. "What are you doing?" I say, removing the cigarette from her mouth. "You don't smoke."

"Excuse me—but that was just a little stressful. I'm in that huge car with you and Mickey Colucci and we're negotiating your production deal and the dawning of a new Bella Feega empire!"

"Welcome to my world," I say. I sit down next to her. "You were really awesome in there."

"Think so?" she asks.

"No doubt," I reply and then add, "So you think we should write a press release for the trades? I'm sure *Inside Hollywood* will give it front-page status."

Corie rolls her eyes in abject horror. "Just what I need!" she exclaims.

One week later, I am at Orso's, the chic Hollywood restaurant where I had lunch with Elaine Dover. This time, I am having lunch with the legendary acting coach Barry Burnstein, porn stars Tess Knight, Lacey Larson and a hot new handsome adult star named Stiff Wand.

Tess had left the business but I tracked her down. I presented her with my new version of the script, specifically tailored for an adult film, but retaining all the character depth and major plot twists of its originally-intended form as a feature. I gave Tess a persuasive pitch to come on board as the lead and suggested she consider this role as her swan song in the adult world and her possible high-flying entrance into Hollywood. She agreed and joins us now for the production meeting.

We are discussing the rehearsal schedule and acting objectives for the upcoming production of the adult version of *The Surrogate*. Walker Smith has agreed to write the original score in return for the first ten videotapes signed by Bella Feega as part of a limited edition. And Adam Berman has agreed to supply background music at a discount rate. I've hired my sex education production staff and we start shooting in five days. Even Cole generously agreed to help me on this one as my cinematographer.

"I need the three of you to practice your monologues before we meet again," Barry tells the talent. "You're almost there. And, Tess, I want you to study Ingrid Bergman's performance in *Gaslight*. Study how she portrays suspicion."

In the last ten days, Barry has witnessed enough positive results from working individually with the talent that his pride as the prima donna acting coach has returned, even to the point of having lunch with the talent in a Hollywood restaurant.

"Thematically, the arc of the lead character is an emotional roller-coaster ride. It's important to remember that when you shoot out of sequence," adds Barry.

Carter Hamson, a huge film star and onetime student of Barry's appears at our table, politely interrupting us. "Barry, how are you?" he says flashing his irresistible smile.

"Great," says Barry, "and you, Carter?"

"Terrific," he says, curiously eyeing our table. "Got your new protégés with you, I see." He turns to Tess Knight and says, "You look familiar. Have we met?"

Tess shakes her head no. Carter looks at her again, "Are you sure?"

"I'm positive," says Tess.

"Well, you guys are working with the best. He'll make you a star. Good luck." Carter leaves.

We seem to have lapsed into the major Hollywood lunch hour because within minutes Sara Stephenson strolls by specifically asking to be introduced to all the talent at the table. "I'm a big fan of your work," she adds with a knowing smile and a slight touch on my shoulder before walking off.

Larry Solomon, editor of *Inside Hollywood,* marches over; "Laura, good to see you! What are you doing these days?"

"I'm getting ready to direct one of my movies. Let me introduce you to the talent, this is Tess Knight, Lacey Larson, and uh, Stiff." I decide to omit his last name.

"Nice to meet you all," says Larry. "Congratulations."

"And this is Barry Burnstein, he's the associate producer."

"The legendary Barry Burnstein?" asks Larry. Barry nods as humbly as he can.

"I take it you have a green light," says Larry. "What's it about?"

"Um, it's an erotic psychological thriller," I say.

"*Sea of Love* meets *Last Tango in Paris* meets *Basic Instinct,*" Barry confidently adds. "It's a very hot story."

Larry's face lights up with interest. "Which studio's behind it?"

"It's an independent," I quickly interject and before Larry can say another word, his pager goes off. As he reaches for it he adds emphatically, "I'm calling you later for the full story, Laura." And he disappears.

From across the room, seated at a corner table, I see Oliver Kleimeister and Joe Schwartz peering at our table, trying to find out why a celebrity buzz surrounds us. Unable to resist any longer, Joe and Oliver rise from their table and attempt to casually saunter over to ours.

"Laura Taylor, right? How are you?" Joe perfunctorily asks, then turns his back on me and faces Barry, his master's guru, "Hey, Barry, you look great! How are you?"

His blatant attempt to acquire brownie points through Nick's acting coach makes me gag. Tess offers me a glass of water.

"I'm great. How's Nick?" Barry politely responds, always the diplomat in maintaining his relations with the stars and their entourage, yet subtly reminding all that they did not achieve their greatness without him. "He asked me to help him prep for his role as Napoleon. Is that still on?"

"The studio didn't approve of the last draft, so it's in turnaround right now," states Oliver Kleimeister.

"So, uh, why do you guys all look so familiar?" Joe asks gazing at the talent; goggle-eying them would be a more apt description. He's clearly hoping for an introduction.

"Especially you," adds Oliver to Stiff. "Haven't we met somewhere before?"

Stiff proudly smiles as his shoulders roll back to expand his chest. "Maybe you've seen me in some of my movies."

"Which ones?" asks Oliver, intrigued and mesmerized by Stiff's good looks and charm.

Stiff opens his mouth, ready to launch into a litany of his most prized roles.

"They're obscure foreign flicks," I quickly say. "If you don't mind, we're in a production meeting."

"Oh," says Oliver. He looks surprised. Surprised that anyone might rebuff his choice to grace him or her with his presence. "Really? Well, uh, we should set up another meeting and have you come to my office to pitch more of your ideas."

"Yeah," adds Joe, desperate to stay in the mix. "I'd like to hear what else you're working on these days, Laura."

"Sure. But they all have female protagonists. And well, that doesn't work for you."

And for the first time in my nonexistent Hollywood career, I no longer cared if I ever pitched another story to Joe Schwartz or Oliver Kleimeister again. The feeling of liberation engulfs me. I hadn't felt this good since I first stepped into Hollywood. It was my turf now and I planted both feet on it with pride.

"Did you say the Bel Air Hotel, Mom?" I ask from my cell phone, as I go over some notes in my hand.

"It turns out that the Getty can't accommodate the size of the wedding, which has now doubled. George's father has added all of his political cohorts."

"Why is he inviting politicians?"

"He wants to groom George for state assemblyman."

"I can't believe he's turning the wedding into a PR campaign for George, who doesn't even want to be a politician.

Besides, I don't think the Bel Air Hotel will be big enough," I comment, when I'm suddenly interrupted.

"When do you want me to fluff?" asks Annie, the fluff girl.

"Are you at the Laundromat?" asks my mother.

"Um, yes. The machines in my apartment broke so I'm here, getting my laundry fluffed and dried…so uh, let me call you back…'bye, Mom."

I turn my cell phone off and focus my attention on Annie. "Oh. Um. When I leave the set, you fluff," I reply. "But only if Stiff needs it. And can you please ask Ian to freshen up Tess's makeup. Thanks, Annie."

Annie heads toward the stage that the crew converted into a bedroom. I am using it to shoot because Cole has surprised me with the use of a crane shot. The crane will sweep overhead to lend the film some high-end production value. In the meantime, lit candles surround the set creating a warm and comfortable mood.

I turn to Cole to go over the shot list one last time. "I can't thank you enough, Cole. What do I owe you for this?"

"Dinner in Hawaii will do," he says with a wink.

Barry ambles over pressing his hands into his head and groaning. "Well, that's it. I believe I've done all I can. This has been the biggest challenge of my career. If Rex Harrison's character in *My Fair Lady* thought he had it bad—he should try this!"

"You're being a drama king, Barry," I say.

"Well, that is what I am," he laments.

Cole laughs.

"Don't be so rough on yourself, Barry. With the right lighting and a little mood music, Tess and Stiff may show us all your tricks onscreen," I say.

Barry rolls his eyes. "I can't bear to watch it. Is there an extra one of those sex-toy blindfolds around?"

While Barry suits up with a blindfold I approach my talent on the set. "Stiff. You are now Xavier. So remember to think of yourself as Don Juan but without the ego. You are an evolved soul. You honor women. You respect women. And you are falling in love with Tess, I mean Tess's character, Jordan. And she trusts you as Xavier enough to fall in love with you."

Stiff nods his head while simultaneously inflating his chest in an air of conceit, "I'm cool. I got it."

I turn to Tess. "Tess, just remember that when Stiff, I mean Xavier, starts to make love to you, that's when you, Jordan, has her big flashback that we'll add in during post. I'll walk you through it when the time comes." Tess nods with quiet confidence.

I move behind the camera next to Cole and declare, "Action."

Stiff transforms, swiftly taking on the persona of Xavier and looking deeply into Tess's eyes as she converts herself into the vulnerable, beautiful and fragile Jordan.

Stiff/Xavier looks at Tess/Jordan, "It's called the Rating Game. When we touch each other we say what we like using a gradation of minus two to plus two. Plus being positive."

"Why can't a client just say it?" replies Tess/Jordan.

"They never learned how to—that's why they're seeing you—the surrogate."

Stiff/Xavier moves his hand under the sheet. "Tell me how this feels."

She murmurs, "One… Two… Plus two…"

He moves his hand under the sheet some more, "And this?"

Tess/Jordan softly responds, "Plus…two…" She moans, unable to help herself.

Stiff/Xavier studies her face, turned on by her beauty and vulnerability. He kisses her fully and deeply on the lips and murmurs, "And this?"

Tess/Jordan begins to moan now, "Plus ten." He buries his face under the sheets between her breasts as she utters, "Plus fifty."

He shifts again. His mouth covers her breasts. His hand disappears. Both are lost in the moment as we imagine him slip his finger inside her—

Barry cocks his ear toward the set; moved by their acting, he removes his blindfold and intensely watches his protégés, revealing hints of pride on his face.

"Okay, Tess, here's your flashback," I interject, guiding her through a visual meditation. "Inside your head you hear galloping hooves and rhythmic breathing as you gyrate into Xavier... You're riding your horse through woods at dawn. Your horse pounds the trail, hard and fast, as you gallop through green pastures... You arrive at the barn. You begin to open the doors when you see shadows shifting through rays of sunlight. You hear panting. You see the body of a man pull the body of a woman toward him. The man and the woman are lost in the moment of heated passion...just as you now are with Xavier."

At this cue, the crane shot rises above the talent and the monitor reveals Tess and Stiff gyrating into one another.

I continue my descriptive monologue, "Then you see the man tug the woman's hair. Tilt her face back. He buries his lips in the crook of her neck, down to her cleavage as their movements thrust back and forth through soiled air in a dance of lust. You jolt the doors apart. Sunlight splashes through thick clouds upon these lovers. Inside the stables you see—the man is your husband. You stand in silhouette—shocked. Your husband stares at you—guilt and ecstasy smeared across his face. You suddenly remember all of this now—in the arms of Xavier as he pleasures you beneath the sheets. And all these feelings of intense and horrible betrayal come back now—in full force."

Tess's body suddenly jerks forward and shudders in a wake of convulsive tears. Stiff tightly holds her, soothing her, rocking her. "It's okay. It's okay," he says. Tess as Jordan sobs into his arms, "I can't stop crying. I keep seeing him humiliate me."

Barry's eyes widen with a combination of surprise and pleasure at their work.

Stiff looks deeply into her eyes. "It's a release of pain and trauma. You've got fresh scars. Let it all out. It's okay to be vulnerable."

Tess/Jordan, "I'm so embarrassed."

Stiff/Xavier, "Don't be. You're healing. They're tears of grief from denying yourself real intimacy."

Tess continues to cry. Stiff continues to soothingly stroke her. "Your tears are beautiful. They're a celebration that you can experience the depth of all your feelings. That's what's valuable. It's what makes you so attractive."

Tess/Jordan begins to breathe and relax between her sobs. She looks into his eyes, "I've never lost it like this before."

"You didn't lose anything. 'Those who lose themselves in their passion have lost less than those who lose their passion.'"

She smiles through tears, "Who said that?"

"St. Augustine." He pauses. "How do you feel now?"

"Like I've been on a long, long trip. And I've finally come home."

"I'm glad, because I'm falling in love with you."

She looks him in the eye. She's falling back in love. Moments pass. Stiff and Tess kiss, deeply, romantically, like Rhett Butler and Scarlett O'Hara in *Gone With the Wind,* like Redford and Streisand in *The Way We Were.*

The crew remains silent. Tears well up in Barry's eyes. Mesmerized by the magic of acting, we all lose ourselves as we watch the talent unleash their passion in an endless kiss. Cole keeps the camera trained on Stiff and Tess.

"Okay. Uh, you can go full throttle now," I pronounce.

Stiff and Tess start humping away. I turn to Cole. "This is the part where I walk off the set so I can see you later."

"Good job, Taylor," adds Cole.

As I leave, Annie sees me and moves into motion in case Stiff needs a fluff.

True to his word, Cole finds me later that evening in my apartment passed out on my living-room couch. I collapsed there before making it to the bedroom. But I am not so tired that I can't resist his insistence that I accompany him to the roof of my apartment building where he then reveals a bottle of champagne and two glasses against a canvas sky of midnight blue dotted with sparkles of light.

"Time for a toast," he says, popping the bottle open. "To Tay. A writer, a director, a producer, a friend, and so much more, you did...great." He lifts his glass up to me. I shyly lift mine in response and clink to his words. Why am I suddenly timid around this wonderful man? A man who passes no judgment upon me, a man who acknowledges me for what I am, for who I am. He looks at me with knowing eyes. "It's okay, Tay. Okay to feel good about yourself."

"I know. You're right. And coming from you... it's really sweet and wonderful." His eyes are full of kindness and comfort. The moment begs for romance. "May I kiss you?"

"Yes, you may." His eyes twinkle.

We set our glasses down on the ledge, looking each other over as our smiles portray a dance of foreplay.

"How would you like to approach the kiss?" he asks, cracking a crafty smile.

I take in the distance between us, returning his stare with a wily glance. "Will you please take me in your arms...no, swoop me in your arms, and then lean in at approximately a ninety-degree angle, tilting my head toward the moonlight? You know, making it sort of...dramatic. Think Rhett and Scarlett, no, not a good ending, think Gere and Winger in *An Officer and a Gentleman*. No, that's not it. Let's be totally original. Think Tanner and Taylor in a new romantic film, *A Naked Truth*."

He offers up a devious grin and swoops me in his arms, arching my back toward the midnight sky. "How's this?" he asks.

I raise a brow ever so slyly. "That's not ninety-degrees. I believe this is more like sixty-eight degrees."

He locks, loads and returns fire with a lifted brow and a leer, then repositions me at what looks pretty damn close to ninety degrees, "How's this for Take Two?"

I glance around me, and then nod at him and whisper, "Action."

The kiss is long and luxurious. And it does exactly what I hoped for; provide the long-awaited impetus for my libido to respond in the most healthy of ways. The rest of Take Two takes place in my bed.

The next morning I ask Cole if he would like to go with me to my sister's wedding. He is pleasantly surprised and says he would love to go if the date does not conflict with his upcoming shoot in Paris on the new big-budget Eddie Quinn picture about college-aged entrepreneurs.

In addition to being a writer, director, and producer of both porn films and adult sex education videos, I now add to the list a new medium, that of infomercial. Yes, George and Ann had indeed convinced me to do it. Of course, it helped that George insisted on paying me a handsome fee for my work. With the exception of the leather socks, George may not bat high RBIs in successfully adopting products into the marketplace, but he always scored homeruns with the way he treated the people he hired.

In the meantime, I am saving George and Bennett a great deal of money on the budget since I arrange for the shoot to take place on one of the stages of the Accent Film

Company at a premium discount of free. Naturally, I schedule the shoot while George is conveniently out of town and Bennett is conveniently out of the country. Unfortunately, Cole is on location in Paris so I have to hire another shooter, which I figure is for the best. I can't always count on Cole to be there for me when it comes to this stuff.

The only one allowed on set is Walt, since he is after all, the spokesperson, and because he is the only one in my family who knows of my dual identity.

After researching infomercials for two weeks, I prepare for a fairly simple, but meticulous shoot. First, I am sure to conduct a marketing research focus group and then second, include the necessary information that was gathered. In addition, I incorporate a variety of well-branded shots of the leather socks with multiple angles to cut back and forth from, so as to depart ever so slightly from the standard stagnant format. I also have to be sure to include room for graphics and sales order numbers as well as the website address and for proper placement of the distribution channel's logo.

While I go over final adjustments to the copy, my father heads to the kitchen for a cup of coffee where he inadvertently meets Ashley Wade, porn star and spokeswoman for the Whale Dildo. My father notices that Ashley has a slight falling of the left arch, and using his suave Bogart/Robards appeal, combined with his knowledge of feet, therein begins a discussion of proper foot care. Ashley explains to Walt how excessive use of high-heeled pumps, staple footwear in exotic dancing, has taken its toll on her. Walt makes several suggestions and then, upon discovery of her spokesperson talents, invites her to where we're shooting for some pointers on his delivery.

For the next half hour, between multiple takes, I endure watching my father and Ashley's excessive but harmless flirtations with one another until an idea pops into my head. I can't believe I hadn't thought of it earlier.

I turn to Ashley, "How about wearing a pair of the socks for a testimonial?"

My father thinks this is a brilliant idea. Ashley is happy to oblige as long as she can get a free pair of the red leather socks for herself. Between the two of them, instinct tells me this will be a very successful infomercial.

Back at the ranch, Tom Kaplan, two longhaired male editors Brandon and Wolf, the shipping guy Juan, Lola Stormrider, and myself, convene around a rectangular table in the warehouse, which I have set up as a makeshift conference room. As an extra treat, I bring in my own variety of bagels and cream cheese for everyone. It's a pleasant diversion from the usual donuts.

As I pass out pens and paper, I ask Wolf how the editing of the infomercial is coming along. He informs me that the rough cut will be done in a couple of days. Once everyone settles into their chairs with their bagels and coffee, I clear my throat to begin. Lola goes into a coughing fit. Tom hands her a glass of water. I toss her a box of cough drops that I bought especially for her. She smiles heartfelt thanks as I pick up where I started.

"Welcome to the first Accent Film Company Creative Meeting. I want this to be an open forum. Anyone who has an idea for a film is welcome to present it. It can be based on something you've read in a magazine or a book or your own imagination. So let's go around the room. Wolf?"

Wolf shuffles his feet uncomfortably on the floor then looks at me and shakes his head. "I can't think of anything."

"That's okay, maybe next time. Brandon?"

Brandon incessantly twirls the strands of hair hanging next to his chin, like a nervous tick. "Well, I saw this DVD of *Me, Myself & Irene* and I was wondering if you could do a spoof on that and call it *Me, Myself, and my Dick,* about a guy who's totally obsessed with his dick."

"Well, um, I like the way you're thinking, Brandon. I just think that might get to be...repetitive. Juan, any ideas?"

A thin, sprightly guy bounces up and down in his seat. Juan's middle name could easily be Mr. Enthusiasm. "I know, I know," says Juan raising his hand in the air. "What about a flick about a guy who works in the shipping department of a porn warehouse?" His eyes dart across the room for reactions.

"That's a good milieu, but what's the story about?" I ask.

He eagerly gropes for one. "Maybe he puts the porn tapes in the wrong boxes and they go to the church by mistake."

"Okay. It's definitely a good start. Let's mull that one over for a while. Tom? Anything?"

"I've always wanted to see an adult spoof on James Bond."

"Hmmm," I ponder. "How about *Jane Bond?*"

"Ooooh, I love it," exclaims Lola, as she adjusts her lipstick, using the blade of her bagel knife as a mirror.

Tom, Brandon, Wolf and Juan all light up. "That works," says Tom.

"Does anyone know of an adult actress who likes doing her own stunts?"

"Dakota Halston," says Tom, Brandon, Wolf and Juan all together.

"Well, that's a unanimous vote," I say.

"The best news is that she's also British," adds Lola, her eyeglasses resting on the floor of her nose. "I think she could even pull off the deadpan humor."

"Is she under contract?"

"Her contract with Vibrant Video ends in a month," informs Tom.

"Great. Let's attach her to star. We'll do a three-part series. I'll start writing them as soon we complete post on *The Surrogate.* Lola, how's it going on the new *Adam & Eve Undercover* series?"

"Great." She clears her throat between more coughs. "In the first episode, Adam and Eve break open conspiracy theories when they take on regimes that suppress human rights. By using their powers of seduction, they undermine those in power and bring about humanitarian change."

"That is intense, man," says Brandon. For a moment, he stops twirling his hair.

"So, it's like a series to influence politics with sex?" asks Juan.

"That is way cool," says Wolf.

"How are we affording this?" Tom asks, skeptical of the whole thing.

"Stock footage," I reply. "They're meant to have a campy charm."

"Does this really work?" inquires Tom dubiously.

"Remember when the Iron Curtain lifted? Or when the Cuban missile crisis was diverted?" asks Lola.

"That wasn't because of porn films that were shipped overseas," Tom replies.

"Think what you'd like," says Lola, "but just remember, when the government talks *covert,* you have no idea what they mean."

"She has a point there, Tom."

"Well, how am I supposed to market these?"

"We'll drive eyeballs through a limited platform release and a streaming media tease that will go on the company website," I say. "Then we can syndicate the promos through other portals to get started. And for *The Surrogate* we can tie in a sweepstakes for who can identify the murderer before Part II comes out."

Tom nods at me. "Okay. I'm down for that."

Then Lola glances around the table and adds, "I suggest we use unknowns and turn them into stars."

"I agree. But let's get into that once you've finished writing the series. Thanks everyone for participating."

The group breaks up. Lola approaches me, beaming with energy and life. "Bella Feega. Thank you for reviving this old series and for launching the Accent Film Company as the first signatory to an Adult Writers Guild Union."

"Well, it's still a long ways away from coming together. But thanks and you just take care of that cough, Lola."

As I gather my pen and paper to return to my office, I think about how nice it feels to get paid for what you do, and what I was doing was writing. But as nice as it was, I wondered if I would ever make it in the big leagues.

"Where are you?" asks Corie.

I swat at a pillow of wet air in front of me, momentarily revealing my face behind ever-emerging clouds of steam. "Right here," I say. "How do you like it?"

"I love this," says Corie. She takes in a deep breath. "I'll be your agent anytime. Does the spa treatment gift certificate come every time with the completion of principal photography?"

"Absolutely," I reply.

"So...how's it going with Cole?"

"Great. I'm finally getting my equilibrium back. All these adult films wreak havoc on my libido. I'm either in overdrive or underdrive. But he's so patient, not like other guys."

The room overloads with steam again.

"I'm getting hot. Want to soak in the Jacuzzi?" asks Corie.

"Sure."

We exit the plush Burke Williams steam room naked and enter a round sunken Jacuzzi tub. Bubbles percolate around our bodies.

I am treating Corie to an afternoon of relaxation as thanks for her help on my deal with Colucci.

"So when do you get your agent wings?" I ask.

"Who knows? But I did move over to Toby Smith's

desk. At least I'll be able to endure the wait. And no more personal errands to run."

"Do you know if she read *The Law of Malus?* Richard Marksman told me he gave it to her to look at."

"I didn't tell you? She did read it. And she loves it as much as I do."

"What happened?"

"She brought it up at a staff meeting. Eric Leve tried to support her but Jason Brand and Brad Isaacs knocked her down. Those guys are ruthless. They only want their pet projects to happen."

"What else is new?" I dunk my head under the bubbles, blowing breaths out into the churning water. I watch my expelled air, filled with expectations, choke between competing bubbles and dissipate into oblivion. When I resurface Corie looks at me.

"Hey, do you want to go to the Triumph Studios premiere of *Demolishing Devils* tomorrow night?"

"No thanks. I'd rather write *Jane Bond*."

"Jane Bond? Does she seduce foreign agents and save the world?"

"That is exactly what she does. And she thoroughly enjoys it."

As Corie and I exit the spa, located next door to the only vegan restaurant in town, we run into none other than Mitchell Mann holding a take-out bag. No matter how hard I try, I can't seem to escape him.

"How's your movie?" he asks.

"Oh, um, it's good. We're in post. How's your six-picture deal?"

"Oh, that. I decided not to work with the Europeans. They're too complicated."

Corie and I trade looks, more lies.

"So I was wondering if you could write me a script?" asks Mitchell.

"Got money?" I ask.

"I thought you could write it on spec for me and I'll give you a producer credit. How about if I pick you up tonight at seven and we can talk about it over a romantic dinner?" His eyes cast that magic seductive spell on me.

"Well, um, I uh..." I stutter, trying to think of something to say. My mind has a habit of going blank in his presence, like a bad chemical reaction that kills all rational sensibility.

"Speaking as her agent," Corie chimes in, "Laura doesn't do spec scripts anymore. But when you get the financing, Mitchell, please give me a call." Corie grabs my arm and pulls me out of eye contact with him.

When we get halfway down the street, I come to. "Thanks," I say.

"No problem," she replies. "You know, being your agent is getting to be kind of fun. I can't wait for the next episode."

Inside my office, I flip my computer on. While it boots up, I lean back in my chair, gazing at the mountains and contemplating the next scenario for *Jane Bond.* The trades lay at my feet. On the cover of *Inside Hollywood* is the latest news about the Cannes Film Festival. Hmmm, I wonder. I could put Jane Bond at an international film festival as an undercover studio executive in charge of film acquisitions. She has to find the antagonist who buys certain films for certain territories. The films have embedded messages for secret operatives living in those territories. She has to find the distributor, find the filmmaker who implants the codes and thwart the deal. Now, where to lay in the "romance." I know—the films she tracks down are erotic films. And of course, she comes into contact with several sexual encounters in the process of thwarting the filmmaker who must get the "talent" to moan certain sounds in the throes of passion that equal some sort of Morse code. And at one point, she has to follow the bad guy to a swing party and go undercover to seduce him there in order to find out what the "moans" mean. Hmmm, I can also incorporate Mickey's line of sex toys that double as hi-tech defense gadgets. And of course, I can have Jane Bond's signature attire be none other than a pair of skin-tight leather socks.

I am about to transport these ideas to my keyboard when Tom Kaplan leaps into my office with stacks of papers and magazines. His face bears a grin as wide as the San Fernando Valley.

"What's up with you?" I ask, lifting my head from my computer, tearing myself away from Jane Bond's next conquest.

"Check out these reviews!" exclaims Tom. He shoves papers marked with Post-its on them in front of me. "Read these," he shouts.

I pick them up. One by one I read the reviews for the adult version of *The Surrogate.* Each one is better than the next, claiming that the quality in the history of adult cinema has been changed forever by the mark of this film. Each review predicts skyrocketing video rental and sell-through results and hands-down adult awards. They all boast of the film's production value, outstanding talent, remarkable cinematography, unique original score, inspiring story line, and ingenious marketing campaign. Reviewers, buyers, and fans all over are striving to guess who might be the prime suspect. Anticipation for the release of Part II reaches record highs.

"This is incredible," I say.

"That's not all," beams Tom. "Lyle Sherkan found out about this and wants you on his show."

"Me and a TV shock jock?"

"Yep," says Tom. "You. As in Bella Feega you."

"I can't show up on that show as Bella Feega. It will destroy my nonexistent Hollywood writing career."

Tom stares at me, "Exactly. Now it's up to Mickey."

The phone rings. In serendipitous style, Mickey Colucci calls from Connecticut.

"Congratulations, Bella."

"Thanks, same to you."

Tom jumps in on the conversation. "Lyle Sherkan wants Bella Feega on his show. How do you feel about that kind of promotion?"

"Don't mention my name."

"Okay." Tom turns to me and shrugs his shoulders.

"Tom, you're crazy. I can't go on national television as Bella Feega while I'm still Laura Taylor."

"Don't worry, we'll put together a disguise for you, with a wig, maybe a padded bra, just kidding. It will be classy, I promise. Ian Bujinski will do your makeup and no one will know Bella Feega is Laura Taylor."

"Gee, thanks," I say.

That evening Corie and I pore through fashion magazines putting together the public persona of Bella Feega.

"She has to have class," I say, leafing through *Working Women* magazine. "After all, she's not just an award-winning writer of adult films, but a certified sex educator and producer of high-end sex education videos."

"Let's give her some glasses," says Corie. "For an academic appearance."

"That's good," I say.

"Think you can handle a British accent?"

"Yes, I think so," I say copying the British brogue I learned so well from my years with Mitchell Mann.

"Excellent. Should we give her an eye twitch?"

I twitch my eye for her.

"No. It looks too weird. Let's give her a mole on her cheek instead. She can be a cross between Cindy Crawford and Annie Hall."

I stare back at Corie. "I have no idea what that looks like."

"Trust me," says Corie. "I'll sketch it out for Ian. But I do think Bella should wear black leather socks."

The next Saturday I'm at synagogue again exercising my muscles of faith. I open the prayer book. I stare at the words on the page. They stare back at me. I close the book and return it to its pew. I hold my father's compass in my hand, gently massaging its gold casing, and patiently wait for the rabbi's words to inspire me.

Rabbi Weiss stands at the pulpit and speaks to the congregation about the one constant in life. "Things change," he says. I smile at the words. How apropos. "They are always changing, and change is what challenges our faith. We have a choice. We can embrace change and renew our faith in order to find and express the greatest light within ourselves or we can wallow in denial and resistance. I propose we embrace change. It's a much happier lifestyle. Trust me on this."

The congregation chuckles en masse. Richard Marksman slips into the seat next to me, and grins. "Hey, you. What's the sermon about?"

"Hey back. Hmmm… Identical themes as *The Law of Malus.* So how come it can't get made, Richard?"

Richard sighs. He looks at me with genuine sincerity. "Doesn't matter how much you push, pull, or package, you know. I learned that long ago. The universe is what gives birth to stories that turn into movies. Agents are only midwives."

"Agents are only midwives," I repeat. "Sounds like a title for a bad novel."

He smiles at me and then sees the compass twirling between my fingers.

"Lose your way again?"

"You know, Richard. I don't think I ever lost it. I'm just on a more circuitous route than most other people. And it makes life a lot more adventurous and a lot more interesting."

Richard turns to look at me. His eyes reveal a renewed sense of respect.

"By the way," I whisper, "Bella Feega will be on the *Lyle Sherkan Show* next week. But don't be surprised if you don't recognize her."

Richard gazes at me. He gently nods his head up and down. Thinking.

"All rise for the Shema," says the rabbi. The congregation stands to repeat the most holy of prayers together. I cover my eyes and sing the words that bring me to a place of repose, at least for a minute or two.

After the service concludes and the blessings are said over the bread and the wine, Richard Marksman and I march around the block as per our usual course of action.

"So what's the subject matter on the *Lyle Sherkan Show?*" he asks curiously.

"The outrageous success of the adult version of *The Surrogate.*"

"What makes it an outrageous success?"

"Numbers—500,000 units in the first four weeks. They can't make duplicates fast enough and they can't ship them fast enough. There's a huge demand in Europe, too. Apparently they're making dubs in foreign languages. That's a first for an adult film."

We come to our usual turnaround corner, but this time Richard turns to me. "Let's go another block or two." I freeze in place. This is a first. He has never taken more than thirty minutes after synagogue to walk with me. And right now we're passing the thirty-five minute mark. He points to the right. We turn and continue walking.

"How much does one videocassette sell for?" asks Richard, eager to do the math.

"Thirty dollars a box. And that's just for Part I."

"That's fifteen million dollars!" exclaims Richard. For the first time during my relationship with him, I hear his voice rise in pitch. "How much did it cost to make?"

"$500,000 and shot on film, I might add. The largest budget ever for an adult film."

"That's incredible." His voice returns to its normal tenor.

"And by the way, that's only the adult market. I plan to edit the original R-rated version and sell that to cable networks."

"Who's repping you on these deals?"

"Corie Berman."

"Who's Corie Berman?"

"She works for you. She was an assistant to Jason Brand, now Toby Smith. Corie's awesome. She helped me negotiate my overall deal."

"But she doesn't have a license yet," says Richard.

"In my industry she doesn't need to." I realize that I have just said the word "my," and that by using that one two-letter word, I have accepted that I am more a part of the adult industry than the Hollywood one, which I have strived so long and so hard to be a part of.

"Why wouldn't you come to me?" asks Richard, surprised that I didn't even try.

"Well, you weren't around at seven on a Friday morning to sit in a big black Lincoln to discuss the matter."

Richard stops and looks at me again. "You have a point there."

"I can't wait for busy midwives, Richard. I need availability and loyalty and that's what Corie gives me. She's the best."

"I hear you," says Richard. And all the way back to our cars, I know his brain is working overtime.

take thirteen

MERGING WORLDS

Ian Bujinski applies blush to my face. I stare at myself in a large mirror framed by bare lightbulbs. We're inside a TV studio's makeup room. I look all dolled up in a blond wig, hair slightly teased, black scholarly glasses, a mole on the bottom of the left jawline, with a wardrobe that makes me look like a college professor who just stepped off a Ralph Lauren runway. I don't recognize myself anymore. Besides the outspoken outfit, the eyeliner, mascara, eye shadow, blush, lip liner, lipstick and fake polished nails, all conspire to make me something I'm not. I glance in the mirror again trying to find the tomboy I once knew who blossomed into a nice Jewish girl who moved out west and became someone I no longer know.

"Okay, that's good enough, Ian. You can stop now. I just want to look natural."

"Any less and it won't look like you have any makeup on at all," he says, blending the blush in across my cheeks.

A kicking sound knocks against the door. "Can you open it up?" says Corie from the other side. Ian reaches over and opens the door. Corie shuffles in, balancing three cappuccinos in both hands.

"Here you go. They didn't have decaf, which is just as well. You might as well be on major alert."

"I'm afraid I might talk too much on the caffeine," I reply.

"You'll be fine, just remember not to mention anything about Mickey."

"Don't talk," says Ian, as he applies a red shade of lipstick on my lips.

"Wow. You look…different…it's really…nice," says Corie.

"It's not too much?" I ask.

"Well, maybe just a little."

"But she needs this under the lights," remarks Ian. "Trust me."

"Where's Cole?" asks Corie.

"He's on location in Paris for the next month."

"Why do you always pick unavailable men?"

"I don't know. Maybe I'm not ready for total availability or maybe I'm not totally available myself yet."

A production assistant pops his head in the door.

"Bella Feega. Lyle's ready for you. Follow me."

Corie, Ian and I traipse onto the set. Corie and Ian stand behind the cameras while I am escorted to the chair next to Lyle Sherkan. As I sit down, I wipe the lipstick off my face. Bella. Laura. Bella. Laura. It's all so confusing.

Twelve minutes later I stomp out of the room. Corie and Ian look at me with astonishment on their faces.

"That took guts," says Ian, with an expression of shock plastered on his face.

"Talk about a mock job on a mock jobber," says Corie.

"I hope it teaches him a thing or two about the golden rule," I spit out.

"You do know mockery is his shtick, don't you?" asks Corie, rhetorically.

"So," I reply, defiant and proud, like Scarlett O'Hara.

"By the way, nice job on sidestepping the mob questions," adds Ian.

"I can't believe you stormed out on him in the middle of an interview," comments Corie, still reeling from the battle of verbiage between Lyle and me.

"Neither can I," I say. "Can we please get out of here?"

But before we exit the doors, there's a flash of light, and a guy with a camera takes off out of sight.

The next day, I am sitting in my office draped inside a blanket, licking my wounds and sipping a hot cup of tea with milk. Across from me on my desk lies an article from *Inside Hollywood* with a photo of a very pissed-off Bella Feega next to a haughtily stunned Lyle Sherkan. The header reads, Bella Feega Shocks Shock Jock.

Tom leans back in the chair across from me. "Hey, you did the right thing. You stood up for your integrity."

"You sure?"

"Yeah. Besides, you know the old adage, bad press is still good press. And Mickey's proud of you. He thinks you've got balls."

"I don't want balls. I want respect."

The phone rings. I hit the speaker button. "Bella—I mean Laura Taylor."

"This is the *James Mallik* show. We'd like to know if we could have Bella Feega on our show for a serious and respectful interview about her work."

Tom and I stare at each other. We are both speechless. Wow, the top broadcast journalist of the top news show of the top cable network. There's no one this guy hasn't interviewed, except God—but I wouldn't put it past him.

One week later, I am seated as Bella Feega in the makeup room of the *James Mallik* show. At the moment I am alone with my thoughts. Never did I expect my notoriety to come from pornography. I look at my reflection in the mirror.

There's a knock on the door. "Come in," I say, flexing my British accent.

A young production assistant enters with a beautiful bouquet of red roses. "These are for you, Ms. Feega." I open the attached card. Inside reads, "Dear Bella Taylor, Good luck with the interview. Love & Faith, Cole." I take in the fresh scent of the roses and smile.

Within minutes I find myself on the set seated across from James Mallik. Corie, Tom and Ian stand behind the cameras. Tom gives me a thumbs-up sign.

Backstage, Corie, Tom and Ian greet me.

"How was it?" I ask, exhausted.

They are all beaming with pride. "I got a call from Juan in shipping. Our sales just went through the roof again," exclaims Tom.

"And I just got a call from Richard Marksman. He wants to know if you would let the two of us represent Bella Feega and sell the mainstream rights of *The Surrogate* to Hollywood?!" declares Corie, in shock and amazement.

I shake my head in wonderment and glance up at the ceiling above me. How did all of this happen? Am I any more talented than before? Or is it the wonders of a little PR?

That night, I soak in my ritual bubble bath with organic bath salts, bath gels and a loofah sponsored by Eva, via Bath & Body Works. A variety of burning candles decorate the bathroom. A stick of my best incense smolders nearby. I sink farther into the bubbles happy to shut out the whir of today's activities when the phone rings.

Cole calls during production from the location site in Paris to see how the interview went and to tell me that he'll be able to make my sister's wedding after all, but barely. His plane lands as the wedding starts. If I still want him to, he'll come straight to the reception. I tell him that would be great and thank him for the lovely roses. I'm about to inform him of Bella Feega's new makeover for the public when we are cut off by the demands of production. His skills to paint with light are needed on set and have become the greater priority of the moment. I hang up thinking about needs. They are always shifting to accommodate basic tenets of survival to achieve our overall lofty goals, but at their core, they exist as self-esteem builders. Cole had a need to do his job well and thus earn money to satisfy more needs that all unite to make him feel good about himself. Even taking care of others is a way to feel good. I have a need to write because it feeds my soul as a means of self-expression, and now, what I've written has brought entertainment to the public, cash flow to Laura Taylor's bank account, and a bit of fame to my alter ego. Perhaps Bella Feega needed that, needed the recognition to justify the role she played. Just like Laura Taylor needed to satisfy cleansing her soul with long hot baths. I wish there was a way for me to merge the needs together for I was getting tired of feeding two souls to satisfy one. What was strange was that Bella Feega had clearly accepted her role in society as a sex writer-educator in the porn world. But Laura Taylor couldn't accept herself for the very same role. I've become my worst nightmare—a hypocrite. There has to come a time and a place where Laura Taylor will accept herself and her needs simply because they are that. When would the need for approval stop and the easy joy of self-acceptance begin?

The phone rings and I pick it up thinking maybe it's Cole

again. Maybe the production needs shifted to someone else, thus giving him time to satisfy other needs of his. But it's Ann, needing to express her reaction to the interview she just witnessed.

"Laura, did you see your friend on TV? I loved what she said, about how her research with sex surrogates changed her whole perspective on the way Americans view sex and that we need to emerge from our puritanical culture and openly embrace the pleasures of sexuality, or at least not judge those who do. I really want to meet her and thank her for what she's given me."

"Okay, Ann. I'll try to get hold of her, but I think she's left town again. Hold on." There's a click signaling call waiting. I switch over. It's Elaine Dover and she has also just seen the broadcast.

"I know you know that woman," she says. "How do I reach her?"

"Hold on." I switch back to Ann. "I have to call you back." I switch back to Elaine. "Why?" I ask.

"I want to talk to her about writing an erotic thriller for us," exclaims Elaine.

"Oh. Well, I think she's on a plane back to Wales or the East End of London. But I think she signed with Corie Berman at STA if you want more information."

I hang up but the phone rings again and this time it's my father. "Honey, did you see James Mallik's show tonight? That woman said she wrote your film *Things Change.*"

Corie and Ian obviously did a superb job with the costume and makeup. "Don't worry about it, Dad. It's okay. I know her, and well, she did help me out quite a bit in the writing of the film, so it's all right."

"Okay," says Walt. "I just hate seeing you get taken advantage of, in any industry you're in. You're always helping everyone else and it never seems like anyone else helps you in return. See you tomorrow night, hun."

"Right, Dad. Good night. And thanks for looking out for me."

"I'm always looking out for you. Every night I visualize a white light around each of you kids, to protect you."

"You do?"

"Yes, I do, Laura. I only want the best for all of you."

We hang up. Instead of feeling clean and whole, however, I feel the dirt of deception on my skin.

The next morning, I discover that the Accent Film Company celebrates momentous occasions with three boxes of assorted donuts from a famous little donut shop in Fairfield, Connecticut called Mary Davis Donuts, compliments of Mickey Colucci.

Tom stands in the hallway near my office picking at a chocolate-covered donut and dunking it in his coffee.

"What is it with Mickey Colucci and donuts?" I ask as I enter my office.

Tom shrugs as he follows me to my desk and attacks the cream inside his donut. "This has only happened twice now in the seven years I've been here, once when the company went IPO and now. I think he may have wanted to own a donut shop or something when he was a kid."

"Have you ever seen him eat a donut?" I ask as I drop my bags of notes, scripts, and combined industry trades next to my chair.

"Never," replies Tom. "By the way, your phone hasn't stopped ringing all morning."

Two lines start ringing at once, then a third, and then a fourth. I glance at the blinking lights then back at Tom, "We need a receptionist here."

"I just hired one. She's out front. Her name is Jodie. She's going to answer the phones and help send out electronic press kits for the movies."

"How did you manage that?"

"Mickey gave me a revised marketing budget after yesterday."

A sprightly, pretty, young athletic-looking girl of about twenty pops her head in my office. "Excuse me, I have messages for you, Ms. Feega."

I cringe as Tom chuckles through an introduction. "This is Jodie. Jodie, Bella Feega."

"Hi, Jodie. You can call me Laura. Laura Taylor."

"Oh." She looks confused as her eyes dart back and forth between Tom and me. Then she shakes it off. "Okay. Was that Bella Taylor or Laura Feega?"

"It's Laura Taylor," I say slowly and carefully.

"Okay. Got it. Laura Taylor. Well, um, where can I find Bella Feega? I have this stack of messages for her—"

"You can give all of Bella's messages to me," I say.

"Okay. Sure." Jodie walks all the way in the office, revealing a perfect body. I glance at Tom. He shrugs his shoulders at me.

"So, Jodie. What are your aspirations? Do you want to be an actress?" I ask.

"Oh, no. I'm here to learn about marketing."

"That's terrific. Do you have a background in marketing?"

"I had the most successful lemonade stand on my block."

"How'd you do that?"

"I included free wet T-shirt throws after every tenth glass of lemonade." Tom and I exchange more glances.

"That's pretty clever," I say, duly impressed.

"After that, I put my brother's homemade snowboard business online and made him a millionaire in ten months. But then he lost it all on a bad real estate deal."

"So you'll be able to help Tom spruce up the online marketing plan."

"Oh, I have two initiatives I'm working on right now for him."

"Great. So, what are my, I mean, what are Bella's messages?"

Jodie takes a big deep breath and then plunges ahead rapid-fire-like, "Sara Stephenson. Janine Tate from Maestro. Eric Leve, Brad Isaacs, and Toby Smith from STA. Natalie Moore from OTA. Joe Schwartz, Oliver Klemenster—I think that's right, and Jeremy Kincaid from Peak Films. Hank Willows from Satellite. Larry Solomon at *Inside Hollywood.* Corie Berman and Richard Marksman from STA. And two producers named Roger Carson and Darlene Green. The executives want to talk to you about the mainstream rights to *The Surrogate* and the agents want to come by and meet with you regarding representation. Oh, and Lola Stormrider's in the lobby waiting to see you." Jodie catches her breath when she's done and checks the second hand on her watch. "Twenty-one seconds."

Her words blur together like a hurricane of sound. I am barely able to decipher their meaning. "Was that like a new extreme sport or something? What would you call that, Word Racing?"

"I call it Efficacious Message Relay," says Jodie.

"Oh. Okay. Do me a favor. Please call all the studio executives back and tell them that my agent is Corie Berman at STA and they should talk to her directly. And do not under any circumstances tell them that Bella Feega is Laura Taylor. But first please bring Lola in. Oh, and can you try not to extreme sport it, unless you want to practice the Enunciation Comprehension Message Relay?" I smile at her.

"Now that sounds dope!" declares Jodie as she exits the office.

I pull out a bag of cough drops and place them on my desk as Jodie leads Lola into my office. Lola enters, lugging a large book bag with her. She smiles and cheerfully drops it on my desk.

"Here they are, the first four episodes in the series," says Lola. "In terms of genre, I would call it a 'modern-day espionage series.'"

I pull them out to peruse their titles; *Adam & Eve Undercover at the United Nations, Adam & Eve Undercover at the International Economic Summit, Adam & Eve Undercover without the Curtain, Adam & Eve Undercover without the Wall.* "I can't wait to read these, Lola."

"I hope you like them," she replies. "I did an extensive amount of research as far as our current foreign policies are concerned."

"Once they're approved we can ask Jodie to help find the right stock footage. Then we'll start casting with new talent." I suddenly realize that Lola no longer coughs. "Hey, you're not coughing."

"The health benefits finally kicked in and the doctor gave me the right medications and antibiotics. I haven't felt this good in years," she says.

Two hours later, Corie and Richard Marksman drive over to see me. They timidly step around the reception area, fascinated by the display of latest releases from AFC, and the Lucite-encased red leather socks.

I watch them and shake my head. "Can I get you guys a care package to take home?"

They sheepishly smile back at me and stick their hands in their pockets while I give them the grand tour, including the editing room where Brandon and Wolf cut together Part II of *The Surrogate.* Corie and Richard become oblivious to all conversation when the hard-core sex starts to play.

"I think they're in a trance or something," says Brandon, still twirling his hair below his chin as Tess gives Stiff a blow job on screen.

"Maybe you should minimize Tess and Stiff for now so we can beam Corie and Richard back to earth," I suggest.

Wolf clicks the scene into the bottom bar and Corie and Richard finally come to again.

Back in my office, Corie and Richard go over the offers

on the table for the mainstream version of *The Surrogate.* The best offers come from Janine Tate at Maestro Films and Sara Stephenson at Eagle Pictures. Janine and Sara want to join forces and make it a co-production deal with STA helping package the picture. I tell Corie and Richard to go for it. Maybe the deal will go and maybe it won't, but I can't let those desires dictate my world anymore. Then I ask them how I am to get around face-to-face story meetings.

"Don't worry about that," says Richard. "Bella Feega will make one appearance walking down the halls of STA for a follow-up meeting. All the agents will then vouch for her existence. After that, she'll always be traveling but available for conference calls."

"All you have to do is keep up the British accent," adds Corie.

"Isn't this just a little on the deceitful side?" I ask.

Richard shrugs. "They did it in *Tootsie.*"

"That was a movie," I remind him.

"And this is show business," he adds.

"I checked with business affairs," adds Corie. "There's nothing illegal about it or I wouldn't be doing it."

"Legalities aside, what about ethics?" I ask.

"Ethics in Hollywood?" asks Richard. "That's an oxymoron, and the reason why I go to synagogue. Remember what the rabbi said, only by doing, committing fully to your actions, will you come to understand them."

"Right," I say.

Later that night, I call Cole in Paris and leave him a message. It is the first time that I tell him I miss him.

The Four Seasons Hotel in Beverly Hills is the perfect posh place for the fancy pre-wedding cocktail party in honor of Ann and George's imminent wedding. George's father, Austin Stern, hosts it. The place is packed with relatives on both sides plus a mere hundred state and local politicians.

Bennett still refuses to talk to me. In preparation for tonight's event, I couldn't bring myself to wear the outfit he had picked out for me two years ago. Instead, Corie helped me find a killer sexy, classy outfit at a boutique on Sunset Plaza, one that I happily splurged on. I can tell I look hot because Bennett does a triple take before moving in a different direction from me. Walt and Eva do their best to tell him to stop this ridiculousness, but as Ann points out, only the fall of fashion could change Bennett's opinion about anything once he's made his mind up.

Aside from Ann's demure affections toward George, he looks absolutely miserable. He finds me in the crowd and grabs my hand. "You look amazing, Laura. I've never seen you look so…gorgeous. You even have makeup on."

"Thanks, George," I say, realizing that all the time spent watching Ian Bujinski prep adult actors on shoots hadn't been for nothing. "I thought a party in yours and Ann's honor deserved as much," I add.

"Come on. You did this for us?"

"Not really. I thought I'd get a syllable or two out of Bennett."

"Oh, don't pay attention to him. He's got too much pride to even tell you how great the infomercial looks. You know it's going to air next month on cable."

"That's great, George. So how are sales doing?"

Ann enters and exclaims, "Rapidly climbing. Ever since Bella Feega wore them on James Mallik's show and talked about them being bundled into *My Red Vibe Notebook,* sales have gone through the roof. Isn't it strange that the woman who unwittingly saves our marriage happens to wear the product that George invested in?"

"That is…really a coincidence," I reply.

"She's amazing," says Ann.

"Yeah," says George. "She's helped one of my ventures finally take off."

"That woman is a disgrace," pipes in Austin Stern, as he suddenly expands our little gathering. "And I'm appalled that my son invested in such a preposterous thing as leather socks, that is with all due respect to Walt and Bennett. George needs to put his focus on politics and less on flimsy fashion trends."

George, as expected, backpedals to his father's views, reminding me once again why I couldn't be with him, "Well, okay, Dad, the venue for her work does discredit herself and offend certain political views but don't you think she's entitled to share her ideas…"

At this, I take my cue and try to squeeze out of the growing circle of opinionated gatherers, but the crowd thickens and I can't quite find an alleyway fast enough.

Ann looks to me, "Laura knows her. She can vouch for the woman's character, can't you, Laura?"

"Me?"

"Laura. You associate with a woman like that?" asks Austin, revealing his gift for making you feel insignificant. I never said George didn't have an uphill battle in standing up for himself against his father's wishes. Outthinking Austin was the only offense I had.

"Well, um, yes, I do, Mr. Stern. And I can tell you that Bella Feega has a master's degree from one of the big universities in England. Cambridge, I think. But more important than her views on sex, she is helping make George a successful entrepreneur, the kind that can legitimately finance his own political campaigns in the near future."

Austin takes a moment to consider the savings this will have on his personal bank account and emits a guttural "hmmph," followed by a "you have a point there," which is quickly evaporated by "writing sexually explicit content is still wrong."

At this I remain silent. It's difficult to separate from and defend myself at the same time, when Ann suddenly ventures a bold reaction.

"Excuse me, Austin, but the underlying subtext of her films promote self-esteem for women and her education videos promote strong family values," retorts Ann. "And those are what your party stands for."

Before Austin can respond to Ann's display of increased self-esteem, another voice unexpectedly chimes in. "Besides, you do support our First Amendment don't you, Mr. Stern?"

Austin, George, Ann and I all turn to see who has suddenly joined our debate. It's Larry Solomon, standing next to us with a martini and a press pass. He smiles at me. "Good to see you, Laura." Then he addresses the rest. "Hello. Larry Solomon, editor of *Inside Hollywood* and former English professor of Laura's. Congratulations to you both."

"Larry, what are you doing here?" I ask.

"Since the ceremony is to be the first live broadcast of The Wedding Channel, it's now a media event, hence my presence."

"Your wedding is going to air on a new reality show?" I ask Ann and George, astonished.

"It was my idea," Austin proudly announces. "Show George as a stable family man in preparation for his run as state assemblyman."

"Nice. Doubling the wedding for both matrimony *and* campaign aspirations," I say in mock deference.

Ann rolls her eyes indicating it's not something she condones.

"It will only be the ceremony and the speeches at the reception. Nothing more, right, Dad?" adds George.

"I'd say it's a good investment," comments Larry. "Live from the Bel Air Hotel."

"Actually, live from the Bel Age Hotel now," says Austin.

"Any more guests and it will be live from the L.A. Convention Center," adds Ann.

"So who has the speaking honors? And do we assume they won't be censored, even for live TV?" asks Larry, ever so slightly goading Austin Stern, for what purpose I cannot discern.

Austin turns to Larry and addresses him, "Larry, are you implying that I'm not for freedom of speech? Because that woman's work, if you will, goes against our national obscenity laws."

"That's a matter of opinion. I've actually seen her work. She has quite a literary style, even making references to some of the classics I taught at Michigan. I was rather impressed to tell you the truth. In fact, if you really want to make a political statement to advance George's run for state assemblyman, I think you should invite her to the wedding. She is after all, indirectly connected to his current business venture."

"That is a great idea," Ann agrees excitedly. "I can't wait to meet her."

"I'm not so sure about that," says George, receiving a direct hit from his father's glare.

"That is a horrible idea," I shriek. "For one thing she's on location on some remote island, off of South Africa, I think." But no one's listening.

"Why not?" asks Larry, adding fuel to his reasoning. "Show that George is a savvy capitalist capable of strong leadership with business acumen, open to the coincidence of good marketing even if it comes from porn. Pardon the pun."

"So you think having this woman appear at his wedding will increase his chances for winning?" challenges Austin.

"I'd stake my own personal editorial view on it," states Larry. "I'm sure *Inside Hollywood* would find it a great front-page article, especially as an exclusive."

Austin digests the innuendo in a flash and before I know it, he turns to Ann and George, "Let's invite her." Then he turns to me. "I'll pay whatever it costs to get her to the wedding."

"Why is everyone looking at me? What if I can't find her?"

"She has an agent, doesn't she? Everyone in this town does," huffs Austin.

"Yes. She's with STA," I respond.

"Fine. I'll handle it myself," Austin says and then turns and leaves.

"There is no way Bella will go to someone's wedding she doesn't even know," I whine to Ann and George.

"If you made her an honorary spokesperson for Leather Footish she would," pipes in Larry. "Plus she'll get good PR for her films and videos on The Wedding Channel. The network expects twenty million viewers."

"Larry, do you have to add a PR angle to everything you say or do? What happened to your views on Marxism and literary criticism for God's sake?"

"I lost it somewhere between the Vegas strip and Hollywood Boulevard," he smiles.

"You are such a sellout. What? If you can't find a good story you have to create it?"

Larry nods, downs the rest of his martini, and quotes, "Necessity knows no law."

"Don't you dare bring St. Augustine into this. And it is not necessary to wag the dog here."

"But..." he quotes again, "Advertisements contain the only truth to be relied on..."

"Please leave Thomas Jefferson out of this, Larry. This is not something you can justify by what others have said before you."

Larry shrugs his shoulders, "I think it's time for a refill." He walks off toward the bar. I turn back to Ann and George.

"You guys have to forget this idea. It's a really bad one. Besides, it's Bennett's socks. And he would hate having Bella Feega near him," I cry.

"It doesn't matter, Laura. Austin always gets his way," says George.

"You are such a defeatist, George," I cry some more.

"Actually, when it comes to his father, that comment would make him a realist," says Ann.

The STA lobby that had once felt so daunting now feels familiar, even inviting, as I announce myself as Bella Feega at the front desk the following day. My outfit affords me a different persona and a whole new attitude, one of quiet confidence, because the receptionist acts not only politely, but immediately as she alerts Corie Berman that I have arrived. Before I can even sit down on the couch, as I have done in the past, an assistant arrives to guide me to Corie's new office. As I walk down the halls as Bella Feega, everyone stares at me the way the paparazzi once did on the beach in Cannes when they thought I was *someone.*

Since Bella Feega's appearances on Lyle Sherkan and James Mallik and the subsequent articles about her in the press, Richard Marksman made sure that Corie was promoted to junior agent with her own office and her own assistant. She proudly shows me her new environs decorated with simple rustic pine furniture, adorned with one photo of her and Adam and one of me. All along the walls of the office lean four-foot-tall stacks of spec screenplays seeking birth into Hollywood.

She shuts the door to her office and beams, "What do you think?"

"It's great," I reply, happy to slip into my regular voice. "I'm flattered that you have a photo of me in here."

"How could I not? Without you, who knows how long it would have taken me to become an agent, if ever."

"Listen, Corie. I have to talk to you before we see Richard," I urge. "I've been invited to appear at Ann and George's wedding."

"You're her sister. Of course you're appearing."

"No, I mean as Bella Feega. I'm a pawn in a political challenge. What am I going to do?"

"What? How did this happen?"

"It's a long story. But not only that, the wedding is going to be on television."

"I know, I know," she says. "I read about it in *Inside Hollywood*. It's the talk of the town. Everyone will be watching. If it scores high on the Neilson ratings, can you imagine the field day advertisers will have? Sex or private lives, that's what sells."

Just then, we are interrupted by a voice coming from Corie's intercom. "Excuse me, Corie. State Assemblyman Austin Stern is on the phone and needs to speak to you."

Corie gives me a look of surprise. I give her a look of utter anguish. She lifts her finger to her mouth motioning for me to keep quiet. "Okay, put him through," she says and then hits another button.

"Hello, Mr. Stern. This is Corie Berman. How can I help you?"

"I'm inviting your client, Bella Feega, to my son's wedding tomorrow for a personal appearance."

"That's very kind of you, but Ms. Feega is…about to leave the country."

"How much will it cost to delay her trip?"

"That's really not the question, Mr. Stern. Ms. Feega simply does not give public appearances. She's a very private person."

"Remind me to hire you when I'm looking for an agent, Ms. Berman. You're very good. Now let's get down to numbers."

"Really, Mr. Stern. I'm flattered that you think I'm deploying negotiating tactics right now, but I'm really not."

"Why, you're better than a politician, Ms. Berman," he laughs. "How about fifty thousand dollars for an hour of her time?"

Corie and I exchange looks. I shake my head no. "I'm sorry, Mr. Stern. But she's not going to be interested. Besides her speaking phobia in front of large crowds, she's not very good at…uh, mingling…"

"One hundred thousand dollars for thirty minutes. All she has to do is sit at her table. And if you'd like, you're welcome to accompany her."

"Thirty minutes? That's all? And she doesn't have to get up and speak?"

"Not a peep," says Austin.

Before Corie can see my hands wildly waving no, she replies, "Fifteen minutes and the table in the back of the room, Mr. Stern."

"Deal," he says.

"See you tomorrow night." She hangs up and looks at me.

"What are you doing?"

"Laura. That's a lot of money. You can give it all to charity if you want. Look, don't worry. I'll cover for you. I'll meet you at the wedding as Bella's agent. I'll say that Bella's on her way and just when she needs to show up, you can do a quick change in the bathroom. That way I can cover for Bella when Laura's around and for Laura when Bella's around. All you have to do is sit for fifteen minutes and nod your head in acknowledgement of any references to your work and then slip back into Laura. Now take a deep breath and relax."

I breathe in and out, calmed by the fact that Corie will be there.

"By the way," she continues. "Before I forget to tell you, I submitted *The Law of Malus* to Rand Chessick. He's now a junior creative exec at ASE and he really likes it."

"Thanks, but I won't hold my breath," I respond, taking in another deep breath with a long exhale.

"You never can in this business. But you can manipulate the heat to create the deal."

"Is that what you've been learning on your way up the ranks here?"

"Under the tutelage of Richard Marksman. Thanks to you."

Her assistant shouts from the hallway, "Corie, Eddie Quinn is on the line."

Corie hits her intercom button and sweetly replies, "Please tell him I'll call him back in an hour and please hold all my calls. Thank you so very, very much."

I raise my eyebrows at her. Corie shrugs her shoulders. "I'm very conscious about being polite to my assistant. If I ever become like Jason, kick me."

"I don't think you have to worry about that," I reply.

"Come on, we can't be late. We're meeting Richard in the conference room to go over Bella's deal."

Ah, the conference room, I remember, my old stomping grounds during the STA Creative Meetings. The room I refer to as power central, where ideas spark into flames, where careers are born, where careers die, and if they're lucky get reborn again.

We're about to leave Corie's office when she notices my mole is missing. We scurry around her office searching for it and finally find it stuck to my coffee mug. Corie reapplies it on my cheek only to realize it's now on the wrong side of my face.

"Fuck it," says Corie. "Let's just walk fast through the halls."

As Corie and I pace toward the conference center, we pass Eric Leve's office. Brad Isaacs leans over Eric's desk discussing a client's deal point when they see Corie and I passing by. They immediately drop their conversation to shower me, as Bella Feega, with attention.

Eric cajoles, "It's a pleasure to meet you, Ms. Feega. I'm a big fan of your work. In fact, I wanted to thank you."

"Why is that?" I ask, laying on the British brogue.

He leans in and whispers, "I think your tapes saved my marriage."

"I'm delighted for you," I reply, perhaps making the accent a bit too thick by the glance Corie shoots me.

"Just one question, if you don't mind my asking you in private..." He whispers out of earshot from Corie. "What do you do if you love your wife, but you've got intense sexual fantasies about someone else that just won't quit? Going on four years. A former assistant of mine."

I look him over and then reply tartly, "You get over it, Mr. Leve. You simply get over it."

"Oh. Thanks," he sheepishly grins. "You remind me of someone."

Before I can respond, Corie politely tells them that Richard's waiting for us and she pulls me away.

Corie and I enter the conference room and shut the doors. Richard Marksman stands near the window, pouring himself a fresh cappuccino. "Hey, Laura, hey, Corie. Would you like one?"

"Sure, thanks," says Corie.

"I'll pass," I say. "I can't have another disappearing mole."

Richard passes an STA mug of cappuccino to Corie. After a few moments of chitchat, he sits down and begins, "Corie, since you're the leading agent on this, why don't you start."

Corie pulls out her notes and dives in. "We think the best offer is still the co-production deal between Eagle Pictures and Maestro with Sara Stephenson and Janine Tate. It's $300,000 against $750,000 with a back-end percentage of 2.5% plus sequel rights, guaranteed sole story by credit, best efforts on sole screenplay credit with associate producer credit in lieu of sole credit if it's shared, with one percent merchandising rights kicking in only after a box office gross of fifty million."

Corie looks up at Richard who adds, "The reason the

fee is low is because Bella Feega is not in the Writers Guild. They know this deal will put you in the Guild, but they're using it against you to lowball the price."

"That sounds like a lot of money to me."

"Not after you subtract the agent's fee, the lawyer's fee, the accountant's fee and taxes. You're looking at about $150,000. Also, here's the sticky point, if you're in the Guild, you can't write adult screenplays anymore."

"But the Accent Film Company is signatory to the new adult writers guild," I inform them.

"The Writers Guild of America doesn't acknowledge that," explains Richard. "At least not yet."

"But I can't turn my back on the adult writers guild right now. Besides, I'm trying to get the WGA to incorporate this little union as a separate division."

"Who knows how long that could take," says Corie.

"Well, why can't Eagle and Maestro create a new production company that's not signatory to the guild? I used to see Eric Leve make those kinds of deals," I say.

"That's what we proposed," states Richard. "We're dangling Raine Foster and Hugo Jeffrey as leads in front of them so they'll push it through. If we package that level of star power for them, then they'll include a production bonus for you of an additional one million."

So this was the power play, the core strategic planning that went into the making of a studio deal. The story had been pushed aside. I'm sure no one even remembered what it was anymore. It was the art of the deal now taking center stage. This kind of leveraging and the stomach it took to maneuver through it was way out of my league. That was when I knew without question that I was first and foremost a writer.

"If we can't get the star power, you'll have to choose between your job at the Accent Film Company and the writing deal," says Corie.

I take a deep breath and let go a heavy sigh, remembering that releasing a large sigh equals liberating a heavy thought. "I guess I've been seduced," I say.

Richard and Corie stare at me, not comprehending. A seduction requires a seducer and a seducee, without one another, there can be no seduction. Consciously or not, I had chosen to be seduced by an industry that commercialized and vulgarized what I had discovered to be some of society's most treasured misfits. I found it no better or worse than the way Hollywood treated its offspring. It was all a matter of comfort zones. For whatever reasons, I felt more comfortable among the porn world's misfits than among the insecurities of Hollywood's elite.

I realize in that moment that if it came down to choosing, I would want to choose the adult industry. I would rather choose to accept myself in this milieu than waffle on Hollywood's quicksand.

I turn to both of them. "Richard, Corie. I need to go make more babies. Just be really good midwives for them."

Richard grins and nods at me. Corie looks perplexed. "What's she talking about?" she asks.

"I'll fill you in later," says Richard. He turns to me and says, "Go home and create your little darlings. Leave Corie and I to deliver the deals."

take fourteen

THE WEDDING

Before leaving my apartment to meet my mother and father, who are picking me up, I drop off the bag containing Bella Feega's face and wardrobe at Corie's. The plan is for her to bring it with her to the wedding so I don't attract any conspicuous attention.

Bennett is not in the car as he has already secured a room at the hotel. This is to make it easier on himself in terms of helping Ann with her makeup and making sure his suit won't wrinkle in anything but a short walk on the way to the ceremony being held on the rooftop. The reception will follow in a giant banquet room, triple in size to what had originally been planned, to accommodate the five hundred guests of family, friends, politicians, live video crew for the Wedding Channel and the journalists from *Inside Hollywood* here for their exclusive.

Eva looks stunning in her gown and Walt appears as

dashing as ever. They both swoon over my dress and my makeup. In fact, Eva barely recognizes me, compliments of Corie and Ian's personal makeover to ensure a difference from the upcoming and last of Bella Feega's appearances. The three of us sit in the car together while Walt drives us to the hotel for the pre-wedding photos. For a brief moment, I feel a wonderfully sweet and long-forgotten sensation of familial harmony, a feeling of pronounced intangible safety. I wish I could keep it with me forever, but as soon as I am conscious of being conscious of it, it disappears.

Then my father turns to me, "You've got your speech all written?" he asks.

"Speech? What speech?" I ask, suddenly petrified.

"I mean the toast," he says. "For your sister."

"Oh…the toast." Between the infomercial and Bella's overnight success in Hollywood, I had completely forgotten about the toast for Ann. "Of course, I remembered," I respond. How could I possibly confess to an Emily Post faux pas with regards to my own sister's wedding?

"Just remember to open with a joke," Eva reminds me. "Audiences always love to laugh before they like to cry."

All through the wedding photos, Bennett refuses to address me. I maintain my composure by occupying myself with long-lost cousins. Then I excuse myself to start jotting down ideas for Ann's toast. There's a pen and some paper in my purse, which has fallen off a chair under a table. I scoot under the table just as George and Bennett pass by making it possible for me to overhear their conversation.

"So you're not upset about Bella Feega coming?" asks George.

"I can't wait to meet her," says Bennett. "I think she's fab."

"I thought you disapproved of anyone involved with sex on film?" asks George. "Like the documentary about strippers that Laura wrote. And that was just a documentary."

"I don't care if Bella Feega does it, just not my sister," replies Bennett.

"You're either a hypocrite or a bipartisan brother," says George.

They pass by and I sigh as I resume my place among the standing. Why is it okay for Bella Feega to do what she does and not me? I wonder.

I look out for Cole and Corie when Ann chases me down. "Laura, our videographer just called in sick. What are we going to do?"

The next thing I know my services are being called upon to help bring in an emergency replacement. Thankfully I've got my pocket PC and cell phone with me. I start by calling directors who own their own equipment and know how to work with video cameras, like Jimmy Hesse and Cliff Peterson, but there's no answer. They're probably out climbing a mountain or shooting a film for the competition. I see Larry Solomon across the room. Behind him comes the Wedding Channel video crew. I tell George if worse comes to worst he can always get copies of the footage from them. But they don't want a sensationalized version.

Corie finally shows up as Bella Feega's agent. The rumor is out that Bella is coming and so when guests ask, she explains that Bella is on her way and expected to arrive momentarily, and so the ceremony, previously touted for its promptness, begins.

Ann and George look genuinely happy throughout the customized ceremony conducted by Rabbi Weiss. I keep my eyes open for Cole, but so far, no sign of him.

"I place this glass in a napkin to be smashed by the groom," announces Rabbi Weiss. "It's become custom for everyone to say Mazel Tov, which is Yiddish for congratulations, immediately following. But the origin of this tradition was not to celebrate a loud noise, but to capture the attention of guests gone wild, particularly a group of Rabbis, I might add, at the wedding of Rav Ashi's son's during the thirteenth century. Rav Ashi smashed a valuable glass to shock everyone back into civilized behavior. But I like to extrapolate another meaning from this tradition, that we all live in a world where temptation to deviate from who we are surrounds us. Let the breaking of the glass redeem us all into our righteous place amongst each other and in our community."

The rabbi's words reach my heart and soul, and I long to be redeemed. George performs the ritual crushing of the glass and then he and Ann kiss—it's a really, really hot, passionate never-ending kiss. Corie and I exchange glances. "Ah, the power of Bella," she murmurs with a cocky grin.

An old aunt of George's sits behind me and exclaims, "That's some kiss!" Then she speaks to Corie and me and asks, "Do you girls kiss like that, too?"

Corie politely whispers back, "Oh, we're not together, but I did once kiss a woman and it was amazing."

My mother leans over. "Is that your special friend, dear?"

"No!" I whisper back rather loudly. I hear a small commotion in back. Cole enters in his staple black attire carrying his prized equipment with him from the plane ride. Apparently, asking for my whereabouts creates a small stir of activity as a message relay begins and before it reaches me it's assumed that Cole is the replacement videographer. Before either one of us realize what's happening, Cole is presented with the job and seeing a need, shrugs why not and whips out his carry-on video camera. He glances at me from down the aisle and behind the camera. I shrug I'm sorry. He offers me a wink and a smile as he catches the remainder of the lengthy wedding kiss and a repeat of *I do's* for his camera's benefit.

As the party moves from the rooftop to the banquet room, Cole and I finally reach each other and hug. "It's good to see you," I say.

"You, too, Tay. You, too, though I almost didn't recognize you," he says.

"Do you like it?" I ask.

"You look beautiful. But I like you any way you dress."

Corie interrupts us. "Is this the famous Cole Tanner I've heard so much about?"

I beam back, "Yes."

"It's great to finally meet you," says Corie. "I've heard nice things about you."

"Likewise," replies Cole.

Eva swoons over to us. "Laura, can you please ask the videographer to film the reception line?"

"Mom, this is Cole. He's my, uh...date."

"Nice to meet you, Cole," Eva says politely, then subtly takes me aside and speaks softly in my ear, "Honey, you don't have to conjure up relationships with the staff to hide who you really are. I'm ready to meet your special friend whenever you are." Then she takes Cole by the hand and points him in the direction of the reception line.

I look at Corie and sigh, "Why me?"

Corie giggles. "Let's recap, shall we? Your mom thinks you're gay and in a relationship with either Bella Feega or me. Your dad knows you write porn but thinks Bella Feega is taking all the credit away from you. Your brother thinks you write documentaries about seedy sexual lifestyles and won't talk to you because of it, but he thinks Bella Feega is fabulous because she's promoting his product and she's not you. Ann and George are now married because Bella Feega's sex ed tapes and porn films saved their engagement and made George an overnight home run venture capitalist. Due to the sensation of an adult movie, Hollywood suddenly wants to buy the work of Bella Feega when Laura Taylor can't get arrested for her writing, and aside from Richard Marksman and me, no one in Hollywood knows that Bella is Laura and Laura is Bella. Am I missing anything?"

I think it over. "Laura can no longer be Bella. It's killing me, Corie. I can't do this anymore. It's one thing to fool myself, because it's only myself I'm hurting, but it's another thing to fool the world and those who love you."

A waiter passes by with a tray of champagne. I grab one and knock it down.

"Okay, calm down," says Corie. "After tonight, we'll figure out a way to off Bella. We just have to do it without making it a scandal so we preserve her reputation. You want her to have a nice epitaph, don't you?"

"What about the, you know, Hollywood writing career?"

"It will die along with Bella. You can't ghost-write for a ghost."

Just then, Austin Stern crosses over to us, "Hello, Laura." He looks at Corie, "I understand you're Corie Berman. It's a pleasure to meet you. So when will I be seeing my investment?" he asks.

"Funny you should ask. I just spoke to her, Mr. Stern."

"Well, I'll let you guys talk shop. I have to find Cole and prepare for Ann's toast," I say and slip away.

As I pass through the lobby looking for Cole, I see a bevy of college-age students stuffing bags with pairs of red leather socks. "Um, what are those for?" I ask.

"Party favors," replies one of them.

"Oy," is all I can say.

Larry Solomon spots me from across the hall and motions me over. "Laura, walk with me while I check in on the live feed for the Wedding Channel."

"Where's the live feed?" I ask. Before he answers, we round a corner into a smaller banquet room where monitors line the walls. One monitor shows Ann and George greeting their guests. Another monitor shows Cole videotaping Table 65. A third monitor reveals Austin Stern getting ready to face the camera. We negotiate our way through a jungle of cables toward a table of producers, talent and crew people.

"Let me introduce you to the producer. If the show takes off, maybe he can hire you."

"There's actual writing done on a reality show?" I ask.

"Laura, don't be so naive," he says.

"No, really, Larry. How can they write what they don't know is going to happen?"

"It's in the narration and the way they cut back and forth between cameras to tell a story. It's like covering a live football game. At some point there's bound to be some drama. Their job is to capitalize on it."

Just then I see the Wedding Channel's celebrity host in the corner of the room under a horde of lights talking on camera. "Well, you've witnessed the ceremony, folks, a ceremony delayed by six months due to wedding jitters, on whose part we don't know. Will the marriage last as long as the kiss that united them? Will George's run for state assemblyman be a hindrance or a blessing to their union? In a moment, we'll hear from George's father, famed politician, Mr. Austin Stern. Meanwhile, stay with us for the reception to follow where we'll be hearing from guests and a special word of advice from adult writer-producer Bella Feega…"

I turn to Larry, "Bella Feega is not speaking. It's in her contract."

"How do you know?"

"Because…my best friend is her agent."

"This is boring! We need some drama," bellows a faintly familiar voice from behind a camera that blocks my view.

Larry looks up spotting the person behind the camera, "There's the producer, let me introduce you. He's a young guy from the JKL Network."

But as the producer steps from behind the camera, I see that he is the pimply-faced kid from the JKL "Authentic Sex" video crew, who rudely tried to interview me at the adult-equivalent academy award after-party. I can't take the chance that he may recognize me either as a journalist covering the porn awards or make some connection between Bella and me.

I quickly do an about-face. "You know what, Larry… I have to go. I just realized it's my turn to speak at Table 32." I hop over the cables before he can say a word.

I find Cole in the banquet room videotaping Table 21. Ann's *Malibu Post* friend Sandra addresses the camera, "I wish Ann and George a very happy union together, for at least three years, because three years in this town is actually a lifetime in Cleveland…"

I interrupt with applause. "That is really beautiful, Sandra, and so apropos. Excuse me, but I need to have a word with the cameraman." I pull Cole away and lead him to the bar, "I am so sorry about this," I say.

"Laura, it's all right. I'm getting to know the terrain and its people."

"Yeah? Meet any interesting souls along the way?" I ask before turning to the bartender to add, "I'll have a double Scotch, no ice. Cole?"

"Pellegrino with a lime twist," he says, and then looks at me. "I'm working."

I roll my eyes. "So am I."

"I thought you didn't drink."

"Only in advance of public speaking engagements."

"What's this I hear about Bella showing up?"

"It's a long story and she has a new and revised look. Just remember that when Bella's here, I won't be."

Walt interrupts us. "Excuse me. Laura, it's time for the

toast." I swallow my drink whole. I hate public speaking. Hate it. Hate it. Hate it.

I stand in front of the waiting crowd. Walt and Eva appear together at the microphone on stage where the band has stopped playing.

Corie finds me, and whispers urgently in my ear, "Everyone's on my case about Bella. As soon as you finish meet me in the bathroom." I nod my head as Walt addresses the guests.

"I'd like to thank all of you for being here, for being a part of Ann and George's wedding, for being a part of our mitzvah. Let's join in prayer over the wine and bread." He lifts his glass of wine and recites the prayers, then he hands Eva the microphone.

Beaming with pride my mother says, "I just want to say how happy I am, for Ann, for George…for me." The crowd chuckles. Eva looks at Ann, "Honey, I couldn't wish for a better son-in-law. And now I'd like to introduce my other lovely daughter, Laura, without whom none of us would be here tonight."

I kick back a glass of water to dilute the alcohol in me and wobble up to the stage. I have no idea what I'm going to say. I'm just praying the god of words will come down and shower me with something that sounds sensible.

"Um, hi, everyone… I really uh, wish my sister hadn't quit her job as a speech pathologist because I, uh, have a pathology when it comes to…speaking."

Everyone laughs. Eva gives me a nod of approval. I see Cole pointing his camera at me as well as the Wedding Channel video crew. I summon up my courage, again hearing the morning TV host's mantra: "And don't be afraid of public speaking, Laura." And then I spot Ann standing next to George and it all starts to come together.

"It's true. You're all here because I introduced Ann and George to each other. I had my chance with George and I blew it, but not really, because I get to have him as a great brother-in-law without having to debate pillow politics or attend a lot of campaign fund-raisers where politicians make promises they can't keep…"

I laugh until I realize no one else is. Wrong crowd. "Actually, the truth is I could never do all of that as gracefully and supportively as I know Ann will."

I see endearing smiles in response. "So what do you say about your sister, your friend, and your confidante on the eve of her marriage? I think back to growing up with Ann. And if there's one unique quality that consistently shines through, it's that Ann has always liked herself. Even when my brother didn't because she wore bell-bottoms when they were out of style."

More laughter. Even Bennett manages to scoff and smile at the same time. I continue. "I believe that because Ann truly loves herself—she's so good at loving others. She knows herself well enough to speak for what feels right and take necessary action to change her course if what she's pursuing suddenly feels wrong, even if it costs her her pride…and thousands of dollars in deposits." More laughter erupts, as everyone knows about the near demise of her engagement.

"It's that Ann is so good at being herself, at having a relationship with herself, and giving it value. There's a story Rabbi Weiss once told about how God hid himself in the hearts of humankind because that's the last place they would look. But Ann's always known where to find God inside her heart. It's in her character to never let fear cloud her convictions. And that takes courage. We only know a character by what he or she says and does, as the novelist Ayn Rand points out." Larry Solomon nods at me in appreciation of the quote I learned from his English teaching days.

"Ann's actions and words are always synonymous with each other," I continue. "When she met George the integrity of those traits crystallized into even greater brilliance.

And in her own shining example, she's helped George to become a man equally synonymous with words and actions. Great character traits for a politician, I might add." The crowd chuckles and the Wedding Channel crew zooms in on me. "I hope one day I know myself as well as Ann knows herself, because she really is the epitome of self-acceptance. And when you've got that, you've got everything."

Tears well up in the eyes of the audience. Ann rushes over to me and gives me a big hug. "That was so beautiful," she says.

I look out at the crowd feeling terribly anxious all over again and start hyperventilating. "Smelling salts, smelling salts," I murmur. Walt dashes over and slips them under my nose. I breathe deep and collect myself. "I'm okay. Thanks. Okay. Gotta go." And I hop off stage to the sound of applause.

Cole reaches me, "Tay, that was awesome, so heartfelt and eloquent. You okay?"

"Yep, fine. Just gotta get to the john. See ya in fifteen."

As I rush to the bathroom, Ann and George prepare to cut the wedding cake. I pass by the room with the live video feed and hear the pimply-faced producer say, "I know I know that woman! I just can't place where. Someone, find the drama in what she said and cut to it! And somebody stay on the entrance for Bella Feega!"

I dive into the bathroom and whisper loudly, "Corie!"

"In here," she says. "Last stall on your left."

I duck in. Corie's got Bella's face and wardrobe ready to go. "Nice job on the impromptu toast, there. Hell, if all else fails, Laura, you could be an inspirational speaker."

"I think not, I'd deplete the world's resources of smelling salts."

I do a quick change, careful to make sure the mole is properly in place. Corie reapplies my makeup, teases the blond wig and dons the glasses while I pull on a pair of black leather socks.

She discreetly hides my Laura attire in the bag and then reads through a checklist, "Tinted glasses, mole, wig, suntan, breast enhancements, hip enhancements, red fingernails, bushy brows." She looks me over. "Ready?"

"Ready," I say, nervously.

"Hello, Bella. Rendezvous back here in sixteen minutes to put Laura back together again."

Corie and I enter the banquet room. The Wedding Channel video crew nearly tramples over me to get a close-up of Bella. I hear that familiar annoying voice again.

"Move over. I'll show you how to make drama for God's sake." The pimply-faced producer shoves his way into me with a microphone in hand shouting in my ear, "Bella, is your appearance here tonight a political statement in favor of George Stern's run for state assemblyman? How do you see your libertarian views in relationship to a Republican wedding party?"

Corie covers for me, turning to the pimply-faced producer. "Bella Feega is not speaking tonight. She has laryngitis. You'll have to get her political views another time. Now with all due respect to the wedding party, please step aside."

All the pushing though has caused my hip enhancements to move off-center. I try tactfully to readjust them as we find our table in the back and sit down. Austin Stern nods at Corie from across the room.

On stage, Ann and George eat cake and thank all their loved ones for attending. I notice Ann sway as she takes another sip of champagne. Then she spots me and suddenly gets all flustered.

"Oh my God, there she is," says Ann. Then she grabs the microphone. "Welcome to my wedding, Bella Feega!"

All eyes turn to look at me. I groan to Corie and politely wave back.

But Ann continues, "I know there are a lot of people with a lot of different opinions about the woman sitting in the back of the room. My sister, Laura, introduced George and I, but it's that woman there who unknowingly closed the deal." Ann looks out over the crowd for the Laura version of me, but I'm nowhere to be found. "Where's Laura?"

Cole covers for me. He relays to Ann, "Recuperating from speaking in public."

"Oh," she says. "Well, it's Laura who introduced me to Bella, sort of. But without Bella's forward-thinking views on relationships I'm not so sure I'd be standing here."

George holds her up and laughs. "You mean swaying here, don't you?"

Ann smiles. "I'm not done. Laura spoke about my acceptance of myself. But I was only accepting the status quo of a marriage that had love but lacked passion. I know it's kind of weird to talk about that here, but Bella's work taught me how to reach higher plateaus of self-acceptance than I've ever known before. My sister Laura is always talking about how the power of story can shape us. Well, Bella's characters do that. I learned about courage by watching her characters demonstrate the power to begin again. I learned to achieve freedom by surrendering to my choices from a place of self-empowerment. It's Bella Feega who epitomizes honesty at all costs. It's Bella Feega who knows how to be true to herself and her ideals and we should all celebrate her for those gifts she exemplifies in the face of controversy. Right, George? And besides all that, she wears my husband's, I can say husband now, she wears my husband's and my brother's invention of leather socks! How incredible is that?"

The crowd applauds and I keep smiling, but instead of simmering down, the clapping builds. People stand expecting me to get up. When I remain seated, they start goading me up to the stage. Corie does her best to stop it but it's no use. The momentum of the guests takes over. Ann holds the microphone out to me. I have no choice.

I stand up and as I feel the mass push me forward, I realize that in my journey to the stage, everything has become surreal. Ann has just spoken out on behalf of everything Bella Feega stands for, but in the body of Laura Taylor, and yet, Laura Taylor doesn't have the courage to be Bella Feega as Laura Taylor. How can I accept the acknowledgement my own sister is now bestowing upon me and still be true to myself? If I can create characters with courage, then why can't I, too, have the courage to accept myself, to be true to myself? The only way I see this happening is to let go of the charade in the eyes of the familiar and in the eyes of the anonymous. I look out and see my family members, George's family members, Cole, politicians, the video crew. And slowly, piece-by-piece, as if summoned by some greater force within me, I begin removing the facade. First, the nails go, which no one seems to notice in the mayhem, then the hip enhancements, creating a stir among the video crew. Everything's a blur as I eliminate the padded breasts, mole, wig, glasses, then finally, I wipe the suntan off my face as I land on stage. The faces around me unexpectedly bear gaping holes of shock and dismay, mouthing the word "Laura," as if my name has suddenly become a question. Hearing my name said en masse in utter bewilderment brings me to a moment where I am immune to my redemption.

The pimply-faced producer quickly jabs the microphone in front of my mouth and I start to hear my voice activate, "Um. Sorry to have 'a come to Jesus' moment at a Jewish wedding. But uh, given that tonight's theme concerns being true to yourself, I thought it only appropriate that Bella

Feega live up to the accolades placed upon her tonight and reveal her true identity. I didn't mean to deceive anyone, but myself. The truth is I wasn't able to accept myself, me, as Laura, until I was Bella. I thought I did, before I started writing adult films, but then…things changed. Bella does live, only she does so inside of me, Laura Taylor."

The pimply-faced producer excitedly announces, "Hello, thirteen more episodes."

Ann, Bennett, George, Walt, Eva, Larry, Austin, Rabbi Weiss, Corie and Cole all look at me in shock. The public speaking makes me dizzy once again, and this time, I promptly pass out.

take fifteen

THE AFTERMATH

After my unexpected plot twist, I didn't know what to expect. But it turned out that it only took a few days for the initial shock to wear off for family and friends, and for them to move past the front-page story in *Inside Hollywood*.

In a strange twist of fate, it turned out that the Hollywood deal got done. And with it came more notoriety. The fact that the mainstream version of *The Surrogate* had been inspired by an emerging adult art form written by Bella-Laura, made headline news in the industry trades and in national magazines.

Soon, my and Bella Feega's photo appeared in print everywhere. It felt strange without the costume. I was totally naked. My life had been uncovered. And Laura Taylor and Bella Feega had become synonymous.

Several things happened after that. First, Hollywood started mining all of the adult industry's catalogues for new content ideas. They scoured for original stories and they even looked to do parodies of the parodies of themselves, optioning the rights to adult movies like *Austin Prowler* to make into an R-rated parody. Even *Jane Bond* got optioned, this time by Hank Willows at Satellite. All the studio executives in town now justified watching adult films on company time in search of adaptable stories. I thought that it would somehow dissolve Hollywood's pretentious veneer, but in essence, it only served to feed it.

The second thing was the bidding war for the rights to my life story. After a tenuous three weeks, Richard and Corie close a deal that places my world at a big cable network, in the form of a TV sitcom in development.

"Two other cable networks wanted to get in the game, but we've already got you the best deal."

I look at Richard, "Whose idea was this?"

"Mine," says Richard. "I've been slowly fanning the flames on it to the right buyers for some time now."

"You'll be guaranteed as consultant on the show and we'll try to get you a guarantee to write the pilot, but we can't promise that," says Corie.

I noticed that even with what one would call success in Hollywood, the uphill battle never ceases.

The third thing that happened was my departure from the Accent Film Company. Hollywood had offered me all sorts of jobs from seedy mystery thriller rewrites to original romantic comedy pitches. One studio even bought an idea of mine based on a two-word pitch: "Bachelorette Party." The career I had fought so valiantly for had arrived albeit in a manner I never expected.

Instead of Mickey waiting for my call, he shows up late one night at my curb. Sam, the chauffeur, calls me, interrupting a deep sleep. "Mickey Colucci would like to see Bella Feega. He's in the car waiting."

I peek outside my window. The big, black Lincoln quietly rests under a maple tree on the street below. I climb out of bed and I throw on a pair of jeans and sneakers and head downstairs.

Walking toward the Lincoln, wiping the sleep from my eyes, I notice a streetlamp emit a massive amount of light onto the car. This in turn creates a shadow that consumes the entire street, making the Lincoln appear larger than life itself. Mickey was no doubt a larger-than-life character who had indirectly found a unique place in my life. I knew it would be the last time we would meet. It was inevitable, as change is inevitable. We would all move on to the next chapter in our lives. But of all the characters I met in the adult world of entertainment, I would miss him the most, for he was the one in an off-center way who had given me the seeds of self-respect.

I knock on the window. Sam pops the locks open and I climb inside next to Mickey.

"Things change," he says.

"Sounds like the title of a hit adult movie," I say.

He smiles, "Your donut's start'n to overbake."

I look at him, still sleepy. "I think I'm missing the metaphor here."

He pulls out a cigar and cracks the window open for me. "Goals are like…circles," he says, lighting his cigar and blowing out a perfect circle of smoke. "Starts with an idea, a notion…which per mutates. Eventually it manifests, and you're back at what started the whole thing. It's like a cycle of life. Birth comes round to death, which comes round to birth. It's all a circle. Everything's a circle. You're back to your original goal, only now…you can taste it. Like a donut."

"Oh," I nod. "I think I get it now." That was the most words I'd ever heard Mickey Colucci say at one time. To my surprise, he continues.

"Before you leave me, I'm gonna leave you. But I want you to know. I don't care for those kooks in Hollywood, so if you ever want to come back you can. And if they don't treat you right, you let me know."

"I don't know what to say. You've given me—"

"Laura," he says, interrupting my farewell speech before I get on a roll. It's the first time I can remember him ever calling me by my real name. "Say goodbye to Bella for me…I'm gonna miss her."

The locks on the doors pop up signaling my cue.

As I climb out of the car, I look at Mickey one last time. "She'll miss you, too. Thank you, Mickey Colucci. I'll never forget you. And I'll never want to."

He nods in mutual acknowledegment, and then I watch the car drive off into the night.

The fourth thing that happened was when Bennett finally grasped the impact I had single-handedly had in the success of his leather socks. He approached me in Malibu shortly after the wedding. He caught up with me as I walked along the shore at dusk. For a while he didn't say a word. Then he finally stopped and lo and behold, he spoke. "I didn't know you were so resourceful."

"Yeah. Well, it's called survival of the fittest."

Silence follows as we continue walking. Then he starts up again. "So how did you know that dermatologist in Florida? I always wondered."

"Sure you want to know?"

"Yeah, I want to know."

"Well, Bennett, believe it or not, he bought me a drink at the strip club the night I went to interview the strippers." I smile at him. "God works in strange ways sometimes, doesn't he?"

"Hmmph," utters Bennett.

I cock my head toward him. "Hmmph?" I determine that the "hmmph" represents Bennett's way of accepting me, at least the hope of acceptance.

"I'm sorry if I was hard on you. Maybe too hard," he says.

"Way too hard. Extreme, severe, and excessive... Approaching the outer limits. Past tough love and moving into cruel and unusual pun—"

"Okay, okay," he says, cutting me off. "I just wanted the best for you."

"You wanted what you thought was the best for me. And I wanted what you thought was best for you. Therein lie our differences."

He stops and looks at me, as if seeing me in a whole different light, with an intense beam of reflection, as if Malus's law was in full effect right now. As if I was suddenly shining, becoming the age I was and a little wiser for it.

The sun was setting into the magic hour, where its rays of soft light glow with reflective colors, making everyone look good, "You're all right, sis, you're all right," he offers.

"Thanks," I reply. We walk a little farther in silence, giving our newfound perceptions a moment to crystallize.

Soon after that, Bennett and George decided to not only make me an honorary board member of their company with stock options, but Bennett personally promised to pay for the trip to Hawaii that I owed Cole. After that, Bennett never made fun of me again. The sibling rivalry from our youth had finally made way for mutual love and respect. Bennett became my biggest champion and one of my best friends.

Lastly, with Mitchell Mann far behind me, and a sense of accomplishment surrounding me, I was able to become more available to Cole. I took some of the lessons I learned in the sex education videos and applied them to our relationship, creating romantic weekend getaways and putting the needs of our relationship above those of Hollywood. In time, we began to find the best parts of ourselves together.

You would think that all is well now that Laura Taylor's writing career has finally taken off due to Bella Feega's writing career. But remember that first impressions are often deceiving and that the unexamined first impression is usually not worth believing. I received my first partial check from Eagle and Maestro for *The Surrogate.* After paying fees and commissions to the agents, lawyers, accountants and the government, I ended up with approximately $37,000. The first thing I did was proudly send bottles of champagne to my family, with notes inviting them to the first day of principal photography. After that, I used the money to start my first IRA account, which made my father very happy.

But then, as usual, something happened. The director who signed on suddenly died from heart failure on a racquetball court. While the studio took its time finding a replacement, the stars had to take other projects and *The Surrogate* languished in purgatory, yes, the dreaded "turnaround." Unbeknownst to me, however, Corie quietly followed up with Rand regarding *The Law of Malus.* Between the two of them, Corie and Rand managed to shepherd the project through and protect the integrity of the story. To my surprise, Rand relentlessly hounded Natalie Moore on the project until she finally gave it to a very talented Academy-Award-winning British actress. It didn't take the actress more than a minute to recognize the value of the role and she immediately signed on as the star, co-producer and co-writer. Needless to say, she rewrote my work, but I didn't care. The story I had been so impassioned to tell finally got told. And it was okay that it wasn't all in my voice. As long as one person finds the strength to beam their brightest light from within and begin again, then my efforts have mattered and the struggle's been worth it.

After that, offers from Hollywood continued but they were always so convoluted. In the end, I missed working with Mickey Colucci. There had been no politics to deal with. No backstabbing. No pretentiousness. I had had all the freedom I wanted to tell the stories I wanted to tell and to create positive social change in the process. But living and working in the adult industry was not my destiny. Though I did stay in touch with Tom and some of the actresses, though the politics of Hollywood became more irritating, rather than call upon Mickey Colucci, I began writing a novel for the publishing industry and found it to be much more civilized.

On the way back from consulting on the TV show, I notice I'm driving past the synagogue where Richard Marksman and I formed our strange and enduring friendship. I decide to stop and enter the sanctuary. Silence dictates the emptiness of the space. I stand behind a pew and open a prayer book to the first chapter of Genesis, and stare at the symbols of the faith I was raised in. My solitude fills the tiny area. Light seeps through stained-glass windows, creating shades of blue and green, orange and yellow, and red. The dancing colors spread across the letters that make up the words that make up the stories that make up the faith on the page. I am reminded of the Crayon Wars that had once surged inside my third grade daydreams. Suddenly, the colors of light streaming in seem to dance together on the page. All conflict dissipates in this moment. I dig inside my purse to find the compass. I pull it out and open it. The needle points to my heart. Hmmm. I watch the colors merge into one on the page. Life is a series of beginnings, I think, one beginning after another. My life uncovered as Bella Feega represents only one chapter in the life story of Laura Taylor. I close the prayer book with the courage to keep my past intact and with optimistic eagerness to see what new beginnings lie ahead.

epilogue

Mitchell Mann continues to call every year to take me out to dinner and rent a hotel room. He still directs straight-to-video horror movies. Corie Berman is now one of the most respected and powerful literary agents in the business. Richard Marksman secretly bought a huge majority stake in the Accent Film Company, making him a multi-millionaire. As well, he helped to establish the Literary Guild for Adult Writers. He now plays golf seven days a week in Bermuda. Sara Stephenson has been promoted to the presidency of a major mainstream Hollywood studio and married Janine Tate. Together they raise children from the sperm of Hank and J.J. All three still work as executives in the industry. Joe Schwartz and Oliver Kleimeister lost their jobs because they had passed on *The Law of Malus,* which went on to win three Academy Awards, including best actress and actor—and one for me as co-writer. So I did get to go up to the podium once again and make another speech, though this time I kept it under the time allotted. Nick Blake was pissed he didn't get the lead male role in

Malus and fired Joe Schwartz when he found out that he had passed on the script and in fact had never read it. Joe now works in his father's business in Wichita, Kansas, managing a shopping mall. Oliver returned to his MBA roots and teaches a course about the business of Hollywood at Boston University.

Lola Stormrider now writes political satire for a top-rated late-night comedy show. Tom Kaplan continues to run the marketing division for Accent Film Company, but now with Jodie, whom he married, alongside. No kids. They like their lifestyle just the way it is. Mickey Colucci retired to Key West, Florida, and opened a chain of donut shops all along the Keys. Every birthday I receive a Fed Ex package of fresh donuts from him.

Cole and I live together ninety miles from L.A. in Ojai, where I juggle my time between writing and consulting, and deciding what color to paint the new baby's room. I drive to Los Angeles three times a week to give my input in the television show based on the double life of Laura Taylor. When I walk down the streets of Ojai, an unknown to the town and its locals, I smile and wave. No posturing exists here. The struggle to prove myself to myself is over. I have surrendered to my choices, found my freedom, and begun again.

P.S.

That day I left the synagogue when I felt in harmony with myself and my world, its past, present and future; there was a message from Scott Sher waiting for me at home on my answering machine. He had called as part of his twelve-step program to make amends for his past wrongs. "You're my one hundredth call. I just wanted you to know that I never did make a deal for your script about Malus's law and well, I hope it didn't screw you up."